BOLD CHALLENGE

"What I question is the Princess's claim that this is a matter of great urgency," said Senator Marook. "Perhaps she can help me understand."

"I'll do my best," Leia said, wary.

"These recordings from the Koornacht Cluster—to the best of your knowledge, they were made days, even weeks ago, yes?"

"That's true."

"So what you've shown us is history. None of these tragedies can be prevented, or even tempered."

"No—"

"Then how is this any different from the unavenged atrocities of the Imperial era? Why are we not meeting to discuss how and when to invade the Core in search of the agents of Palpatine's rampages? Isn't the real urgency here the waning of your political power, and your desperate need for a dramatic victory to restore your prestige?"

The Black Fleet Crisis
Book Two

◆

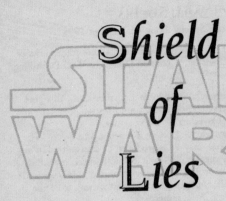

Shield
of
Lies

◆

Michael P. Kube-McDowell

™

SPECTRA

BANTAM BOOKS
NEW YORK TORONTO LONDON SYDNEY AUCKLAND

SHIELD OF LIES

A Bantam Spectra Book / September 1996

SPECTRA and the portrayal of a boxed "s" are trademarks of Bantam Books, a division of Bantam Doubleday Dell Publishing Group, Inc.

ISBN 0-553-57277-6

Published simultaneously in the United States and Canada

Bantam Books are published by Bantam Books, a division of Bantam Doubleday Dell Publishing Group, Inc. Its trademark, consisting of the words "Bantam Books" and the portrayal of a rooster, is Registered in U.S. Patent and Trademark Office and in other countries. Marca Registrada. Bantam Books, 1540 Broadway, New York, New York 10036.

PRINTED IN THE UNITED STATES OF AMERICA

OPM   0 9 8 7 6 5 4 3 2 1

Dedication

For Matt, Amanda, and Gwen,
in gratitude for
their love, support, and understanding.

And for all the twelve-year-olds
everywhere and anywhen
who, like me,
believed they would journey into space someday—
most especially for those who really did,
and for those who *still* believe.

Acknowledgments

The STAR WARS universe has been so greatly expanded and enriched in the years since *Return of the Jedi* appeared that even the best-intentioned of us can hardly hope to master all its details unaided.

I'm therefore grateful for the assistance of the many writers and fans in the extended STAR WARS community online—on Genie, CompuServe, and the Internet—who took the time to answer (and even undertook to research) my questions. In particular, Kevin J. Anderson, Roger MacBride Allen, Matt Hart, Robert A. Cashman, Laurie Burns, Jim Fisher, Cathy Bowden, Tim O'Brien, Wm. Paul Sudlow, and Steve Ozmanski each added at least one page of helpful facts to my reference binder this time around.

Other invaluable references included Bill Slavicsek's *A Guide to the Star Wars Universe,* Shane Johnson's *Star Wars Technical Journal,* Dan Wallace's planet research, and the various time lines, lexicons, and concordances provided me by Sue Rostoni of Lucasfilm, Ltd., and Tom Dupree at Bantam.

Once again, I owe a great debt of thanks to my family and first readers, all of whom made sacrifices so that I could devote my time and attention to this project.

viii ◆ *Acknowledgments*

Without Gwen, Matt, Amanda, Arlyn, and Rod aiding and abetting the effort, this book would still be a work in progress, and my editor and agent would have even more gray hair than I've already given them.

Finally, I remain grateful to George Lucas for giving me a chance to add a few pages to the continuing saga of the STAR WARS universe. It's been a pleasure and a privilege to serve as a *de facto* historian for the maturing New Republic and biographer for some of its legendary figures.

—Michael Paul McDowell
February 6, 1996
Okemos, Michigan

Dramatis Personae

On Coruscant, capital of the New Republic:
Princess Leia Organa Solo, president of the Senate
 and chief of state of the New Republic
Alole, aide to Leia
General Han Solo, on detached duty
Admiral Hiram Drayson, chief of Alpha Blue
General Carlist Rieekan, head of New Republic In-
 telligence
First Administrator Nanaod Engh, administrative di-
 rector of the New Republic
Senator Behn-Kihl-Nahm, chairman of the Defense
 Council and friend and mentor to Leia
Senator Tolik Yar of Oolidi
Senator Tig Peramis of Walalla
Senator Cion Marook of Hrasskis
Ayddar Nylykerka, chief analyst for the Asset Track-
 ing Office, Fleet Intelligence
Plat Mallar, sole survivor of the Yevethan raid on
 Polneye
Belezaboth Ourn, extraordinary consul of the
 Paqwepori

With the Fifth Battle Group of the New Republic De-
fense Fleet, in Farlax Sector:
General Etahn A'baht, Fleet commander

Captain Morano, commander of the Fifth Fleet flagship *Intrepid*

Esege "Tuke" Tuketu, K-wing bomber pilot

With the Teljkon Task Force:

General Lando Calrissian, Fleet liaison to the expedition

Lobot, chief administrator of Cloud City, on vacation

See-Threepio, protocol droid

Artoo-Detoo, astromech droid

Colonel Pakkpekatt, expedition commander, New Republic Intelligence

Captain Bijo Hammax, foray commander

On N'zoth, spawnworld of the Yevetha, in the Koornacht Cluster, Farlax Sector:

Nil Spaar, viceroy of the Yevethan Protectorate

Eri Palle, aide to Nil Spaar

Vor Duull, proctor of information science for the viceroy

Outbound from Lucazec in the skiff Mud Sloth:

Luke Skywalker, a Jedi Master

Akanah, an adept of the White Current

On Kashyyyk, homeworld of the Wookiees:

Chewbacca, attending coming-of-age ceremonies for his son Lumpawarump

I.

Lando

Chapter 1

♦

The Teljkon vagabond was on the run once more. But this time, there were hitchhikers aboard.

"Hyperspace?" See-Threepio echoed in a dismayed tone as he struggled to free himself. The droid's limbs were tangled up with Lobot, R2-D2, and the equipment sled in one corner of the vagabond's airlock—a chamber that had suddenly become a spacegoing prison. "You must be mistaken, Master Lobot."

"I am not mistaken," said Lobot, pushing a flailing golden leg away from his faceplate. "All my data links terminated at the same moment, in exactly the same manner I associate with a hyperspace jump."

"There was a course change, too, during the acceleration," Lando said from the opposite corner of the lock. He flexed his ungloved right hand, trying to drive the bone-chilling cold from his aching fingers.

"Master Lando!" See-Threepio cried in his most plaintive voice. "Can't you make it stop?"

"I didn't make it start, Threepio," Lando snapped.

"With all respect, Master Lando, you most certainly did," Threepio said huffily. "Now, you just reach back in that hole and undo whatever you did, and quickly, too. Colonel Pakkpekatt will be *most* upset with us for running off with his starship."

"Colonel Pakkpekatt is probably inventing new words in Hortek right now," said Lando. "But at least he's on a ship that he can boss. We're not. Any damage over there? Lobot? Artoo-Detoo?"

The little astromech droid emerged from the jumble of bodies and chirped once.

"Artoo-Detoo reports that all his systems are operational," said Threepio.

"I'm uninjured, Lando," said Lobot. "My suit took the impact of the equipment sled. But my data links are still all down, and I am finding it disorienting."

Lando nodded. "Artoo, can you help Lobot out?"

Rotating in midair with the aid of its microthrusters, the droid chittered disagreeably.

"Don't be rude," Threepio chided.

"What's going on?"

"Master Lando, Artoo says that he prefers to keep his systems private."

"Yeah, well, I don't like telepaths, either, Artoo," said Lando. "But I'd sure like to be able to think at the colonel right now. Give Lobot a link to your event log. There might be something in there we can use to figure out what happened. Does anyone see my right glove?"

Lobot was clinging with one hand to the equipment sled. "I think your glove blew out the airlock in the decompression."

"Just perfect." Lando looked at his purpled hand, then at the inflated wrist cuff that was keeping his suit sealed. "What's the pressure in here now?"

"Six hundred forty millibars," said Lobot. "Repressurization began after the entry sealed."

"Repressurization? That's interesting. From where?" Lando craned his head and looked at the seamless, featureless bulkheads. "Artoo, see if you can find the vents."

The droid acknowledged the order with a beep and rose to begin cruising along the bulkheads at close range.

"All right—here's the way it looks to me," said Lando. "We're no longer invited guests and welcome visitors. She shook off *Lady Luck* and tried to spit us out. Probably would have succeeded if she hadn't been trying to run away from the task force at the same time."

"Which raises a question," said Lobot. "Why didn't she know?"

"I'm listening."

"It appears to be a misjudgment. Two defense routines were activated without consideration of their combined effect. The repressurization of this compartment appears to be another inconsistency."

"Do you have an explanation?"

"These events suggest to me that the ship is either under the control of systems with limited intelligence, or under the control of beings with limited intelligence." When he saw Lando's expression, Lobot added, "At this point, it's not possible to distinguish between those possibilities."

"Maybe if we figure that out, we'll know something that can help us get on top here," said Lando. "I'm sure of this much—that lock closed because of the jump, not as any favor to us. We're not wanted here. And if we're not clear of this compartment by the time the vagabond leaves hyperspace, I don't think too much of our chances."

"Master Lando, I am certain Colonel Pakkpekatt and the armada are pursuing us," said Threepio. "The sooner we leave hyperspace, the sooner they can rescue us."

"Yeah, they're going to be looking for us," said Lando. "But finding us—we could pop out five light-years from where we were, or fifty, or five hundred. And normal evasive tactics would call for an immediate course change, then another jump. Once *that* happens, you might as well be playing hide-and-seek with the Ewoks on Endor."

"But, Master Lando—there must be *some* way they can rescue us. Surely they wouldn't abandon us. If they do not come for us, we are all doomed to perish as prisoners, lost in space—"

"Threepio, we can't afford to wait for them." Lando tapped his faceplate to remind the droid why. "The chrono's already moving. Lobot and I could be dead before this ship even decides to leave hyperspace. That's why we have to act now. We can't count on any help from the armada, unless we can figure out some way to give them some help finding us first. Until then, we're on our own."

Threepio raised his arms and his voice together. "We *apologize*," he called to the ship. "Please, believe me, I never meant to harm anyone—"

"Shut up, Threepio."

"Yes, sir."

"Lando," said Lobot.

"What?"

"It couldn't hurt," said Lobot. "Someone *might* be listening."

Lando frowned. "As far as this ship is concerned, we're pirates, burglars, tomb-robbers, or worse. Not too likely they'll forget that just because we suddenly develop better manners after breaking down the front door."

"The probability of success may be low," said Lobot. "But diplomatic words are the tool Threepio is best equipped to wield. And perhaps an apology will prove to be the key that will open the next door."

Sighing, Lando waved his gloved hand toward See-Threepio. "All right. But, Threepio, a little dignity, please."

"Of course, Master Lando," the droid said, a hint of defensiveness in his tone. "I am programmed to conduct myself in a dignified manner at all times. Why, it's one of the fundamental principles of etiquette and protocol—"

"Right," Lando said, cutting him short. "Just get to it. We have no idea how much time we have. Use the secondary comm channel so Lobot and I can still hear each other."

"Very well, Master Lando," Threepio said, then seemingly fell silent.

"Lobot, you have access to Artoo's event log?"

"Yes, Lando."

"See if you can figure out our new heading from his gyro and accelerometer readings leading up to the jump. Maybe that, plus Artoo's astrographic database, can tell us something about how much time we have—"

New Republic ferret *IX-26* came out of hyperspace close enough to its destination for the planet to fill most of the forward viewscreen.

"Check the coordinates," Kroddok Stopa ordered, frowning. "Absolute reference."

"The astrogator says forty-four, one-niner-six, two-one-oh." The pilot spun the index wheel on the ship's log with a swipe of his palm. "Yeah, that's what you gave me."

"Those numbers came directly from the Third General Survey." Stopa pointed at the astrogation display. "But if I'm reading your board correctly, it says that this planet is Maltha Obex. That's a Tobek name."

The pilot cocked his head toward the astrogator. "Maltha Obex, that's right."

Stopa, expedition chief for the Obroan Institute's mission to Qella, shook his head as he studied the data coming in from *IX-26*'s sensors. "My stars. What happened here?"

Glancing up at the viewscreen, the pilot said, "Why, what d'ya mean? Looks just like ten thousand other iceballs."

Josala Krenn, the other half of the Obroan expedition, moved forward from her station. "That's just it. The Three-GS survey mission reported this as a temperate world. It had a population of seven million and a primary ecosystem rated provisionally at complexity two."

Shaking his head, the pilot said dryly, "We must have missed the summer season."

"That was expected," Stopa said. "When the Three-GS contact mission came here, they found a third of the landmass glaciated." He left unspoken that the contact team had found the planet dead, the Qella civilization in ruins.

"When the Tobek came, they must have thought this world was theirs for the taking, and gave it a claiming name," said Josala.

"What difference does the name make? This is where you wanted to be, right? What am I missing?"

"The last Three-GS contact was a hundred and fifty-eight years ago," Stopa said. "The planet should have begun its recovery by now."

"I still don't see the problem."

"Yes, you do," Josala said. "The problem's *all* we can see. The problem is the ice."

"Try me again."

Josala sighed. "Where'd you pick us up?"

"Babali," the pilot said. "Wait—you don't have ice drills? Snow shelter? Cold suits?"

"Babali's a tropical dig. For some reason, ice drills weren't on the equipment list," said Josala wryly. "Our rover isn't even rated for this kind of weather."

The pilot whistled sympathetically. "Now I see the problem. But why'd they send *you*, then?"

"We were the best solution to a two-variable equation," said Josala. "The nearest bioarchaeologist and the fastest available transportation."

"It is not all bad," Stopa said thoughtfully. "We were sent here to recover biological samples. The glaciation virtually ensures that good samples still exist to be recovered."

"Unless what triggered this climatic episode was a dirty war—with incendiaries, or surface-burst weapons," Josala pointed out.

"Not much atmosphere left, but I can drop a probe to take a sniff," said the pilot. "We ought to be able to settle that question pretty quickly."

"No," said Stopa. "Put us in a mapping orbit. Let's have a look at the other side. We only need one landing site—a few grams of material. There could be a geothermal field, or some other sort of hot spot—a warm current from a deep vent, perhaps, that kept a portion of some seacoast ice-free. If so, surely the Qella would have fled there before the end."

"You don't expect to find anyone alive, do you? Look at the surface temperature readings."

"No, not alive," Stopa said. "But I would be grateful for a single corpse that is not buried under three hundred meters of ice."

"Mapping orbit it is," said the pilot, reaching for the controls. "Maltha Obex, here we come."

"Qella," Josala amended quietly. "If at least a little bit of this planet doesn't still belong to the Qella, we're going to be a big disappointment to the folks who sent us here."

From the close vantage of a standard mapping orbit, Qella's face proved no more inviting. The land was blanketed in ice to a depth of up to a kilometer, while the shrunken oceans, too salty to freeze, were thick with bergs and growlers.

"That's it," said Stopa, studying the data from the final pass. "Some of the Qella might have tried to live on the ice—we might get lucky and find their remains only fifty or a hundred meters down. It's something we can work on while we're waiting for reinforcements. But we have to assume the worst, and call for help."

"Maybe we can get Dr. Eckels's team," said Josala. "They were supposed to be finished with the Hoth excavation by now."

"We can try. Open a hypercomm link to the Obroan Institute," Stopa said.

"Ready," said the pilot.

"This is Dr. Kroddok Stopa, verification code alpha-eager-four-four-two. I want Supply and Dispatch in on this call."

"Done. Go ahead, Doctor."

"I have an urgent requisition for additional equipment and staff for my current assignment." Stopa quickly rattled off the detailed list he had composed. "Have all that?"

"Supply here—I have it. We'll get working on it right away."

"We also need a crack cold-site team out here. Is Dr. Eckels's Hoth crew available?"

"They reported back yesterday. I don't know what their status is," said the dispatcher. "But I'll send this up to the committee right away, and get you an answer pronto."

"Assuming that they *are* available, what's your best estimate of when we see them and the gear out here?"

"If we can push the turnaround on *Penga Rift* and get the team and gear aboard by midnight—you're looking at sixteen standard days. Add on hour-for-hour for any delays getting off."

"Is anything faster than *Penga Rift* available?"

"Not under institute registry—sorry."

"Explore other options," Stopa said shortly. "This has the highest priority. Stopa out." He signaled the pilot to end the link. "Now you'd better get me Krenjsh at New Republic Intelligence. They need to know there'll be a delay getting them what they asked for."

*   *   *

There was little talking among the quartet trapped in the vagabond's airlock. Everyone had a job to do.

Artoo searched for the inflow vents, while Threepio made entreaties to the vagabond's masters. Lobot analyzed the acceleration and astrographic data while he inventoried the equipment on the equipment sled. And Lando returned to the control handle in the corner of the compartment to see if it would respond to him.

The handle proved immovable, and Lando's touch alone elicited no detectable response from the ship. But through his efforts, he realized that his bare hand was puffy, stiff, and aching—the pressure from the wrist collar was compounding the damage done by the decompression.

"Do we have any sample bags?" Lando asked, returning to where Lobot and the equipment sled floated.

"Yes. Six small, six large, and two capsules of free-form sheet gel."

"The bags—they're self-sealing, right?"

"Yes, Lando." He paused. "I'm sorry—I don't have any more information. Do amnesiacs know that there are things they cannot remember? If so, then I know how it feels to have amnesia. What I know best is making links and browsing for information. I do not seem to have much other expertise."

"Save the self-examination for another time," said Lando. "Grab one of those small sample bags and see if we can't improvise a mitten for me."

Before long, they managed to attach the mouth of the sample bag above the wrist lock for the missing gauntlet. By squeezing the locking pins, Lando was able to make the wrist cuff relax. Almost immediately the swelling in his fingers began to subside.

"I do not know if the bag or the adhesive is strong enough to withstand another depressurization," said Lobot.

"I'm not counting on that," Lando said. "I just don't want to lose consumables, or the use of my hand.

The odds are bad enough already. Did you get anything out of Artoo's data?"

"I believe I have our heading prior to the jump to within half a degree," Lobot said, then rattled off the numbers. "I apologize for the imprecision."

"That would put us on a course toward Sector One-Five-One," Lando said.

"Yes. The boundary is eight light-years from our original position."

"Is there anyone out in 'Fifty-One who might be able to help us?"

"I'm sorry," said Lobot. "Artoo has navigational data only. There is no geopolitical or sociological data."

Lando nodded. "Stop apologizing for what you can't give me. We haven't the time to spare. How far is this road open?"

"The imprecision of the heading becomes more significant the farther out we look, of course," said Lobot. "The nearest body that is close enough to the center flight path and has a large enough gravity shadow to force a ship out of hyperspace is forty-one-point-five-three light-years away."

Frowning, Lando said, "That doesn't help me much. Turn the question around—how far to the spot along this flight path that's the farthest from everything else?"

Lobot closed his eyes and concentrated. But the answer came from Artoo-Detoo as a long series of beeps and chirps.

"Artoo says that in twelve-point-nine light-years, this vessel will enter the most isolated region along this flight path," Threepio offered. "At that point, there will be no charted bodies larger than a class five comet for nearly nine light-years in any direction."

"Sounds like a good place to make a course change," said Lando. "And far enough out to give us a little time to work with."

"But we do not know how fast this vessel is capable

of traveling in hyperspace," Lobot pointed out. "That region could be twelve hours away, or eight, or six—or even fewer. The conventional upper limit on hyperspace velocity may be technological rather than theoretical. And there's something else—"

"What?"

"If we *do* clear that gravity shadow forty-one light-years from here, we'll be heading straight for the border of the New Republic, in the general direction of Phracas, in the Core."

"All the more reason not to just stand around waiting," said Lando. "Artoo, what did you find?"

Artoo beeped, and Threepio translated. "Master Lando, Artoo says that there are no inflow vents anywhere in this chamber."

"What? Then how was this chamber repressurized?"

"According to Artoo, the atmospheric gases are passing through the bulkheads molecule by molecule. He says that most of the surface area of the compartment is involved."

"Let me get this straight—these bulkheads are porous?"

Artoo chittered, and Threepio offered the answer. "No, Master Lando. Artoo says that molecules of gas simply appear on the surface."

"Curious," said Lobot. "I wonder if the bulkheads could be actually *producing* the gas."

"Artoo, is there any area that's more involved with this process than the rest?" asked Lando.

The little droid jetted down to the center of the chamber and illuminated a band across the inner bulkhead with a beam of orange light from his holographic projector.

"Got it. Threepio, give me a report on your progress."

The golden droid cocked his head. "Sir, so far I have hailed the masters of this vessel in eleven thousand, four hundred sixty-three languages, offering our abject apologies and asking for their assistance. There has been no reply on any band I am capable of detecting."

"Do those six million languages of yours happen to include the Qella?"

"Alas, Master Lando, they do not."

"Do you have any information at *all* about the Qella language? Maybe it's related to some other language you *are* fluent in—the way that if you know Torrock, you can almost get along in Thobek or Wehttam."

"I'm sorry, Master Lando. I am completely at a loss."

"What about matching up geographically?"

"Sir, it is a standard first contact procedure to attempt contact with regional languages when the native language is unknown," Threepio said with a note of indignation. "I began with the eight hundred seventy-three languages spoken in the sector where Qella is located, and continued with the three thousand, two hundred seven languages with direct links to those linguistic families."

"And now you're just going A to Z on the rest?"

"I am continuing by astrographic proximity."

"How long will it take you to try them all?"

"Master Lando, by reducing the wait time to the minimum specified by my protocols, I will be able to complete the initial series in four-point-two standard days."

"That's about what I figured," said Lando. "Lobot, dig out the cutting blaster. We're going to have to make our own door."

With a grim expression on his face, Admiral Hiram Drayson sat on the edge of his desk and studied the final contact report from Colonel Pakkpekatt at Gmir Askilon.

The recordings from the spotter ships were dramatic

and alarming. Moments before the vagabond broke away, a ring of six rounded bumps—accumulator nodes or beam radiators, Drayson thought—appeared at the forward end of the ship. A fierce blue light began to dance over the bow.

Moments later, twin beams of energy shot out from two of the nodes and scissored back through the gap between the vagabond and *Lady Luck,* slicing them apart. Another pair of beams knifed out from two other nodes and carved through the interdiction generator on the underbelly of the picket *Kauri.* The blowback surge from the fully charged generator destroyed *Kauri*'s power compartment and left the ship afire and dead in space.

The instant *Kauri* was neutralized, the vagabond began to move, turning away from *Lady Luck* and accelerating out past the disabled picket's position, well clear of the remaining interdictors. Just forty-two seconds after it began, it was over, the vagabond vanishing into the center of a hyperspace cone.

The final tally for the contact:

One drone ferret destroyed.

One interdiction picket disabled and abandoned, with twenty-six casualties, including six fatalities in the power compartment.

One yacht recovered and returned to a mooring on *Glorious*'s hull, undamaged except for the primary airlock.

One successful boarding of the target.

One successful escape by the target.

One expedition armada scattered across space, with four ships in pursuit of the target and the others pulling ambulance or cleanup duty.

And, most troubling of all to Drayson, one contact suit gauntlet recovered in the debris—right hand, in Lando's size.

The report contained some positive information as well. It was beyond dispute now that the vagabond's weapons were compound—the intersection of two or more beams did the damage, probably through some sort of harmonic resonance. Unless there were more weapon nodes concealed amidships, it seemed as though six targets were all the vagabond could handle. Possibly as few as four ships, properly spaced, might overwhelm its defenses.

But first Pakkpekatt would have to find the vagabond again—a task that had taken two years the last time.

Drayson called up the chart of the pursuit and studied it closely. Three ships were racing for search stations along the vagabond's last heading: *Lightning* ten light-years out, *Glorious* twenty, and *Marauder* thirty. The improvised plan called for them to drop sensor buoys with hypercomm repeaters at those entry points and then begin making short jumps out to the limits of sensor range, hoping to catch a glimpse of their quarry.

The precision of the plan did not mask its weakness—its slim chance of success depended on the vagabond's making a single short jump. If it followed a short jump with a second jump on another heading, where there were no eyes to see or sensors to track—or if it carried the first jump out fifty, a hundred, five hundred light-years, beyond the borders of the New Republic and into the chaos of the Core—

Drayson knew that Colonel Pakkpekatt had addressed an urgent appeal for more ships to both New Republic Intelligence and the Fleet Office before *Glorious* jumped out from Gmir Askilon. He also knew the likely answer to that appeal.

"The only real chance for us to catch her lies with you, Lando," Drayson said softly. "You must help us find you."

But it was not Drayson's way to abandon someone he had sent into danger. His fingers danced over his controller, bringing an inventory of Alpha Blue's assets in Sector 151 to the screen. There might be little he could do, but he would do what he could. And there was always some way to alter the odds.

The habits of the Senate's Council on Security and Intelligence were not unlike those of the institutions over which it reigned. It announced no meetings, released no public reports, and met only in closed session in the field-shielded Room 030, deep in the subbasements of the old Imperial Palace.

So earnestly secretive were the seven sitting members that, in Coruscant's own dialect of Basic, the phrase "CSI agenda" had become a benchmark for the unattainable, the impossible item on a scavenger hunt. Discouraged suitors would despair that they had "a better chance of taking a CSI agenda home." Subordinates handed a daunting task could comfort themselves with the thought *It could be worse—he could want a CSI agenda, too.*

Even Drayson found it difficult to discover when the CSI would take up Pakkpekatt's request. And when he finally did learn about that session, it was too late to find a way to listen in.

"Last item on the agenda is the Teljkon expedition," said General Carlist Rieekan. "May I assume that you all received your copies of the report?" He waited a moment, then, hearing no dissent, went on. "Discussion, please."

Senator Krall Praget of Edatha, chairman of the CSI, leaned back in his chair and combed his fingers back through his skulldown. "What is there to decide? The mission was a failure. Close the books."

"Lando Calrissian and his team are still aboard the vagabond," Rieekan reminded him gently.

"What reason do you have to think they're still alive?" Praget asked. "Why would any captain capable of acting as surely and decisively as the captain of the vagabond did in escaping make the mistake of not repelling boarders with equal vigor?"

"It is possible that they were taken prisoner," said Rieekan. "It is even possible that they escaped capture."

Praget pulled his datapad toward him. "How do you account for the contact suit gauntlet found by the recovery teams? It's Calrissian's, I believe."

"I don't have an explanation," Rieekan admitted.

"General Rieekan," said Senator Cair Tok Noimm. "Do I understand correctly that the gauntlet is undamaged and there is no blood on it?"

"That's correct."

She nodded. "In that case, this gauntlet does not seem to me to be reason enough to abandon these people to their fate."

"It's not clear to me what we can do for them," said Senator Amamanam, who represented the Bdas on Coruscant. "Unless Senator Noimm would like to lead us in prayer to the Star Mother—"

The laughter around the table was cold, but Noimm's eyes were colder. "There are two lives at stake here—the lives of two valuable friends of the New Republic. And please remember that the droids are of no small value, either—they had their own role in making it possible for there to *be* a New Republic. I doubt there are any droids anywhere who are better known than these two—or better loved, for that matter."

"If they are so important to the New Republic, they should be in the museum, along with all the other beloved icons," said Praget curtly.

"Along with Luke Skywalker, to whom they belong?" asked Senator Lillald. "I must agree with Cair Tok. I would not want to face the questions that would come if these four were to disappear in our service and we were to make no effort to recover them."

"In our service? Have you read the account of how they came to be on that ship? They can hardly be said to be in our service," said Senator Amamanam. "General, could you kindly explain to us how it is that the Baron Calrissian and the others came to be involved in the first place? I don't recall there being any mention of them in the expedition plan you brought to us."

"*General* Calrissian was representing the Fleet on this mission, at the request of the Fleet Office," Rieekan said deliberately. "The others comprise his support staff, apparently assembled specifically for this mission."

"This is all so absurd," Praget fumed. "If it were Hammax and his men on board the vagabond, as it should have been, we would not be having this discussion. Either they would have disabled the ship, or we'd be sending our regrets to the families of the missing in action."

"Senator—"

"But Pakkpekatt allowed these meddlers, these outsiders, these *amateurs,* to intervene, and suddenly it becomes impossible to write off our losses in a professional manner."

Rieekan tried again. "Senator, have the reports from Colonel Pakkpekatt led you to reevaluate the potential gain if we succeed in recovering the Qella vessel?"

"No, General," said Praget, with a touch of impatience at being handled. "I'm still quite convinced that this artifact is worthy of our interest. But I don't see that the circumstances justify sending a Force Two armada wandering through a thousand cubic light-years on what is very likely to be a futile effort."

"With all the uncertainty in Farlax, we could surely find better uses for those ships than chasing a phantom," said Senator Amamanam. "The vagabond will turn up again."

"Will you be personally handling the apologies to Luke Skywalker, then?" Senator Noimm asked cuttingly. "Will the chairman make himself available to the newsgrids to explain exactly under what circumstances these notables disappeared?"

"If I might make a suggestion—" Rieekan began.

"By all means," said Praget.

"A contact suit isn't designed for long endurance. Its recycling systems are simple and relatively inefficient. Its consumables, if managed wisely, might last the wearer perhaps two hundred hours—certainly no more than two hundred and twenty," said the intelligence director.

"So we simply wait a few days to declare them dead, is that your point?"

"Not quite," Rieekan said. "If they *are* still alive, the general and his team will be highly motivated to act expeditiously. Anything they *can* do to impede the flight of the Qella vessel, they will do in the next several days. So it seems only prudent to me to allow Pakkpekatt to continue the search for, say, another fifteen days."

"If nothing else," said Senator Amamanam, "doing so would cut the heart out of the charge that we abandoned the Baron to his fate." He glanced expectantly down the table toward Senator Noimm.

"If you'd truly like to protect yourself, I suggest you go one step further and propose that we send Pakkpekatt the additional vessels he requested," said Noimm. "Otherwise the search might be seen as the token gesture it is."

"No, no, no," said Praget. "Pakkpekatt gets no more ships. That incompetent Hortek spook—what he *ought* to get is a review board and a dishonorable separation. But I suppose I'll have to settle for the general's finding a deep, dark hole to drop him in once this is over."

"I wouldn't support sending additional ships," said Rieekan, ignoring Praget's other comments. "The way I see it, we now have assets aboard the target vessel. That changes the tactical equation. We're not going to be trying to run it into an interdiction net, or firing on it. We just need to find it and be on hand to pick up our people."

"I see Pakkpekatt only has four vessels actively committed to the search at this point."

"That's right," said Rieekan. "So I think we can reasonably talk about downsizing our commitment to this project. If everyone will look at page fifteen in the mission outline, the ship assignment list—"

Chapter 2

◆

"Have you ever used a cutting blaster before, Lando?" Lobot asked with concern.

"Lots of times," said Lando, bracing himself between the inner bulkhead and the equipment sled. "But don't ask me for a list. The statute of limitations hasn't run out on all of 'em. Artoo, can I have a little more light in here, right in front of me?"

The dome-topped droid drifted up and forward on tiny puffs of thruster gas, changing the angle of the light slightly.

"That's good, Artoo—hold right there."

"Be careful not to cut too deeply," Lobot said. "There may be mechanisms behind the wall—"

"If Artoo's right, there's nothing behind this part of the wall. The sonogram showed a thin bulkhead and another compartment beyond, five meters in diameter."

"I know. But a ship this size could have waste ports five meters in diameter. Or fuel conduits."

"You know, Lobot, when you're cut off from your databases, you're almost as much of an old lady as Threepio here," Lando said, but not without affection. "Threepio, any change?"

"No, Master Lando. There has been no response to my first nine hundred sixty-one thousand, eight—"

"Save it for the log," Lando said. "Lobot, Threepio, I know how much you want to watch over my shoulder while I do this. But if I were you, I'd move around to where my contact suit is between you and the blaster. That way, if I make a mistake, you might still be around to learn from it."

"If Artoo would give me a link to his video processor—" Lobot said.

"Do it, Artoo." Lando held the cutting blaster up before his face with his right hand, and with his left set the selector for hairline and depth for shallow. "Maybe we'll finally get a response to *this* message," he said, and activated the cutter.

Under Lando's steady hand, the blue-white energy blade drew a straight line down the face of the bulkhead. But when Lando pulled the blaster away to inspect his work, he found that the blaster had left no mark—the bulkhead was intact.

"Guess I was a little too careful," Lando said, frowning. "Move the sled in just a little for me, Lobot."

When he had finished adjusting his position, Lando reached forward and drew the blaster blade slowly down the face of the bulkhead once more.

"What the—"

"What is happening?" Threepio asked worriedly. He rose from behind Lando to peer over his shoulder at the wall.

"A lot of nothing," said Lando in disgust. "I can't even scorch it."

"I think you are mistaken, Lando," said Lobot. "Please try again, and this time move the cutter more quickly."

Lando slashed the cutter downward across the face of the bulkhead. The brilliant glare of the blade left a thin black line in its wake—a clean, straight cut that closed up and vanished a fraction of a second later.

"Self-sealing bulkheads?"

"It would appear so," said Lobot.

"Well, that's just dandy," Lando said, shutting off the cutting blaster. "I can't cut us a door, because it hasn't the manners to stay cut."

Lobot tapped Lando on the helmet, then gestured at the blaster. "May I try something?"

"Be my guest." Lando surrendered the blaster and moved aside, pulling himself hand over hand toward the aft end of the equipment sled.

Lobot studied the selectors on the blaster for a few moments, then opted for the medium drill setting. The blade appeared this time as a pointed cone, which Lobot pressed against the wall until half its length had disappeared. When he withdrew it, there was a hole a few centimeters across in the bulkhead.

The hole began to close at once, but it took noticeably longer to vanish than the cut had—long enough for Lobot to pull himself down to eye level and catch a quick glimpse through the breach.

"Very clever, Lobot. Very interesting. Between one and two seconds, I think," Lando said.

"I was hoping for this result," said Lobot, turning toward Lando. "Whatever mechanisms are involved, substantially more material must be transported or replaced to fill a hole than to seal a cut."

"Did you see anything?"

"Nothing useful. An open space of some kind, dimly lit. Everything had a yellowish cast."

"Let's try a bigger hole," Lando said. "Artoo, do you have some sort of remote sensor you can stick through this time?"

"The limpet," Lobot suggested. "We could reach through and attach the limpet on the other side of the bulkhead. Both Artoo and I are capable of receiving its sensor data."

"I don't want to make quite that big a hole," Lando said. "Not this time. Every time we cut into that bulkhead, we're reminding this ship we're here. I don't know how many times we can bite before we get swatted. Artoo, what about it?"

Artoo tootled pridefully as a small equipment panel on his body popped open and a slender wand topped by a small silver ball unfolded from within.

"You needn't be snippy about it," Threepio chided.

The response from Artoo sounded like an electronic raspberry.

"Well, I'm sure it's not his business to keep track of those details," Threepio said, bristling. "I've been in your company for longer than I care to remember, and *I* certainly don't keep track of every gadget in that ugly little chassis—"

Lando whistled sharply. "Whoa, you two—save it for later. Threepio, was there any part of that I need to know?"

"Master Lando, Artoo says that astromech droids must frequently inspect systems which are located in confined spaces," Threepio said curtly. "He apparently believes that R2 units are important enough that this should be common knowledge. He has quite the little ego, you know."

"Yes, well, I've often thought it's a shame he doesn't have your modesty, Threepio," Lando said, flying himself back to the middle of the equipment sled and reclaiming the cutting blaster from Lobot. "Have you made any new pen pals since we started cutting?"

"There has been no response whatever from the masters of this vessel since I began trying to hail them," said Threepio. "I suggest you proceed with whatever you are planning."

Lando changed the selector to medium drill and activated the blaster. "Artoo, come in close—I want that sensor wand through the hole as quickly as possible. But don't let yourself get caught when it closes. And Lobot, Artoo, between the two of you, I want to know exactly how large a hole I make and exactly how long it takes it to close. Is everyone ready? Let's do it, then."

The medium setting allowed Lando to open a hole that was nearly large enough to admit a man's clenched fist. Switching off the blaster, Lando pushed off from the wall and did a backward somersault, floating out of Artoo's way. The droid moved smoothly and surely into position, extending the wand through the very center of the opening and snatching it back at the last moment as the hole disappeared again.

"Show us, Artoo. Holoprojector," Lando ordered. The droid chirped an acknowledgment and offered up a fish-eye perspective of a round-walled passage that seemed to bend around or through the ship in both directions. There was no sign of life or machinery, nor any response to the cutting of the hole and the invasion of Artoo's scan probe.

"Looks promising," said Lando. "Whatever it is, it could give us access to at least part of the ship. Artoo, Lobot, what's the verdict? How big a hole do I need to cut to get us all through?"

"I am afraid there is a problem, Lando," Lobot said. "Artoo's measurements show that the larger hole closed faster, per unit of area, than the smaller one."

"It looked that way to me, too," Lando agreed. "Bigger holes probably get higher priority from the ship's systems. What, don't you think we can get through?"

"The short dimension of the common wall between that passage and this chamber is approximately one-point-seven meters," Lobot said, pointing. "My estimate is that a hole that size will take only six or seven seconds to close down to the point where it will be impassable for any of us. That is not enough time to move the sled and the four of us into the other chamber."

"It might be enough time. Jump troops go out the drop chute of an assault boat at a rate of one per second."

"Jump troops have the benefit of training and gravity. I have modeled it with Artoo's nav processor. At best, one of us would not make it through."

"Well—that *is* a problem," said Lando. "Because I have a sneaking suspicion that when we cut a hole that size, this ship's going to get fed up with us and try to spit us out again. I don't think we'll get a chance to do it twice." He thought hard for a moment, then waved the blaster in the air. "Everything off the sled. I need to make some modifications."

The equipment sled was an uncomplicated device. Its thick rectangular frame contained the gyros, fuel cells, and thrust stabilizer system, and also provided cut-out handholds at regular intervals. The standard diamond-pattern metal grid that filled the frame provided a wealth of lockdowns for gear kits and tools. Both sides of the grid on the team's sled were heavily loaded.

"Modifications?"

"Yeah," said Lando. "I think we need a frame for our door."

Clinging to the sled with one hand and wielding the cutting blaster with the other, Lando slashed away where the grid joined the sled frame. When he was finished, the sled was in two pieces. Lando pushed the wobbly, heavily loaded grid toward Artoo. "You tow that through to the other side."

The droid's grappling clamps appeared and latched onto the grid securely.

"Give me a hand here, Lobot?"

Lobot eased forward and grabbed a handhold at the opposite end of the gutted sled frame. "I am remembering something I accessed earlier," he said. "The chief designer of the Ma'aood funerary temples directed his draftsmen that all obvious passages should be booby-trapped, and all traps should be made as inviting as possible."

"Thank you for that uplifting thought," said Lando.

"If we get out of this, you should think about a new career as a morale officer. Everyone ready?"

"Master Lando, what should I do?"

Lando checked his combat blaster in its holster, then slid the selector on the cutting blaster to WIDE. "Add this to our apology," he said, and pointed it at the bulkhead. "Hang on."

The brilliant flare of the cutting beam momentarily dazzled the viewscreen of Lando's contact suit, and the vaporized material from two and a half square meters of bulkhead filled the air as a gray cloud. Before Lando could even see clearly, the hole began to close.

"Let's go, let's go—get it lined up!" Lando shouted. The two men maneuvered the frame into position, and the bulkhead closed around it as though it were a tailored fit.

But as they did, they heard a deep, rumbling groan from the ship, a sound that had no direction. Though the surroundings were alien, the sound was familiar—the signature of a form of stress that aged large vessels' hulls and led to the spectacular form of self-destruction known as an exit breach. It was the exit growl, the characteristic sound caused by portions of the ship emerging from hyperspace nanoseconds before the rest as the jump field collapsed.

"I hate it when I'm right," Lando said, gesturing with his free hand. "Move it, Artoo. Now!"

The little droid jetted quickly toward the opening, towing the heavily loaded grid behind it. For a moment Lando thought the frame looked too small for Artoo to pass through it. But the droid retracted his treads as far as they would go, turned his body, and cleared the opening by bare centimeters. The equipment grid smoothly passed through behind him.

"Wait for me, Artoo!" Threepio called, flailing his arms and legs in midair.

"Go ahead," Lando said to Lobot, passing him the cutting blaster and waving him on. "I'll get Threepio."

Lobot didn't wait to be told twice, swinging himself feetfirst through the improvised doorway as neatly as a gymnast taking a turn on the parallel bar. Meanwhile, Lando clipped the safety line from the contact suit's belt to the handhold of the frame and launched himself toward the droid, his gloved hand extended to him.

"Oh, *thank* you, Master Lando," the droid said relievedly as he grabbed hold of Lando's arm. Then Threepio saw Lando's eyes suddenly widen in alarm. "What is it, sir?"

Watching from the inner passage, Lobot saw the same thing Lando had seen when he looked past Threepio toward the outer bulkhead: a small opening appearing and quickly irising into an airlock that revealed a stark, starry blackness beyond. Moments later the external mics on the suits picked up the hiss of outrushing air.

Lando did not take the time to answer Threepio's concerned inquiry. "Heads up—incoming!" he bellowed, and swung Threepio by the arms toward the inner doorway. Bracing himself against the frame, Lobot reached through, caught Threepio's right foot, and dragged him into the inner passage.

But the rush of air through the inner passage and out through the wound kept building, and it was all Lobot could do to keep himself from being sucked through.

Nor was he the only one in trouble. Artoo's thrusters could not hold against the screaming wind, and he squawked loudly as he was dragged inexorably back down the inner passage toward the opening, clinging determinedly to the equipment grid.

Meanwhile, Lando dangled helplessly at the end of his safety line, his feet banging against the edge of the outer airlock as the air grabbed at him on its way into the vacuum beyond.

Only Threepio was relatively secure, his metal body braced across one end of the sled frame, blocking part of the opening. But he was waving his arms wildly like a shell-spined mud crawler that'd been flipped on its back. "Oh, Artoo, we're doomed!" he cried. "I never did like space travel. Look where your adventuring has led us—"

"You have to cut the frame," Lando was shouting into the comlink. "Cut the frame and it'll pull out—the rest of the hole will close. Do it!"

"Not with you on that side," Lobot said, climbing across Threepio to where the safely line was attached. "There's a take-up crank on that belt line. See if you can pull yourself up that way."

"No good," said Lando. "Too much load. Just cut the frame, will you?"

Lobot glanced sideways down the corridor to see if he and Threepio were in danger of being knocked through the hole by an out-of-control Artoo and his cargo. But to Lobot's relief, he saw that Artoo had made his way to the edge of the passage, burned a small hole with his arc welder, and let the hole close around a repair arm. So far, the anchor was holding against the current—which seemed to Lobot to be weakening.

"Forget it," Lobot directed, reaching down between his braced legs and catching hold of the thin safety line. He began hauling on the line hand over hand, reeling Lando in like a great white fish. The cyborg's wiry body concealed surprising strength, and soon he had hold of the tow ring on Lando's suit, at the back of the neck. "Use your thrusters now—full vertical."

"Full vertical," Lando echoed.

With one smooth, powerful motion, Lobot pulled Lando up between his widely spaced knees, lying straight back to drag Lando's legs clear and hurl him free down the passage.

Quickly sitting back up, Lobot pulled out the cutting blaster and slashed the frame in two places. There was a shower of sparks each time, then a puff of D20 propellant from the broken lines as he kicked out the section between the cuts. It spun free and tumbled out through the airlock on the breeze.

The bulkhead groaned under Lobot, and the rest of the frame began to collapse, twisting sideways as it did, until it, too, was carried away. Seconds later the hole had closed under them, the pitch of the roaring air rising to a shrill note before it cut off entirely, leaving them in silence.

"I guess we only get to use that doorway trick once," Lando said. The inside of his faceplate was fogged with sweat. "Where'd you learn that?"

"I learned it wild-water rafting on Oko E," Lobot said. "It is the preferred method for getting a raftmate out of the river before the sulfur ice pulls him under. That was my *last* vacation," he added.

"You have unexpected depth, Lobot," said Lando. "Is everyone all right?"

"I am certain that several of my circuits are over-heated," Threepio pronounced. "With your permission, Master Lando, I would like to perform a self-diagnostic."

"Go ahead," Lando said. "While you're doing that, we'll get Artoo free. And then we can start figuring out what to do next."

"That should not prove too taxing," said Lobot. "The choices appear to be to go that way"—he crossed his arms over his chest, pointing a finger in each direction—"or that way."

"Shhh," Lando said, craning his head. "Wait. Listen."

They listened in silence, with sinking hearts. In the mysterious hollow spaces of the vagabond, the fading rumble of the entry growl echoed for a long time.

"Blast." Lando sighed. "She's jumped again."

"Something interesting here," said Josala Krenn. Kroddok Stopa bent forward over the surface scanner. The false-color image mapped the undulations of a great glacier as it crawled its way along a widening, steep-sided valley toward a frozen sea. "Where?"

"Here," said Josala, pointing out a string of small blue blotches scattered along the northeast edge of the glacier. "The side-scanning radar pulled these up— they're sitting anywhere from eleven to nineteen meters down in the ice."

"Rock from the lateral moraine?"

"No, for two reasons. First, they're awfully regular in size, oblong, between one-point-five and two meters in the long axis. And second—do you know anything about the flow lines in the accumulation zone of a glacier?"

"Not a thing."

"Something that falls on the surface of a glacier moves down-valley with the ice and down into the body of the glacier as more snow falls on top of it," Josala said. "The lateral moraine running through that part of the glacier is made up of rock coming off this cliff face." She pointed at a side valley well back along the path of the glacier.

"So by the time that rock gets to here—"

"It's fifty meters down. These other objects, they haven't been in the ice as long as that rock underneath them. And they would have had to come onto the ice somewhere in here." Josala traced a circle with her finger over a flat area up-valley.

"That's out in the middle of nothing," said Stopa.

"Right." She wrinkled her face in thought. "It's hard to be sure of the timetables with cataclysmic climatic change, but I'd guess that whatever these are, they've only been in the ice for fifty to a hundred years."

His eyes widened. "Bodies. Burials on the ice."

"That was my thought."

"It makes sense. Nomadic groups, or perhaps caves somewhere nearby—ice caves, possibly—"

"It doesn't matter where they lived, so long as we've found where they died."

"How deep is the shallowest of those bodies? Eleven meters?" When Josala nodded, Stopa turned to the pilot. "We're going to want our rover."

"Kroddok—"

"I know, I know. But hear me out—we'll wait until the weather's good there," Stopa said, his eyes animated by anticipation. "We'll set the rover down right on top of the site. We leave the engine running at idle so there's no chance for anything to freeze up. We work right out of the gear bay, because all we have to do is take a core. Our equipment ought to be able to handle that."

"You want to drill a core?" Josala said in horror. "That'll mangle the remains."

"Yes," Stopa said. "I know it violates the usual protocols. But we weren't sent here to recover bodies. We were sent here to recover biological material. When our reinforcements arrive, they can go down and excavate the other sites. But in the meantime, we'll have something we can analyze and report back on."

Josala shook her head. "I'd really rather wait for the people who know what they're doing."

"But we know how to take a core," Stopa said. "Krenn, a first-year apprentice knows how to take a core. We'll be out of there in thirty minutes. Twenty."

Josala's reluctance still showed on her face.

Kroddok drew closer and dropped his voice. "The bonus from the NRI would be enough to fund the expedition to Stovax," he said. "But if we wait until *Penga Rift* arrives, we'll have to share the bonus. We might even end up being cut out completely."

He waited to see if that would sway her, then added, "I give you my word that we'll withdraw at the first sign of any trouble. No, better, I'm making you expedition boss. You say 'That's it,' and that's it."

Josala looked up at him with a frown, then past him to the pilot. "What Dr. Stopa said. We're going to want our rover."

*   *   *

The archaeologists' little Mark II World Rover skimmed across the top of snow-covered southwest range and began its descent into the glacier valley.

"You're on the beam, eight hundred fifty meters out," said the voice of *IX-26*'s pilot, continuing to talk Stopa and Krenn down to their destination. The navigation and sensor arrays of the rover were no match for those of the ferret.

"Copy," said Stopa, who was at the controls. "I'm going from glide to hover mode now."

"Seven hundred. Six hundred. Five fifty—"

Several small shield doors on the rover's fuselage and delta wings slid open, revealing vector nozzles for the thrustjets. With the rover's nose stall-high and the nozzles perpendicular to the wings, the little ship quickly lost its forward velocity and began to settle.

Josala was peering out the starboard cockpit viewpane, studying the ground below them. The steep inner slope of the southwest range wore a smooth blanket of snow, but the surface of the glacier itself was a field of jagged ice blocks, some as large as the rover itself.

"It looked a lot smoother on the SSR display," Josala said.

"The rover can cope with a forty-degree terrain tilt. We'll be all right."

"It's going to be like drilling through rock."

"But ice won't wear the bits, like rock does," said Stopa. "We'll get through."

"Two hundred twenty," the pilot was saying into Stopa's headset. "Ease her a hair to port."

"Copy," Stopa said. "Krenn, we have to at least give it a try—"

Just then a cloud of swirling white particles billowed up around the rover from below, closing in around the cockpit viewpanes and cutting visibility nearly to zero.

"It's our downblast," Stopa said quickly. He raised

the control handle, and the rover climbed nimbly out of
the cloud, which immediately began to dissipate beneath
them. "Not a problem."

"One fifty."

"You can't land us in a whiteout," said Josala. "If
you set us down on the edge of one of those ice boulders,
we'll flip over before the strut levelers can do anything."

"Ninety-five."

"I'll just hover at ten meters until the thrusters blow
the site clear of loose material," Stopa said confidently.
"If I can't get definition on the undercarriage holo, I
won't try to land. All right?"

"All right," Josala said with a sigh.

"Sixty," the pilot said. "Ease off, or you're going to
overrun the site."

Stopa tapped the air brakes lightly and pulled back
on the control handle slightly. As the rover settled
toward the glacier, it was once again engulfed in a billow
of jet-driven snow. But before long, the swirling cloud
began to thin, and the horizon returned.

"Twenty-five."

Josala peered forward. "I can't judge distances
without a referent. That big slab of ice—"

He patted her arm. "It's bigger and farther away
than you think."

"Ten. Eight. Five. Easy—"

"Take me to plus-sixteen. I want to put the rover's
tail right down on top of it."

"It's under you now. Plus-six. Plus-nine. Plus-
fourteen—"

Stopa pushed the control handle sharply down, and
the rover dropped hard and shook from the impact, nose
tilted down and sliding sideways. It came to a stop with
another small jolt, then slowly came to level.

"There," he said, switching quickly among the undercarriage scanners and studying the display.

Those closest to the thrusters were frozen over with
steam ice, but the forward and aft scanners were clear.

The front landing strut seemed to be wedged in a small crevasse, though no damage was evident. Aft, the body of the rover was sitting comfortably above the ice.

"That wasn't half bad," he said with a grin, setting the systems to STANDBY.

"Let's just get it done," Josala said crossly.

One behind the other, they made their way through the crawlspace over the orbital engine compartment to the crowded gear bay. There they helped each other into their improvised snow gear—the ferret's sole emergency spacesuit for her, a standard digger's isolation suit for him, augmented by the ferret pilot's spacesuit glove liners.

Neither of them was prepared for the blinding dazzle of the glacier when the gear bay doors swung open. The sky was clear, and the blue-white sun lit the landscape with cold crystal fire as hard to look at as the sun itself. Josala's viewplate adjusted for it, but Stopa had to avert his eyes and squint to keep from being overwhelmed.

"Spectacular!" Stopa exulted.

"Sightsee when we're finished," Josala chided.

Everything took longer than it should have. The core drill base didn't want to latch in the working position, giving Josala reason to worry about whether the bay doors would seal properly when it was time to leave. The gloves made them both clumsy and turned the routine assembly of the first sections of the coring tube into a test. Josala's sounding for the body beneath them was marred by crazy echoes. The drill's gimbal mount froze up until the drill was turned on, complicating the alignment on Josala's sounding.

But at last the coring bit chewed its way into the surface of the glacier and headed down into its depths.

"Seven sections!" Stopa shouted over the rumble of the drill. "At this angle, we'll need seven sections."

Josala waved her hand in acknowledgment and turned away to pull the next section from the rack. It danced under her touch, and she drew her hand back. She pressed her gauntlet against the wall of the bay and felt it shivering. It was then that she realized that what she had thought was her own body shivering was the deck of the rover vibrating under her feet. The drill was roaring now, as though its bearing rings had disintegrated, its lubricants turned to grit.

"Turn it off!" she cried, pulling her way along to where Stopa was leaning out the back of the bay, looking down at the core drive and measuring the drill's progress. "Turn it off!" He looked up at her dumbly, and she reached behind him for the controls.

The core cylinder spun to a stop, but neither the vibration nor the noise ceased. Just the opposite, in fact—the rumble was growing louder and the shaking growing worse.

With a desperate fear already in their eyes, they looked out from the gear bay at the mountain ridge behind them, the ridge they had flown over just minutes before, the ridge that had been like cotton bathed in sunlight. The middle of the ridge was now hidden behind an onrushing wall of snow and ice, spreading and climbing the sky as it hurtled closer.

There was no chance to escape into that sky. The avalanche was on them before they could even quite remember the word. It tumbled the rover before it like a toy, packing its every crevice with snow, engulfing the ship in the furious turbulence of the icy maelstrom.

When the flow finally slowed and ceased, its leading edge reaching nearly halfway across the valley, there were two more bodies buried on the ice for *Penga Rift* to recover.

"The first thing we need is a way to find this spot again, and this passage is notably lacking in landmarks," said Lando. Using the cutting blaster, he sliced a small triangle off one corner of the equipment grid. "Where was our doorway? Here?"

"Lower," said Lobot. "There."

"I'm glad you're sure," said Lando. "I'm all turned around." He cut a slit in the bulkhead, inserted one edge of the triangle, and held it there until the bulkhead closed around it. Then he placed one palm flat against the bulkhead and tried to tug the metal grid out of the wall. "That should do it."

Lobot drifted up with a short length of cord in one hand. "We might want more than one marker before we're done," he said, looping the cord through one of the diamond-shaped openings and tying the ends together with an overhand knot. "One knot equals the first marker. We'll put two knots on the next one."

"Okay," said Lando, turning away from the wall. "There's one thing I overlooked when we took inventory. I burned about sixty percent of my thruster propellant trying to get up here."

"I have ninety-one percent remaining," said Lobot. "Unfortunately, there is no way for me to share my supply with you."

"You might end up sharing it by carrying me around on your back," Lando said. "Threepio, how are you doing for thrust mass?"

Artoo burbled, and Threepio offered the translation. "Artoo says that his propellant supply is adequate, but he would like to be informed when any of us locates a power coupling."

"With any luck, it'll be right next to an oxygen valve," Lando said grimly. "All right—we are in a survival situation. This ship has now jumped twice, and we have to assume that it lost any pursuit that was mounted with that second jump. That means our first priority is to locate and disable the hyperdrive, and stop this ship."

"But Master Lando, if we disable the hyperdrive, we would be stranded," Threepio protested.

"We don't know how long the vagabond stays in

hyperspace—weeks, months, years. The galaxy is one hundred twenty thousand light-years across. I like our chances better stranded."

"Master Lando, would it not be more prudent to find the masters of this vessel and petition them to take us back to Coruscant?"

"Threepio, I think we're the masters of this vessel now," Lando said. "We have to be, if we're going to survive." He ticked off the priorities on his fingers. "First, we find some way to stop this ship. Second, we find out where that leaves us. Third, we find out who our nearest friend is. Fourth, we find some way to signal them. If we get that all done before Lobot and I run out of air and the droids run out of power, *then* we can worry about who built the vagabond, and why."

"We may need to engage those questions in order to achieve those objectives," said Lobot.

"Maybe," said Lando. "But in my experience, you really don't need to know much about a precision machine in order to smash it." He pointed a finger to the left, then to the right. "What's your best guess—hyperdrive aft, or forward?"

"Center of mass is the most efficient placement," Lobot said. "Forward."

Lando nodded. "Then let's get going."

Colonel Pakkpekatt hovered near the communications station as the cruiser *Glorious* dropped out of hyperspace. The chase armada was strung out along forty light-years, and *Glorious* was the second bead on the string. "Give them to me as fast as they come," he said to the tech at the station.

"Yes, sir. I'm seeing six dispatches—an emergency action directive from the Fleet Office, copied to Captain Garch. A blue letter from the NRI, copied to Captain Hammax. A dispatch marked 'Urgent' from the Obroan Institute. Reports from *Lightning, Pran,* and *Nagwa.*"

"The three ships behind us," said Pakkpekatt. "Very well. Make the dispatches available at my station."

Crossing the bridge with long, light-footed strides, Pakkpekatt eased himself into his flak couch and brought up the secure display. Neither his face nor his carriage betrayed any emotion as he read through the dispatches one after another. When he was finished, he tipped the screen away and let out a long hiss.

"Major Legorburu."

Ixidro Legorburu, the M'haeli intelligence officer who was serving as Pakkpekatt's tactical aide, hurried to his station in response to the summons. "Colonel."

"We have just received a Fleet-wide level one alert," Pakkpekatt said, tipping his display upward so that the major could read the emergency action directive. "My request for additional ships for the search has been denied. I am under orders to release *Marauder, Pran,* and *Nagwa* from their duties here so that they may return to their respective commands at best possible speed."

"That's nearly half our remaining strength, sir," Legorburu said, shaking his head. "What do they expect us to do?"

"Fail, apparently," Pakkpekatt said curtly. "I have also been placed on notice that *Glorious* may be recalled as well. We are to remain on one-hour alert status, which means no jumps greater than one half light-year."

"At least that allows us to proceed with the search," said Legorburu. "But we should call *Kettemoor* forward to fill the gap in the line when *Marauder* pulls out. She should be finished with recovery work by now, anyway."

"*Kettemoor* has already jumped to Nichen with the dead and injured from the *Kauri,*" said Pakkpekatt. "We will not have her back for another day at least—if they allow her to rejoin us at all."

Legorburu peered intently at the display. "I don't get it, Colonel. Why the sudden change of priorities? What's happening back there? It must be something big if they can't spare a thirty-year-old gunship and a couple of interdiction pickets."

"That information was not made available to me," said Pakkpekatt. His mouth curled in an unhappy threat-snarl.

"Maybe I can get something out-of-channel," said Legorburu. "Would you like me to try?"

Pakkpekatt nodded. "Please do," he said. "I would like to have a better idea just who I must wrestle to keep this mission alive."

Chapter 3

◆

The procession through the passageway of the Teljkon vagabond was led by Lando Calrissian, combat blaster in hand. Following close behind was Artoo, towing the equipment grid protectively behind him. Last in line was Lobot, with Threepio riding on the back of his contact suit like a child perched on the back of his father.

"This is my fault," Lando said, peering over his shoulder at them. "I should have gone ahead and gotten a thrust belt for Threepio, maybe even a complete thrust harness and powerpack. Consumable refills for the contact suits, too."

"We have them—had them—on *Lady Luck*," said Lobot. "Everything could not fit on one sled."

"I'd trade most everything on that grid for a couple of refill packs. I never thought we'd be in zero-G as long as it looks like we will be." *Forever, maybe,* Lando thought grimly.

"It is an interesting design choice," Lobot said. "The Qella appear to have done everything they could to make it hard for us to move about in here. There is no artificial gravity, no spin. The bulkheads are nonmagnetic and have no friction tracks, handholds, or zip lines."

"What's so interesting about that?"

"The Qella were planet-dwellers," Lobot said, surprised by the question. "How did *they* expect to get around in this ship?"

Lando grunted. "Maybe the Qella are giant slugs as wide as this tunnel."

"Perhaps," said Lobot. "But even giant slugs are probably more comfortable in a gravity field. I can't help thinking that somewhere in this vessel there must be a switch that would make all of this much easier."

The passage seemed to have no end. It curved away in front of Lando like an ever-receding horizon, teasing him with a promise it never fulfilled. "How long has it been now?"

"Artoo's event recorders say we entered the vagabond three hours, eight minutes ago. We left our entry point forty-seven minutes ago," Lobot answered.

"Seems even longer than that," said Lando. "Am I the only one who's noticed? Shouldn't we have run out of ship by now?"

"Obviously we haven't."

"Nothing's obvious here," Lando said. "We're cruising at a meter per second, minus overhead for a couple of stops. Forty-five minutes is twenty-seven hundred seconds. And this ship is only fifteen hundred meters long. We should be a kilometer out in front of the bow by now."

"The conduits we saw on the surface of the vagabond wind around it in complex patterns," Lobot said. "If we are inside one of those, as I believe we are, that could account for the length of this passage."

"No, it couldn't, because we're still heading forward. Aren't we? If this passage had turned back, we'd have noticed."

"Would we?" asked Lobot. "Without landmarks and referents, I find it difficult to be sure."

"You're right about that. No matter how I try, I can't keep a picture of this place in my head," Lando complained, turning to face the others. "Artoo, let me see your map again."

Artoo's holoprojector flickered into life. The map superimposed the data from Artoo's inertial movement sensors over the scans of the vagabond performed by Pakkpekatt's technicians, showing their path through it as a bright red line. The line wiggled back and forth like a low-frequency sine wave across the hull of the ship and extended out beyond it.

"See?" Lando said. "We *are* out in front of the ship."

"Artoo, are your gyros operating normally?" Lobot asked.

The droid's affirmation was indignant.

"Then how do you explain this data?"

Artoo chirped a curt reply. "The ship is longer now?" Threepio translated incredulously. "What an absurdity. Even you can't be *that* foolish. You are obviously malfunctioning."

Lando sighed and surveyed the passage's face—they had dropped the words "wall" and "bulkhead" as inappropriate some time earlier. "It makes as much sense as anything else," he said tiredly. "We've seen something of the tricks their technology can do. Maybe nothing about this ship is immutable, not even its dimensions. Maybe the Qella don't play fair."

"You have beaten rigged games in the past," Lobot said.

"Yeah—I guess I have," said Lando. "But it helps a lot if you can watch the table for a while first. Kill the map, Artoo, but keep tracking us as best you can. We're going to pick up the pace a little. Two meters per second, on my mark—"

*   *   *

Most of another hour dragged by before Artoo made a discovery that set him to beeping agitatedly.

"What is it?" Lando demanded.

"Artoo says that there is an irregularity ahead," Threepio said. "It may be an artifact of some kind."

Lando jetted ahead, scanning the passage face hopefully. "Which side?"

"Ahead and high to your left, Master Lando," said Threepio.

"I see it," said Lando. "Blast, it's tiny. Wait—oh, no."

"What is it? Lando?"

Lando did not explain, but when the others joined him, they got all the explanation they needed. A fragment of metal diamond grid protruded from the face of the passage, and a short cord waved from its anchoring knot.

Threepio gave voice to the unspoken. "Why, we're back where we started."

"That's impossible," Lobot said, with a touch of irritation.

"Yeah, you'd think so, but how else do you explain this?" Lando said, gesturing.

"Perhaps it was moved," said Lobot.

"How? You think there's someone else on this ship?"

"I do not know," said Lobot. "This could be a copy of our marker, a deception. Artoo's sensors still indicate that we're heading toward the bow."

"Oh, we are—for the second time, most likely. What kind of crazy ship are we on? This passage doesn't go anywhere, and it doesn't do anything."

"It occupied us for two hours," Lobot pointed out.

"So it did. And we've wasted those two hours and"—Lando checked his readouts—"about nine percent of my thrust mass. Same for both of you, I'd guess."

"This is most distressing. What do we do now?" Threepio asked.

"We start playing smarter," said Lando. "How much carbon line do we have?"

Lobot knew the answer without looking. "Two spools, five thousand meters each. Why?"

"If we keep going around in circles, we could find ourselves unable to get anywhere for lack of propellant. There's not enough grid to spare to make handholds the length of the passage, but there might be enough for line anchors. I think we'd better start stringing some hand lines now," Lando said. "And they'll help keep us from getting fooled again."

"Yes—we can build a topological map rather than a representational one," Lobot said. "We will at least know the relationships between the places we have been, even if the exact geometry escapes us."

Lando nodded. "*Something* had better start happening. I'm starting to get seriously annoyed."

According to the counter on the line spool, they had gone 884 meters down the passage, staking four improvised line anchors along the way, when they came to the junction.

"This is nuts," Lando said, hovering in midair before the twin openings. "This passage didn't branch the last time we were through here."

"If we've been through here before."

"Don't start with me," Lando said, turning.

"It was not a jest," Lobot said. "It remains a possibility that these passages are channels or conduits, related in some way to the operation of the ship. What we have seen in here may have nothing to do with us."

"Conduits for what? They're dry as a bone."

"There are other types of fluids and flows—gases, energy plasmas, electrical charges," Lobot said. "And conduits generally require stops, valves, and switches of some sort. This is likely to be one, directly ahead of us.

There may be another somewhere behind us that placed us on this path."

Lando slowly spun back to face the junction. "If I had a fat toe, a short toe, a black toe, a new toe, I would know, where to go," he chanted softly.

"What?"

"Pardon me, sir. It is a children's counting rhyme, from Basarais," Threepio said. "Master Lando, may I make a suggestion?"

"Anytime, Threepio. The last thing I want is for the last thing I hear to be someone saying, 'You know, I wondered about that earlier—I guess I should have spoken up.'"

"Very well, Master Lando. My suggestion is that we should separate into two parties and explore both passages at the same time. This would be the most efficient method. If each party consists of a human and a droid, I believe we should be able to maintain communications even if we become separated by some distance."

"Not bad, Threepio," said Lando. "We have two spools—we could set lines in both passages. Lobot?"

"I strongly advise against separating," Lobot said. "Valves and stops which open seemingly at random can as easily close. It is also possible that we have been presented with this choice precisely for this purpose—to divide us."

Lando frowned. "If we don't separate, which passage do we take?"

Lobot shook his head. "It will not matter, Lando. Just choose."

It did not matter. The passage Lando chose ended three hundred meters later, after turning downward—inward?—nearly ninety degrees. When they doubled back, the alternate passage led them to another junction that was the reverse of the first, and to another short passage that turned sharply before ending abruptly.

"There's something down there," Lando said, lingering as the others turned back. "Both dead ends go to the same place. The hyperdrive could be down there."

Lobot could tell that the baron was powerfully tempted to test his theory by blasting a hole in the wall, and touched his shoulder with an outstretched hand. "Come," the cyborg said.

"I'm tired of this."

"I know," said Lobot. "But *you* know that disabling a hyperdrive and destabilizing one are two very different matters. We will find a better way."

Lando glanced at his telltales. "All right," he said. "But if we haven't found it by the time these numbers reach single digits, I'm coming back here. I'm not just going to wait for death, Lobot."

"I would not expect that of you," Lobot said. "But for now, please, my friend."

They jetted back up the passage together, side by side.

With an artfulness born of desperation, Lando and Lobot managed to improvise forty-one line anchors from the equipment grid and the supplies attached to it. Spaced two hundred meters apart, those anchors secured more than eight kilometers of hand lines, covering three major passages and more than fifteen branches.

In the course of their explorations, the team cataloged eleven stop valves, eighteen switch valves, and three different routes back to their original marker. The purpose of the mechanisms and the pattern of their movements remained impenetrable, but Artoo-Detoo's holographic map steadily took on more useful form, framing the unknown with the known.

Through it all the vagabond bored on through hyperspace, seemingly oblivious to the passengers within. The early fears faded. The vessel remained mysterious, giving up few of its secrets, but it was no longer menacing in its own right. The threat to their lives was as impersonal as the graph of an equation—one in which none of the variables was under their control.

At a point when yet another unexplored passage had disappointed them by leading them to a passage already hung with hand lines, by unspoken mutual consent they lingered there—to rest, and to recover their resolve.

Lando looped the slack of a hand line around one wrist and let it hold him in place. "How long is this jump now?"

"A little over thirty-seven hours," Lobot said.

"Going a long way to somewhere," Lando sighed. "Let's see, four times three-point-one-four times thirty-nine cubed divided by three—by now we could be anywhere in a quarter of a million cubic light-years of space. They'll *need* a telepath to find us."

"You and I should sleep," said Lobot.

"Why?"

"Sleeping will conserve our consumables. And human beings do not perform at peak efficiency when fatigued."

"We don't get very much done when we're dead, either," Lando said. "The five hours we spend napping might be five hours we need to get out of this fix."

"And the five hours we do not spend 'napping' may result in one of us making a nonrecoverable error."

"We have the droids to keep us from making mistakes. They don't get tired," Lando said. "Besides—I'm hungry. I'm kinda counting on turning up an after-hours café somewhere around here."

"Lando, that is not a rational expectation."

Lando chuckled tiredly. "I know when I'm being silly," he said. "Do you know when you're being stuffy?"

"Master Lando—"

"What is it, Threepio?"

"Is it possible that this vessel could already have exited hyperspace, without our knowing? Perhaps we were distracted by our other activities. We may not have gone as far as you fear."

"No," Lando said curtly. "I've never heard a ship growl like this one does going in and coming out. We couldn't have missed it. I couldn't have, anyway. That's something I've been thinking about. Thinking about how long this ship's been jumping at shadows, hopping in and out of hyperspace. About how long it's been since it was in for a structural inspection and an overhaul.

"I had a friend in the yard at Atzerri who showed me scanning holos of the ships that'd come through there—microfractures in the hyperdrive cage, the inner stringers, even the keel of a Dreadnaught.

"No, even if we had all the oxygen, all the water, all the hot café food we could eat, all the time we could ask for, I don't think I'd want to hang around here long enough to hear that growl too many more times. Because someday soon, no matter how well the Qella tightened the nuts, this old crate is going to turn herself into a deep-space junkyard."

Artoo cooed worriedly.

"I wonder where *Glorious* is now," said Threepio.

"*That* I won't think about," said Lando, and laughed. "I don't want to get depressed." He released the hand line and floated free. "You rest if you want. Show me the map, Artoo. There's still a lot of ship to explore."

They found the coupling panel in the seventy-first hour of their imprisonment. It was pure luck that they did, since it appeared in a section they had already passed through twice and would not have returned to if a new passage they were marking had not brought them there.

Nearly two meters long and more than a meter wide, the round-cornered panel was inset flush in the "ceiling" of the passage. (Lando had established by fiat that the hand lines defined the "right" face of the passage and all other directions derived from it.) The panel was liberally decorated with sockets and projections of various heights, depths, and diameters, with the sockets clustered symmetrically in the center third and the projections flanking it.

"Master Lando, what do you think it is?"

"Some sort of intelligence test, maybe," Lando said, trying to peer through one of the larger-diameter sockets. "Anyone feel up to taking it?"

"Why, it *does* bear some resemblance to the busy box Ambassador Nugek gave to Anakin Solo," Threepio said. "My, how he enjoyed spinning the wheels and pushing blocks through the holes—"

"Shut up, Threepio."

"Yes, sir."

Lobot was carrying out his own examination of the artifact. "Twenty-four sockets, in two sizes. Eighteen projections. I can see no obvious moving parts. The metal has a high sheen and reflectivity, and no protective finish. Yet there are no scratches or scars, even in and around the sockets."

"It looks like some sort of bus port to me," Lando said. "Like the diag rack on the *Falcon,* or the maintenance cabinet on *Lady Luck.* Plug in here and you have access to the ship's systems."

"That is what you have been looking for," said Lobot. "How likely is it that you would find it?"

"It's the only mechanism we've seen in nine klicks of passageway."

"It is the only mechanism we have been able to recognize," said Lobot. "But the design of this vessel apparently provides for mechanisms to be concealed until they are needed. I ask you to consider why this mechanism has appeared now."

"You tell me."

"Most likely because the ship will shortly need whatever function this mechanism serves—"

"Which gives us a chance to slip in and take care of

ourselves," Lando said. "These couplings weren't designed for us, but maybe we can make use of them anyway. Energy is energy—Artoo can cope with thermal, plasma, or electrical ports. And data is data—if Artoo can read it, Threepio can interpret."

"Lando, you have no basis for concluding that this is a system port," Lobot pressed. "It is more likely that the function of this mechanism is related to the function of these passages."

"Which is what?" Lando snapped. "Holding cell? Ventilator? Rodent maze? A fungi farm? Are you saying we're not supposed to touch this, either? Blast it all, how long are we supposed to wait before we *do* something?"

"You have not had more than two hours' sleep in nearly three days," Lobot said. "Your sense of urgency has been heightened—"

"That's right," Lando said. "I haven't had anything to eat in so long I'd cut a friend dead for a fracking cracker. My water supply tastes like it's gone around half a dozen times already. Are you more machine than man? Doesn't any of this affect *you*?"

"I am as human as you are," Lobot said. "I doubt that you could be any hungrier than I am. My water supply is as disagreeable to me as yours is to you. But I do not understand the discoveries we have made—"

"Then don't you want to learn more? I want the droids to try to interface with this port. That's all. No blasters. No creative structural renovations."

"Please listen," Lobot said earnestly. "I do not understand why structures as extensive as these have been inert throughout our tenure on this ship, or why we have been permitted to move about in them unimpeded. These questions trouble me. And I am concerned that the appearance of this artifact may signal the end of either or both of those conditions—"

"All the more reason for us to make the first move," Lando said. "Artoo, Threepio, come on up here. I want you to try to interface with the vagabond."

Lobot turned toward the droids. "Threepio—Artoo—I ask you to wait until we know more. None of our supplies are critical yet. We do not know what we are dealing with."

"I am sorry, sir, but Master Luke placed us in the care of Master Lando," Threepio said, allowing Artoo to tow him toward the panel. "We are obliged to follow his instructions, no matter what reservations you may have."

"Thank you, Threepio," Lando said, fixing Lobot with a baleful gaze touched with a hint of smug triumph. "I'm glad to know that you're still on the team."

Whether it was due more to Lobot's misgivings or to Artoo's innate sense of self-preservation, the astromech droid proceeded cautiously in carrying out Lando's instructions, and Lobot was glad to see it.

At first Artoo stopped a safe distance from the panel and began to scan it, his dome rotating back and forth as he brought different sensors to bear—optical, thermal, radionic, electromagnetic. Threepio called out the results of each reading to the two men, who were watching from opposite sides of the passage.

Lobot already knew the results by the time Threepio pronounced them, for the droid—on his own initiative, and without any notice to Lando—had opened another of his data registers to the cyborg's neural interface. It was a signal of support that Lobot accepted in silence, saying nothing that would betray the small mutiny.

When the initial scans produced no obvious red flags, Artoo moved in closer and extended his sensor probe. The scan head was too large to fit fully into the smaller sockets, but Artoo brought it as close to the first of them as he could without actually touching it.

"Field, zero-point-zero-nine gauss," said Threepio. "Flux density, one-point-six-zero-two. Alpha rate, zero. Beta rate, one hundred sixteen. Charge polarity, negative—Artoo, I don't understand a word of this. Will someone please tell me what it means?"

Artoo swiveled his head and emitted a sharp series of whistles, which Threepio did not translate.

"I am *trying* to hold still," Threepio said as Artoo moved the probe to the next socket. "It's not my fault I wasn't designed for weightlessness. Most sensible beings live on planets, where they belong."

The response from Artoo sounded churlish even to Lobot's ears.

"I don't care what you think," Threepio said. "Why, you're only a mechanic. I was meant for nobler purposes. I should be at a diplomatic reception, helping to forge peace between bitter rivals, arranging a dynastic marriage— Oh, how I miss the old days—"

Artoo's response was an electronic bleat. "Very well, then," Threepio said haughtily. "See if I care. I don't need your help." With that, the golden droid released his grip on Artoo's right tread support and folded his arms across his chestplate.

"But I need *your* help, Threepio," said Lando. "So stop squabbling with your brother and call out the numbers."

"Why do you keep making that error, Master Lando? That egotistical little tyrant is no kin of mine," Threepio sniffed.

"I can help you, Lando," Lobot said quietly, without explanation. "Field, zero-point-eight-two-two gauss. Flux density, one-point-seven-four. Alpha rate—"

Lando looked at Lobot with annoyance, a sight that gave Lobot surprising satisfaction. Neither of them saw Threepio reach out and clutch one of the projections on the panel to steady himself. But both heard a loud burst of static on the contact suit comm unit and saw a blue glow in the passage.

"Gracious me!" Threepio exclaimed.

Quickly looking that way, Lobot saw that the end of the panel was crawling with blue-white snakes of energy. They were crackling between the tips of the projections, dancing up Threepio's arm nearly to the elbow joint, and rapidly growing more intense.

"Threepio—*don't let go*—" Lobot began.

The warning came too late. The moment his surprise abated, Threepio pulled back his hand in a reflex of squeamishness.

An instant later a massive, squirming bolt of energy leaped from the panel to Threepio's hand, flashed up his arm and one side of his head, and sprang from there to the face of the passage. Before anyone could react, it had raced away down the passage and disappeared, spreading as it went until it was dancing over the entire surface like a halo of blue fire. One finger of the bolt ran along the hand lines, leaving them crumbling into black dust in its wake.

The bolt left Threepio convulsing and spinning in midair. His right arm was burned black and smoking from the servos and energizer controls, his head was frozen at an odd angle and quivering as though an actuator were caught in a feedback loop.

Lobot loosed a string of curses he had forgotten he knew and started toward the injured droid. Lando stared dumbly for a moment, then did the same. But Artoo beat both of them to Threepio, latching on and dragging him away down the passage in the opposite direction from the one the bolt had taken. As Artoo passed Lando, the droid made a hostile noise.

"I'm *sorry*," Lando said, throwing his arms up in a gesture of surrender. "It's not my fault. Lobot—tell him it's not my fault."

Hastening up the passage after Artoo and Threepio, Lobot jetted past Lando in purposeful silence.

Artoo would not allow Lando to approach Threepio. He had to content himself with watching from several meters away while Lobot and Artoo hovered over the protocol droid and tried to assess the damage.

From several meters away, the damage looked to be considerable.

An R6 or R7 could have survived the jolt handily. The latest combat-rated droids were armored against power surges and induced currents up to and including a near-direct hit from a class one ion cannon.

But Threepio had been designed for wars of words. His buffers and breakers were minimal, and the bolt of energy from the panel had overwhelmed them. If the charge had passed across his body, through the primary processors, instead of up one side, Threepio would be dead.

As it was, Lando could see that Threepio's right arm was rigid and useless at his side, the servo controllers burned and the linkages fused. Even worse, his speech synthesizer or vocal processor had been crippled. When he spoke, his voice phased and changed timbre, as though he were a million klicks away on a pocket com-link. Twice already he had halted in midsentence, as though stuck searching for the most ordinary of words—something Lando had never heard him do before.

After a few minutes, Lobot left Threepio with Artoo and joined Lando. To Lando's surprise, there were no words of recrimination—only a businesslike coolness barely distinguishable from Lobot's usual demeanor.

"Threepio's arm is beyond repair, given that we have no spare parts," Lobot said. "Artoo is trying to free the lateral actuator and restore freedom of motion to Threepio's head." He nodded past Lando at the equipment grid, which Lando had towed away from the scene of the accident. "I need the tool kit."

"In a moment," Lando said. "What happened back there—have you thought about it?"

"I need the tool kit, Lando," Lobot repeated, and moved to pass between Lando and the passage wall.

Lando reached out and caught Lobot's forearm.

"You were right about these passages. They're getting ready to—" Something moved at the periphery of his vision, and Lando's gaze flicked past Lobot to the droids, then past the droids to the growing glow where the passage bent out of sight. "Blast!" he exclaimed. "Get away from the wall. Artoo, look out!"

"What?" Lobot craned his head.

Using his grip on Lobot's suit, Lando dragged him toward the center of the passage, just as the energy halo appeared at the horizon of their vision and sped toward them. It surrounded them for only a moment as it raced through on its course, but its passage made the hair rise on the back of Lando's neck.

"It's gone all the way around?"

"Yes."

"It doesn't seem to have lost any strength at all," Lobot said in wonder.

"No," Lando said. "That's what I was trying to tell you. You were right. These *are* conduits—superconducting accumulators. Perhaps even some sort of gas-tube cascade generator."

"For the weapons," Lobot said slowly. "It has to be for the weapons."

"That panel is the ballast, the source of the spark. Threepio created an arc path while it was building up to fire—probably prematurely. He may have caused the system to report a failure, buying us a little time as it resets."

"The weapons are useless in hyperspace. That explains our reprieve."

"It also answers your question about the panel—about why it showed up now," Lando said. "Smart. She's a smart lady. The last thing I do before I enter an unfriendly room is check my weapon."

"Testing the integrity of the system. She must be getting ready—"

"Wait," Lando said. "Listen."

*　　*　　*

All at once, all around them, the ship began to groan and growl in a slow, deep voice.

Lando released Lobot and dove toward the equipment grid, wresting the sensor limpet from its restraints. The limpet was secured in a harness of silk line, with a single trailing cord ending in a loop.

"I have to do this now," Lando said. "Artoo! Map! What's the shortest way to the outer hull?"

Artoo's reply was a squawk.

"Point out the direction—I can't understand you!"

"He's not answering you," said Lobot. "He's asking me why I'm not back with the tools yet." He closed his eyes. The lights on his interface blinked at a furious rate. "Through there," he said. "Eighteen meters. But I don't know what's between here and the hull."

"I'll tell you when I get back," Lando said. He drew his blaster, burned a hole in the direction Lobot had pointed, and was gone.

With his thrusters holding his widely set feet against the outer bulkhead of the vagabond, Lando pointed the cutting blaster down between his legs and squeezed the actuator. A perfect circle of hull vanished in a puff of gray smoke, which was instantly sucked out through the opening.

The limpet had been floating freely, tethered to Lando's left wrist. Now it strained at the end of a taut line, rocking as the compartment's air rushed past it. Pocketing the blaster, Lando let the line play out through his gloved fingers until the limpet slipped through the opening. Only the cord on Lando's wrist kept it from escaping completely into space.

Then he simply waited, watching the hull breach knit closed. When the opening had shrunk enough to prevent the limpet from being pulled back inside, Lando took up the slack and pulled the limpet back against the hull. Reaching through, he pressed the dual switches that activated the limpet's sensors and armed its attachment system. Letting a little line play out again, Lando waited until the hole had closed to the size of a peephole, then yanked the limpet toward him.

There was an audible *thwack* as the crisscrossing anchor spines fired and drew the limpet flush against the hull. For insurance, Lando knotted the cord around the safety tab that had covered the limpet's switches, pulling it snugly against the inner face. Lando hoped that even if the ship was somehow able to slough off the limpet's barbed anchor spines, the harness and improvised stop would keep it in place.

That job accomplished, Lando turned away to examine for the first time the compartments he had crashed through en route to the outer hull.

Unlike in the accumulators, where the entire face of the passage itself gave off a pale yellow glow, the only light in the outer compartment came from the twin "ear lamps" located on either side of Lando's helmet. When he swept their beams through the dark volume that enclosed him, a great emptiness swallowed the light forward, aft, and around the circumference of the ship. It was as if he were alone in the darkest corner of space.

Only when he looked up, away from the outer hull near which he hovered and back the way he had come, did the light catch and reflect to him any of the substance of the ship. And what the light revealed there made Lando shiver with a chill no warmer could drive away.

For the lamps showed that the inner wall was covered with alien faces—a collage, a portrait gallery, a mural, a memorial, stretching as far as the light could carry, and likely beyond. There were thousands of different faces, or thousands of variations on the same face, each gazing out from its own hexagonal cell. The faces were unlike any Lando had ever seen, and yet he keenly felt the intelligence in the large, round eyes that seemed to seek him out.

More than by any other gift, Lando had found his

way by reading the faces of strangers and knowing them better than they knew themselves. He read in the sculpted, deeply lined faces of the Qella both strength and surrender, a settled wisdom and a thwarted curiosity, and most of all a terrible knowledge of the impermanence of life. The beings who had sat for these portraits, and the artisans who had created them, had known when they did so that these images might be all that survived them, and they had held nothing back.

There was a circular gap in the mural where Lando had burned his way through it from behind. The supporting wall had healed, but the overlying portraits had not—four were damaged in varying degrees, one obliterated forever. Lando fought off sharp pangs of guilt as he jetted up toward the mural and reopened a hole at that same spot.

"I'm sorry," he said to the surviving faces as he left them behind. "But this is your tomb—your memorial. I'm trying to keep it from becoming mine. I like to think that if life meant this much to you, you'd be rooting for me to succeed."

Lando found the others where he had left them, still tending to Threepio. The golden droid was the only one to react strongly to his return, turning his head toward Lando and greeting him cheerfully.

"Master Lando!" he said in a crackly voice. One glowing eye flickered. "What are you doing on Yavin Four? Why are you wearing that costume? Do you know, you look rather like a droid?"

"Threepio, take a look around," Lando said. "Do you recognize this place?"

The droid's head swiveled. "Oh. Oh, yes, I see. The Qella vagabond. I seem to have had an accident." He turned and clanged Artoo on the dome with his good arm. "And it's all your fault, you good-for-nothing sabo-

teur. You belong in a waste compactor, along with all
the other—"

"No," Lando said sharply. "It was my fault. I gave
the orders. I made the mistake. I'm sorry, Threepio. I
promise you, we'll get you put back to specs as soon as
we get home."

"It is I who should apologize, Master Hambone,"
said Threepio. "I am sure that my clamminess was the
approximate corpse of my mishop."

"Don't try to talk, Threepio," Lando said. "Just
keep running your diagnostics. Your parser will map the
damaged regions and relocate those functions."

"Fairy wall, monster lambda." The droid's head returned jerkily to the neutral position.

Lobot shook his head in sympathy. "Lando, the test
charge—if that is what it was—has been around four
more times. I could see it weaken when it passed your
new hole, but other than that, it did not seem to lose any
strength at all. I expect that it would still be circulating if
the panel had not reabsorbed it the last time it passed."

Lando acknowledged the report with a nod. "These
passages are a nearly perfect energy bottle," he said.
"This explains a lot about the power of their weapons. It
must get pretty exciting when they're running a capacity
charge through here."

"I believe our consensus is that we have had enough
excitement for now."

"You're right—we need to get out of here. But
there's something that has to be done first," Lando said.
"Artoo, I was able to place the limpet on the outside of
the ship. I need you to pick up its signal and make it
available to Lobot."

The little droid turned its dome away from Lando
and remained mute.

"Artoo, we need to find out where we are. Step two
of our plan, remember? I don't know how long we can
count on getting data from the limpet. And we don't
know how long we'll be in realspace."

Still the droid was silent.

"Lobot?"

Lobot cleared his throat. "Ah—Artoo just said something rude to me about your leadership ability. Then he told me to tell you that he's on strike."

Working to restrain a flaring temper, Lando said evenly, "Artoo, you're the only one of us who can receive the data from the limpet. If we don't have that data, we can't plan an escape. If we don't escape soon, we're going to run out of air, and you're going to run out of power. Is whatever point you're trying to make worth the four of us expiring?"

Artoo emitted one small beep.

"Receiving data," Lobot said. "Artoo said to tell you that he's doing it for Threepio, not for you."

"I don't care if he does it for the Blood Prince of Thassalia, as long as it gets done," said Lando. "How long will it take to get a navigation fix?"

"Artoo is calculating the triangulation now," Lobot said. "Lando, only one local star is in the spectral database. Artoo is searching for other reference stars."

"What? Where the frack are we?"

"One moment," Lobot said. "Coordinates zero-nine-one, zero-six-six, zero-five-two. Uncertainty due to measuring error, two percent."

"Triple zeroes? That can't be right. That would put us in Sector One."

"Correct," Lobot said. "We are presently one hundred six light-years past the border of the New Republic, in the Core. The nearest inhabited system is Prakith."

"Prakith," Lando repeated. "Foga Brill."

"Excuse me?"

"At last report, Prakith was controlled by the Imperial warlord Foga Brill."

"I see. Prakith is eight light-years away."

"Are there any other ships out there? Any security buoys, drones, probes, anything?"

"None that the limpet can detect. However, the hull of the vagabond blocks a substantial portion of the sky."

Lando muttered grimly, "Well, we're sure not going to be putting out any calls for help in this neighborhood. All right—let's get out of this accumulator while things are still quiet. We'll go right back through where I just came out. I don't know quite where it puts us, but nothing bad happened the first time."

Artoo trilled.

"What?"

"Never mind," Lobot said. "You don't want to hear."

Lando thought dark thoughts about lax maintenance schedules and the consequences of letting droids go too long without a memory wipe. *Your decision, Luke, but they've both got entirely too much personality for my taste.* But he kept those thoughts to himself.

"Once we're through," he continued, "I'd like to see if we can avoid blowing any more holes in the walls—"

Lobot nodded approvingly at that.

"—but that means one of us is going to have to solve the puzzle of what a Qella door looks like and how to open it," Lando said. Then he looked directly at Artoo. "So the first thing we're going to do when we get over there is get six hours' rest—all of us. I should have insisted on it sooner. I'm sorry, Artoo. I don't know if it would have changed anything. But I never meant for Threepio to get hurt."

Artoo's dome swiveled back toward Lando. *"Chirr-neep-weel,"* he said.

"He told me to tell you that he is considering giving you a second chance," said Lobot.

Lando nodded, drawing the blaster from its pouch. "You tell him for me that that's all a smart player should need."

Chapter 4

◆

The nudge that finally awakened Lando was provided by a dehydration headache and a stomach knotted with hunger. The dream that lingered in his awareness was of being pursued through a dark city by a soft-voiced, unseen assassin, and he was eager to chase it from his senses. Reaching up, he switched his helmet lamps to the low setting and looked for the others.

Lando found he was the only member of the team who was conscious. Lobot was floating near the wall below him, a few meters away. His arms were raised beside his face and his legs drawn up and bent at the knees like a child's. Artoo was still holding Threepio protectively with his grasping claws, and the duo spun slowly in the air at the far end of the chamber as though dancing to music only they could hear.

Glancing down at the controls on his left forearm, Lando checked the timer he had started before closing his eyes. He was startled to see that the six-hour rest he had proposed had stretched to more than sixteen hours. He and Lobot had both slept through their alarms, and the droids were still powered down, waiting for an awakening touch.

For a moment he felt a flash of guilt over the lost hours, but he swept that away with the realization of how necessary the rest had been. *The body knows what it needs,* he thought, looking at Lobot's blissful expression.

But sleep had not healed all the insults. Lando's hunger was keener than ever, and the water from the helmet pipestraw only spurred wishful thoughts about bottomless ice-filled glasses of *charde* and *skoa*.

More than anything, though, he wanted out of his contact suit. The air inside was decidedly rank, and his own breath came back to him off the sneeze-spotted faceplate as a foul cloud. His scalp and a half dozen other unreachable places itched maddeningly. His skin felt greasy, and he craved a hot shower. And the suit was a prison, preventing him from stretching out tight muscles and deep aches.

The makeshift glove on Lando's right hand was clinging lightly to his fingers, a sign that the atmospheric pressure in the compartment was slightly higher than the one-normal of the suits. Lando began fingering the helmet release with his other hand, absently betraying his thoughts.

It's not as if there's anything poisonous in the ship's air—it's just a bit on the chewy side. I held my breath for six minutes once in a tank test. That's plenty of time to wipe my face and scratch my—

Lobot's voice interrupted Lando's thoughts. "I would like to know," the cyborg said, "which agency you used to make the arrangements for this vacation. The accommodations have not been up to expectations."

An easy smile creased Lando's face as he turned toward Lobot. "You're just cranky because I ate your complimentary breakfast while you were sleeping in."

"Which is just one of several hundred reasons why I'm never traveling with you again."

"Stop complaining and help me wake up the children," Lando said. "I hear today's going to be one of the highlights of the tour."

By mutual agreement, they activated Threepio first, so that Lando could have a few minutes to diagnose his status without Artoo's protective interference. It took only a short conversation with Threepio to discover that the droid had regained most of his verbal faculties—and with them, most of his dignity. All that remained of his vocal injury was a background buzz when he spoke, a rasp in the speech synthesizer that made it sound as if the droid were suffering from a sore throat.

"Threepio, I'm very glad your language systems came around," said Lobot. "I may have to raise my estimation of Bratan Engineering's cybernetic products—my first neural interface was from Bratan, and I had nothing but trouble with it."

"Thank you, Master Lobot," said Threepio. "I, too, am greatly relieved. A protocol droid with a malfunctioning synthesizer is hardly any use at all."

"Unless you want to do business in one of the nine thousand fifty-seven sign languages," said Lando.

The droid looked down at his damaged arm. "In my present conditon, I would not be able to offer you even that service. If my synthesizer fails, I would be nothing but a burden to you. You might as well cannibalize my power cells and leave me behind. I'll understand—"

"Don't worry, we're not going to leave you behind," said Lobot. "I don't want to have to depend on me to communicate with Artoo."

"Why is that?" Lando asked. "You seemed to be doing fine back in the passage."

Lobot shook his head slowly. "Artoo thinks in that same binary polyglot he speaks, and I can't understand a byte of it. He can leave short messages in Basic for me in his memory registers, but that limits us to whatever he knows of Basic. And from what I've seen so far, he seems to have learned most of his Basic vocabulary from a nerf-herder."

"Oh, he can be *quite* rude," Threepio agreed conspiratorially. "He constantly says the most outrageous things—you can't imagine. I don't dare repeat half of his comments. Sometimes I think that he means to trick me into embarrassing myself." Threepio looked past Lando to where Artoo was floating at an angle, his STANDBY lamp still glowing, and added worriedly, "He hasn't been damaged, has he?"

"No—he's just the last one up this morning," Lando said. "I'm going to take care of that right now."

"Perhaps it would be better if I did it," Lobot said, stopping him with a touch. "Artoo may not have recovered from Threepio's accident as well as Threepio has."

"Just how many diplomats are on this mission?" Lando asked lightly. "No, if Artoo still has a problem with me, he can start getting over it right now. This is my mission, and I'm not handing it over to a petulant droid. No offense, Threepio."

"None taken, I'm sure," said Threepio. "I know exactly what you mean."

Artoo's system lights came on all at once, and his sensor dome rotated a half turn in each direction. Rising, he moved away from Lando and jetted toward Threepio, loosing an unusually long chatter of sounds.

"What's he saying?" Lando asked.

Threepio chattered back at Artoo in the same dialect before answering, and Artoo replied at even greater length.

"Well?"

A crackle of static made it sound as though Threepio had cleared his throat. "Master Lando, Artoo says that he has the greatest enthusiasm and confidence in the mission."

"Threepio—"

"Lando, I suggest you take it at face value," Lobot said quietly.

Lando looked hard at Lobot for a moment. Then, frowning, he said, "Thank you. I have trouble sometimes hearing clearly over what's not being said." He reached for his control pad and brought his helmet lamps up to full brightness. "Lobot, is there anything going on outside?"

"All of the limpet's sensors are clear. The vagabond's forward speed is negligible."

"Just another oblong asteroid, drifting along a long way from anywhere, eh? All right, then. Artoo, can you help us with some light? Let's see what we have here."

What they had was a chamber fifteen meters long and nine meters wide, and as infuriatingly seamless and featureless as the airlock.

"Kind of have the feeling that I've been here before," said Lando, scanning. "And I don't mean yesterday, when I burned through here on the way to the hull."

"I understand," Lobot said. "Perhaps the highest form of art on Qella was the locked-room mystery."

Lando laughed. "Which would make this ship their hall of fame anthology, I guess. But it wants for variety."

"The apparent consistency of design principles should serve our interests."

A grin appeared. "You want me to see if I can lose the other glove this time?"

"The Qella esthetic demands that nothing be evident until it is needed," Lobot said. "But how does the structure know when a concealed feature is needed? How do the Qella communicate their desires to their creations? We know at least one answer—we know that it responds to touch."

The grin faded into a frown. "The last time I touched this ship, it tried to leave us out as a meal for space slugs."

"I am not convinced that this vessel means to do us harm."

"What exactly would you consider compelling proof? A fatality?"

"I've been reconsidering the incident in the airlock in light of Threepio's accident," Lobot said. "It's possible that we misinterpreted the message which Artoo found in the airlock. It's possible that the control you activated was an emergency lock close switch, which functioned exactly as intended."

"What? No, that doesn't make sense."

"It's even possible that we *asked* the vagabond to attempt an escape," Lobot continued. "The prominence given to the symbology Artoo detected parallels the use of red and yellow as alert and caution colors, and arrows as pointers, in human artifacts."

"You're saying that if Threepio could read Qella, we'd have seen a sign saying 'In case of emergency, pull here.'"

Lobot nodded. "Isn't the most prominent marking on the outside of a snub fighter the canopy release? What if we walked up to one knowing the meaning of an arrow but unable to read the word 'Rescue'?"

"Here's the problem with your theory that *we* hit the panic button," Lando said. "The next time this ship had a chance, it tried to spit us out again—without us ever getting near that control yoke."

"That 'next time,' we were burning a hole in an element of the primary defense system—a hole that the repair mechanisms were unable to close in the usual amount of time."

"I take your point," Lando said. "But after we did that, the ship has to have known we weren't Qella and we weren't friendly."

"If the ship had the consciousness you attribute to it, and had formed an intent to remove us, it could have done so at any time while we were in the accumulator," said Lobot. "It could have disposed of us while we slept just now. It could have opened the hull under your feet while you were placing the limpet. Yet it has done none of these things."

"Hmm. And what kind of security system would forget about us once we'd managed to break in, eh?" Lando said. "As though once we'd put our weapons away, we were no longer suspect. 'Terribly sorry, forgot our keycode, had to blow up the entryway'— 'Oh, that's all right, come in and make yourself comfortable—' "

"I've been asking myself from the beginning what kind of intelligence we were facing," Lobot said. "It's the most interesting question before us—"

"I'm still going with 'Where's my next meal coming from?' " Lando said. "And Artoo would probably vote for 'Who put him in charge, anyway?' "

Lobot patiently waited out the interruption, then went on. "I have projected how this ship would behave if you, or I, or Artoo, or Threepio were its master. Its real behavior does not match any of these models."

"Pardon me, sir, but why should it?" asked Threepio, who had been listening attentively. "This vessel was not built by humans, or droids. We are *not* its masters. Its behavior can only be properly evaluated in the appropriate cultural context."

"I disagree, Threepio. The conditions of the test dictate the form of the answers," said Lobot. "If that were not so, the millions of species in this galaxy would have so little in common that there would be no need for your services."

"He's got a point, Threepio," said Lando. "No matter where I've gone, or who I've been dealing with, the one thing that holds the deal together is that everyone's looking out for their own end. I call it enlightened self-interest, and it's the motor that powers the universe."

"The conditions of the test are sentience and survival," said Lobot. "The form of the answer is to identify and neutralize threats. This ship has failed the test. Therefore I conclude this ship is neither sentient nor controlled by sentient beings. It is a work of great ingenuity, but it is not intelligent."

"I see," said Threepio. "Master Lando, should I discontinue my efforts to contact the masters of this vessel?"

"Just hang on, Threepio," said Lando. "I'm still not sold on this. Lobot, a ship of this size and complexity, successfully evading capture for more than a hundred years—there must be something or somebody in charge."

"Something, yes. But not something sentient. I believe we were deceived by the apparent complexity into invoking a god hypothesis."

"A god hypothesis?"

Lobot nodded. "When we spoke of the masters of this vessel, we assumed there was a consciousness observing us and controlling events in our environment," he said. "We even turned to these masters to save us, respectfully offering entreaties and hoping for their intervention on our behalf.

"But there's no indication the ship is aware of us, beyond its local awareness of our effects on it. Its responses have the character of autonomic functions. I now believe the vagabond is an automaton of great sophistication, employing rule-based responses incorporated into its fundamental structure."

"What rule could it have been following when it tried to suck me out into space?"

"You were using a blaster, and caused a breach which did not heal," said Lobot. "You could have triggered a rule specifying that fires be extinguished by exposure to vacuum."

Lando's cheeks wrinkled as he weighed Lobot's argument. "So you want us to start pushing buttons at random, is that it?"

"We know it responds to touch. We were probably wrong to conclude that it responds negatively."

Lando continued to vacillate. "Still quiet outside, Artoo?"

Artoo chirped a single beep, recognizable as "Yes."

Looking back at Lobot, Lando shrugged and gestured with an open hand. "After you."

Nodding, Lobot unlocked and removed his gauntlets one at a time, clipping them to tool stays on the contact suit. Then he jetted to the nearest part of the enclosing wall, reached out both hands, and pressed the palms lightly against the surface. When nothing happened, he started sliding to his left. The wall of the chamber began to rise under his hands, as though it were shaping itself to an invisible mold.

"My goodness gracious!" Threepio suddenly cried out. "Artoo, do you see?"

Lobot retreated hastily to the middle of the chamber, but the transformation continued. Broad disks appeared and grew into squat cylinders. Ridges defined long arcs across the display, shadowing the rippled patterns spilling down the curves of a hemisphere. Color appeared but did not overwhelm—there were swirls of a pale blue and spikes of a soft yellow, and none respected the boundaries of the geometries they overlaid.

Lando's eyes twinkled with delight. "I never thought you were the artistic type, Lobot."

Returning to the wall, Lobot touched the drumlike surface of one of the cylinders. The chamber was suddenly filled with music, a haunting duet of intertwined melodies that rose and fell like swells in a gentle sea.

"I'm not letting you have all the fun," Lando said with a grin, peeling the makeshift glove off his right hand and jetting to the opposite wall.

It answered his touch with a great rectangle pierced by two long channels and filled with finer detail than the sculpture it faced. Lando did not know the meaning of the pattern, but he could see the scar his blaster had left in it—a circular bite out of the upper edge of the rectangle, obliterating twenty or more of the myriad smaller cells within it.

The damage did not dampen Lando's enjoyment for long. The two men flew about the chamber like nimble, persistent insects until they had tested its entire surface. There was something marvelous about the way a simple touch of the hand brought the empty chamber to life.

But the most splendid discovery of all—in Lando's eyes, at least—was the doorway that opened for him at one end of the chamber, and its twin, which Lobot manifested at the other.

Lando did not know where either might lead them, but he much preferred an uncertain choice to no choice at all.

In the captain's wardroom aboard *Glorious,* two pieces of metal rested on a table beside a contact suit gauntlet. The longer of them was badly twisted. The ends of both were scorched with matching burns. Colonel Pakkpekatt held the shorter of the two lightly between two fingers, turning it over for examination.

"You're certain?" he asked.

"Yes, Colonel," said Taisden. "This is the frame of a Hired Hand CarryAll, a common self-stabilizing equipment sled."

"Ownership?"

"The registry code indicates it is the property of a Hierko Nochet, a Babbet adventure guide and onetime acquaintance of Lando Calrissian. We believe that the general acquired this and certain other property from Nochet in a sabacc tournament two years ago."

"Have you had it analyzed for biological identifiers?"

"It was swept immediately after retrieval," said Technical Agent Pleck. "There are trace markers consistent with human handling, but I cannot confirm that either Calrissian or the cyborg is the source."

"Why not?"

"Sir, it's, uh, a bit awkward—we have no bioprofile of the general to compare it to."

Pakkpekatt bared his teeth. "A flag officer of the Fleet? To say nothing of his history before joining the Rebellion, and since leaving it. How is this possible?"

"I don't know, sir. We have found records that indicate his bioprofile was recorded at least three times, but the profiles themselves have disappeared. And the clerk of records on Cloud City refuses even to answer our inquiries, citing something he called the Founder's Contract."

Shaking his head, Pakkpekatt said, "Under his uniform, General Calrissian remains a smuggler and a scoundrel. Was anything else found in the sweep, Pleck?"

The agent frowned. "Yes, Colonel—though I don't know what significance to assign to it."

"Tell me what you can."

"Yes, sir. We recovered a relatively large amount of an unidentified biological material from the facing of the sled—this area, here," the agent said, pointing. "The quantity is on the order of two million cells—I should say cell fragments, because most were mechanically damaged."

"Mechanically? As if these pieces had been used as weapons?"

"No, sir. The distribution was too uniform. More like—well, sir, more like you'd sat down and sanded the outside of the frame with a roughskin rat. I'm sorry, sir, I know that's rather unscientific."

"You said the cells were unidentified."

"Yes, sir. And they may stay unidentified. The leading theory is that they may be artificial cells, a mechanism rather than an organism. The genetic sequences are much too short and seem to have little extro material. With your permission, we'd like to use one of *Glorious*'s hyperspace probes to send a sample back to the Exobiology Institute on Coruscant."

Pakkpekatt bared his teeth. "See to it, Lieutenant," he growled. "It should have been done when you first thought of it."

The agent hurriedly left the room under the heat of Pakkpekatt's glare, and the colonel turned his attention back to Taisden. "Was anything else recovered from the location where these were found?"

"No, sir. Nothing else. *Stendaff* is still on station, sweeping the area, but it looks clean down to decimeter resolutions."

Pakkpekatt picked up the short section of sled frame. "A most curious kind of flotsam, Agent Taisden. Difficult to construct a scenario to account for it."

"Yes, sir."

"Are all of our people off *Marauder* now?"

"Yes, sir. The section came over with me, and Captain Garch had quarters assigned to them on X Deck."

"Then I suppose I have delayed as long as I can, hoping that these foolish orders would be withdrawn," said Pakkpekatt. "Advise Captain Hannser that I am releasing *Marauder* from this command effective immediately. He is to return his ship at best possible speed to Krenhner Sector Station and report to the commodore there."

Taisden nodded. "I'll see to it immediately, sir."

Left alone in the wardroom, Colonel Pakkpekatt slowly cupped his right hand and began to smack it against the table, driving his friction pads against the retracted points of his nails. The pain proved unequal to the anger he was wrestling, so he methodically increased both the force and frequency of the blows.

There was an eerie deliberateness to his self-abuse, and his face remained expressionless throughout. He did not stop until the pads were swollen and pulpy-soft, and the pain shooting up through his arm and deep into his chest had bled off the restless need that impatience and frustration had bred in his *pedrokk* gland—the fighter's heart.

By that time *Marauder* was ready to depart, and Pakkpekatt waited until he had watched it go, jumping toward Krenhner the moment it cleared convoy radius.

Then he turned to his recording log and began at last to dictate a report he did not want to make for a supervising committee he no longer could say he respected.

Four little ships, groping through the dark for a few short days. That is all your lives are worth to them. I never would have thought I would see such dishonor. I never thought I would feel such shame.

Over the next several hours, Artoo added twenty chambers to his map of the vagabond, numbering each in turn as the team visited it. To help them remember where they had been, he also recorded for each a fish-eye holo of what Lando had dubbed "the pop-ups."

So far, they had discovered two basic patterns for the pop-ups. Eight of the chambers were like the first—one side of the chamber would reveal a large figure that might have been a sigil, a sculpture, or symbolic writing. The opposite face would reveal a finely detailed geometric design that Lando and Lobot both were convinced was the map of a temple or small city. Somewhere in every map room was a key that triggered Qella music, though every "song" was different from the others.

Apart from the music, the pop-ups in the map rooms appeared to be static. They remained on display as long as the team lingered; when the team moved on to another chamber and the connecting portal closed, the pop-ups collapsed and vanished as quickly as they had appeared.

Next in sequence after every map room came one or more of what Lobot dubbed "gadget rooms." In them the team found a variety of mostly mysterious pop-ups that might move, change color, hum, or change shape when touched. But with a very few exceptions, the gadgets had no decipherable function, and none caused any detectable change in the status of the ship.

"I still think these could be control rooms," Lando said as they prepared to leave chamber 20. "We just don't know what we're controlling. We could be driving the custodian crazy, lowering the heat in the 'freshers and changing the channel on his CosmiComm service."

One welcome discovery was that when they entered a chamber by conventional means—through the portals—the chamber provided its own illumination. Power had become critical enough for Artoo that, back in chamber 11, Lando had coupled him to Threepio for an energy transfusion. The protocol droid, carried everywhere by Lobot or Artoo, was consuming very little power directly.

"Yes, by all means. You should take it all," he said, looking down at his chest as Lando snapped the transfer cable into the recharge coupling. "I'm nothing but a burden to you. I don't know why you ever brought me on this mission, Master Lando. I'm completely useless to you. Give all my power to Artoo and go on without me. Leave me here in the dark."

With a will, Lando resisted the temptation to take the droid at his word.

Chamber 21 was another map room, the ninth. The sigil resembled a feathered V embracing a cluster of fist-size spheres. The map was an irregular pentagon, with one side twice as long as the others and the same shape echoed in the open area at the very center. Neither Lobot nor Lando could find a music key, but their attempts seemed to trigger something quite different, and startling.

At first, there was just a pale pink glow slowly pulsing in a structure near the long outer wall. Then, suddenly, that part of the map erupted in a gout of fire that leaped a full meter up from the wall.

The team fell back in surprise. "They've found us!" Threepio cried. "Artoo, save yourself!"

"It's a holo—a recording," Lobot said.

"No, it's real," Lando said. "Look at your suit sensors—wait, Artoo, don't!" He lunged toward the droid, who was busily unlimbering the nozzle of his fire extinguisher. By the time the struggle was over, the entire map had been replaced by a five-sided black scar, and the chamber was half choked by a white-soot smoke.

Lando herded them back into chamber 20, where they waited the two minutes they had learned it took for a room to reset. When they reentered 21, the black scar was gone, and with it the smoke. With their backs practically pressed against the sigil, they then watched a replay.

The initial blast came from the same structure, after the same pulsing glow. As the pillar of fire rose, the shock rippled out through the rest of the city, destroying the neat symmetry. The fire quickly fell back but spread into a firestorm that raced across the shattered city and consumed it. In a matter of seconds the wall was scorched black as before, the map destroyed.

"Artoo, please run an analysis on the atmosphere in here," Lando said.

Threepio reported the results. "Oxygen five percent—oxygen eight percent—oxygen eleven percent—would you make up your mind?" the droid asked, clanging Artoo on the dome with his working arm.

"It's not him, Threepio," said Lobot. "The ship is restoring the chamber to its status before the fire, for the next demonstration." He looked to Lando. "These are history lessons. Something terrible happened to the Qella city that was under this sign."

"Maybe this is our first clue about what happened to them," Lando said. "But there's something else going on, too. Artoo, what's the oxygen component now?"

The answer, relayed through Threepio, was fifteen percent.

"Son of a— Lobot, Threepio, you stay here. Artoo, come with me. There's something we have to check."

"Where are you going?"

"Back to chamber one, express lane. Sit tight—it won't be so long. We won't be sight-seeing this time."

The patrol frigate *Bloodprice* bore the colors of the Prakith navy and the crest of Governor Foga Brill. Both were more prominent than the sigil of the Imperial Moff for Sector 5, which was consigned to the armor panel above the frigate's chin turrets.

The displays mirrored the allegiances felt by Captain Ors Dogot and his crew of nearly four hundred. The officers owed their commissions and their postings to Brill, not to Grand Moff Gann. It was Brill who collected the commission fees and the annual posting assessments. It was Brill who paid off favors to wealthy families with command ranks that drew pay in goods and gold instead of Prakith scrip.

The specialists and ratings, draftees all, owed the security of their families to Brill's promise of the protection of the Red Police for the daughters and wives of those who protected his power with their lives. To be drafted into the navy was a far better thing than to be drafted into the slit mines or the foundries, or to be one of the hundreds rousted nightly from the riverbanks in Prall and Skoth to dig their own graves.

Graft and fear were inferior flavors of fealty, but they were the best Foga Brill could command, and they sufficed.

"Course change maneuver complete, Captain," the navigator reported in a clear, loud voice. "Now heading nine-zero, mark, negative four-five, mark, two-two at deep patrol standard."

"Towmaster, report," said Dogot.

The listening array *Bloodprice* towed behind it on deep patrol was a hundred times longer than the ship itself. It was a spiderweb of passive antenna cables, tiny noiseless amplifiers, steering jets, and tension vanes, with a drag gondola the size of a troop transport at the end of the antenna's main cable. The three crew members in the gondola had the difficult job of flying the array through the turn when *Bloodprice* changed heading.

If there was too little tension, the elements could tangle, or the whole array could tear itself apart in what the manuals called dynamic destabilization and tow crews called tail whip. If there was too much tension through the turn, the likely result was an overstrain disconnect and a two-hour delay for the recapture procedure.

The towmaster on *Bloodprice*'s last patrol had allowed two disconnects. Along with the gondola crew, he had spent the last half of the patrol in the brig, awaiting the return to Prakith and a court-martial on a charge of treasonable incompetence.

So it was with great relief that his replacement announced, "The array turned cleanly and deployment is nominal."

"Very well," said Dogot. "Lieutenant Sojis, you are master of the bridge. I will be in my quarters, working on crew reviews. Inform Yeoman Cligot that she is to report to me there immediately."

"Yes, Captain."

When the portal closed after Lando and Artoo, Lobot watched, fascinated, as the smoke thinned and disappeared, the scar faded and vanished.

Even the tiny white bits of soot smudging the outside of his faceplate seemed to evaporate. He watched on his suit monitor as the temperature plummeted thirty degrees, to the slightly chilly norm for the vagabond.

"Pardon me, Master Lobot—"

"Yes, Threepio, what is it?" Lobot said automatically, still distracted.

"I was wondering, sir, if you could tell me—do droids meet the conditions of the test?"

Lobot's head snapped around. "What did you say?"

"The test of intelligence," Threepio repeated. "Am I sentient, like you, or simply another work of great ingenuity, like this ship?"

Taken aback, Lobot looked away from the droid's waiting face as he groped for an answer. "Ah— Threepio, you know, most droids are built to have self-aware artificial intelligence. Especially third-degree droids like yourself."

"But that must be something different than sentience," Threepio said. "Otherwise, the Senate of the New Republic would not consist solely of organics, served by droids."

"It *is* different," Lobot said, as gently as he could. "Artificial intelligence is programming. Wipe a droid's memory and it disappears. Replace it with different programming and a translator becomes a tutor, or a med droid becomes a chem droid."

"I understand, sir," said Threepio; he was quiet for a long moment. "Then can you tell me how it feels to be sentient? How is it different from what I feel?"

"I'm not sure that I can say," Lobot replied slowly.

"Perhaps it is a thing that you just *know,* because you are an organic and not a machine? Perhaps if I were sentient, I would not need to ask you these questions. I would know who I was."

Lobot said nothing for a time. "What do *you* think, Threepio?" he asked at last.

"I do not know, Master Lobot," the droid said. "But I have noticed that when someone speaks of memory wipes, I am seized by an inexplicable panic."

"I don't find that inexplicable," said Lobot.

"Really, sir?"

"Self-preservation is an elementary part of self-awareness—even artificial self-awareness. It's the part of us that feels that awareness which matters to us," Lobot said. "I expect you would give that up"—he pointed at Threepio's immobile arm—"to keep your programming intact. As I would surrender this"—he pointed through his faceplate at his neural interface—"to preserve my consciousness."

"I do not recall having this reaction when I was younger, sir," Threepio said. "Why, I have seen many droids of my acquaintance taken for memory wipes. I felt nothing but gratitude that their masters cared enough for their well-being to schedule proper maintenance." The droid cocked his head. "My own maintenance record, I'm afraid, is something of a horror. It's a miracle that I can still function at all."

Lobot mused on that answer for a while. "Just out of curiosity, Threepio, have you thought about asking other droids what *they* think about this?"

"Yes, Master Lobot," Threepio said. "But they seemed not to understand the question. Why, one even had the ill manners to call me a computational defective with deviant specifications. Can you imagine?"

"I know something of such prejudice," said Lobot, then sighed. "I don't have any answers for you, Threepio. All I can say is that the questions would seem to be worth revisiting when some time has passed."

"Thank you, Master Lobot," said Threepio. "I will do so."

Except for blind spots caused by *Bloodprice* and the drag gondola, the towed array could scan several light-hours in every direction. As the outermost of Prakith's three concentric spheres of defense, the first purpose of the deep patrol was to detect possible military threats long before they could come near the planet. For that reason, the ship's patrol route took it through the most likely final staging areas for an attack on Prakith, outside the range of its ground-based and orbiting sensors.

But an equally important purpose was to intercept and claim as a prize any merchant or private vessel unwary enough to pass within reach. Ship seizures were not only an obligation, but an opportunity. A rich enough prize could advance the entire crew to a better post. And every deep patrol captain knew stories of other captains who had come home with a prize rich enough to earn the favor of Foga Brill himself.

So when Captain Dogot was called away from his examinations of the new female crew members and saw the size of the contact on the optical displays, he quickly forgave the interruption. "What identification have you made?" he asked, peering over the shoulder of the security master.

"None so far," said the officer. "The image is too crude, and the target is silent in all spectral bands except the optical."

"Interrogate the navigation transponder."

"There is no transponder response at that location."

"Range?"

"Three-point-eight light-hours—nearly at the limit of detection."

Captain Dogot weighed the possibilities. A warship of that size would be more than a match for a patrol frigate. He would need reinforcements from the inner fleet. But a freighter of that size would be a prize of the first rank, and one he would much prefer not to share with other captains.

For a brief moment he considered cutting the array adrift, rather than allowing the hour necessary to reel it in. Abandoning the array would ensure that *Bloodprice* was the first ship to reach the target. But if the contact proved spurious, or the target escaped, the loss of the array—or even any substantial damage to it—would cost him his post, if not his life.

"Bring in the array," Captain Dogot ordered. "Prepare the ship for hyperspace. Notify patrol command that we are in pursuit of an unidentified contact, vector zero-nine-one, zero-six-six, zero-five-three."

The navigation master turned at his station. "But, sir, the last coordinate for the contact is zero-five-*five*."

"I am sure you are mistaken," Dogot said evenly. "Communications master, send the message as I instructed. Patrol command will want to send additional ships to support us. Navigation master, what would an error of two degrees over this distance mean?"

"The, uh—the ships would be hours away at sublight, but too close to safely microjump." Understanding belatedly came to his eyes, and he glanced down at his console. "Yes, sir, zero-five-*three*. Thank you for catching my error before it had any undesirable consequences."

"Sleeping on the job again, I see. Did you know that you snore like a power saw in ironwood?"

Lando's voice, sharp and clear in the helmet's comm speakers, startled a dozing Lobot awake. He looked up to find Lando and Artoo back in chamber 21, the portal quickly closing behind them. Lando was holding his helmet under his arm and grinning broadly.

"Lando—what are you doing?"

"Master Lando, have you gone mad?" Threepio demanded in alarm. "You must replace your helmet immediately, or you'll suffocate!"

"I've had it off for most of an hour now," said Lando. "Didn't you wonder how anything could burn in an atmosphere that was ninety percent nitrogen and carbon dioxide?"

"It seems I did not have the necessary data to wonder," said Lobot. "And I was thinking about other things."

"Well, the answer is, it can't," said Lando. "What I had to find out was whether it was just this room that had been oxygen-enriched."

"And it apparently wasn't."

"No. Something happened while we were sleeping. Every chamber back to number one now has a breathable atmosphere. Go on, take your helmet off—try it."

The air was cold, dry, and sweet in Lobot's lungs. He looked at Lando in puzzlement. "Why should this be?"

"You said it first—this ship isn't out to harm us. It was expecting visitors."

"But we took a wrong turn after we entered," Lobot said thoughtfully, scratching his bald head with vigor. "We weren't supposed to be wandering through the weapons system, which has its own specific environmental needs. We were supposed to be going through the museum."

"Which was in cold storage until we arrived," said Lando. "It makes perfect sense. Oxygen is highly reactive—a reducing agent. Keeping the oxygen pressure low and the carbon dioxide high protects the ship from fire, the exhibits from corrosion. Imperial Star Destroyers flood key equipment compartments with an $N-CO_2$ mixture before going into battle."

"Then what happened to all the carbon dioxide that was in the air? Scrubbers?"

"The original and best kind," Lando said. "The ship breathed it in, locked up the carbon, and gave back the oxygen. Lobot, don't you see? This ship is alive."

On Captain Dogot's orders, the *Bloodprice* began charging its primary ion cannon battery immediately after exiting hyperspace.

There would be no negotiations, no warning shots, no demands for surrender. Dogot did not intend to allow the captain of the intruding vessel any latitude at all. Unless a closer look at the target showed it to be a friendly, or a warship of cruiser class or heavier, Dogot intended to use the big guns quickly. The talking could begin after his gunners had disabled the other ship.

"Target acquired," called the gunnery master. "Twenty seconds to full charge."

"Target is confirmed unknown," called the senior

analyst. "Design class is unknown. Estimated displacement class, gamma-plus. Detecting no weapons ports forward."

"Target real velocity is fifty-two meters per second," called the navigation master. "Target closing velocity is one thousand, eight hundred sixteen meters per second."

Captain Dogot studied the image on his command display. It seemed almost too good to believe—a huge, unarmed and unprotected vessel barely crawling through space. "Are there any other Prakith vessels on the board?"

"Showing the light cruiser *Gorath* and the destroyer *Tobay* approximately twenty million kilometers astern," said the navigation master. "They won't be here for a while."

"Very well," Dogot said. "Then we must do what we can ourselves. Gunnery master, you may fire when ready. Ion batteries only—I want that ship disabled, not destroyed. Troop master, prepare your units for boarding—"

Lando and Lobot had both temporarily shed their contact suits to stretch, scratch, and even scrub away their accumulated annoyances, sacrificing some of their precious water to restore a measure of dignity and comfort.

The convenience of the waste management facilities in the suits alone dictated that they would eventually climb back inside them. As a practical matter, they also couldn't afford to sacrifice the maneuvering and communications systems. But neither man was eager to give up his unexpected freedom. The pieces of both suits floated around the chamber like dismembered corpses while Artoo and Threepio looked on, nonplussed by the display.

"Pardon me, Master Lando, but should we not continue searching for the vessel's control room? I do not see that this has significantly altered our situation—"

Artoo suddenly began squawking shrilly.

"*I'm* talking to them now, Artoo," said Threepio. "Just you wait your turn— What? There's another ship? Heading directly toward us? Oh, Artoo—we're *saved*. I knew that the colonel would come for us—"

"Slow down, Threepio—what's going on?"

"Artoo says that the sensors on the limpet are detecting another ship on an intercept course."

Grabbing his helmet as it floated by, Lando shot a worried look toward Lobot. "*What* ship? Ask him what ship—"

"The holoprojector," Lobot interrupted. "Artoo can relay the signal from the imager."

A few seconds later half the chamber was filled with the limpet's wide-angle view of space outside the vagabond's hull. The approaching ship was clearly visible to the extreme left of the projection, toward the bow.

"Imperial escort frigate," Lando said immediately. "The original KDY design, with the heavy stuff forward. It looks like the gun ports are open, too."

"Shouldn't we signal it somehow, Master Lando?" asked Threepio.

"It's not from our armada, Threepio," said Lobot.

"The only signal I want to send that ship is a wave good-bye," said Lando, reaching out and touching the wall of the chamber. "Come on, old lady, don't wait around for an introduction."

"Master Lando, Artoo says that there are two other ships approaching as well, but much farther away. Perhaps one of *them* is *Glorious*."

"Not coming from that direction, it isn't— Oh, hell!"

The bow of the onrushing frigate had suddenly disappeared behind the yellow-white plasma bubble of an ion cannon burst. A fraction of a second later the holoprojection turned a crackling white, then disap-

peared. Artoo yelped unhappily. At the same time, the
ship shuddered under them.

"The limpet's been fried," Lobot said, spinning in
midair as he struggled to pull the lower half of his contact suit up over his legs. "Artoo isn't getting anything
from it now."

Lando pressed his palm against the wall, hoping to
feel the tremor of a hyperspace jump beginning. "Of all
the luck— What's going on?" he demanded. "Why is she
waiting so long to jump?"

They fell silent as one, listening to the ship, hoping
to hear her sinews groaning in protest as the jump engines punched her across into hyperspace, and fearing
any sounds that might mean their journey would be ending here, a long way from home.

The captain of the cruiser *Gorath* was cursing the
name of the captain of the frigate *Bloodprice* even before
his ship's forward scanners lit up with the glow of a
battle begun. When he saw the frigate open fire on the
strange vessel, his fury knew no bounds.

"I swear, this man will dig his own grave, and I will
see his children bury him alive there," the captain said
with an icy venom. "He will hear his daughters screaming, his mother pleading, while his lungs fill with dirt and
his eyes are ground blind by sand."

They were too far away, the image too jumpy and
coarse, to tell what effect *Bloodprice*'s barrage had had
on its target. But they were close enough to witness what
followed—together with the crew of *Tobay,* they were
the only witnesses.

The great hull of the target brightened fore and aft,
and something almost invisible struck out across the
emptiness toward *Bloodprice*. Seconds later, the frigate
exploded with a ferocity that could only mean the ioni-
zation reactor had gone critical. It vanished from the
sensor displays.

"Too quick for you," the captain of the *Gorath* said coldly.

Meanwhile, the intruding vessel was turning away from the shattered hulk, away from Prakith and toward the Rim.

"Notify *Tobay* to prepare for hyperspace. Propulsion master, ready on my mark!" the captain cried out. "We will erase this humiliation and capture this invader ourselves."

A bright circle of light flared out around the vagabond. "Now!" the captain screamed. "Match headings! After them!"

The captain's crew was well trained to his voice. *Gorath* jumped into hyperspace close enough behind the vagabond to be able to detect her quarry ahead by its soliton wake.

"We have them," the captain said with grim satisfaction. "Wherever they are going, we will be there. They are ours."

Colonel Pakkpekatt's new orders read simply, MISSION TERMINATED EFFECTIVE YOUR RECEIPT THIS NOTICE. BREAK OFF ALL OPERATIONS IMMEDIATELY. NRI OPERATIONS CENTER.

"This will not do," he said, and swept out of his quarters. The threat ruffles blossoming down his back and the crimson expanse on his throat warned away any who might otherwise have tried to speak to him on his way to the bridge.

"Secure channel, isolation," he said as he dropped his body into his combat lounge. The enclosing shell came forward from the back of the chair and closed him in. "NRI Operations Center, Coruscant, highest priority."

It took several seconds for the hypercomm link to be made and verified.

"Operations," said a briskly professional voice. "Go ahead, Colonel Pakkpekatt."

"I need to talk directly to General Rieekan."

"I'll see if he's available, Colonel. One moment."

Pakkpekatt's impatience made the wait seem longer than it was.

"Brigadier Collomus, operations senior staff," said a new voice. "How can I help you, Colonel?"

Pakkpekatt showed his teeth. "You can help me talk to General Rieekan, as I asked."

"General Rieekan isn't available at the moment," said Collomus. "If you have any questions about your orders, I should be able to resolve them. I was in the planning loop for the Teljkon expedition."

"I know who you are, Brigadier," said Pakkpekatt. "When General Rieekan becomes available again, please advise him that his last orders were garbled in transmission. I will require a verified voice confirmation to proceed."

"I can give you that, Colonel."

"No, sir, I'm afraid you cannot."

Pakkpekatt relaxed into the cushions and left the isolation shell up. The callback came twenty-four minutes later.

"General Rieekan," Pakkpekatt said with an acknowledging nod.

"Colonel, Brigadier Collomus tells me that you have a problem with your orders which for some reason only I can resolve. Would you care to explain what's going on?"

"Sir, I must contest the decision to terminate the mission. This is a betrayal of—"

"Colonel, this is not open for discussion."

"There are six men dead and a contact team still missing."

"Colonel, those facts are not relevant to the decision."

"Not relevant? You—"

"No, Colonel, they are not. All agents must be considered expendable, always. And your ships are needed elsewhere, most especially *Glorious*."

"With all due respect, sir, you don't understand the ramifications—"

"Colonel, I wouldn't finish that sentence," Rieekan said sharply. "Your reports have been carefully reviewed. The probability of any positive outcome at this point doesn't justify further investment. The decision has been made, and your exception is noted. The mission is terminated. Bring them home, Colonel."

"Sir, I request permission to take an all-volunteer team and continue the search in General Calrissian's yacht, *Lady Luck*. This would not—"

"Denied."

"Then I request immediate leave, in order to continue the search on my own."

"Denied. All leaves have been canceled due to the crisis in Farlax Sector."

"Then you leave me in an impossible position."

"Why is that, Colonel? Do you find it impossible to follow orders?"

Pakkpekatt bared his teeth. "General, a Hortek does not leave the bodies of comrades in the hands of the enemy—ever."

For the first time since the call had begun, there was silence. "I understand, Colonel. But I can't help you."

"I think you can, General."

"I'm listening."

"You said that all agents must be considered expendable. I am asking you to count me among the missing from the Teljkon expedition. Because even if I did return, I would still be *here* in ways which would compromise my ability to do any other job for you."

"This is that important to you," Rieekan said, settling back in his chair. "Even though these missing men were not part of your command, flouted your orders, and are principally responsible for the failure of your mission."

"One's comrades and allies do not come neatly out of a mold, General," Pakkpekatt said. "They are inevitably a mixed lot, and never without flaws. And I find I often must hope for as much tolerance from them in that regard as I am able to offer to them."

Rieekan pursed his lips. "Very well, Colonel. I will extend you a little tolerance. *Lady Luck,* no more than three additional volunteers, and whatever unexpended mission supplies you choose and the yacht can carry. Report any substantive developments promptly. And, Colonel—"

"Sir?"

"My tolerance is fairly inelastic. Don't try to stretch it."

"Thank you, General."

Slightly more than an hour later, Pakkpekatt, Captain Bijo Hammax, and technical agents Pleck and Taisden watched from *Lady Luck*'s tiny flight deck as the cruiser *Glorious* and the escort *Kettemoor* turned together and jumped toward Coruscant.

"It begins," said Pakkpekatt to the empty sky.

Penga Rift found the pilot of *IX-26* keeping a lonely watch over the bodies on Maltha Obex.

"What took you so long?" he demanded. "You were supposed to be here days ago."

"Copy, this is Joto Eckels," came the reply. "Sorry about the delay. Frankly, we weren't even expecting you to still be here. Our original sponsor withdrew just before we lifted, and then we got word about the accident. We were going to have to go to a contract ambulance to recover Kroddok and Josala when another sponsor came along and picked up the contract."

"This is all news to me," the pilot said. "I don't

know why I wasn't recalled if the NRI pulled out. Who's sponsoring you now?"

"A private collector—name of Drayson," said Dr. Eckels. "He hopes to authenticate some Qella artifacts. I think he's going to be disappointed, and very expensively so. But it helps us, and we'll do what we can for him. Do you still have a good fix on the bodies?"

"Affirmative, *Penga Rift*," said the pilot. "Nothing's moved down there since the avalanche, unless you want to count the snow that's fallen on top. You're in for a cold dig."

"We're ready for one."

"Then tell me how you want the data, so I can light this candle and get out of here," the pilot said. "Because this is hands down the creepiest duty I've pulled in sixteen years, and I have a great need to get myself somewhere warm and crowded—and soon."

"Understood," said Eckels. "Ready to receive your coordinate system reference data. We'll take the next watch here at Maltha Obex."

II.

Luke

Chapter 5

♦

The skiff *Mud Sloth* was outbound in realspace from Lucazec at top speed—which, considering it was a Verpine Adventurer, was not enough to satisfy Akanah.

"Luke—can't you make it go faster?"

"How? Get out and push?"

"Why—yes. Can't you use the Force to speed us up?"

"You need a lever *and* a place to stand," Luke said wryly. "The Force isn't a magic wand—there *are* limits."

"All limits exist in the mind, not the Universe," Akanah said. "I'm surprised your tutors never taught you that."

Luke shook his head. "Obi-Wan and Yoda both taught me to see that we limit ourselves by not trying and sabotage ourselves by believing we'll fail."

"Then why do you—"

"—But even Obi-Wan, in our worst moments, with millions of lives hanging in the balance, couldn't make the *Falcon* go any faster." He gestured at the navigational display. "Besides, it looks like no one's taken enough interest in our departure to try to follow."

"They don't need to, yet," said Akanah. "We're days from clearing the Flight Control Zone, aren't we?"

Luke glanced down at the controls. "Three days, more or less."

"Then they can just watch us for now, let us think we're away free and see where we're going. There aren't many ships that *couldn't* catch us before we reach the jump radius."

"The agents who ambushed us are dead. No one tried to stop us at the port. The flight controllers gave us clearance without a peep. The skies are empty. What will it take for you to feel safe?"

"I won't feel safe until we've found the Fallanassi," Akanah said. "I can't bear the thought of failing. I've waited so long—and so have you. If anything should stop us this close to the end—"

"How close are we?" Luke asked. "What did the Current writing back there say?"

"I already told you—it pointed the way home."

"But you didn't tell me where that is."

"I was afraid to say anything until we were away from there," said Akanah. "I couldn't risk having anyone else hear."

"We're alone now," Luke pointed out.

"But they could have placed a listening device in the ship while we were on the North Plateau. I want to wait until we're in hyperspace. Then I know they won't be able to follow."

"No one's been in the ship but us," Luke said firmly. "And this isn't going to be much of a partnership if you're keeping secrets from me. Don't you trust me, Akanah?"

"I know you to be a good man," said Akanah. "But some of what you do and believe makes me uncomfortable. In the long run, I have never known a warrior or a soldier to be a friend."

"I'm not a soldier," Luke said softly. "And the lightsaber now only comes to my hand to protect people I care about. Is that a warrior, or a friend?"

Akanah was silent, looking down at her lap. "We have to go to Teyr," she said at last. "The circle may not have been able to stay there, but that is where they went from Lucazec."

"Teyr is—um, that way," Luke said, pointing up and to the right.

"More or less," she said, and reached out to raise his arm slightly. "That's closer. I was planning on a double jump, in case anyone is thinking about following us."

Luke nodded his approval. "That's one of the worlds the children were sent to."

"Yes," she said.

"Didn't you say you'd already been there, looking for them?"

"No. I said I couldn't find them there," Akanah corrected. "I was never able to make the journey. I made inquiries, from Carratos, when I could." She looked up then. "But the Fallanassi change names, styles of dress, habits of speech, even the way we groom our hair, to blend in, to disappear. Unless I can be face-to-face with them, exchange the signs, let them feel me beside them in the Current, they would not reveal themselves, out of fear that I was not what *I* seemed to be."

"You think they're still hiding?"

"After what just happened, can you not say we have reason?"

Luke nodded. "I think we need to talk about what just happened."

"So do I," she said. Her eyes flashed darkly. "But I would prefer not to have that conversation with an Imperial interrogation team. Can't you do something so we can jump out of here sooner rather than later?"

"I don't really want to. I think so far, we've managed to slip out of here without attracting any special attention," Luke said. "But if we suddenly blast out of a

Flight Control Zone, especially in *this* bucket, we're going to go right to the top of the alert list. And when we arrive at Teyr, they're going to insist on talking to us. They might even insist on inspecting our ship and pulling its license."

"I had not thought of that," she said, frowning. "But what if you're wrong, and six hours from now an Imperial warship comes out from behind Lucazec, or drops out of hyperspace in front of us? Wouldn't you like—"

"To be able to show them our tail? Yes." He squeezed his eyes shut, as though trying to visualize something without distractions. "Maybe there's a way to do this without getting near the motivator. What do you have for tools?"

"I—I'm not sure. I thought you would use the Force somehow," she said. "Bend a contact, or break a trace—"

Luke shook his head. "You have to know *exactly* how something's put together before you try that sort of trick—and I've never even had my hands inside the access panel of an Adventurer."

"You're destroying all my illusions about the all-powerful Jedi," Akanah said with a hint of a smile.

Laughing lightly, Luke climbed out of the pilot's seat. "The truth is that, most of the time, the Force is no substitute for a tech droid or a tool kit. And I've never known a Jedi who wanted it to get around that he could fix broken appliances."

Her smile broadened at that.

"Did you get a key to the equipment bay when you bought this thing?"

"No," she said, suddenly worried.

"It's all right," Luke said, touching her shoulder as he slipped by her. "I *can* handle an idiot lock without a tool kit. Stay here and keep an eye on the nav scanner. I'll see what I can do about giving us another option."

*   *   *

Luke sat on the edge of the open drive compartment, his feet dangling inside, just above the fuel pumps for the realspace thrusters. It felt both strange and pleasantly familiar to be tinkering again. It took him back to the hot breezes of Tatooine, to surprisingly fond memories of his years in the Lars household.

"Boys and machines," he could hear his Aunt Beru saying with bemusement. "What is it about boys and machines?"

His life then had consisted of little more than tinkering. The greater part by far of his chores on the farm had been trying to keep Uncle Owen's motley collection of secondhand droids and second-quality moisture vaporators running. After chores, Luke had invested his free time in coaxing a little more speed from the XP-30 landspeeder he had rescued from the Anchorhead salvage yard, and tweaking the performance of the family's T-16 skyhopper for those races in Beggar's Canyon.

Teenage impatience had made him view Tatooine as a wasteland and the farm as a prison. But that world looked better seen through a filter of time and experience. And he realized belatedly just how much he had enjoyed those hours with his head and hands inside an engine service panel, in a simple, knowable world of which he was the master.

"You look happy," said Akanah softly. She had returned from the flight deck without his noticing.

"I am," he said, twisting and looking up at her. It was a surprising discovery.

She nodded toward the drive. "Do you think you'll be able to fix it? Or break it—I suppose that's more descriptive."

"It's already done," he said. "It wasn't that hard once I got into it. The lockout doesn't go into the drive at all—it's here at the nav controller, see? If it doesn't get a signal from the FCZ interface, the controller can't enable the drive—" He saw her expression and stopped himself.

"Anyway, I'm just studying up for the next problem now."

"Already done? That's wonderful!" she said. "I'm terribly impressed—I've never had so much as a single home tech course, and when I look down in there, I have no idea what I'm seeing. You could probably tell," she added.

"Well—we should test it before we need it. I need to know if any of this was important," he said, letting a small handful of metal plugs, clips, and wires cascade to the deckplate.

When he saw the sudden alarm in her eyes, he laughed and quickly said, "Just kidding. About the parts, anyway. We ought to test it, though. I was thinking we could jump out just a little early. Even fifteen minutes would be enough."

"What about the alert list?"

"The boundary of the FCZ isn't a hard line—there's a yellow zone. We can jump out of there without attracting any attention, but it'll still be a fair test. I'm sure it'll work, though."

"So you do fix appliances," she said mischievously, sitting on the deck in a spill of skirt. "What were you thinking about when I came in?"

"Home," he said simply.

She settled back against a wiring panel. "It's funny—I spent most of my life on Carratos, but 'home' always means Lucazec to me."

"Tatooine," Luke supplied. "Which I always said was a better place to be from than to be. I'm not so sure about that now."

"Almost all of my memories from Ialtra are good ones," Akanah said. "I suppose that's one reason what you did there upsets me so much. Now I have *that* memory, too, and I would rather not."

"At least you're here to have it," Luke said. "I'm sorry, but I'm not going to feel guilty about saving you."

"What about killing those two men—do you feel anything about that?"

"One of them killed himself," Luke said, pulling his feet up out of the hatchway and turning to face her.

"Commander Paffen."

Luke nodded. "He said something about poison, remember? I didn't want him dead. I was trying to question him."

"And the other? The one you eviscerated with your lightsaber? Were you trying to kill him?"

"He had a personal shield," Luke said. "It takes a lot of force to get through one—and when your blade does pop through, it's hard to stop it before it does a lot of damage."

"I understand. Were you trying to kill him?"

"Didn't I just answer that?"

"I don't think so," she said with a shy smile.

Luke eased himself back against the bulkhead on his side of the compartment. "I guess the truth is that, at the moment, I wasn't particularly worried about whether I killed him or not."

She shook her head slowly. "That is so hard for me to understand—how you could not be aware of the power in your hands."

"The power that mattered to me was the power to protect you from them," said Luke. "You told me afterward that you weren't in any danger, but that wasn't how it looked."

"Yes," said Akanah. "I understand that. But, Luke, there's something I must ask of you—that you never again kill to save me. I am glad that you cared about me, but it makes my heart sick, my spirit heavy, to have the screams and the blood of those men in my memory, in the ruins of a place that I loved."

"I don't know if I can make you that promise," Luke said. "I have my own conscience to satisfy. And sometimes it demands that I fight for my friends."

"That you kill for your friends."

"When it's necessary."

"Is that how you see the Jedi? Are they ready to kill to protect their friends on Coruscant?"

Luke's gaze narrowed. "What are you trying to say?"

"I'm trying to understand," Akanah said. "I want to know what your Jedi mean to the New Republic, and what the New Republic means to you. Are you training the Jedi Knights to be Coruscant's warrior elite? What are you willing to do when the commander-in-chief calls on you?"

"That isn't the way it works," Luke said. "Leia doesn't give orders to the Jedi. She can ask us for help— one of us or all of us—but we can refuse. And sometimes do."

"But the Republic supports your academy. You had a military spacecraft in your hangar. Can you afford to offend them?"

"The Jedi aren't mercenaries," Luke said, an edge in his voice. "When we fight, it's an individual choice—and it's in defense of the principles of our creed. Coruscant supports the academy because the memory of the Jedi is a powerful force for stability. Our presence is what they want most."

"That's the part of the tradition that concerns me," said Akanah. "The guardians of peace and justice in the Old Republic for a thousand generations, or so the legend has it. But if you cannot have both peace and justice, which will you choose?"

"Which would you have me choose?"

"I would choose for you to keep your great gifts beyond the reach of politicians and generals," she said. "For you to owe them no debts, and take on no causes—"

"I've been careful to protect our independence," said Luke. "Despite appearances."

"You aren't sworn to uphold the government on Coruscant? You've taken no oaths of allegiance?"

"No. Only those few who've chosen to serve in the Fleet, or the ministries. It's not forbidden. But it's not common. The Jedi aren't the Republican Guard. And never will be."

"That's something," she said. "But how much better it would be if the most powerful symbol of your order—the very emblem of that long tradition—was something other than a deadly weapon."

"We didn't ask for that," Luke said. "It just happened. Old weapons have a cachet."

"All weapons have a cachet," said Akanah with sorrow. "Too many men want to either conquer the world or change the world. The second is nearly as dangerous to living things as the first. Can you tell me why is it not enough to find a safe and comfortable place *in* the world, or—at worst—to find shelter *from* the world?"

Luke frowned. "No. I can't." He nodded toward the work bay. "But I can tell you how to disable the FCZ lockout on a Verpine Adventurer. Which I couldn't have told you this morning. Maybe tomorrow I'll figure out something else."

She smiled ruefully at him. "I guess that will have to do for now."

In the end, three days of watching the nav scanner like a nervous mouse watching for the predator in the dark yielded only a handful of wholly innocent contacts. No warships appeared, and the few private and commercial craft that left Lucazec after them or passed the *Mud Sloth* inbound took no apparent interest in the little skiff.

"Whoever Commander Paffen was reporting to must have been far enough away that his controller simply wrote him off," Luke said, leaning forward over the controls.

"But they'll be looking for us everywhere now," said Akanah from behind. "For you in particular."

"Looking and finding are two different things. I've

had to make a habit of disguising myself in public just to be left alone, to go where I please without being gawked at," Luke said.

"How do you do that?"

"Oh—I make myself look older where youth is honored, and younger where age is honored, female where males are the ones who strut, male where they aren't. It's the nearest thing there is to being invisible, being unattractive."

"Show me."

Akanah saw his shoulders rise and fall, heard the deep breath that came out almost as a sigh. When he turned his couch toward her and looked up, she saw a sixty-year-old face that reminded her at once of everyone and no one. The eyes were unguarded but vacant, the expression open but bland. There was nothing distinctive about his features, nothing at all to remember him by or for.

"Very good," she said. "May I try something?"

He gestured silently with open hands.

Drawing a shuddery breath, Akanah closed her eyes and moved the focus of her senses behind where Luke seemed to be, groping for an anchor in what was real. When she found it, she opened her eyes again and blew away the illusion with the soft breath of disbelief.

"There you are," she said, and smiled.

"Very good," he echoed. "It takes a strong mind to penetrate the illusion."

"I wanted to make certain *I* could find you, if we had to separate on Teyr. Do you change your voice, too?"

"I can. It requires more concentration, because the ear isn't as easily fooled. I'm not sure why that is, but it is—with humans, anyway. Speaking of Teyr—we're in the yellow zone."

"Is it safe to jump out now?"

"I don't see why not," said Luke. "And we'll pick

up almost an hour, jumping from this point. Assuming that I didn't break more than I meant to back there."

She smiled. "Let's find out."

"Let's," he said, turning back to the controls. "Do you still want to make a misdirection jump, or shall we go directly to Teyr?"

"I still want to," Akanah said, letting one hand settle lightly on his shoulder. "Someone could still be watching us from Lucazec. But a short one, please. I want to get to Teyr as soon as we possibly can. I just know that we'll find something more than ruins there."

Her touch caught Luke momentarily unguarded and made her mind open to his as well. He felt the barely restrained urgency of her need for reunion, the brightness of her hope, the depth of her anxious fears.

"Well, better strap in, then—just in case," he said.

The jump-out was reassuringly uneventful. By the time the *Mud Sloth* would have been released from the FCZ, it had already completed its first jump and turned to the heading for Teyr.

Then there was time to think, in the quiet, undisturbed hours while Akanah slept and nothing could touch them. Luke thought most about Ialtra, returning to his mother's dusty, crumbling cottage, searching his sense-memories again for her presence.

Luke knew he would have to return there when it was safe to do so, and wondered if something should be done to preserve the site. He wondered how the authorities on Lucazec would react if he asked them to protect his mother's onetime home. If the burned-out ruin of the Lars farm could be rebuilt as a historic monument, perhaps the ruins of Ialtra could be rescued from a hostile neglect by the Skywalker name. Perhaps the reputation of those who had been driven from there could even be rehabilitated.

But that would have to come later, when there were

fewer secrets to protect. For now, Luke would have to count on the shame of the Fallanassi to shield Ialtra from being further disturbed.

Let the nackhawns take the bodies, he thought, *and the shadows keep Ialtra undisturbed. Let her memories sleep until I can return to awaken them.*

When Luke heard Akanah moving in the bunk behind him, he planted a bare foot on the control console and pushed off, spinning the couch around to face aft.

"Hey—are you awake?"

"It's hard to sleep," she said, invisible behind the privacy curtain. "Perhaps we should change places."

Luke looked back over his shoulder at the displays. "It's only two hours to the end of the jump," he said. "And there'll be plenty of chance for me to rest up during the crawl to Teyr."

"Couldn't we use your military waiver, now that you've disconnected the interlock?" Her voice was clear and unmuffled, and Luke pictured her lying on her back. "We could microjump right in, couldn't we?"

Luke's surprised laugh was a loud noise in the confined space. "Not in this bucket. The navigator won't take microjump parameters. And even if it would, chances are the resonances would shake her to pieces. There's an entry shock wave in hyperspace, and when you microjump you have to let it catch you just when it's at its strongest. We'd arrive at Teyr as a bright smudge in the sky."

"Oh," she said. "But we could have jumped all the way in if we'd planned to back at the last waypoint."

"Right. If we were willing to answer all the questions and deal with the extra attention. I hate the crawl as much as you do, but, trust me, this is better."

Akanah sighed. "I'll try to sleep, then. It's the easy way to make the time pass."

"Good luck," he said, and started to turn back to the console.

Then he realized it had almost happened again—the conversation he had started for a specific purpose had wandered away and disappeared before he could get to his question.

"Akanah?"

"Yes?"

"Before you fall asleep—there's something I've been wondering about."

"What is it?"

"Back at Ialtra—was there a date in that message you found?"

"A date? No."

"Could you tell how long it had been there? Maybe scribing fades with time, or something like that—"

"No—not if it's done well. I can't tell you when the message was left—except that I'm sure it was left before the Fallanassi left Lucazec. Why?"

"I'm wondering how two Imperial agents could hide for so long in a place where everyone knows everyone else and nothing changes very quickly," Luke said. "I'm wondering *why* they would."

"Why—because they still want us—want the White Current as a weapon."

"But why would they think anyone would be coming back there? Why would they be expecting you?"

She was quiet for a time. "I've been asking questions for a long time, trying to find the circle," she said. "I haven't always been as careful as I should have been, either in what I asked or who I asked."

"Who did you tell that you were planning to go to Lucazec?"

"Only you," she said. "But I tried sending messages to the circle, to Wialu. I talked to the customs and immigration office on Lucazec. I applied for every starliner job posted on Carratos, hoping to get a working passage.

I checked open ticket prices constantly, every time new rates were posted."

"So people started to know who you were, and something about what you were interested in."

"More than that," she said. "I made rather a pest of myself. I hung around the spaceport dives when a ship came in, hoping the crews might know something. I found ways of getting passenger lists. I talked to everyone I could who might know anything." Her smile was full of regret. "It wasn't until later that I thought to be more discreet."

"The people you'd been left with—"

"I didn't get any help from them," she said. "They forbade me to speak to them about the circle, and punished me for looking on my own."

"They must have been afraid for you—maybe for themselves, too. They were supposed to hide you, weren't they? And you refused to stay hidden."

"It's easier to understand than it is to forgive," she said. "They kept me from being where I belonged. I can't forgive that until I find the circle again. If I never do, I don't think I can ever forgive her."

"Her?"

"Talsava," she said. "My guardian on Carratos. But if I start talking about her now, I'll never get to sleep."

"All right," he said. "Sorry."

"You didn't know," said Akanah. "I'll tell you about it, sometime."

"When you're ready."

He thought that had ended the conversation. He heard Akanah changing position and pictured her lying on her side, her head on her folded arms. He was surprised when she spoke his name.

"What?"

"What do you think the chances are that someone will be looking for us on Teyr?"

"Greater than zero," Luke said. "But we'll be careful. Go to sleep, now."

She did not argue or answer, and Luke lapsed into silence as well, wondering why he felt as though none of his questions had been answered, and the most important ones had never been asked at all.

Where Lucazec was rustic, Teyr was bureaucratic.

Located near the juncture of three busy spaceways and wearing a spectacular four-thousand-kilometer-long canyon like a dueling scar, Teyr was one of the New Republic's boom worlds. Most of the boom was in visitors and vacationers. Fearing unbridled growth, Teyr's leaders purposefully discouraged would-be immigrants with a maze of regulations, a series of successively higher application hurdles, and a determinedly officious Citizen Services Corps. The unofficial tourism motto was "Come see spectacular Teyr Rift. Then go home."

While still inbound, Luke and Akanah were offered the unattractive choice of parking their craft at one of the vast orbital parking areas and shuttling down to the surface, or paying four times as much in landing fees to bring the skiff down at a spaceport of Teyr's choosing.

"I don't like the idea of being down *there* and having to depend on third parties to get back to our ship up *here*," Luke said. "If someone should decide they want to delay our departure, I like our chances better if we don't have to jump quite so high."

"But I don't have that kind of money, Luke," said Akanah. "You know that."

"I think Li Stonn is good for it," Luke said. He flashed a wry smile that disappeared behind his illusion of age, then tapped the comm key. "Teyr Flight Control, this is *Mud Sloth*—I'd like to request landing authorization."

"Copy, *Mud Sloth*, your queue number is alpha-three-nine, confirm."

"Confirm, alpha-three-nine," Luke said. "Could you tell me, is there any chance that we could possibly put down at Turos Noth? We're going to be meeting some friends—"

"Landing sites are allocated on a space-available basis according to standard protocols. Ground transportation is available at all spaceports. The Rift Skyrail connects all spaceports with all major population centers and with visitor centers, trailheads, and resort destinations in the Rift Territory. Monitor this channel for further landing instructions. This is Teyr Flight Control, end transmission."

Luke and Akanah exchanged bemused looks.

"They wouldn't have dared give Luke Skywalker number thirty-nine," she said.

"Too bad he couldn't join us for this trip," Luke said, allowing his disguise to dissolve.

"I wonder how many times a shift they have to recite that," Akanah said.

"I don't think they care," said Luke, then explained, "It was a droid. I couldn't touch it." He nodded past Akanah. "Are any of the stuffed koba left? I think we might have time to eat before the skids get dirty."

As Luke had suspected, there was more than enough time. Following directions from Flight Control, *Mud Sloth* joined a long queue of yachts and liners in a high orbit over Teyr. Six full revolutions later, they were still there, though most of the ships in front of them—and several behind them as well—had already made their descent and been replaced by newer arrivals.

"Nice view," Akanah said. "Do you think they'll ever let us any closer?"

"No," said Luke. "I knew we should have told them we had eighty-two paying customers aboard, all eager to start shopping."

"Eighty-two?" she said, raising an eyebrow skeptically.

"Ewoks," Luke said, shrugging. "You should see

the way they live. It's nothing like in the holos. Twenty-four to a room, stacked in layers, boy, girl, boy, girl—"

"You've been in space too long," she said, with a disapproving frown. "Maybe we didn't hear our call."

"—Queue number alpha-eight-one, proceed to approach—"

"Eighty-one!" Akanah exclaimed indignantly. "Why is everyone going before us?"

"Because whatever kind of priority list they're using, they put people who own Verpine Adventurers at the bottom of it," Luke said.

"Will you please stop making jokes?"

"Sometimes there's no other recourse," said Luke. "What happened to your implacable calm?"

"This is making me crazy," Akanah said.

"I can tell."

"Can't we just disguise ourselves as some other ship and take its landing instructions?"

"There's a little problem about two objects occupying the same space at the same time."

"Luke—"

The tone of her voice made him look toward her. He saw anguish on her face, anxiety in her pleading eyes. "Do you think they might be holding us up here until they can get everything ready to grab us, or follow us?" *Please do something!* her expression cried.

"No," Luke said, and reached across to touch her hand. "Teyr runs the shuttles themselves, and the space-lines have contracts with Teyr for priority landing access. They get to go first—we get to wait for an opening. It's all right—they're treating us the way we want them to. No special treatment, no special notice. They'll get around to us soon. They want our money, too."

"—Queue number alpha-three-nine, proceed to approach corridor for landing at Prye Folas—"

"There—see?" He squeezed her hand reassuringly, then moved his own hands back to the flight controls.

Relief was evident on her face. "Prye Folas—that's

good. It's a long way from the Rift, but that doesn't matter to us—it's only one stop east of Turos Noth."

"I'm glad someone studied their geography," Luke said. "Snug up those straps, Lady Anna. Did you know that most crashes take place within sixty seconds of liftoff or touchdown?"

She frowned crossly at him. "Did you need to tell me?"

"I think I did," Luke said, firing the braking thrusters to drop the skiff out of her parking orbit. "You seem to need something to worry about—I thought it might as well be something real." He looked sideways at her and grinned. "One way or another, we'll be on the ground in ten minutes."

"You think this is helping, don't you?"

"It's just my way of saying, relax—"

"I can't," she said with a nervous sigh. "I've been waiting too long. I have too much at stake."

Luke nodded understandingly. "In that case, I promise to try for the *soft* landing."

For just a moment, he thought Akanah was going to punch him.

Luke's landing at Prye Folas was better than soft. It was flawlessly smooth, the kind pilots call a first kiss.

It also put *Mud Sloth* right back in a line—this time, the long taxi line leading to the vast field of open-air tie-down berths. Teyr's exorbitant landing fee didn't buy "Li Stonn" a spot in a docking bay, or even secure covered stowage, for his ship.

"One good storm, and the shipbuilding trade has a record year next year," Luke said, surveying the expansive, and expensive, assortment of vessels.

When the tow droid finally reached the assigned berth and backed *Mud Sloth* into its space, its port wing nestled under the thrustpods of a big Toltax Starstream, the port manager's official voice—another droid—came over the open channel.

"Welcome to Prye Folas. In order to help ensure the safety of all visitors to Teyr, port regulations forbid occupancy of vessels in tie-down berths," the droid said. "Please remove whatever personal articles you will need during your stay and seal your vessel, then wait for the arrival shuttle. In order to help ensure the safety of your vessel, access to this parking area is limited to arriving and departing visitors. This area is patrolled by port security. Thank you for including Teyr in your travel plans—"

"I'm ready," Akanah said impatiently.

Luke powered down the skiff's primary bus. "Let me grab my bag and put on my face."

The arrival shuttle, a low-riding, slow-moving landspeeder, was piloted by still another late-model droid. Akanah and Luke caught two of the last three open seats, and the third was taken by the Elomin who emerged from the airspeeder parked across the towpath from *Mud Sloth*. When the shuttle was full, it rose several meters above the ground and sped off in the direction of the terminal. An empty shuttle immediately moved in to take its place.

"Quite an operation, don't you think, dear?" Luke said. The voice of "Li Stonn" had a little tremble, a little added huskiness. "When you see this many droids, you know someone's doing well."

Akanah seemed inhibited by the other travelers close around them—the Elomin, immediately to her right, towered over her by more than a head. She answered only with a glance and a polite smile.

Luke patted her hand reassuringly. "I know, you don't like open landspeeders. But we're almost there," he said. "Look—you can see the track for the Rift Skyrail. The guidebook said it's the fastest aboveground train in five sectors—"

*   *   *

The last hurdle was Arrival Screening—another line, a droid greeter, an IRR screening for their bags, a discreet security sweep of their persons, and three questions from a human examiner who had much the same demeanor as the district censor on Lucazec.

"How long do you plan to stay on Teyr?"

"We're not sure, are we, dear?" Luke asked. "How long does it take to really see the Rift at its best? Our reservation is only for three days, but we're hoping that we can extend it now that we're here."

"Three days," the examiner repeated. "Are you now, or have you recently been, infected with any transmissible class B or class C agent?"

"No, no," Luke/Li said, smiling at Akanah. "We're fit as can be. I just hate to travel when I'm sick, don't you?"

"Do you have in your possession any lethal weapons, proscribed drugs, unlicensed technology, or other articles in violation of the General Visitor Agreement?"

"Oh, gracious, no," Luke said. "We're here to have fun."

The examiner passed two traveler's aid cards through an encoder. "Welcome to Teyr," he said, handing the cards to Akanah. "Enjoy your stay with us."

Between the Prye Folas spaceport terminal and the Skyrail station was the broad green expanse of Welcome Park. Luke and Akanah stopped at the first open bench they spotted, tucking their bags protectively behind their feet.

"I think we're finally officially here," Luke said. "How are you doing?"

"It's not what I expected," said Akanah, looking around.

Luke held out a palm. "Let's see that," he said, nodding toward the traveler's aid cards Akanah still clutched in her hand.

Distractedly, Akanah handed one of the cards to Luke, who began to study it. The card had a tiny display screen that took up half of one side, with some universal-symbol command keys below. On the back was a line drawing of the structure that stood at the center of the park—a ring of more than a hundred small kiosks surrounding a two-story-high carousel display.

"I have to go do a Li Stonn thing," said Luke. "Stay here—I'll be right back."

When Luke got closer to the structure, he could see that the band at the top of the carousel said "Visitor Information Center" in Basic and several other common languages.

There were short lines of people waiting at every kiosk for a chance to select their areas of interest and have that information transferred to the cards, where they could browse it at their leisure. While they waited, most looked up at the carousel display, which was offering colorful one-minute documentaries on the geology of the Rift, the building of the Skyrail, and the shopping opportunities in Prye Folas.

"Pickpocket's paradise," Luke muttered, and turned away.

Just then, Luke felt the momentary tickle in his senses that meant he was being watched. He scanned the park carefully as he returned to the bench where Akanah sat, but the feeling did not return, and nothing he saw raised his alarm.

"I need to know what region we'll—" He stopped as he saw that she was struggling against tears, her eyes faraway and forlorn. "What's wrong?"

"Everything's wrong," she said. "I just know they're not here."

Luke sat down sideways beside her. "Why? You thought you'd be able to feel them, and you can't?"

She was not too upset to be indignant. "No—we're not that careless, to broadcast our presence even on the Current."

"Then what's the matter?"

"I told you—everything's wrong." She shook her head sadly. "This isn't our kind of world. It's everything we're trying not to be. It's too crowded, too loud, too organized and artificial. If they were ever here, they won't have stayed very long." Bowing her head, she began to sob quietly. "It's too late. It took me too long to get here—"

Edging closer, Luke drew her into a comforting embrace, brushing away the worst of her despair with caressing thoughts. "You don't know that," he said. "It's too soon to be giving up. Come on, where do we start?"

Akanah rested her head on his shoulder. "I'm sorry—I'm not doing a very good job of being invisible."

"No one cares," Luke said. "No one's watching. All these people have tunnel vision—all they can see right now are their own plans and worries and hopes. They're all eager for confirmation that this really will be the vacation of a lifetime."

Raising her head, Akanah sought confirmation of his words. "On Carratos, everyone notices public tears," she said, wiping her cheeks. "My ears expected to hear ridicule."

"Looks like you'll have to do without, this time," he said. "So where do we start? Who are we looking for?"

"The city of Griann," she said. "It's in what they call the Greenbelt Region. That's where they were taken—Jib Djalla, Novus, Tipagna, and Norika. The first three are boys," she added. "Novus is Twi'lek, the others are human."

"Okay. Let's go see what the machines can tell us about Griann," Luke said, reaching down and shouldering both bags.

As they stood in line for an information kiosk, Akanah's mood seemed to brighten, as though she were absorbing some of the joyful energy around her. But Luke again felt someone's curiosity as a sudden shiver, as if someone had lightly touched his face, trying to recognize him.

Looking back across Welcome Park on a pretense of casual crowd-watching, Luke focused in on the tall, slender form of an Elomin male, already turning his horned face away. Luke watched his quarry move aloofly through the gathering until it disappeared behind the curve of the information center, but the Elomin never glanced his way again.

You're getting twitchy, Luke told himself. *There's no way that an Elomin would be working for Imperial intelligence.*

But the fact that an Elomin—perhaps this same one—had parked an airspeeder directly across from *Mud Sloth* would not leave his awareness. And the noise and the bustle of the crowd in the park suddenly seemed less a joyful party and more a potentially deadly distraction.

Maybe they were *holding us up for a reason, Akanah,* Luke thought worriedly, patting the bulge of his lightsaber along his thigh to reassure himself that it was there.

But though he stayed protectively close, Luke said nothing to Akanah beyond the kind of inconsequential chatter a couple as accustomed to each other as they were to traveling might share while waiting in line. *There's something here that I still don't understand—some question I've failed to ask.* He shook his head in annoyance, with such vigor that Akanah noticed.

"Is something wrong?" she asked.

"Oh—I've just done it again, that's all," said Li Stonn. "The lines on either side are moving faster than ours. I shouldn't ever pick. You pick the line next time, all right?"

She slipped her hand into his. "Be patient, dear," she said with an affectionate smile. "We're almost there—and maybe this will be the last line we have to stand in."

Someone behind them chuckled deeply. "This is

your first time on Teyr, isn't it?" the stranger called out. "You haven't seen anything yet. Wait until you get near the Rift."

"Oh, it'll be worth it, I'm sure," Akanah said brightly, tightening her grip on Luke's hand. "I just know it will be worth the wait."

Chapter 6

◆

Luke and Akanah rode the Rift Skyrail as far as Cloud Bridge, the southernmost of the West Rim stops. That treated them to a breathtaking view of the last eighty kilometers of the Rift—one of the narrowest sections, and consequently one of the most spectacular. The elevated track was perched right on the edge of the chasm, leaping across side canyons that would have been major attractions in their own right anywhere else.

At Cloud Bridge, Li Stonn rented a bubbleback, a local landspeeder variant popular with visitors who wanted to explore the canyon bottom. But instead of heading for the elevators at the Cloud Bridge Rift Access Point, Luke turned the bubbleback west along Flyway 120, toward the Greenbelt.

An hour and a half at the top speed allowed on the flyway brought them to the intersection with Harvest Flyway, which Akanah's traveler's aid card told them was an important cargo route connecting the heart of the Greenbelt with Turos Noth. There was no speed limit on the lightly traveled cargo route, which put the agricultural city of Griann not quite two hours away at the bubbleback's top speed.

"Need to stretch?"

"No," she said, pointing behind them. "I can manage." As "getaway" vehicles, bubblebacks featured a compact waste station and reprocessor, with a full set of standard humanoid fittings. "Do we need to refuel?"

"No. Griann has fuel stops, I assume."

Akanah checked her aid card. "Yes. Though 'local prices may vary from published visitor area rates.' Please, let's push on."

They had nearly reached Griann when Akanah finally noticed the outline of the cylinder in the right thigh pocket of Luke's walk-arounds.

"You brought your lightsaber?" she asked, leaning toward him.

"Yes," he said. "You sound surprised."

"How did you get it through Arrival Screening? You can't fool a scanner with Jedi mind tricks. Can you?"

"You can fool the person whose job it is to respond to scanner alarms," Luke said. "But even that wasn't necessary. Lightsabers are still the rarest weapons in the galaxy. There's only one model of general security scanner that's programmed to recognize them, and Teyr doesn't use it."

"Then what do they think it is?"

Luke smiled. "Most scanners misidentify a lightsaber as a type of shaver. Which I suppose it could be, in a pinch—if you were *very,* very good with it."

She settled back in her seat. "I wish you had left it in the ship."

"That's asking too much," Luke said. "I don't carry it every minute, but I don't like to be that far away from it. I've gotten in more tough spots because of not having it close enough than I ever have for carrying it."

Looking out her window at the gently rolling fields and the day moon that was setting over them, Akanah said, "Please remember what I asked of you—it's important to me."

"I remember," Luke said. "I hope you remember that I didn't make you any promises."

"Is there that much pleasure in killing, that it becomes something difficult to give up?"

Luke shot a hard glance across the bubbleback at her. "What makes you think I take pleasure in killing?"

"That you won't renounce it," she said, turning to meet his gaze. "If I had caused a million deaths, I don't think I could ever pick up a weapon again. I don't understand how you can."

With no ready answer, Luke turned his gaze back toward the flyway ahead. It wasn't until years after the Battle of Yavin that Luke had first become aware that the Death Star he had destroyed at Yavin had a complement—officers, crew, and support staff—of more than a million sentients.

In retrospect, it was something he *should* have realized without prompting. But it took a new Battle of Yavin display at the Museum of the Republic on Coruscant to point it out to him. When Luke thought of the Death Star, he associated it with Vader and Tagge and Grand Moff Tarkin, with the stormtroopers who'd tried to kill him in its corridors and the TIE pilots who'd tried to kill him above its surface, with the superlaser gun crews who had obliterated defenseless Alderaan.

But the signs at the massive cutaway model of the Death Star in the museum had spelled out the numbers in its table of specifications, and Luke could still recite them: 25,800 stormtroopers, 27,048 officers, 774,576 crew, 378,685 support staff—

"One million, two hundred five thousand, one hundred nine," Luke said quietly. "Not counting the droids."

The calm precision of the recitation brought a look of startled horror to her face.

"But you have to look at both sides of the ledger," Luke went on. "Alderaan. Obi-Wan. Captain Antilles. Dutch. Tiree. Dack. Biggs—" Luke shook his head.

"Sometimes your enemies don't give you much choice—kill them, give up, or be killed. And if you think I should have done anything other than what I did—"

"The past is fixed, unalterable," Akanah said. "What I care about is what you'll do today, or tomorrow. I know your past—I know your heritage—and I have already seen you kill once. Can't you understand how alien and abhorrent this is to me—to those who gave Nashira shelter?"

"You don't trust me."

She folded her hands on her lap, and her voice became small. "I am trying, Luke—but you don't know how hard it is for me to trust someone who believes as you do, and who has your power."

Luke stole a sideways glance to catch her expression. "Are you saying you're afraid of me—because of this?" He rested his hand over the concealed lightsaber.

"I suppose I am," she said. "I don't want to be."

"I would never hurt you, Akanah," Luke said. "I brought this with me in case there were any surprises waiting—not to threaten you."

"I move through the world without one," she said. "Could you not do the same?"

Luke slowly shook his head. "Not while I still call myself a Jedi. It's more than a weapon—it's a tool for training the mind and the body. And it's become part of me—an extension of my will."

"And a way to enforce your will on others."

He shook his head. "Most of the discipline of the lightsaber has to do with defense."

"What about the rest?"

"The rest—the rest requires that you get close to your adversary, close enough to have to look them in the eye," Luke said. "An old-fashioned idea, and a civilizing one. If all you want is to kill quickly, efficiently and impersonally, a blaster is a much better choice—the Emperor's stormtroopers didn't carry lightsabers, after all."

"All of my nightmares are of places where there are

men who want to kill 'efficiently,' " Akanah said, turning her face back to the viewpane. "And the worst nightmare of all is to think that the only Universe that is, is such a place."

Griann had been laid out on the plains of Teyr with a compass and a square. Its regularly spaced streets of regularly sized houses intersected with right-angle precision in a grid five kilometers square. At the heart of the city was a small commercial zone serving both the residents and the traffic on the Harvest Flyway. Around the boundary of the city was an enclosing wall of silos, granaries, ag domes, sheds for the autoharvesters and skyhoppers, control towers for the irrigation system, and all the other facilities necessary for servicing the fields beyond.

"Welcome to scenic Griann," Luke said, guiding the bubbleback into a refueling stall. "What now? Do you have a plan?"

"I have an address," Akanah said. "North Five, Twenty-six Down. My friend Norika lived there."

Luke shot her a questioning look. "I thought the children were supposed to be hiding. How did you get a lead as specific as an address?"

"From Norika," Akanah said. "I got one letter from her that first month, hypercommed to Carratos from a public terminal at something she called the committee office. I wrote her back, a dozen letters at least, but she never answered—I never heard from her again."

"Hmmm. Someone probably enforced on her the idea that 'hiding' means you don't tell anyone where you are," Luke said.

"Or the circle came for them, and took them away."

Luke glanced out his window at the display on the refueling droid. "It's been nineteen years—you may not know her even if she's still here."

"I would know Nori no matter how many years

have passed," Akanah said fervently. "Wialu said we had the bond of twins. I've never been closer to anyone."

The refueling over, Luke started the repulsorlifts. "Well, let's go find out how close we are. North Five, Number Twenty-six?"

"Yes."

"I think I can find that."

From city center to city edge, Akanah's anticipation built until it bubbled over in nervous smiles and a restless bouncing in her seat. But when the bubbleback turned onto North 5, her face went pale, and her hand shot out and clutched Luke's wrist tightly. A strangled noise was all that escaped her parted lips.

Luke did not need an explanation—his eyes saw the same thing hers did. The double row of lowhouses along North 5 ended at Number 22. Where Number 24 should have been was an expanse of patchy grass. Beyond it, the grass gave way to several lots' worth of bare, yellowish dirt. The next even-numbered lowhouse was at the corner of the next intersection, Number 38.

"Well, I'll—there's no 'there' there," Luke said, peering over his shoulder as he brought the bubbleback to the curb in front of Number 38.

Popping the bubble, Akanah jumped out before the landspeeder came to a stop. She ran back down the street in a staggered gait, hugging her arms to her chest, her gaze darting from one side of the roadway to the other. Her steps slowed as she neared the lot opposite Number 25. She looked frantic and frail standing there, staring at the bare ground and the broken outline of a foundation.

Leaping out of the landspeeder, Luke hurried after Akanah. Before he could reach her, her legs buckled under her, and she dropped to her knees in the dust-dry rain gutter.

"No!" she screamed, her anguish stretching the single syllable into a wounded howl. "No! It's not fair!"

"Akanah—"

She raised her head and turned her face toward him. Her eyes were full of pain, her cheeks streaked with tears. "I'll never find them," she whispered hoarsely. "What am I going to do, Luke?"

"You're going to keep looking. All this means is that Nori's not here," Luke said, crouching beside her. "You weren't counting on that, were you?" But he saw in her eyes that she had been, and what might have been a minor disappointment was a bitter blow.

"Something the matter, folks?" a new voice said from behind.

Both Luke and Akanah turned their heads quickly to see a stubble-faced middle-aged man in blue-black tech coveralls approaching them from the direction of Number 27. Luke stood as the man neared, and offered Akanah a hand to help her up. She remained on her knees and took Luke's hand to steady herself instead.

"Is the lady having a problem?" the man asked again, a hint more suspicion in his appraising look. "Do you want to call out to Medi-Aid?"

"No—she's all right. She just had an ugly surprise, that's all," Luke said. "We're looking for someone who used to live in Number Twenty-six."

"Ah," the man said with a nod. "Po Reggis—Jiki and I live over in Twenty-seven Up. So you didn't know, did you? You must be visitors." He glanced down the street. "Why, sure you are, and I'm a fool for not see-ing—bubbleback's not practical in a working city."

"Was it the war?" Akanah asked, her voice shaky.

"The war? No, Teyr was never bombed. Cyclone," Reggis said. "Eight—no, nine years ago. Took out eight houses here, then skipped and hit another five over at the end of North Three. The committee used to talk about rebuilding, but there's no demand—half the houses in the city are single-family now, Up and Down. It's all the field droids they've brought in—city's slow-dying, if you ask me."

Luke urged Akanah to her feet. "The people who lived here—"

"Kritt and Fola. Good folks. Our kids played with their kids, till they all moved to Turos Noth."

"Kritt and Fola are in Turos Noth now?" Akanah asked, a spark of hope entering her voice.

The spark was quickly extinguished by Po Reggis. "What? No, dead, the whole family. Sorry. Killed by the cyclone. It was the supper hour, and the weather radar failed. Fifteen dead on this street alone—I knew them all."

Akanah sagged against Luke. "How long have you lived here?" Luke asked.

Reggis squinted. "Twenty-seven—no, twenty-eight years."

"The person we're looking for would have moved here nineteen years ago," Luke said. "A girl, eleven years old. Akanah?"

"She was—dark-haired. Willowy. Her name was Norika, or Nori."

"I don't know," Reggis said. "Maybe Jiki remembers—did you say the name was Rika? Oh, Twenty-six *Down*. Who was it that lived there then? Trobe Saar, I think was her name."

"Yes!" Akanah said eagerly. "You remember her? Where did she go? Please tell me she wasn't one of the fifteen—"

"Sure, I remember little Rika. She was shy as a shadow. Wasn't there very long—one season at most. The Dormand family moved into Twenty-six Down the spring I transferred to Irrigation. I'm sorry—I don't know where they all went. That was all a long time ago, you know."

"Is there anyone else on the street who might know something?" Akanah asked, trying desperately to sustain hope.

"I don't think so," Reggis said slowly. "Jiki and I are the last of the old crowd. I guess we're the only ones who could take looking across and knowing what happened, what's down there. They just collapsed everything into the holes and covered it over with dirt, you know—"

"Thank you, Po," Luke said. "You've been very kind."

"Sorry I couldn't be more help. Do you want to talk to Jiki? She'll be up from her nap soon."

"Yes—" Akanah started to say.

"Thank you, no," Luke said, steering Akanah back toward the landspeeder with firm pressure on her arm.

She looked up at him in puzzlement. "Li—the others—maybe she remembers the others—"

"We must have the wrong address," Luke said, gently pressing that thought into Po Reggis's consciousness. "We'll try over on North Three."

"That's right," said Reggis. "There hasn't been a Twenty-six on this block for years."

"I think I hear Jiki calling you," Luke suggested.

"Well, I need to get back—Jiki's calling me," Reggis said, retreating slowly. "Good luck, now."

"Thank you."

Akanah waited until the ag tech disappeared into his house, then turned on Luke with fierce indignation. "Why did you do that? He might have been able to tell us something more."

"He already told us enough," Luke said. "Norika lived here for a little while, in the underground half of the house, with a woman named Trobe Saar. And that structure is still down there—it's just filled in. Wouldn't she have left a marker for you here when she left? Can you read scribing through the fill?"

"I—I don't know." She stepped forward, out of the street and onto the crumbly yellow dirt. "Maybe, if it's there. Let me try."

Luke waited and watched as Akanah slowly walked across the buried ruin of the lowhouse several times, pausing here, crouching there, reaching out to touch a small bit of foundation protruding up from the ground. Her expression offered no encouragement, and in time she sighed deeply, shook her head, and rejoined him.

"It's the deaths," she explained glumly as they returned to the bubbleback. "The Current is still tangled here. It's as if—as if someone made a delicate sand painting, and ten minutes later a meteorite fell right in the middle of it. If there was anything here, it's gone now."

"Don't give up," Luke said. "I've been thinking—a society as orderly as this one keeps records. Let's find the committee office. I'll bet some gray-hair there knows everything about everyone who's ever lived in Griann."

The Recorder of Assignments and Transactions for the Supervisors' Committee turned out to be completely hairless—a brand-new fat-bodied TT-40 library droid. Like all factory-fresh droids, TT-40 was long on formality and short on personality, lacking even a nickname. They found it busily moving its three spinning data probes from port to port in the U-shaped firewall switchboard that surrounded it.

"We need some information about—" Luke began.

"In accord with Ordinance Twenty Twenty-five, Privacy of Official Records, all requests for current records must be approved by the supervisor of your district, or, for nonresidents, by the general supervisor," the droid pronounced.

"That's nice," Luke said under his breath. "Nosy but discreet."

"—Commercial requests for historical records must be accompanied by a completed application and bond guarantee. Individual requests for historical records for purposes of personal scholarly or genealogical research will be processed at no charge on a time-available basis—"

"Whoa—stop right there, Chuckles. That's us," Luke said. "What counts as 'historical'?"

"For income, sales, and employment data, all records one fiscal year or older are deemed historical. For birth, death, bonding, and dissolution certificates, all records one hundred days—"

"What about census data—names and addresses, residences?" Akanah interjected.

"For biennial census data, all records fifty years—"

"*Fifty!*" Luke exclaimed.

To Luke's surprise, Akanah was unfazed. "Clerk," she said. "I have a package to deliver to Po Reggis. Can you tell me his current address?"

The data probes spun. "Po Reggis resides at North Five, Twenty-seven Up."

"Clerk," she said. "I have a package to deliver to Trobe Saar. Can you tell me her current address?"

"Trobe Saar is not in the current city directory."

"Can you tell me her last known address in Griann?"

"In revision eighty-one of the city directory, Trobe Saar's address is North Five, Twenty-six Down."

"Are other city directories available?"

"Yes." One of the data probes seated itself in a new port. "Connected to Central Directories."

"Can you tell me Trobe Saar's last known address on Teyr?"

"In Revision eighty-nine of the Sodonna city directory, Trobe Saar's last known address is Kell Plath, Thirteen."

"Thank you," she said, taking Luke's arm. "Let's go, Li."

"Are you sure?"

"I'm sure."

Outside the committee office, Luke tried to stop Akanah for an explanation, but she could not be headed off until they reached the spot where they'd parked the bubbleback.

"Why are you in such a hurry? We could have tried the children's names," Luke said. "Getting Chuckles to look in the city directories instead of the census was working like a charm."

"You can't search the directories with nothing more than the first name of a minor," Akanah said, rapping on the landspeeder's dome with her knuckles. "Would you open this up, please?"

Luke complied, and they climbed in together. "I know that because I tried, from Carratos, years ago," she continued as the bubble sealed around them. "It's impossible without knowing the family names they were using. Are we going to get started, or not?"

"Started where?"

"Sodonna, of course."

"Revision eighty-nine was more than fifteen years ago. And we don't know that Norika went with this Trobe Saar, or even if Trobe was part of your circle. Chances are this is going to be another North Five—a disappointment."

"No," she said. "Not this one."

"Why are you so sure? An hour ago you thought this was hopeless. And this morning you were sure they would never make their home on Teyr. Why so upbeat all of a sudden?"

"Because Kell Plath is a Fallanassi name." She hesitated, then added, "It means 'held breath'—an allusion to our meditation exercises. Besides," she said, "what other leads do we have?"

"You've got me there." Luke fumbled in his pocket for the traveler's aid card. "All right, where *is* Sodonna, anyway?"

The river city of Sodonna was on the far side of Teyr from Griann and the Rift, straddling the Noga River at what traditionally was considered its upstream limit of navigability. Five hundred years earlier, Sodonna had been the gateway to the entire Inner River District, with bustling docks and a job for anyone who wanted it.

Repulsorlift transports had taken the focus of commerce away from the river, and in large part from Sodonna as well. The docks were gone, and the Noga River now tumbled through the city as an elaborate water sculpture of falls, rapids, ponds, and fountains. Sodonna was the smallest Teyr city with a spaceport, and the terminus of the single-track River District spur of the Rift Skyway.

Luke followed the Harvest Flyway to Turos Noth, paying a hefty premium for dropping the bubbleback at the Skyrail station there. As night closed in, he and Akanah boarded a westbound railtrain and found seats in the single car that was programmed to separate from the rest and follow the spur to Sodonna.

But that intersection was hours away in the darkness. At Luke's urging, Akanah napped. She was not the only one in the nearly full cabin to do so. The ride was smooth, with just a slight and soothing side-to-side sway, the cabin lights were dimmed to unobtrusiveness, and the individual self-adjusting tour couches cradled them comfortably.

Luke did not dare sleep. Only his consciousness could hold the Li Stonn mask in place—there were suggestions in the old records of great Jedi Masters who could cast illusions even when sleeping, but neither Luke nor any Jedi he knew had attained that level of facility with the Force skill known as alter. And Luke could not risk dropping his mask in public—even if he were not recognized as himself, shape-shifters and mentalists were so widely assumed to be thieves, spies, and brigands that he could expect nearly as much commotion.

So he sat up awake, watching over Akanah, listening to whispered conversations, gently sensing the energies of those around him, looking out into the night as distant lights betrayed their swift passage and the cities along their route embraced the railtrain with their restless energy and then surrendered it back to the darkness. He wondered if somewhere out in that darkness the woman Akanah had known as Nashira was asleep as well, peacefully or restlessly, tranquilly or fearfully. *What would my mother think of me?* he wondered, and it was the first time such a thought had ever confronted him.

The thought perplexed and distracted him. He recalled Akanah's words on the night she had appeared: "The gift of the Light came from your mother—and your mother was of our people. There is an emptiness inside you where memories of your mother should be, a weakness where what she would have taught you would have strengthened you." Presumptuous words, but knowing words. In that moment, he felt that emptiness acutely, unable even to imagine what might fill it, or even that it might ever be filled.

Perhaps Nashira has stayed away because she's ashamed, Luke thought. *Perhaps she sees too much of Father in us, just as this woman does. You may have been right, Leia. If I do find the truth, I may not find it to my liking—*

Then Luke's sense skill tugged at his consciousness, calling his attention to a change in his surroundings. Clearing all other thoughts from his mind, he swept his awareness and his gaze together across the darkened railtrain. Both quickly fixed on the same point—an Elomin passenger, sitting near the front of the car on the opposite side. The Elomin's back was turned toward Luke, his horned skull-crown just visible over the top cushion of his tour couch.

Now, where did you come from? Luke thought, intent with suspicion. *You weren't there ten minutes ago—how could I have missed you coming in? Something doesn't feel right about this—*

He stole a quick look at Akanah, reassuring himself that she was sleeping blissfully. He wondered how badly his attention had wandered, whether he had let his mask slip.

Everything I know about you says that this isn't

really your sort of vacation spot, he thought, staring at the back of the Elomin's couch. *Even if the Teyria share your fetish for order, they keep letting in all these unpredictable alien types. And I can count on the fingers of one hand the number of times I've seen a solitary Elomin out in mixed company. Two of you in one day—or the same one twice—*

This feels like more than a coincidence. What I can't figure out is what would make an Elomin go rogue and hook up with Imperial agents—or why someone else might be interested in us. And I just may have to have a few answers—

Just then the Elomin left his seat and moved forward with slow, long-limbed strides. He was empty-handed, as the Elomin at the spaceport had been. At the end of the aisle he paused for a moment and looked back into the cabin. Then, ducking his head, he passed through the connecting doorway and was gone. Luke waited, torn between wanting to follow and not wanting to leave Akanah.

The Elomin had still not returned when the porter droid made an appearance, trundling down the aisle reciting a soft-spoken warning. "Attention, passengers. If you are not continuing to River District Spur destinations, please move into one of the forward cabins. This car will be separating from the train at Podadun. Attention, passengers—"

Still the Elomin did not return. As the chime sounded and the status light above the connecting door changed to yellow, Luke reached out with his senses and searched the train for the Elomin. But Luke could not find him. Fearing a bomb, he rushed forward to where the Elomin had been sitting.

Luke stared. There were no bags or articles there—just a sleeping Gotal infant.

The chime sounded again. Luke looked up as the connecting doors slid shut and the status light turned red. There was an almost imperceptible deceleration as the cars separated and the lights of Podadun began to flash through the unfiltered viewpanes.

The infant stirred in its sleep, and Luke retreated. *What is wrong with me?* he demanded silently as he made his way back to his seat, the aisle tilting under him as the car swung off the main line and onto the banked spur to Sodonna. *Why am I jumping at shadows?*

Akanah had slept through it all, oblivious. When she finally woke to the spectacular salmon-and-pink sunrise warming her face, Luke said nothing to her about it. He didn't know what he could have said, except that he had had another waking dream and still didn't know its meaning.

The name Kell Plath no longer appeared in the Sodonna directories, but not because Teyr's winds had ripped it from the map or because the name had become burdened by shame. An hour at the city library uncovered not only its location, but also the petition under which its new owners had asked for the more marketable name of River Gardens.

Kell Plath had been a commonal—a walled and gated space enclosing a group of small residences surrounding a common green space. The design was popular in Sodonna. Standing in front of the gate to River Gardens, Luke and Akanah could see more than a dozen other commonals along the road winding along the high bank above the river.

According to the traveler's aid card, the commonal was a piece of the region's history, as well—a reminder of rougher days when the walls and gates protected unmated children and other valuables from the less refined types who came to Sodonna to work the docks.

As a matter of form, Luke and Akanah approached the security droid at the gate and asked after Trobe Saar, Norika, and the other children. In each case, the answer was the same: "I am unable to identify the resident requested."

"I'm interested in purchasing a share in River Gardens," Luke said, trying another tack. "Who could arrange a tour of the facilities for us?"

"No shares are currently available for purchase," the security droid said. "When shares become available, they will be listed with Indal Properties of Sodonna."

Akanah stepped forward. "I'm researching the history of commonals for *Teyr Tours* subscribers," she said. "I'd like to know more about the history of *this* site—is the property manager available to talk to me for a few minutes?"

Directed for a second time to Indal Properties, they retreated to the other side of the street to regroup.

"So much for the front door," Luke said with a sigh. "I hate trying to wiggle past a security droid. They're too dumb to deceive and too single-minded to finesse."

"We have to get inside."

"They're not there—you know that. They've been gone for fifteen years."

"But they *were* here," she said. "And the way will be marked."

Luke looked back over his shoulder. "You don't think they were considerate enough to leave their mark on the *outside* of the commonal, do you?"

The wall of the commonal was three meters high and slippery smooth, curving slightly outward and topped with a line of sharp-edged fracturestone that was both decorative and functional.

"I can vault this," Luke said. "It isn't a problem."

"It is for me."

"I can get us both over."

"Give me a chance to read here first."

She moved down the wall at her own pace, trailing

her fingertips along the surface. Luke followed a few steps behind, trying to sense the interaction between her and the wall, to understand what opening she was looking through in search of the Fallanassi scribing.

When they rounded the third corner, Akanah cried out in surprise and fell back a step. With two quick strides, Luke was beside her. It was then that he saw the security droid blocking her way.

"This is your only warning," the droid said. "You are loitering on private property. Your likeness has been recorded. Your suspicious behavior has been documented. Remove yourself from this vicinity immediately. If you do not, you will be detained, and a complaint will be made against you. If you return to this vicinity, a complaint will be made against you. This message constitutes a lawful and sufficient notice under Article Eighteen of the Criminal Statutes of the Sodonna Syndic."

Akanah opened her mouth to protest, but Luke knew better than to argue. "We're leaving," he said, pulling her along by the arm.

Unswayed by the promise, the droid followed them back to their landspeeder and waited until they moved off to return to its post by the gate.

"Have I mentioned that I hate security droids?" Luke grumbled. "How are you going to check the other side and a half now? Did you find anything?"

"There was writing by the front gate," Akanah said. "It marked this place as Kell Plath."

"That's all?"

"That's all. What we need is inside." She looked back to see if they were out of sight of the gate at River Gardens. "Stop here."

"Why?"

"I have to go back."

"And do what?"

"What I did the night we met," she said. "Or have you forgotten?"

"I haven't forgotten that you never explained how you got into the sanctuary without me sensing you."

"Are you going to stop?"

Frowning, Luke brought the landspeeder to an abrupt halt.

"Thank you," she said, and tipped open her door.

"You're not going to explain?"

"No, I do not intend to explain."

"Wait—" he said. "What can I do?"

"I do not expect to need anyone killed," she said, clambering out. "Do what you just said—wait. And try not to attract the suspicions of any droids in *this* neighborhood. Our ship is halfway around the planet, and it might be difficult to get back to it if we're criminal fugitives."

He stared after her as she strode back down the street, wondering how many different women he was traveling with, and whether he would ever learn all their stories.

Twenty minutes later, Luke felt Akanah approaching.

"Let's go," she said as she climbed in.

"Did you get inside?"

"Let's go," she repeated insistently.

Luke looked back along the street. "Is someone following you?"

"I got inside. No one is following me—yet. Now, can we go?"

The landspeeder surged forward. "And?"

"I found it," she said. "We're done here."

"Are you going to tell me this time?"

"When we're away from here, and I know it's safe."

"So it's not *me* you don't trust."

"These things are never to be spoken to one who cannot read them," Akanah said. "To tell you at all violates an oath. To tell you now, here, when there are so many ways a secret can escape, compounds that offense with needless risk."

Luke frowned. "Is there any reason we can't return by Skyrail?"

"No," she said, looking out her side viewpane. "I wasn't seen."

She seemed determined not to talk, but there were things Luke needed to say before they reached the terminal.

"You weren't the only one who was successful," he said. "I turned up some information, too. And I'll even tell you now."

"Please don't. Whatever it is, it will keep," she said. "All that matters now is to get away from here."

"Knowing where we're going next matters a tiny bit," Luke said. "I got curious about *how* your friends left."

"It's of no consequence. We leave no trail that an outsider can follow."

"You may think so," Luke said. "But I found out some interesting things, all the same. Like the reason they sold the commonal."

She looked at him disdainfully. "That's no mystery—to buy passage. They had no more use for it except for any value they could take with them."

"Akanah, they bought a starship." Luke waggled the traveler's aid card. "Can't judge things by their size. In addition to the maps, the food guides, the attraction lists, and the ads, this has a wireless link to the Teyr Commerce Bureau and an information hotline. Your friends may be long gone, but there's still a corporation registered here called Kell Plath. And it owns a starship named *Star Morning*."

"It must have taken everything they had," Akanah said.

"And a little more," Luke said. "*Star Morning* is a Koqus liner—the better part of fifty years old, mind you, and too small to compete with the big Expo ships, but still no small purchase."

"How many could it carry?"

"A Koqus? Maybe sixty, depending on the cargo allocation."

Akanah nodded. "That would be enough."

"You don't seem overly surprised by this," Luke said, raising an eyebrow. "I was. I thought we were trying to track down refugees, not stockholders."

"Just because we choose to live simply doesn't mean that we're without resources," Akanah said. "To be poor is to be powerless. The Fallanassi are as old as the Jedi, and we've hidden and husbanded our resources well."

"Then why were you left on Carratos?" Luke asked. "I can see that they might not want to risk bringing their ship there to pick you up, but why couldn't passage be bought for you?"

"You forget that Carratos fell under Imperial control soon after I was sent there," she said. "There were head taxes that had to be paid at the port by anyone leaving—high taxes, to discourage people from fleeing the planet."

"Then why couldn't the tax have been sent for you?"

"I don't know that it wasn't," said Akanah, her eyes misting. "I don't know that Talsava didn't keep it for herself."

"Your foster mother?"

"My custodian. She was never more than that." She tried a smile, which fell short of conviction. "There was a morning, you see, when I woke up and she was gone."

"Gone?"

Bitterness owned her voice. "Her clothes, her little precious geegaws, every personal possession small enough to pack in a bag and carry away in the night, all gone. I never saw her again. She abandoned me there to fend for myself—at fifteen, in a port city that made your Mos Eisley look quiet and genteel."

The unvoiced suspicions behind Luke's questions left him feeling ashamed.

"We'll find them," he said firmly as the Rift Skyway appeared ahead of them. "When we get back to *Mud Sloth,* I can access the New Republic Ship Registry's traffic logs. We should be able to find out where *Star Morning* has been, and when. We can surely find out where she is now."

"That isn't necessary," Akanah said. Reaching out, she laid her hand across his, as though she were trying to reassure *him.* "Atzerri. We need to go to Atzerri now. And I know that it may not, but I pray this ends there."

Chapter 7

◆

For hours after *Mud Sloth* lifted from Teyr, Luke sat at the pilot's station studying the traffic leaving the planet behind them.

The traveler's aid card helpfully informed him that there was no direct regular service between Teyr and distant Atzerri by any commercial spaceline. So Luke concentrated on the private vessels, monitoring and logging the ID profiles their transponders sent as they passed the inner Flight Control buoys:

Star Hummer, RN80-440330, owner Joa Pqis, registry Vobos, Tammuz-an—

Rode to Ruin, RN27-382992, owner Fracca, registry Orron III—

Amanda's Toy II, RN18-950319, owner Unlimited Horizons Inc., registry Kalla—

"What are you looking for?" Akanah finally asked him. "No one bothered us on Teyr. No one saw me in the commonal."

"I'm just being cautious," Luke said, keeping his eyes on the code reader. "Just because no one confronted us doesn't mean no one was aware of us."

"Aware of us—what does that mean?"

"Whoever those men on Lucazec were working for,

they wanted what you know as much as they wanted you. I don't know what they think they can do with you, but the Fallanassi are the prize."

"I would never betray the circle. And there is nothing anyone could do to compel me. Not even you."

"But you're taking me there," Luke said. "And if they simply keep touch with us, you'll take them there, too. All they have to do is follow us, and be patient. That's what I'm looking for—someone following. If any of these ships leaving Teyr now show up at—show up later, we'll have to do something about it."

"The circle can protect itself."

"I'm sure the Jedi thought they were safe, too," said Luke. "But they were wrong."

"The Jedi faced a terrible enemy, and the betrayal of one of their own," said Akanah.

"There are enough enemies left," Luke said. "All the assorted dictators and warlords in the Imperial sectors—including Admiral Daala, who isn't likely to have found a new hobby. Then there are the hundreds of thousands of inhabited systems in the Borderlands, the Corporate Sector—"

"And there is the New Republic."

Luke turned toward her. "What?"

"The New Republic stands now where the Empire stood—as the single great power in the galaxy," said Akanah. "They have the most to lose if their power is successfully challenged. And their power is the greatest threat to those who choose to stand apart, who take a different view."

"You can't think that the New Republic is hunting the Fallanassi."

"Why not?" she asked calmly. "It was you who decided those men on Lucazec were Imperial agents. How do you know they weren't from Coruscant? How do you know they weren't from your NRI?"

The suggestion was absurd, laughable—but it silenced Luke all the same. He looked back to the controls, trying to sort out his thoughts. For some reason, he couldn't now remember why it was he had been so sure the men at Ialtra were Imperial sleepers. And Akanah's suggestion offered an explanation for something he had no explanation for—the Elomin were so principled that the prospect of one's working for an Imperial spy network was beyond imagining. But the NRI—

Out of Touch, RN40-844033, owner Tok-Foge Pokresh, registry Bothawui—

"They would have to have been tipped off by me," Luke said finally, then shook his head. "But I only spoke to Leia and Han that night. And Leia didn't even give me a chance to tell her what little I knew. No one knew I was going away, or why."

Akanah touched his shoulder. "Please don't think that I suspected you," she said. "The men at Ialtra were not expecting you—and if the NRI could count on your assistance, they would have no need to shadow us."

"I don't know that *anyone* is shadowing us," Luke said. "I just want to make sure that no one tries—and if they do try, that they don't succeed. We can jump out of here at any time if we need to. And before we make our final jump, I'm going to go over this ship from bow to baffles and make sure we didn't acquire a tracking device while we were parked on Teyr."

"I trust you to take the right precautions. I know you have as much at stake as I do," she said. "Do you mind if I go lie down? I did not sleep well on the Skyrail."

Adela, RN32-000439, owner Refka Trell, registry Elom—

"Sure," Luke said. "Go ahead. I'll call you if anything unexpected shows up."

Akanah squeezed his shoulder. "Thank you," she said, and started to turn away.

"Akanah?"

"What?"

"How much do you know about our destination?"

"I know it's a Free Trader world—not much more."

"I didn't even know that much," Luke said, turning toward her. "I'd like to query the Ministry of State atlas on Coruscant and request a diplomatic backgrounder."

"You can do that?"

"I think so," Luke said. "I'd be using a point-to-point channel, not broadcasting, so no one else will be listening in."

"But they'll be listening in on Coruscant," Akanah said. "You might as well be announcing where we're going."

Luke shook his head. "I know what you just said, but I can't treat those people as the enemy," he said. "But I could make a series of queries, so the one for Atzerri is just one in the crowd. Would that make you feel any more at ease?"

"Do what you think is necessary," she said with a small, quick smile. "There are risks in ignorance, too. Balance them against the risks of showing our hand. If you think the weight falls in favor of making the query, and you'll wait until we've jumped out from Teyr to do so, I won't question your decision."

Shortly after the reorganization of the government, Nanaod Engh had given Luke keys to most of the real treasures of the New Republic—the central data libraries maintained by various branches of the General Ministry. Thanks to Admiral Ackbar's intervention, Luke also carried the highest-grade security clearance held by any civilian.

Between the two, Luke had—potentially—a great deal of information at his fingertips. But the access he had been granted was a courtesy, not a necessity. Luke's most urgent curiosities were in areas of little interest to bureaucracies, and he had never found reason to make much use of the favors extended him.

But he found himself with reason now.

So far, it seemed, his contribution to the expedition had been modest to the point of invisibility. Luke was completely dependent on Akanah for information, and it was difficult to see what she needed from him. Companionship, perhaps, and a bit of piloting, but not protection—she was emphatic about that.

She had offered him a gift of great value by coming to him, and had gone to some lengths to do so. Luke felt himself not only uncomfortably dependent, but also involuntarily in her debt. And he had little to offer to right the balance.

But the lead on *Star Morning* gave him an opportunity to make himself more useful.

If asked, he would have said that suspicion had no part in his decision to contact the New Republic Ship Registry under his military access code. Even though Akanah had plucked their next destination from the Current, a great deal of time had passed since the Fallanassi had left Kell Plath. The prospect of another Griann causing them to lose the trail was reason enough to follow up on his discovery.

Still, Luke waited until Akanah was asleep to open the hypercomm link, and his reason for doing that wasn't entirely clear to him. True, he didn't want her to think he was checking up on her. But Luke was also aware that *he* didn't want to think he was checking up on her. He had to be able to trust her. Everything he had done, his very presence, was predicated on that.

"Ship Registry."

The Adventurer had no secure-entry touchpad, so Luke had to offer the voice codes.

"Authorization verified," said the registry clerk. "Go ahead."

"I need a report pulled on a private vessel."

"Yes, sir. Quick or comprehensive?"

"The difference is—"

"The comprehensive includes everything that's in all of the linked databases—taxes, transfers, ports of call, whatever we have. On anything but a brand-new ship, that can be quite a bit."

"Comprehensive," Luke said. "The ship is the *Star Morning,* Teyr registry, owned by—"

"I have it on my display, sir," said the clerk. "It takes up to an hour to pull a comprehensive. Would you like it forwarded to your current hypercomm identifier when it's ready, or held here for your next call?"

"Forward it," Luke said.

"Very well, sir. Is there anything else?"

Luke looked back over his shoulder and extended his senses to confirm that Akanah was asleep. "Yes," he said on impulse. "I'd like a comprehensive pulled on a skiff, a Verpine Adventurer, registration number NR80-109399, no name currently profiled, owner and home port unknown—"

"I have it, sir. Would you like this report forwarded with the other?"

"No," Luke said. "Hold this one for me."

"Very well, sir. Is there anything else?"

"No."

"Clear to close link."

"Closing link," Luke said, and reached for the controls.

Then he wondered why what he had just done made him feel so unclean.

Akanah's nap lasted more than three hours, but the report from Ship Registry had not yet arrived when she stirred. She said nothing to him when she emerged from the sleeper, disappearing for several minutes behind the privacy screen of the refresher unit.

When she emerged, she had forgone the more flowing, multilayered garment she had worn on the planet for the simple, close-fitting, long-sleeved one-piece she had worn for much of the jump to Teyr. When she joined him at the flight controls, he caught the faint scent of the freshener cabinet on her clothing.

"So, have we a shadow?"

"None clumsy enough to give itself away yet, anyway," Luke said. "There are eighteen ships—make that nineteen, now—in this outbound corridor. In theory they're all heading for the Foless Crossroads, or for Darepp."

"In theory?"

"Under free-navigation rules, they don't have to file flight plans and announce their destinations—they just have to announce themselves as they leave here and when they get there."

Akanah leaned forward to study the navigational display. "How did you make it display those identifiers? When I was coming into Coruscant, all it showed me were those green bars—it didn't tell me what they were."

"The display options are on the command menus. But the basic display really tells you all you need, most of the time," Luke said. "A green bar means a ship that is a safe distance away on a noncollision course. Yellow bar, a ship that's closer than the standard spacing, but not on a collision course. Red bar, something on an intercept course. Same rules for rocks, except the symbol is a circle—like that one."

"So any red symbols mean danger."

Luke nodded. "I'm sure this ship has some fairly obnoxious alarms, and collision-avoidance protocols."

"What if someone fired a missile at us? Would it show up as a red bar?"

Frowning, Luke considered. "Probably as a circle, as though it were a fast-moving asteroidal body. Missiles don't send out recognition signals, and skiffs don't have threat-recognition modules in their scanners."

"I have never been in a warship," Akanah said. "Tell me—how does this compare with the cockpit of a military spacecraft?"

"Oh—worlds apart," Luke said.

"How, exactly?"

"Well—in a military ship, the automated systems are there to support the pilot—most everything that matters is done with your hands on the controls," Luke said. "A ship like this is designed to have the expert systems take over as much as possible, to protect casual pilots from making mistakes."

"So there are more controls in a fighter."

"A lot more. Heck, a combat flight stick has almost as many controls on it as there are on this whole panel," Luke said. "Most of what this ship will let you do by yourself is buried three levels deep in the command option displays."

She nodded. "Tell me, if we were pursued by a warship, or intercepted by a fighter—how much could you do?"

Luke ran his fingers back through his hair. "Less than you're probably hoping," he said. "It's not a test I'd look forward to."

"Not even with your reputation as a pilot?"

"She's underpowered for realspace, which means we can't run away. She doesn't have true vector thrusters, which means she's not very agile, despite her low mass. The nav shields would pop on the first hit, and the hull would breach on the second—unless the second hit was from an ion cannon."

"What would happen then?"

"All the systems would sizzle, and we'd be dead in space." He showed a rueful smile. "Piloting ability doesn't count for much then. And reputations count for even less."

"So our only hope would be to jump to hyperspace before we were hit."

"That's about the size of it."

Just then a sweet-toned signal sounded from the console, startling Akanah. "What is it? What's that?"

"Nothing to worry about," Luke said as he leaned forward. "Incoming hypercomm file transmission. A report on the *Star Morning*. I requested it from Coruscant while you were napping."

Her eyes flashed angrily. "I asked you to wait until we'd jumped."

"You also asked me to use my judgment," Luke said. "We can't do a quick jump-and-go if we're sitting out there somewhere waiting for a report to come in. And I thought this report might have information we'd want in hand *before* we commit to Atzerri."

"We're already committed to Atzerri," she said stiffly. "That's where the scribing at Teyr told us to go."

"I want to look at the report," Luke said. "The way I see it, the more information we have, the better."

"All it can do is mislead us," Akanah said. "I told you that we leave no trail an outsider can follow."

Another, low-pitched tone signaled the end of the transmission.

"Then I'll count on you to keep me from getting lost," Luke said, bringing up the secondary display panel. "You can look at this or not—but I have to. I never have liked making decisions in the dark."

Luke had anticipated two possible reasons for the delay in the report's arrival—and either a very thin or a very thick file, depending on which was to blame.

It was a thick file, almost overwhelming with detail. *Star Morning*, a.k.a. *Mandarin*, a.k.a. *Pilgrim*, a.k.a. *Congere*, had had a long history before passing into the hands of the Fallanassi and a busy history since.

Built by the Koqus Design Syndic as a variation on an even older Republic Seinar design, it was classed as a short-route liner despite the sleeper configuration of its fifty-eight-passenger main cabin. At forty-four meters long and twenty-eight meters across the spade-shaped twin-deck main hull, it was readily capable of planetary landings at even the smallest spaceports—and a good pilot might even try a dirt-field touchdown and get away with it. The hyperdrive was a rather ordinary Block I, with dual fusion generators. But the ion engines, a pair of SoroSuub Viper 40s, would have been adequate for a ship with a keel mass half again greater.

With legs like that, she could give the Falcon *a run for her money,* Luke thought.

More interesting than the specifications, though, was confirmation that *Star Morning* was still the property of Kell Plath Corporation of Teyr, and had been so continuously for the past fifteen years. The port call list for that period ran to more than two hundred entries, with no single port appearing more than three times, and most entries unique.

You've tramped around, Luke mused as he skimmed the list. *I haven't even heard of most of these places.*

The list was spotty, obviously incomplete. There were many stretches of a month or longer—well more than the ship's rated stand-alone endurance—with no port calls listed. But a footnote explained that early records from some Alliance worlds were unavailable, records from worlds heavily involved in the war were incomplete or had been destroyed, and some recently acquired records hadn't yet been processed.

"THE ABSENCE OF DATA SHOULD NOT IN AND OF ITSELF BE CONSIDERED INDICATIVE OF PROSCRIBED TRAVEL OR ILLEGAL ACTIVITIES," read the disclaimer at the top of the port call list.

That didn't stop Luke from wondering and speculating. The longest gap, a few days short of a year, started just three months after the name *Mandarin* had been burned off the hull. The gap began weeks before the Battle of Endor and continued through the worst of the fighting of the last year of the war against the Empire.

According to the record in front of Luke, *Star Morning* had left Motexx fully loaded, heading for Gowdawl under a charter license. The liner wasn't seen again until she turned up, cabin and cargo holds empty, at Arat Fraca some three hundred days later.

All things considered, that was a good time for an unarmed liner to lie up in port or another safe haven. But where had she gone? Motexx and Arat Fraca lay nearly two sectors apart, separated not only by thousands of light-years, but also by the unnavigable Black Nebula in Parfadi, with its twin supermassive neutron stars. And what had happened to the passengers from Motexx? There was no record that *Star Morning* had ever berthed at Gowdawl.

Another port conspicuous by its absence was Atzerri. *Star Morning*'s first destination after Teyr had been Darepp. In the weeks that followed, it wandered erratically toward the Rim, stopping at colony worlds named 23 Mere, Yisgga, New Polokia, Fwiis, and Babbadod before turning back toward the heart of the galaxy and, in time, its appointment at Motexx. As best Luke could determine with the Adventurer's navicom, the closest *Star Morning* had come to Atzerri was en route to Fwiis—but without enough unaccounted time for it to have made a 150-light-year side trip.

Luke felt himself girding for an argument with Akanah. *The Fallanassi didn't go straight to Atzerri from Teyr—so why is it so important that we do? Did they know when they left that they would end up there? Why didn't the pointer point to Darepp? I wish I knew exactly what the message at the commonal said.*

But it was the third discovery Luke sifted from the report that seemed the most urgent. That was the one that prompted him to leave his couch and go back to the service access compartment, where Akanah was putting on a good show of being otherwise occupied.

Akanah's vehicle for that was what Luke thought of as her stretching exercises and what she called active meditation. At that particular moment she was sitting with eyes closed and, without evident stress, with her ankles crossed behind her neck. A light touch of the tips of her forefingers on the deck pad maintained her upright balance.

"Found something," he said quietly, and waited for her to acknowledge him. When that acknowledgment was slow in coming, he added, "Akanah?"

Drawing a deep breath, she let her body roll forward and unfold, then sat back up in a more conventional position. Her eyes opened slowly, and her gaze was steady. "What did you find?"

"*Star Morning*," Luke said. "For most of the last few months, she's been way over in Farana, on the far side of the Corporate Sector. But she put in at Vulvarch not twelve hours ago."

"Why do you think that that's important?"

"Vulvarch is just thirty-four light-years away," Luke said. "We could be there in half the time it would take us to get to Atzerri. Less than half."

"The ship is not important," Akanah said. "Our path leads to Atzerri."

"That path's overgrown with fifteen years of bramble," Luke said. "Look at what's happened so far—the chances are that all we'll find on Atzerri is another message telling us to go somewhere else, to Darepp, or Babbadod, or Arat Fraca. *Star Morning*'s been all over the galactic map."

"The ship is not important," Akanah repeated. "It's a tool—property. We were told to go to Atzerri."

"Anything or anyone waiting for us on Atzerri has been waiting fifteen years and can wait a few more days," Luke said, growing frustrated with her stubbornness. "But *this* lead is only twelve hours old. If we jump right now, we should be able to reach Vulvarch before *Star Morning* lifts again."

She shook her head. "We won't find the circle there."

Luke's tone betrayed his impatience. "The same pilot's been listed for the ship since Kell Plath took it over. She has to be one of you, or at least in the know.

Akanah, we could spend months following the circle's movements over fifteen years. But *Star Morning* could send us—maybe even take us—right to where the Fallanassi are today. I thought that was what you wanted."

"I'll follow the way left for me," Akanah said. "It's what I know. It's what I was promised—the way home will be marked."

Luke turned his face away, one hand clenched in a fist at his side, then retreated to the forward compartment. When he had shed the anger, he returned. She had already resumed her meditation.

"Will you at least *talk* to them before we jump out of here?" Luke asked. "I have *Star Morning*'s hypercomm receiver address—I can set up a secure link for you. You can have all the privacy you want to exchange whatever recognition signs you need to with the crew. Maybe they can save us at least one wasted trip."

"No," Akanah said without looking up. "They can't."

"Why not?"

She paused and turned her face to him. "Even if the crew of the ship *is* of the circle, they will never reveal themselves to a stranger such a distance away. As I will not reveal myself to anyone I cannot feel in the Current. The outward signs and spoken words are only ritual— the recognition lies in sensing another adept beside you. I'm sorry."

Her refusal left Luke wordless with frustration, and she saw it in his eyes.

"You should understand," she said. "It's the same with you and those like you. The only recognition that matters is what you feel here." She tapped between her breasts with three fingers of her left hand. "That is the truth that can never deceive."

The dispute hung in the air between them as unspoken suspicion and resentment.

Akanah did not try to forbid Luke to contact *Star Morning* on his own. But she hovered close enough to the flight stations to make it impossible for Luke to do so without her knowledge. It was absolutely clear that she meant to prevent any more surprises like the one that had greeted her after her nap.

For his part, though he had said nothing of it, Luke had already concluded that hailing the other ship without Akanah's cooperation could only be counterproductive. And since he had reluctantly accepted her decision and resigned himself to taking *Mud Sloth* to Atzerri, he resented her vigilant scrutiny.

Her scrutiny also prevented Luke from collecting the report on the *Mud Sloth*'s history, which was surely ready for him in Ship Registry's Pending queue. His discoveries in the *Star Morning* report and Akanah's stubbornness over Atzerri made him more curious than ever to see it. But that curiosity was being thwarted, leaving him doubly resentful and harboring some suspicions of his own.

When the time came to jump out from Teyr, Luke handled the details without announcing them to Akanah, then climbed into the bunk to sleep through the short hop he had programmed. When he did, he purposefully left the *Star Morning* report open on the flight station's secondary display. Whether Akanah was tempted by that invitation, he did not know. Opening wide his connection to the Force, Luke allowed the discordant emotions to bleed away, and he was asleep within minutes.

Three hours out from Teyr, the Verpine Adventurer dropped out of hyperspace as programmed. Climbing out of the bunk, Luke found a friendly smile for Akanah, who managed a quick, somewhat tired smile in return.

"I'm going to query the Ministry of State now, unless you know some reason not to," Luke said, sliding into the pilot's seat.

"No," she said. "Do you need privacy?"

Luke shook his head and keyed the hypercomm. "Nothing secret here—just limited access." He tried another smile and found it still felt sincere. "There's a shortage of privacy here, anyway."

It took only a few minutes to put in his requests, and the responses started coming back immediately. Luke chose not to mention that all seven additional worlds for which he requested backgrounders were one-time ports of call for *Star Morning*. If she recognized the names from reading the report, she would know his reason. If not, it would never be an issue.

"I'm going to start my inspection," Luke said, standing.

"May I look at these files?"

"Of course," Luke said. "It's better if you do, in fact. As I said, no secrets. I'll be in earshot—feel free to talk to me if you find something you think I should know."

The interior inspection took nearly an hour. Beginning at the rear of the skiff's small service compartment, Luke systematically opened every removable panel and access door inside the ship, searching for anything that looked as if it might not belong. His examination turned up a clumsy retrofit to the water recycler that accounted for one of the *Adventurer's* eccentricities, and half a dozen lost objects of the slipped-through-the-cracks variety, but nothing more.

"I don't understand why the spaceport wouldn't allow service work in the parking area," Akanah said when he rejoined her.

"Probably protecting the interests of the ship services licensee. Have to keep those maintenance bays full, you know." Luke gestured toward the displays. "Interesting reading?"

"There's no Flight Control Zone at Atzerri," she

said. "We can jump right into orbit if we like and pick our own landing site—all the spaceports are independent. There's not much government of any kind there, it seems."

"I've been on Free Trader worlds before," Luke said. "Free Traders are the closet anarchists of the galaxy. If they could figure out how to do without any government at all and not risk losing their finer things to bandits, they wouldn't hesitate. Even as it is, they tend to tolerate a lot of fighting over the scraps. You don't want to be poor or slow on a Free Trader world."

Luke missed the look that crossed her face, but he felt the shiver of revulsion. "Carratos was a lot like that, after the Imperial garrison left," she said. "I should feel right at home."

"But would the Fallanassi?"

"What do you mean?"

"It just doesn't strike me as any more your people's sort of place than Teyr was," said Luke. "Did you find anything in the backgrounder to suggest why they would go there—much less stay there?"

"They're your people, too," she said with a sad little smile. "I don't have an answer to your question. Perhaps being what it is made it a better place to disappear."

"I suppose that could be an answer."

"Let's not guess," she said. "Is the ship clean?"

"I couldn't find anything."

"Then let's go. Let's go directly to Atzerri."

"I'm not saying there aren't people who could hide things I couldn't find," Luke warned.

"I know that."

"Well—let's see if a direct route is available from here," Luke said, turning to the astrogator. "I'd been planning to line it up with the next one."

They jumped out twenty minutes later, with the report on the *Mud Sloth* still waiting for him on Coruscant.

*   *   *

The skiff had a way of getting smaller the longer they were in it, and the recent tensions had accelerated the process. As soon as they were on their way to Atzerri, Akanah and Luke resumed sleeping in shifts.

It worked largely because the active noise-canceling system in the bunk was effective enough that the curtain divided the ship into two worlds, dark and light, awake and asleep. For most of a day's cycle, no matter which side of the curtain they were on, both Luke and Akanah could enjoy the illusion of being alone on the ship. They allowed just enough time between shifts with both awake to avoid military-style hot-bunking—though Luke could usually catch Akanah's gentle scent on the pillow even after he turned it.

The jump to Atzerri was a long one. The travelers did not have much to say to each other at the first turn— she was impatient for bed and he to read the diplomatic files. It was little different at the second turn, when the conversation was polite and perfunctory.

By the third, they were both just lonely enough again to welcome some company and to linger together in idle talk. And by the fourth, Luke ventured to broach a subject that had kept touching his thoughts in the time he spent alone.

"Akanah—if telling me what the scribing says violates your oath, why do you do it?"

"Because I consider you one of us," she said, her expression carrying a hint of surprise. "You are untrained—you are not an adept—but you are Fallanassi."

"Why? Because my mother was—is?"

"That, and because of the potential within you, given proof by your skill with the Force."

Luke returned to the pilot's couch and curled up sideways in it. "How do people become part of the circle?"

"Curiosity is not sufficient—which I hazard you know. Some are born to it. Some come to it. Is it any different in your discipline?"

"Born with the gift, do you mean, or born to someone who already belongs, to a trained adept?"

"Is the gift not in the blood?"

"Sometimes it seems that way. Sometimes it seems as if the talent goes wild, almost as if the Force chooses its own," Luke said, turning on his back and propping one foot on the control panel.

"Why, what do you mean?"

"Look at the way the Jedi are coming back," said Luke. "The Empire hunted us so relentlessly that most everyone who escaped thought they were the only Jedi left. But it isn't just that a few solitaries who were hiding have resurfaced. I've found students with no family history whatsoever, in species that were never represented before in the Order."

"Some of your number may have been adventurous travelers," said Akanah. "On Carratos, I heard many jokes about how the Emperor spent his evenings. If a Jedi sleeps alone, surely it must be by choice, as it is with you."

"Are you saying that you expected me to warm a bed with you?" Luke said. "I didn't think that was our bargain."

"No," she said. "I never expected that."

"Then what are you saying?"

"That Luke Skywalker could have a hundred children by now. A thousand."

"That's crazy."

"No—that's the simple truth. There are different rules for heroes and royalty, and you're seen as a little of both. You can't be unaware of that."

Luke frowned and looked away. "I don't know how to be a father to one child, much less a thousand."

"You wouldn't need to know," she said. "Their mothers wouldn't expect it. They would be grateful enough for the gift."

"I'd expect it of me," he said, and firmly steered the

conversation back on course. "We were talking about my being an honorary member of the circle—"

"Not honorary," she corrected. "Novice."

"Novice, then. But there's an exception in your oath for people like me?"

"Every adept has the right to judge and the duty to teach," she said. "I've made my judgment."

"And the rest?" Luke asked. "We've had many hours together—why haven't you started to teach me?"

"But I have," she said. "I've asked you to think about what you know and believe. To go beyond that, the novice must ask for the door to be opened. But you aren't ready to think of yourself as a student again—not yet. You run too well and easily to go back to crawling."

"No," Luke said, shaking his head. "To be a Jedi is to be a seeker. A Jedi is always learning. It's only on the dark side that one becomes obsessed with knowing, and impressed with doing."

"There's a touch of the dark side," Akanah said slowly, "in the way you cling to the privilege of killing, and resist the teaching I've offered you. A hint of a mind that has settled on answers and resents being challenged with new questions."

Luke toyed with the lacing on his longshirt as he considered her words. "You may be right," he said finally. "I found the Force at a time when what I needed was power. I wanted a weapon to protect my friends, not enlightenment. I was thinking of war against the Empire, not peace with the universe. Perhaps something of that lingers in how I see myself. I'll think on it."

"Good," she said. "Your words give me hope. And hope is the beginning of everything worthwhile."

Luke sat up and turned toward her. "Akanah—I do want you to teach me," he said. "I want to learn to read scribing. You were able to help me see it. Can you teach me to see it without your help?"

"Yes. But that isn't the first lesson," she said. "That will come later."

"Don't you think there's reason enough to change the curriculum?"

"What reason?"

"Insurance," Luke said. "If we're going to follow your way, the marked way, to the circle, finding and reading the signs left in the Current is crucial. But if only one of us can read them—"

"I won't miss any signs," Akanah said, shaking her head. "Or misread them."

"What if we become separated? You said that in your mind, I'm Fallanassi. If that's so, then these signs are meant for me as well."

"Commitment must be based on more than need," Akanah said. "I'm sorry. The time isn't right for what you ask."

Luke frowned. "Are you afraid that I'll go off and try to finish this journey without you?"

"No," said Akanah. "Would you allow your student's impatience to dictate the sequence and timing of his instruction? Would you give him the secret that could most compromise you before he had affirmed the principles that most define you?"

"Do you want me to take the oaths of the circle, too?"

"Yes," she said. "But only when you're ready, and you are not ready—and only for the right reason, and this is not the right reason."

"Then how can I give you the assurances you want? How do I show you that I'm ready?"

"Choose to leave your weapon behind when we land at Atzerri," she said. "If you do that, you will have shown me something. That would be a beginning."

Resting his elbows on his knees, Luke pressed a fist into a cupped hand and stared down over it at the deck. "I'll have to think about that, too," he said finally, standing. "If I do it, I want it to be for the right reason—not just to pay a tutor for my next lesson."

She smiled warmly. "I knew I was right about you,"

she said. "You will be welcomed by the circle, when the time comes."

He nodded, lips pressed together, as he edged between the couches and toward the bunk. But his face must have said something more to her, for she stood and called after him, "Are you having doubts about me, Luke?"

Luke paused, one foot in the bunk's step-up, and looked back. "There are things I don't understand, and things I wonder about," he said. "Is that the same as 'having doubts'? I don't know."

"It is," she said. "Why don't you ever ask me about these 'things'? I'm not afraid of your questions. Are you afraid of my answers?"

"Hardly that."

"Of giving offense with your curiosity, then."

"Perhaps."

"I'm not easily offended. Ask me something now, and perhaps there'll be one less mystery to trouble your sleep."

Luke turned toward her, bringing both feet back to the deck. "All right," he said. "How is it you came to buy this ship? Why didn't you go to Lucazec when you'd saved the price of passage? That had to be far less than the price you paid for this ship. It seems you could have gone there years ago. I don't understand why you didn't."

"I almost did, six years ago," she said, with a wistful smile. "I had the price of passage, as you say. I could have gotten myself to Ialtra. The temptation was almost beyond resisting."

Luke gestured with one hand. "And?"

"If I had gone, I would have been trapped there," she said. "I would've been on Lucazec, yes, but I would've been poor again. On Carratos, at least, there were busy ports, and I knew how to earn enough to keep some. You saw Lucazec—there's not enough wealth there to take by theft or marriage, much less by honest work."

"So you waited."

"There was really no choice," Akanah said. "I realized I needed to buy myself more than passage off Carratos—I needed to buy myself freedom from ever living like that again. I have nothing but this ship, Luke, and a few credits—but I have this ship. Though with your perquisites as a hero, you may not understand how much that means to me."

"No," Luke said. "I understand. I remember what it felt like to be trapped on Tatooine."

"Then have I answered your question? Do you understand now?"

Luke nodded. "All except for this—when you finally got the ship, why did you come for me first? Why Coruscant and not Lucazec?"

"Because when I dreamed of returning to Ialtra, you were always there," Akanah said gently. "Which puzzled me, until I realized what it meant—that I was supposed to take you with me. That I was to bring you to the circle. That you belong there."

Almost to his surprise, though not to his displeasure, Luke found that he believed her answers. They had the simple directness of emotional truth.

But for some reason, they did not make it any easier for him to sleep.

Chapter 8

♦

"Talos Spaceport, Atzerri."

Akanah glanced sideways at Luke. "May I?" she asked.

"Of course," Luke said with an offering gesture, settling back in the pilot's couch.

"Talos Spaceport, this is *Mud Sloth*," Akanah said. "What's your berth price for twenty meters and under?"

"What currency will you be paying in?"

"New Republic credits," she said.

"Nine hundred for the first two days, including landing fees and topping your consumables. One hundred a day beyond that. But if you're staying longer than ten days, we can start you with long-term rates from the third day."

"Talos, you must have mistaken me for a rube," said Akanah. "Because those can't be anything but rube rates."

"Those are the published rates as of the first of the month," the spaceport controller said. "Nine hundred to plop and fill, a hundred a day for the lockup. I don't have any latitude on that."

"Talos, I said twenty meters, not two hundred," said Akanah. "And I'm only renting the berth, not buying it. So why don't you start again, and this time try not to be insulting."

"Nine hundred to plop, a hundred a day for the lockup," the controller repeated. "Do you want it, or not? There aren't that many spaces available."

"Really? I would have thought all your berths would be empty, seeing as Skreeka is landing the little stuff for six hundred, with five days' lockup included."

"Skreeka is run by thieves," the controller said. "Their lockups have the worst security on the continent."

"You'll have to give us a better reason than that not to go there," Akanah said. "After all, you've already tried to rob me."

"One moment, *Mud Sloth*." A yellow light glowed on the comm display.

"Watch," Akanah said to Luke. "He'll come back with a better offer and say his supervisor authorized it. But it's all a matter of how much of his margin he's willing to give up to keep us from going to Skreeka. Whatever he comes back with, you can be sure it's above the port's internal rates—he'll make sure he gets something out of this."

"I didn't think you were so well traveled."

She smiled. "I stayed close to the ports on Carratos, and I listened well."

"When did you get the quote from Skreeka?"

"Oh, I made it up."

The yellow indicator winked out and was replaced by a green one. "Talos Spaceport. We see this is your first visit here. My supervisor doesn't want to see you taken advantage of by those scoundrels at Skreeka. He's authorized a one-time courtesy rate—five hundred to land and load up, seventy-five a day. That's the very best I can do for you, and I'd take it, if I were you. Trust me when I tell you, we're not making a credit at those prices. And I don't care where you go, anyone who asks you for less is gonna find some way to get the difference back from you."

"Thank your supervisor for me," Akanah said. "We accept."

"A good decision," the controller said. "As soon as you transmit your authorization, we'll put you on the beam."

The indicator turned red, then blacked out completely as Akanah turned her head toward Luke. "All yours, dear," she said, smiling sweetly. "We have a reservation."

Docking Bay A13 reminded Luke of a smaller version of the Mos Eisley facility in which he first encountered the *Millennium Falcon*. The design was similar, and the amenities were as old-fashioned—hand umbilicals, a machine shop without a single tool-and-die droid, mechanical locks, and no storm cover.

"I can't believe I paid them five hundred for this," Akanah said with disgust, raising her hands wide. "This berth must be a hundred years old. It's been paid for twenty times over."

"Discount rates," Luke said, securing the last of the umbilicals to the Adventurer's three propulsion systems. "Can't expect luxury accommodations."

"Or to be dealt with honestly. We overpaid by half, or more. I hope they enjoyed their little joke."

"It doesn't matter," Luke said. "This will do. Shall we take a look in ship's supplies and see if there's a food pack old enough to fit *Mud Sloth*'s reprocessor?"

"I'll leave that to you," Akanah said, shouldering her bag. "I have to go."

Luke emerged from under the repulsorlift "wing" of the skiff. "What are you talking about?"

"I have to do this by myself," said Akanah.

"Why?"

"If the Fallanassi are here, I must approach them

alone," she said. "If I take you with me, they won't let themselves be found. They won't see you as I see you. They'll only see you as an outsider."

"What am I supposed to do while you're off by yourself?"

"You can stay here. I'll come back for you if I find them—you know I will. And I'll come back to you if I don't."

"What if I don't want to stay here?"

"Then do your own exploring in the city. Go where you like. Do what pleases you. If you're not here when I return, I'll wait for you," Akanah said. "All I ask is that you not follow me. You'd only hinder our purpose here."

"This doesn't feel right to me," Luke said. "Why can't we go together, like we did on Lucazec, and Teyr?"

"Because I knew that the circle had left Lucazec, and Norika had left Teyr," she said. "But I do not know that they have left Atzerri."

"I didn't realize you were embarrassed to be seen with me," Luke said wryly.

"Please understand—if you leave the docking bay, it will be as Li Stonn. Yes?"

"Yes."

"But the others can pierce that illusion, just as I did," Akanah said. "If we're seen together, or you follow me, they'll think you're a deceiver, a threat. They'll wait for a chance to approach me when I'm alone. But if you're recognized, I don't know what they will do. They might decide to stay hidden from me, fearing I've been turned. They might even decide to leave Atzerri. We can't risk that. I have to go alone."

A deep frown creased Luke's face. Everything she said was perfectly reasonable. But everything she said felt completely wrong. "I don't like the idea of us being separated. Especially here."

"Do you still think I need your protection?" she asked. "I've been living around this kind of petty evil for most of my life. I know them—street bangers, body slavers, drug dealers, turf warriors, blackmailers, and the cold-eyes who just enjoy making someone scream. I got caught a few times and hurt a few times, but I learned. I got stronger, I got smarter, and I became my own protector. I'll be fine, Luke."

"All right," Luke said, reluctantly surrendering. "But I should at least know where you're going—in case you don't come back. In case you run into something you're not expecting. Something not so 'petty.' "

"That's fair," she agreed. "But give me enough time to do what I need to. Promise that you won't come looking for me until—let's say until I've been gone three days with no word."

Luke shot her a disbelieving look. "Three days? That's long enough for someone to grab you and be half-way to the Tion Hegemony."

She laughed. "The last man who tried to grab me only wanted to take me as far as the alley," she said. "Three *minutes* later, he knew he'd made a mistake."

"All right," Luke said. "But I still don't understand why you need three days."

"I shouldn't," Akanah said. "That's why you should come look for me then. I'm going to the Pemblehov District, north of the park."

"That's all you're going to tell me?"

"That's all I can tell you," Akanah said. "Good-bye, Luke. I'll be back for you as soon as I can."

After Akanah left, Luke first took some time to explore behind all the doors of the docking bay.

The public showers and refresher were overdue for a cleaning, no doubt due to the fifty-credit cleaning fee. But the prospect of a real six-head unlimited-water spacer's shower was too appealing to resist. Luke vouched for the additional charge and secured the door so that the automated scrubdown and sterilization could begin.

Luke tried to get even on the day rummaging through the lockers of ship's supplies. To his surprise, there were *two* K-18 food packs—both out of date, but not too badly so. He installed the older of the two in the skiff's reprocessor and tested it, then found stowage for the other in the crowded belly bay. The portmaster would nick his account again for returning only one empty, but not enough to dissuade him.

When scavenging paled, Luke turned to tinkering.

The control systems terminal offered an extensive list of flight system upgrades, with a data card burner right beside it. Most of the skiff's flight systems were out of date, but Luke located half a dozen aftermarket upgrades and coaxed *Mud Sloth* into taking them. All of them came up virus-free—something he hadn't expected, considering the source. But the navigation upgrade spotted Luke's handiwork on the FCZ interlock, forcing him to restore the original, blissfully unaware package.

In time Luke had done all the tinkering he could without risking having something crucial arrayed in pieces on the bench or the bay floor at an awkward moment.

He then took advantage of the open space inside the bay to work his first complete set of Jedi training drills since leaving Coruscant. Working both with and without his lightsaber, he patiently went through the complex exercises which brought him to a profound state of restful clarity.

It was in this state that he felt most keenly the truth and the wisdom of the simple words: *There is no emotion; there is peace. There is no ignorance; there is knowledge. There is no passion; there is serenity. There is no death; there is the Force.* The peace, the knowledge, and the serenity were gifts that came with his surrender to the Force and with his connection through the Force to all that was.

Sustaining that clarity was always the challenge. In the isolation of a Dagobah, the Jundland Wastes, or a hermitage on a frozen shore, an experienced Jedi could preserve that inner state indefinitely.

But the chaos of the real world was another matter. When ego returned, so did will. The surrender became tainted, the connection flawed. The clarity gradually slipped away under the continuous assault of elementary drives and passions. Even the greatest of the masters needed to perform the practice regularly lest they lose the discipline that made them what they were.

The drills were as much a test for the body as for the mind, and the docking bay's newly sanitized shower brought a blissful peace to muscles that were telling Luke they had not been properly exercised in too long. He stood for a long time in the place where the six needle jets converged, letting the water flowing down his body become another meditation.

When Luke finally emerged from the shower and once again donned his clothes, he allowed himself to check the skiff's chronometer and see how long Akanah had been gone.

Barely six hours had passed.

Standing beside the skiff's bow, Luke looked around the bay. Inexplicably, it seemed much smaller when viewed through the prospect of spending the next several days there.

Donning his hooded cloak, Luke secured the skiff, locked the docking bay—bending a pin so that only he could unlock it again—and went out into the night.

As he looked out across the spaceport and at the lights of Talos beyond, his hand—out of habit—went to the place at his hip where his lightsaber usually hung. His fingers found only air, which puzzled him for just an instant. Then he drew the face of Li Stonn down over his own and walked on.

*   *   *

It was a much-remarked irony that very little was free on a Free Trader world. Walking and breathing were among the few activities without a price tag—though some said that was only because the Traders' Coalition hadn't figured out how to deny those amenities to those who wouldn't pay.

But there was a twenty-credit service fee to enter Talos, which crowded up against the spaceport boundary in classic Free Trader fashion. Virtually anything could be bought on Atzerri, and no small part of the catalog could be had within five hundred meters of Talos spaceport's three entrances. Every major trader in the city had at least one of the kiosk-size satellite storefronts that crowded along the broad boulevards leading to the cabs and hire shops along the flyway ramp.

The narrow little stores were aggressively gaudy and loud. Multistory display panels above their doorways graphically hawked their wares while door barkers made promises and entreaties shoppers were well advised to ignore. Every shop along the boulevard was willing to refund service fees and provide express transport to the sponsor's main location. Some sent small armies of droids out to stand outside competitors' doorsteps with even sweeter offers.

The entire purpose of Traders Plaza was to snap up as many newly arrived "greens" as possible. Once they were safely away from competitors, they could be worked at leisure or steered to other members of a trading alliance—a scratchback, in Atzerri argot. The scratchback networks were elaborate. There was nothing a Free Trader hated more than having a willing buyer and seeing a competitor get the sale.

Luke surveyed the offerings in Traders Plaza with a mixture of wonder and horror. The last time he had been on a Free Trader world, it had been to try to buy weapons for the Rebellion, and there had been no time for browsing the commercial districts. Few of the offerings in the plaza had any appeal to him now, but his curiosity went beyond the personal.

Information brokers offered religious, political, and technical secrets. The forbidden vices of ten thousand worlds were available openly and without shame. Traders who called themselves facilitators arranged personal experiences. Embargoed technologies were readily available alongside unlicensed copies of commercial products. Librarians sold entertainments in every known medium without respect to content or copyright.

Though Luke had prepared himself to resist the blandishments of the sellers on Traders Plaza, his resistance was broken down by one unexpected offering on the display board of The Galactic Archives. He accepted a credit tab from the barker outside, then stepped into the tiny storefront.

"Welcome! Welcome to The Galactic Archives, your one-stop source for everything that's worth knowing," said the hook, greeting him with a broad, oily smile. "Whatever you want, we have—or we'll get it for you, free. What did you say your name was?"

"Li Stonn."

"Li Stonn, walking through that door is going to be one of the best decisions you ever made. When you leave us, you're going to leave satisfied—but you're not going to want to leave, because we have everything. Did you see something particular that you were interested in? Don't be shy about asking—"

Luke pointed upward. "You had an ad up just a few moments ago. Something about the lost secrets of the Jedi—"

"Oh, excellent choice—a real find. We just added that to our catalog, and it's already a best-seller. Absolutely authentic material, answers all the questions we all have about the secret masters of the galaxy." The hook pressed a bright blue tab the same size and shape as the credit tab into Luke's hand. "For security reasons, all our sensitive documents are available only at our central archives location. Just give these tabs to any trading agent when you arrive. Would you like a courtesy cab?"

Dual display screens in the back of the cab subjected Luke to a concentrated dose of Galactic Archives advertising—advertising that seemed to be tailored to the request he had made at the satellite shop.

The offerings included Emperor Palpatine's *Principles of Power*, a private publication for Imperial Moffs; the Sith book of offerings and rituals; the H'kig book of laws; and the secrets of forming Bilar-type *claqa* groupminds, among others—with a special discount if Luke took any three or more. Most of the documents were undoubtedly frauds, and none tempted Luke beyond idle curiosity over the skillfulness of the fraud.

When Luke reached the traders' central site, negotiating the price of his purchase required most of an hour, two attempts to leave empty-handed, and a promise to bring a friend back to The Galactic Archives with him. The final agreement brought the price down from two thousand credits for the Jedi file to nine hundred for the file and a pocket datapad.

By then night had settled solidly over Talos, and the bustle of activity had shifted away from the commerce district, leaving the flyways and walks there nearly empty. Luke walked west, drawn by a bright nightglow in the sky. Twice he was approached from the shadows, but the weak minds of his would-be attackers were easily influenced by a simple projection of doubt, and they retreated to await easier prey.

The nightglow came from the lights of a sprawling and boisterous entertainment district, The Revels. He could hear that it was well named long before he reached the district boundary and paid the general admission. The walks were jostling-full with visitors bent on pleasure, and the air was full of loud voices, laughter, and the music escaping from dozens of rec centers, casinos, and club bars.

Li Stonn wandered The Revels looking for a place to sit undisturbed and read about *The Secrets of Jedi Power*. Luke Skywalker wandered The Revels listening, watching, and trying to understand what drew so many and stirred in them such a desperately fevered energy. With the effects of his exercises lingering, the pleasures offered on the banner displays of the clubs and rec centers seemed shallow and uninviting.

Be a pirate for a night at Tawntoom Territory—

Play Point 5 where it was invented! New games every five minutes! Ninety-percent payoffs!

Near-Death Experiences! Walk Right to the Edge with our Master Torturers and Million-Credit Insurance!

Melee!—Any Weapon, Any Target! The Ultimate Personal Combat Simulator!

The Daughters of the Empath Princess Know Exactly What You Need—

Arena Shock-Ball—Now with Ultracharge!

Li Stonn was no more interested than Luke. But there were no places to sit outdoors—not even a half-wall or a ledge—and no peace from the crowd or the hookmen. The managers of The Revels had cannily decided that if a visitor needed to rest, it should be somewhere indoors, where the average seat turned a hundred credits an hour in drinks, food, and services.

Facing that prospect, Luke decided to leave The Revels and return to the docking bay. It was possible that Akanah had already returned—and if she had not, he would at least have quiet for his reading.

But making his way to the outgate, Luke turned a corner and was taken aback by the brilliantly lit exterior of a club bar called Jabba's Throne Room. *Performing Nightly—The Original Max Rebo Band,* said the scroll. *Visit Jabba's Guest Quarters with a Pleasure Slave. Face the Mighty Rancor in the Pit of Death—*

Driven by an outraged curiosity, Luke joined the

line and paid the membership charge without haggling. Inside, he descended a curving flight of stairs into a remarkably faithful copy of the throne room in Jabba's desert palace on Tatooine. Some of the dimensions had been stretched to accommodate more tables in front of the bandstand and around the rancor pit, but the architecture and atmosphere were authentic.

"Why, it's just like the Palace Museum," Li Stonn said to the tall and elegantly dressed Twi'lek barring the way at the bottom of the stairs.

"I'm afraid my master Jabba is away on business," said the Bib Fortuna look-alike, nodding toward the empty dais. "But I'm having a little party in his absence, and I hope you'll enjoy yourself." His head-tails stirred in signal, and one of the scantily clad dancing girls hurried to him.

"Yes, Lord Fortuna," the server said.

"Oola, this is a friend of mine," said the major-domo. "Treat him well. Find him a seat at my best table."

The same fiction was carried through everywhere else—an Ortolan keyboardist leading a jizz-wailer trio on the bandstand, the roaring of the rancor underfoot, an annoying Kowakian monkey-lizard skittering around the room stealing food and cackling rudely, even a carbon-frozen Han Solo hanging in the display alcove. But a busy kitchen was concealed down the corridor to the servant's quarters, and the price card "Oola" left for him included various services available upstairs in the guest quarters and downstairs in Jabba's dungeon.

It was tasteless and exploitative, but the music was surprisingly agreeable, the roast nerf was tantalizing, and the clientele was markedly more subdued than their counterparts out on the walks. Li Stonn ordered a drink and the executioner's cut of nerf, refused all other offers with a polite smile, and settled in to discover the truth quotient of *The Secrets of the Jedi*.

Shortly after his meal arrived, Luke's consciousness was pricked by hearing a familiar name spoken at a nearby table: Leia's. He looked up, fearing that the evening's entertainment at Jabba's Throne Room would be a dance by a slave-girl-Leia look-alike. But the band was on a break and the transparisteel dance platform over the rancor pit deserted.

Luke extended his awareness, seeking the voice and the conversation that had intruded.

"This'll lead to war," the woman was saying. "And bravo for that. The Republic has every right to slap the Yevetha down for what they've done."

"That's nonsense," her companion—a slender Lafran—retorted. "It's like going into someone else's home to break up an argument. Completely inappropriate."

"We're not talking about an argument. We're talking about murder."

"It's still their business, not ours."

"You can't just let them get away with murder."

"What does it matter to us what anyone does outside our borders? If we try to police the whole galaxy, we'll always be at war. Organa Solo should just grow up and accept that the universe is an imperfect place."

"That's awfully cold," the woman said. "It sounds like if you heard me screaming next door, you'd just complain about having your sleep disturbed."

"We're all responsible for protecting ourselves—and no one else," the Lafran said, shrugging. "We have no business going into Farlax to pick a fight over someone else's business. If a single Fleet pilot dies there, the Princess should be put on trial—for murder and treason."

That brought a chilly end to the conversation. The woman left the club alone; shortly after, the Lafran disappeared up the stairs leading to the guest quarters. Luke returned his attention to his meal.

But when "Oola" came by with an unordered second drink, Li Stonn asked if it would be possible to get a

newsrecord on the troubles in Farlax. She smiled as
though he had asked a foolish question, and returned
with it before the last bite of nerf disappeared. The price
of that convenience was added to his bill as a stiff service
charge, along with the cost of the drink.

Shortly after, a holographic Jabba made an appearance on the dais above the main floor. That signaled the
start of an elaborately scripted show that promised to
involve not only "Bib Fortuna" and the dancers, but additional actors and the audience as well.

Luke took that as his cue to leave. His decision was
affirmed when, climbing up the curving stairs to the
street, he encountered the bounty hunter Boushh coming
down them with an unconvincing Chewbacca in tow.

"Aren't you a little short for a Wookiee?" he muttered under his breath as they passed.

When Luke reached the docking bay, the door was
still locked, the skiff was still secure, and Akanah was
still away. Nor was there any sign she had returned and
left again. Checking the chronometers, he found that she
had been gone more than sixteen hours.

Where are you? he thought. *What are you doing so
long out there? You have so little money, and asked me
for none—and that's all this place respects—*

But Luke resisted the impulse to collect his lightsaber and head off in the direction of the Pemblehov
District. Climbing up to the *Mud Sloth*'s flight deck, he
settled in the flight couch with his reader and two expensive data cards. As the balance of the night slowly
ground by, he diverted himself with absurdities about
the Jedi and the troubling news about what sounded like
a coming war—hoping that wherever they were at that
moment, neither Akanah nor Leia needed his help more
than she needed him to stay away.

Akanah stood before the housing block known as
Atrium 41 and viewed it with dismay.

Even in the forgiving early-morning light, the fifteen-level tower looked like a home for people who had made a habit of leaving everything they had in the casinos. Every other letter was missing from the unlit sign, and the entry arch's security doors were propped open with metal bars. There was an unpleasant smell in the air that seemed to arise from the sun shining on the stone.

Akanah's journey to reach this point had taken her through dozens of shabby clubs, shops, and nightspots in the second-tier outer districts of Talos—the optimistically named New Marketplace, the tawdry flesh auction that was Pemblehov, the rough-tempered Demon's Lair. She had bought and traded information as she could, walked long distances on now aching feet, fended off three attacks and at least twenty propositions without drawing blood, and been granted an unexpected measure of compassion by a street captain, who gave her a sheltered place to rest without expecting anything in return.

Now she stood before her objective brushing a streak of alley grime from the sleeve of her dar-cloak and trying to fight off disappointment. She found herself hoping that her last informant had lied to her—it would be better to be played for a fool than to have to accept this as the truth. It was that hope, as much as anything, that finally moved her forward through the entrance arch.

The tower's atrium was barely deserving of the name. Just four meters across and ten meters long, it was more truly an open stairwell with a skylight at the top. Metal-grate balconies with bent and broken railings circled the atrium on each level, linked up and down with companionways at the narrow end. Triangular doors aping the gratings led to each level's four apartments.

Akanah made her way to the third level unmolested, but there her way was blocked by a gray-furred Gotal wearing a black Imperial Navy officer's tunic with a blaster hole scorched through it, and a vibroblade slung in a smuggler-style hip belt.

"Nice trophy," Akanah said. "Vice admiral, isn't it? Did you take him yourself?"

The Gotal answered with a wordless growl. "What's your business?"

"Does Joreb Goss live here?"

"Who asks?"

"I am Akanah."

"Who sends you here?"

"I am here on my own, on business of my own, in search of Joreb Goss."

"Master Joreb owns all of this, and by his graciousness allows his friends and servants the comforts of his domain. Are you to be one of his girls?"

"Yes," Akanah said. "I am."

"You're early," the Gotal said. "Don't be disturbing the Master. Wait in the playroom for the others."

"I'm not part of the morning auditions," Akanah said, growing impatient. She washed the Current gently across the Gotal's sensitive head-cone receptors, hoping to make him more pliant. "Take me to him, please."

"When the Master rises, I will tell him that the woman Akanah comes, asking after him on business of her own," said the guard. "He will decide what meaning that has to him." The Gotal pointed at a door one level up on the opposite side. "Wait there."

Joreb Goss had the swagger of petty self-importance and the presence of someone who believed he was the power in the room. Tall and trim, with pale blue eyes in a lined but otherwise unmarked face, Joreb was handsome despite his age. His long, thick silver hair was swept back to a vertical comb and hung to the small of his back.

But his mock flight suit was gaudy and cheap, his black boots buffed to an unlikely shine. His smile had the same false cast, and those alert blue eyes appraised Akanah familiarly before meeting her gaze.

"So you are my visitor," Joreb said.

"No," Akanah said, holding herself erect. "I'm your daughter."

Joreb's eyes widened, but he said nothing at first. Clasping one wrist behind his back, he circled her slowly. "My *daughter*," he repeated. "Who is your mother?"

"My mother was Isela Talsava Norand," Akanah said. "She's dead now."

Completing his circuit, Joreb stopped facing Akanah and leaned in toward her. "I don't know this name," he said. "What is it you want, daughter of Isela?"

"That you not lie to me," Akanah said. "You knew my mother well—let me remind you when. You met her on Praidaw, came to live with her on Gavens, where she had a house in Torlas—the house in which I was born. You moved with us to Lucazec. And within the year, you left us there."

"You speak of things older than my memories," Joreb said. "How am I to know the truth of them?"

"What do you mean?" Akanah said, a sudden flare of anger in her eyes and her tone. "I was the child, not you. I'm the one who had to learn about you in a story told by my mother."

"I have not heard this story," said Joreb. "Perhaps you will tell it to me."

"I came so far to find you," she said in a small voice. "How can you be so cold to me—"

"You are not unattractive, and perhaps there is something about your eyes I find familiar," Joreb said. "But, you see, I have developed a fondness for Rokna blue." HIs tone was sorrowfully apologetic. "Do you know it?"

"It's a deadly poison," Akanah said. "From a tree fungus that grows on Endor."

Joreb brought one hand forward and waggled a finger at her. "Yes, that's right—Endor. I had forgotten. But you see, Rokna blue is not so deadly as some think. The smallest amount brings an exquisite state of bliss. It magnifies all other pleasures for hours—indescribable. You must try it to know. I would be happy to stand you to your first—"

"No, thank you," Akanah said curtly. "What does this have to do with your memory?"

Joreb looked momentarily lost. "What— Ah, yes. I was saying, in the proper doses—a microgram, no more—the blue is not deadly. But it still does demand a price for its blessings."

"A price?"

Joreb touched his temple with two fingers of his left hand. "My memories do not go back even as much as a year. Everything is new to me. No, do not pity me—I have chosen to live in a vivid present rather than hold on to what is now the forgotten past."

Akanah wore her horror openly. "How could you make such a choice?"

A smile spread slowly across Joreb's face. "Bliss beyond imagining," he said. "I could show you."

"No," she said firmly.

Joreb shrugged. "I find your choice as puzzling as you find mine. Do you have memories worth treasuring? It seems I did not."

"*I* would have treasured them," she said, and tears ran freely from her eyes. "I came here to find my father. What am I to do now?"

"You can stay if you like," he offered. "There are rooms open on the upper levels. Or, at least, I think there still are. Trass will know for certain. But I'm afraid I will never be able to add anything to the story your mother told you. You may be my daughter, as you say," Joreb said, then shook his head regretfully. "But I am not your father."

Chapter 9

♦

Akanah returned to Docking Bay A13 twenty-two hours after she had left it, her face pale, her clothing dirty, her eyes dull.

"They aren't here," she said wearily as she climbed into the skiff, waking Luke from an unplanned nap in the pilot's couch. "We can go."

Then, without saying anything more, she tried to crawl into the bunk and draw the curtain against Luke. But he followed close behind her, unwilling to settle for so little after so long.

"Go where?" he said, catching the curtain with a hand and throwing it aside. "Did you find anything?"

"I found enough," Akanah said, turning her back to him. "I'll tell you when we're outbound."

"You said you'd come back for me. I'd like to see the scribing. I'd like to see where they lived. There might be something I can pick up."

"I'm too tired," she said.

"You're a mess, too, but I'm not keeping score," Luke said. "Look, I paid to have the shower cleaned. I think you should go make it dirty again, and we'll talk after. You'll feel better, no matter what comes next."

To Luke's surprise, Akanah allowed herself to be

directed. She lingered a long time under the water, longer than Luke himself had. When she emerged, she was standing a bit straighter, with better color in her face and a little life in her eyes.

But it seemed to Luke that whatever strength the shower had returned to Akanah went directly into stubbornness. She flatly refused to take him back out into the city, or to talk about what she had done and where she had gone.

"I want to sleep," she said, standing at the foot of the mounting ladder with her soiled dar-cloak draped over one arm, the sun glistening in the last drops of water beaded on her bare shoulders. "I'm *going* to sleep, or I'm going to fall down where I'm standing."

"I'll hire a speeder—"

"No!" she said sharply. "We're finished here—I didn't miss anything, and I can tell you everything I found when I'm rested. Just take us away from here. Lift ship and jump us a few hours toward the Core. I should be human again by the time you're done doing that. But right now, I need to be alone, and I need to sleep. And that's what I'm going to do."

Brushing close enough past him that he caught the scent of soap on her hair, Akanah clambered back up the spindly ladder into the skiff. Frowning resignedly, Luke walked to the bow of the skiff and started his preflight inspection. By the time he made his way up the ladder into the flight compartment, the bunk was sealed as tight as a cocoon, with as little clue to what would eventually emerge.

He slipped back into the pilot's couch with a sigh, switching off the datapad and tucking it under a tiedown. "*Mud Sloth* to Talos tower," Luke said. "Departing A-Thirteen, requesting clearance to orbit."

"Talos tower. Please hold, *Mud Sloth*. There's traffic ahead of you."

Luke glanced at the chronometer and shook his head with a wry expression. They had been on Atzerri a few minutes short of a full day. His reply was far more Luke than Li Stonn.

"Talos tower, copy, I have the traffic on my sensors, and it looks from here like a slow accountant making an extra pass," he said. "Do you think it'd help him along if I rattle the walls with my thrusters while I'm waiting for him to count to one?"

Clearance to lift came a few moments later. But Luke was not greatly surprised to find that the final bill, transmitted to him as he cleared the atmosphere, still assessed him for two days' berthing.

Free Traders, Luke thought with disgust. *Thieves with business cards.*

Just before jumping the skiff out from Atzerri, Luke remembered to retrieve the report on the *Mud Sloth* from the New Republic Ship Registry on Coruscant.

It was much shorter than the report on *Star Morning,* as befitted a ship that Luke guessed had probably spent most of its life grounded. The little ship was impractical for anything more than the occasional businessman's vacation or off-the-spacelanes sales call. Most of its value was as a status symbol, something a Have could talk about where the Have-Nots could listen in envy. To judge by the skiff's lines and detailing, Verpine had very consciously traded comfort underway for a design that looked fast while sitting still.

But Luke's only interests were the ownership records and the most recent entries in the traffic log. After Akanah's behavior on Atzerri, Luke had developed a renewed interest in independent confirmation of the things she had been telling him. He still wanted to believe her, but was no longer sure that he could. And, one way or another, he had to know.

Luke also found he had developed a renewed curiosity about the things Akanah was *not* telling him. It had occurred to him, for instance, that almost every time

Akanah spoke about her past, she spoke about her life on Carratos, not Lucazec. Knowing how hungry he was for information about his mother, he had expected Akanah to be generous with anecdotes and remembrances about the part of her life she claimed to look back on most fondly.

But such remembrances had been few, and Nashira had figured in even fewer. It made Luke wonder, and wondering led to doubt, and doubt to suspicion—a highly undesirable state of affairs.

So Luke was relieved at first when the initial screen of the report informed him that NR80-109399, a Verpine Adventurer, Model 201, production group E, belonged to:

Akanah Norand Pell, being an adult resident of Chofin, a settlement belonging to the autonomous state of Carratos, under the authority of which this registration is granted.

And the recording date for the articles of registration was recent—not quite half a year past.

Turning to the traffic log, Luke found more welcome news. The only planetfalls recorded for *Mud Sloth* since Akanah had taken ownership were at Golkus and Coruscant, and Golkus was near enough to being on a line from Carratos to Coruscant that a stop there en route needed no explanation. Curiously, though, there was no record of their departure from Coruscant, nor of their stops at Lucazec, Teyr, or Atzerri.

The latter omission Luke could explain by the update cycles—there must not have been time for the routine transmission of data from those flight control centers to Coruscant, or for the addition of that data to the master record. But the former omission was puzzling. Luke's cloaking work as they left Coruscant should only have concealed their point of origin from watching eyes and discouraged curiosity about any out-of-trajectory alarms at Flight Control.

But as far as Coruscant was concerned, *Mud Sloth*

had never left. The skiff had never requested clearance to lift to orbit, had never requested clearance through the planetary shield—except they never could have left without it. And shield passage required not only that the skiff answer a transponder interrogation, but also that Ship Registry verify the ID. It was impossible to imagine how their passage had gone unrecorded.

Luke wondered what would happen when the outworld updates arrived and *Mud Sloth* was suddenly in two places at once.

Then, just for a moment, he toyed with the idea that both places were really the same—that they *were* still on Coruscant, perhaps even still in his hermitage, and some elaborate deception was under way.

He quickly rejected the idea as too extreme a solution to the mystery. But it left a worrisome question in its wake: Just what was Akanah capable of? What were the limits of *her* power?

May I cloak us as we leave? she had asked.

And he had not thought to question it.

What had she done? Something that could hide them completely from the best planetary security the best engineers could devise? He realized he had missed a pattern. How had she gotten into his hermitage without his knowing it? How had she gotten past the security droid and into the commonal on Teyr? All the questions pointed toward the same answer—some gift of deception, illusion, or concealment that went well beyond what he himself could call upon.

She can pierce my projections, he realized. *I wonder if I can pierce hers. I wonder if I can even tell when she's using one.*

Distracted by such thoughts, Luke almost overlooked the other surprise in the report from Coruscant. It waited for him in the section on ownership history, and fell under his eyes while he was wondering why, if she had such a talent for concealment, Akanah had needed to buy a ship at all.

You could have stowed away on any ship at any time, he was thinking. *You wouldn't have been trapped on Lucazec. Stang, you could have stolen the price of passage, even the price of the ship—*

Then he noticed that the sole prior owner of the skiff was a man named Andras Pell, and that the transfer category given was:

CLASS III NONTAXABLE—INHERITANCE BY MARRIAGE

He rose out of the couch and turned to stare at the closed curtain screening the bunk. *Just how* did *you buy your freedom?* he thought at Akanah. *And what else are you keeping from me?*

Akanah hibernated—or hid—for nearly ten hours. But rather than frustrating Luke's curiosity, her absence redirected it. For the last five hours of her isolation, *Mud Sloth* drifted in realspace on the fringe of Atzerri's Oort Cloud with only the cold methane-ice comets for company. With all his inhibitions about making inquiries behind Akanah's back gone, Luke made full use of the time, his credits, and his priority access codes.

From Carratos he requested any information available from newsgrid, political, or police records on Akanah Norand Pell, Andras Pell, and Talsava. He sent the same query to Coruscant's criminal records office and citizen registry and to the home offices of both the Coruscant Global Newsgrid and the New Republic Prime Newsgrid.

From the New Republic Reference Service, he requested a quickreport on naming conventions on Lucazec and Carratos, thinking he might parse another lead from the names in hand.

A second request to the same source asked for five-hundred-word excerpts from all matches on the key words "Fallanassi" and "White Current." After a short debate with himself, and despite the pathetic and sensational inaccuracies of *Secrets of the Jedi,* Luke also contacted an information broker on Atzerri and paid a hundred credits for a search on the same keys.

He also requested a Current Terms & Conditions brochure from the chief librarian's office on Obroa-skai. The library computers there were the only resource offering both a greater variety and a greater volume of records than those held by Coruscant.

But Obroa-skai's generosity with its planetary treasure was limited. To protect against theft of the library, and to provide the resources needed to maintain it, accessing the records meant either going to Obroa-skai or hiring one of the library's own trained contract researchers.

In either case, Obroa-skai was not a resource one turned to for quick answers. The official language of New Republic recordkeeping was Basic, and everything held by Coruscant was kept in one of several readily searchable data specifications. But the Obroa-skai library was a collection of primary documents, in ten thousand storage formats and uncountable languages. The most complete general index covered only fifteen percent of the library's holdings, and all the specialty indexes combined added only a few percent to that.

Those were the principal reasons why the brochure—which Luke received within minutes of requesting it, as the first response to any of his inquiries—reported that a normal single-part library search was averaging eight days. The waiting list for terminal time was holding at fifteen days, and the backlog for contract researchers had climbed to seventy.

Discouraging as those numbers were, Luke dispatched a command-control message to Artoo and Threepio on Yavin 4, instructing them to go to Obroa-skai and search the library on his behalf, as they had done once before.

The only request he made that was refused outright was for the Fleet Office's daily Tactical Briefing Memorandum, also known as the trouble map—a compendium of situation reports from all the various Fleet and base commands. Unlike that aboard his E-wing, *Mud Sloth*'s hypercomm wasn't military-rated, and there was no persuading the Intelligence Section to send a white-star file to what they considered an unsecured receiver.

Luke thought about comming Admiral Ackbar directly to ask his appraisal of the trouble in Farlax—the news digest Luke had picked up on Atzerri was almost as sensational and unbelievable as the Jedi document. But doing so promised to invite questions Luke wasn't ready to answer, and possibly force a decision he wasn't ready to make.

Instead, he chose to contact the public information offices of both the Senate and the General Ministry. He asked for the official record of the past twenty days, hoping he could read between the lines well enough to know if it was time to head home.

Then he lowered the lights in the flight compartment, stretched out on the deck behind the control couches, and closed his eyes. All his pending requests required patience, from minutes to hours to days. But just reaching out had left him feeling better about his circumstances. Even if some of his efforts returned nothing useful, the next time he and Akanah talked, he expected to be in a much stronger position.

Sorry as I am to say it, what I have to have now is reason to trust you, not just reason to want to, he thought. *If we're going to go on any farther together, you're going to have to start trusting me.*

Prompted by a sensation like a feather tickling somewhere inside his skull, Luke became aware of two things at once: that he had fallen asleep on the deck, and that he was being watched.

He turned his head in the direction of the sensation and opened his eyes. He found himself looking directly at Akanah. She was sitting on the edge of the bunk, hands folded on her lap, her hair bed-tousled.

"Hi," she said. "I'm sorry I monopolized the bunk for so long. I didn't mean to do that."

Taken aback by her apology, Luke pulled himself up to a sitting position. " 's all right," he slurred. "You must have needed it. You looked like you did, anyway, back at Talos."

She nodded. "About Talos—there's some things we have to talk about," she said. "You've been very patient with me, and I've been terribly unfair to you. You deserve to know what's been happening with me."

Having had his own opening speech preempted, Luke could find nothing more to say than "Go on, then—I'm listening."

Akanah nodded toward the foredeck. "You have some messages. You'll probably want to look at them first."

Eyeing her quizzically, Luke moved to the copilot's couch and browsed the list of waiting replies.

There was an acknowledgment from Streen on Yavin 4, which Luke skipped for the moment. He also skipped the press folders from the Senate and General Ministry, which were irrelevant for the moment.

The New Republic Reference Service had responded with a short précis on naming, ending in the messages:

Search Key: FALLANASSI—Not Found

Search Key: WHITE CURRENT—Not Found As Single Term

Search Key: FALLANASSI + WHITE CURRENT— Not Found

It was the same with the response from the information broker on Atzerri—an apologetic note and an offer to apply half of the search fee to Luke's next request.

With increasing agitation, Luke skimmed through half a dozen more replies from various agencies and companies on Carratos and Coruscant. All were singularly uninformative—a few dates, a few facts that fell into the category of vital statistics, and several NO REC-ORD and NOT FOUND messages, with a pair of RE-QUEST DENIED rebuffs scattered among them.

"Let me tell you what your messages say," Akanah said gently. "My full name was Akanah Norand Goss, now Akanah Norand Pell. I was married on Carratos to Andras Pell, a man thirty-six years my senior. Andras died a year later, and I inherited this ship and a few thousand credits. His obituary says it was an innocent death, and no one official seems to have taken any notice of his passing, but you wonder if I might have both married and killed him to escape from Carratos. And no matter who and where you asked, there's nothing at all to be found about the Fallanassi."

"How do you know?" he demanded, twisting around to face her. "Did you read my mail?"

"No. I didn't need to."

"You knew I was going to check up on you," he said.

"Oh—I thought you would, eventually. I rather thought it would be sooner."

"So you checked yourself, and you knew how little I'd find."

"I checked *for* myself," she corrected. "You're not the only one looking for pieces of your past."

He sat down on the edge of the copilot's couch. "Why are there so few?" he asked, the accusatory tone leaving his voice.

"Talsava and I lived in the shadows on Carratos. We came in unregistered. We lived in a part of Chofin where people come and go without notice. When Talsava left, I became one of the invisibles—I owned nothing, did nothing that put my name in the identity records of the occupation. The only time I ever lived above the line on Carratos was the last two years—the years I was with Andras."

"No one questioned who you were, where you came from?"

"No. The old records were seized by the Empire, and the occupation records were destroyed by the liberty movement. Everyone was given a fresh start. I took a name in the local custom for women—given name, mother's name, father's name. But it means nothing anywhere but there, anytime but then."

"So there's no reason for it to be anywhere in Coruscant's records."

"Or Lucazec's, or Teyr's. It's not that there are other names behind which the records hide—"

"As far as the bureaucrats and census-takers were concerned, you didn't exist."

She smiled. "On Carratos, the census is of property and the owners of property," she said. "When I owned nothing, I did not count. When Andras took me, I was *his* property. Now that I own this"—she raised her hands to indicate the skiff—"I am a person."

Luke nodded slowly. "I guess that all makes sense, the way you explain it," he said. "But something else I learned still doesn't have an explanation. The traffic records say we're still on Coruscant, and I'm starting to think that we're still going to be there no matter how many systems we visit."

Inexplicably, Akanah giggled. "Did your tracking report mention a visit to Golkus?"

"Yes," Luke said. "On your way to Coruscant."

"And did it say why I went there?"

"No. I didn't think about it much, either," Luke admitted. "I guess I figured that, it being your first trip in the skiff, there was either some little problem you needed fixed, or you just didn't like being alone out here."

"Well—the second is true, absolutely true. But so is the first. The problem I needed fixed was the ship's identification transponder. I told you—we leave no trail that an outsider can follow. There was someone on Golkus who could help with that."

"Someone? Altering ID profiles is no mean trick."

"His name would mean nothing to you but could

harm him," Akanah said. "I believe he once worked with—or for—Talon Karrde."

"How do you know him?"

"He came through Carratos once, years ago," she said. "When I heard why, I arranged to meet him and to do him a favor. But the price was still dear. I paid him with most of the credits I had, plus favors I had collected from others."

"So he changed the profile—what, to some other Adventurer? So some *other* ship left Coruscant."

"Oh—he did more than change it," Akanah said. "If that's all I'd asked for, it wouldn't have been quite so dear. No, he put what he called a smuggler's kit in the transponder."

"This ship's black-boxed?" Luke stared wonderingly.

"I guess that's what it's called. Every time we jump, the profile changes—to something that looks legitimate but isn't. If I'd had the price, I could have bought bootleg IDs instead of counterfeits."

"And I suppose the system doesn't activate until after you've jumped out from wherever the work was done, so the trail doesn't point back to this gentleman." Luke frowned. "Stang, the days we've wasted—we *could* have jumped out from Lucazec, or Teyr—"

"I encouraged you to," she protested. "I'm the one who asked you to disable the interlock."

"Yeah, but you neglected to mention that it'd be safe to do it," Luke grumbled. "We blast out of one system under one ID, tiptoe into the next under another—and no one connects the two. Very sweet. This fellow on Golkus is going to do a brisk business."

"He chooses not to," Akanah said. "I had the impression he considers himself retired. He says he's very selective about who he'll do this kind of work for."

"Well—I guess the fact he's on Golkus and not in Talos backs that up," Luke said, shaking his head. "Why didn't you tell me?"

"I did," she said. "Just now."

"That's a cheat," Luke said.

"Yes," she said. "The truth is I wasn't ready to trust you with that information. I didn't really know whether I might need to hide myself from *you* at some point. I have a lot to protect."

"But you're ready to trust me now."

"If I don't trust you, I'm completely alone," she said, a hint of an old sorrow in her eyes. "And I can't do that anymore. I never wanted to, and now I just can't. I can't hold you out when what I need is to be close to someone again."

"Akanah—"

"Secrets are like walls, aren't they? They separate people. And I've been alone behind these walls for as long as I can bear," she said. "I'll teach you to read scribing, Luke. And if you want it, and you allow me enough time, I'll teach you the rest. You will become one of us in full measure—an adept of the White Current. You will finally walk your mother's path."

Luke understood the significance of what he was being offered. "Thank you," he said in a voice drawn tight by emotion. "Even the chance that I might find her—I want to bring as much of her into my life as I can—I want that balance—"

"But you still have questions," she supplied.

"Yes."

"Please don't hold them back because you don't want to seem ungrateful. Ask them."

Her words captured the flavor of his reluctance exactly. "Is telepathy one of the adept's skills?"

She laughed lightly. "Are people now so afraid to look closely at Luke Skywalker that ordinary attentiveness seems remarkable?"

Luke's smile was rueful and faintly embarrassed. "Perhaps."

"They should not be," she said. "Now ask me the real question. Something else in those reports, I think."

"Something that wasn't there," he said. "You were right. There wasn't a word about the Fallanassi—not on Lucazec, or Teyr, or Coruscant, or Atzerri. Not *that* word."

"You must wonder whether there really is a circle," she said, "or if this is just a fable spun by a lonely madwoman to lure you away with her." She showed a small smile, inviting him to demur.

"I just expected there to be *something*. Rumors, myths, legends, superstitions—it's hard to understand how a people as powerful as the Fallanassi, with as long a history as you've suggested, could leave no trace of yourselves—"

"Because we have made it so," she said quietly.

"—Or are the traces there, and I don't know the right names to ask after— What did you say?"

"Because we have made it so," she repeated. "When such traces appear, we remove them. But there are not many to remove, because we have not made it our purpose to leave a mark."

Luke nodded slowly. "Not to conquer—not to convert—but to find the place where one belongs—"

"Yes. If you understand that, you understand the most important truth of the Current," she said. "If you let it, it will carry you to where you need to be, for the lessons you need to learn, the work you need to do, and the people who need you in *their* lives."

Nodding, Luke slid across to the pilot's seat. "Speaking of which—we've been sitting here a long time. We should get going," he said. "But I need to know where."

"J't'p'tan," she said. "The world is called J't'p'tan."

Luke turned away toward the controls. "Well— you've stumped me again. I'll have to look that one up in the navigation atlas."

"Luke—"

"What?"

"Isn't there a question you haven't asked?"

Luke thought for a moment. There were many he still could ask, but the urgency had left them. He believed she would answer them all, in their turn. "Yes, one," he said finally. "Did you love Andras?"

"That isn't the question I expected," Akanah said, and bit her lower lip. "Yes. I loved him. He held me lightly. He found something in me that he thought was beautiful, and he never tried to change me. And he was never cruel. It was like being a child—like being a child should be. I wish that it could have lasted."

Curiously, J't'p'tan wasn't in the skiff's navigational database. Since the spelling was so odd, he pressed Akanah about it.

"It isn't a Basic word," she said, calling forward to him from the refresher. "It's the Basic transliteration of four mystical glyphs in H'kig—'jeh,' the immanent; 'teh,' the transcendent; 'peh,' the eternal; and 'tan,' the conscious essence. Only 'tan' may be written out in full. The H'kig consider the others too sacred. The spelling I gave you is the convention that respects that belief."

"You could have just said 'I'm sure,'" he said with mock grumpiness.

"Next time, I will."

The failure of the skiff to identify their destination forced Luke to make a query to Coruscant, and *Mud Sloth* to linger a while longer near the Oort Cloud. When the Astrographical Survey Institute returned the requested coordinates, they caused Luke's eyes to widen.

"A long way," he said, zooming and scrolling the nav chart across the primary display. "And we can't go there directly, because that'd put us on the wrong side of the Borderlands for the whole middle third of the trip."

"Which would be unsafe, I take it."

"There are Interdictor patrols all in through there," Luke said. "But that's okay, because it's too far to go in one jump anyway. We'd be twenty hours over the skiff's endurance. I'm going to have to pick a stopping place somewhere along the way." He waggled a finger over one section of the map. "Somewhere in here—that'll keep us on the right side of the line."

"I'll leave that decision up to you."

Luke drew a small square around their destination and zoomed the map in to a more familiar scale. Legend marks and other identifiers popped into view. "Farlax Sector," he said under his breath.

"What?"

"Talking to myself," Luke said. "I'm tired. My mind's already lying down in the bunk."

He zoomed the map another order of magnitude. *Not just Farlax—Koornacht Cluster,* he realized with a troubled frown. Pulling the datapad from the tie-down keeper, he brought up the news abstract and searched it for J't'p'tan. It was a relief not to find it listed among the worlds involved in the fighting.

Still frowning, Luke next turned to the PIO reports still waiting in the message queue. Skimming, he found confirmation for the key element in the news reports— some colony worlds within Koornacht had been attacked, and their populations exterminated, by the Yevetha. Some colonies were given by name, some only by the origin of the colonists. But J't'p'tan was not mentioned. Nor were the H'kig.

He zoomed the navigation map once more and studied the geography of Koornacht Cluster. J't'p'tan lay in the interior, out of scanning range for a ship on the edge of the Cluster. If something had happened there, Coruscant might not have any way to know.

Do I tell her? Do we wait here until we know more, or do we go?

As he plotted an alternate course—one that would take them as close to the border as possible without crossing the line—he allowed himself to consider the horrendous possibility that the Yevetha had fallen on J't'p'tan and exterminated the Fallanassi. It was possible that he and Akanah had set out on their journey too late—by no more than a few tens of days. It was possible that Nashira had been alive that short a time ago—and was now dead.

Akanah emerged from the refresher, and Luke pushed the datapad back in the keeper as she came forward. *I can carry this. I can tolerate this uncertainty—she can't,* he told himself as he blanked the secondary display.

"We have a good line to Utharis," he said to her. "A Tarrack world, just inside the border. We should be able to take care of the skiff there with no problems."

"Have you ever been there?"

"No," Luke said, sending the coordinates to the autopilot. "You?"

"No."

"Can't get a better recommendation than that," Luke said, suddenly feeling as tired as he had pretended to a short time before. "When we get there, I'll buy you a souvenir hat."

He did not wait for Akanah to settle in her couch. Thumbing the hyperdrive safety and throwing the actuators forward, Luke bent time, stretched the stars, and hurled the ship toward Utharis.

Lying on his back in the bunk, Luke stared up into the mesmerizer that covered the bulkhead above the bunk.

The thin panel offered several holographic depth illusions intended to combat shipbound claustrophobia, an array of hypnotic sleep-inducing light and color patterns, and several other displays of a purely recreational nature. Playing before Luke's eyes was the slowly spinning disk of a great spiral-armed galaxy as viewed from outside, a thousand light-years above the galactic plane.

Luke had seen such a sight once before—from the Alliance's medical frigate, at the deep rendezvous point they had code-named Haven. The sight took him back. That had been after the debacle at Hoth, after the escape from Bespin. He held his right hand, the bionic hand, up before his face and flexed the fingers, remembering— trying to remember.

Even more than leaving Tatooine in the *Falcon* with Han and Obi-Wan, it was his encounter with Vader, there in Cloud City, that divided his life into two halves. Before that, Luke had been little different from any of the Empire's many casual victims—uprooted from his home by Imperial brutality, recruited into the Rebellion more by rage and tragedy than ideology. The blaster bolts that killed Owen and Beru had destroyed one fu- ture and sent him tumbling into another. But it had seemed a matter of chance, not destiny.

His meeting with his father, though, had laid a greater weight on his shoulders. Not until he was hang- ing from the power gantry, hearing the voice from be- hind the black mask speaking unthinkable words, had he understood what was being asked of him. Not until then had he known that he and no one else could carry that weight. Looking back to that moment was looking back to the moment he became himself. Looking back beyond that moment was almost impossible.

You can hardly see twenty-one from thirty-four, he thought.

The soft click of the curtain release interrupted his introspection. A moment later, Akanah slid the sections apart.

"Somehow I knew you were still awake," she said, showing that now familiar quick smile. "What did I leave you wondering about?"

He shook his head. "I was just thinking about when I stopped being a kid. And how long ago it seems."

"What if you live to be as old as Yoda?"

He smiled ruefully. "Then I'll probably laugh at my- self for feeling the way I feel right now."

"It's not the time. It's the responsibility," she said,

and the smile left her eyes. "Luke—I'm sorry to intrude on you this way. But there was something I didn't tell you, and should have. And I didn't feel right letting it wait."

Luke sat up far enough to prop himself up on his elbows. "Okay."

She sat down on the wide sill at the edge of the bunk where the curtain track ran. "Even though I held back some things you might wish I'd told you, I've tried to always tell you the truth," she said. "But I did lie to you about Atzerri."

Luke sat up a little farther. "Oh?"

"I took you to Atzerri under false pretenses," Akanah said. "The circle was never there. You were right about *Star Morning*. The writing at Teyr said to go to J't'p'tan."

"Then why?"

"I had to," she said. "I had to try to find my father."

Luke looked hard at her for long seconds, but his words were surprisingly soft. "Did you think I wouldn't understand?"

"I was afraid of what I might find," she said, dropping her eyes. "I was afraid of what you might think of me if my father turned out to be someone even I can't respect."

"Well—I understand that, too," Luke said. "I think Leia's been afraid to look for our mother. Maybe if I were Leia, I would be, too."

"Why?"

Luke considered for a moment before answering. "Her memories of our mother—few as they are, and little as they've told us—are very precious to her. They're a child's memories, innocent, idyllic. And she's protecting them."

"Protecting them? From what?"

"Reality," Luke said. "There's nothing Leia could possibly learn about Mother that could improve on those memories—and a lot she could learn that could damage them. Leia's never had to consider our mother in her full complexity. What kind of relationship did she have with Vader? Why did she have his children? Why did she give us up? When you start letting yourself ask questions like those, you risk getting an answer you don't like."

"But it's different for you?"

"I don't have any memories to protect," he said, with a hint of wistful regret in his voice. "I just want to know who I come from—what else I carry inside me. I'm not as worried about being disappointed." He smiled wryly. "Though if I discovered that Mother had something to do with turning Anakin Skywalker into Darth Vader—"

"Oh, no," Akanah said, looking up and touching his hand reassuringly. "I promise you—Nashira is nothing like that. Please believe me."

He nodded. "I do."

"That's so important to me—and I'm afraid I've destroyed it," she said, her voice quivering with anguish. "I didn't want you to have any reason to doubt me, any reason to question coming with me." She smiled sadly. "So, of course, I lied to you. I'm so sorry, Luke. I knew better. I knew I would never be able to deceive you."

Luke folded his fingers around hers and squeezed. "Did you find him?"

"Yes," she said, and her eyes began to glisten. "In a way, I did. I found him in Trasli District. He's the very minor chief of a shabby little tribe, puffed up with flattery and brain-burned on Rokna blue. He didn't remember my mother. He didn't know he had a daughter." She bravely tried a smile. "These little pieces of us that others hold inside them—some know their value, and others are careless with them. When you find Nashira, I know that she will have more to give you than Joreb Goss did me."

"You didn't have much time," Luke said. "You can go back."

"No. My father is dead," she said simply. "Someone else lives in his body. I will never speak to that person again."

Luke could tell that her composure at that moment was simply an exercise of will. There was a tremble in her hand, her eyes were tear-bright with loss, and her skin was hot with her misery. But she would not let herself ask him for anything but forgiveness.

"I understand that, too," he said gently. "I know how that feels, to have that door locked, and only an empty space beyond. I'm sorry. I know it hurts."

"He was my last hope for a key," she said, unable to keep the pain from her voice. "They're both gone now—my mother and my father. If we don't find the circle, I'm always going to be alone."

Words no longer offered any hope of comforting her, and her need was too acute to ignore. With a gentle tug on her hand and a meaningful, confirming look, Luke invited her into the bunk with him.

After a moment's hesitation, Akanah climbed in through the gap in the curtains and curled up against him, nestled in the crook of his arm. Before long, she was sobbing quietly, her body shaking beside his.

But the tears felt to Luke more like welcome relief than distress. Saying nothing, he held Akanah close and tried to wrap her in a blanket of comfort.

The galaxy turned like a wheel high above them, all its tumult far away and, for the moment, forgotten.

IIII.

Leia

Chapter 10

◆

Viceroy Nil Spaar returned to the spawnworld of the Yevetha as more than a hero and just less than a god.

On the day of his return, more than three million of the Pure gathered to watch the gleaming sphere of *Aramadia* descend through the leaden sky of N'zoth. By means of Imperial hypercomm and planetary net, the vast throng at Hariz was joined by the entire population of the Twelve and the new worlds of the Second Birth. The consular ship was so brilliantly lit by spotlights that it seemed as though a fragment of a star were delivering the architect of the Purification back to his people.

"*Ni toi darama,*" they whispered. "The Blessed comes to us."

Overhead, smoke generators on the escort fighters flying cover created descending spirals of crimson and purple. The roar of *Aramadia*'s undampered pulse-lifters beat down on the upturned faces of the vast gathering, lifting their hearts. They embraced the concussion waves as though they were caresses by the viceroy's own hands.

"*Hi noka daraya!*" they cried. "The Brightness touches me!"

Thousands of those standing closest along the barricades were struck deaf in the last seconds before *Aramadia* touched down on the landing baffle, the fine haircells sheltered in the line of pits along their temple ridges shaken until blood ran from them. The maimed fell to their knees in joy, screaming the viceroy's name as they ecstatically daubed their blood across their chests as a badge of honor.

"I was there at Hariz to welcome *darama* Spaar," the deaf would say with pride in the days to come. "My ears remember the glorious sound of his pure and loving power, and no lesser sound will ever make them forget it."

Aboard *Aramadia,* Nil Spaar stood at the curving viewport in the gallery of his quarters and looked out over the throng. The viewport's security screen concealed him from their eyes, but he could see that his Yevetha carpeted the landscape nearly to the horizon.

"Viceroy," said his aide, Eri Palle, standing a few steps behind. "Let me tell you how beloved you are today. Each and every *nitakka* below would gladly give his blood to feed your nesting. Each and every *marasi* would gladly offer herself as your breeding mate."

"You flatter me with exaggeration," said Nil Spaar.

"No, *etaias,*" the aide protested. "I have been told by the proctor of labor for your office here that they have been overwhelmed by offers. The gate guard at your estate counts more than a thousand hopeful *marasi* who have shown themselves there."

"Indeed," Spaar said, glancing back over his shoulder. "If you hear that he took any for himself, I trust you will see that he pays for his error publicly and painfully."

"He wouldn't dare show such disrespect to you," Eri Palle said, aghast. "He is as loyal to you as any of us—as I myself am."

"There is always someone who will dare, Eri," said Nil Spaar, turning away. "In that way ambition makes a place for itself. I dared, once. Or do you forget how it was that Viceroy Kiv Truun left the palace?"

The ship shuddered under them as the landing pads touched down and the stabilizers took up the weight of the vessel. Then the distant rumble of the lifters ceased, and the smaller sounds of *Aramadia*'s systems and machinery became audible once more.

"I remember," said Eri. "I still have my tunic, stained with Kiv Truun's blood, to remind me."

Nil Spaar nodded, then drew himself up to his full height before the viewport. "Have the spotlights dimmed, and drop the screens, Eri. Let them see me."

The aide turned away to the viewport controls. A few moments later the crowd saw a narrow band encircling the ship at its middle draw inward to create a balcony.

Standing on that balcony was a tall Yevetha in ceremonial scarlet, who raised his hand to them in salute. The projected, polarized image was repeated at intervals around the ship. No matter where the faithful stood, each could look up at *Aramadia* and see the Yevethan leader.

The crowd roared its welcome with one fevered, joyful voice. The sound they made rivaled the noise of the ship's lifters and set the hull of *Aramadia* vibrating in sympathy.

Nil Spaar basked in their devotion. The feeling was almost as sweetly intense as the embrace of his nesting but left him shimmering with desire. Both his fighting and his mating crests were vividly swollen.

The roar went on and on, with no sign of abating. Finally Nil Spaar could stand it no longer and stepped back from the viewport, gesturing to Eri.

The aide quickly closed the screens, making the gallery a private place again. Then he retreated before the viceroy, mindful of the engorged fighting crests.

"You see, *etaias*," said Eri, backpedaling. "How glorious for you."

"I want to go down to them. Is my skimmer ready?"

"The tender of the port has supplied a car—a processional car, built for this occasion by the guildsmen of Giat Nor as a gift to you. I am told that the craftsmanship is flawless."

"Then I shall go accept this gift," said Nil Spaar, moving toward the entry. "Thank you, Eri. Please see that my family is transferred to the palace after the crowd clears."

"Yes, Viceroy," said the aide, his face falling as he realized he was not to be allowed a place on the viceroy's processional car. Then, fearing his thoughts had been read from his expression, he quickly fell to one knee in obeisance. "I am honored to serve you, *darama,*" he said softly.

Nil Spaar's fingertips grazed the back of Eri's neck as he strode past him toward the corridor. "I am glad to hear it," said the viceroy. "Be careful not to hunger too much for more."

Blind, silent, and isolated from one another, the 106 ships of the Fifth Battle Group of the New Republic Defense Force bored through hyperspace, counting down to their arrival at Koornacht Cluster.

"I don't like to make this long a jump into a hot zone," General A'baht said under his breath, shaking his head.

Captain Morano, captain of the Fleet carrier *Intrepid,* flagship of the Fifth Fleet, was the only one on the bridge close enough to A'baht to hear his words.

"A hot zone, General?" Morano asked. "The last report from our prowlers, before we left Coruscant, said that everything was quiet outside the Cluster. I thought we were going in to draw a line in the sky, nothing more."

"A lot can happen in three days, Captain." A'baht glanced up at the mission timers. "We'll know soon."

The task force would leave hyperspace as it had entered it, with the spacings, velocities, and timings all pre-

determined. Before leaving Coruscant, the Fifth had
dispersed into the widest formation the jump lanes to the
target coordinates would allow. The signal ferret had
jumped first, followed by the forward scouts and pickets,
then the well-spaced capital ships and their screens. No
change was possible en route. New Republic engineers
had still not found a solution for the hyperspace blackout. Once the jump began, the Fleet was committed.

So 106 sets of decisions had had to be made before
the Fleet moved out, and the number of possible solutions to that matrix was uncountable. Some solutions
were ideal for one tactical situation, and disastrous for
others. It was a guessing game, then a waiting game, and
A'baht hated the long hours with nothing to do but wonder if he had guessed right.

The worry, always, was that the tactical situation
might have changed. The worst version of that fear was
that the enemy might have learned the jump vectors from
spies or a prowler and prepared a deadly surprise.

That was why A'baht preferred to jump first to a
staging area, where he could pick up updated reports
from Fleet Intelligence and make any necessary adjust-
ments before a final jump to enter the target zone. By
doing so, he could shorten the window of opportunity
created by the blackout to an hour or less.

But caution had its price, and the price was paid in a
precious commodity—time. A'baht had been ordered to
take the Fifth back to Koornacht with all possible speed.

It was too late to help Polneye or New Brigia, but
Princess Leia and Admiral Ackbar wanted a quick show
of strength. Only that, it seemed, would discourage the
suddenly predatory Yevetha from eyeing Galantos,
Wehttam, or any other settlement outside the Cluster.
Captain Morano's figurative description, drawing a line
in the sky, was perfectly apt.

The final report from the prowlers General Solo had
left in Farlax Sector had shown no enemy ship activity
outside Koornacht, and very little traffic of any other

kind in the area—just a pair of tramp freighters and a gypsy scoop miner in more than a hundred cubic light-years of space. There had been no attacks on New Republic territory, no confrontations between New Republic and Yevethan forces. And the mission had begun in secure territory, the Coruscant system. The risks of a direct jump seemed small.

But there were always risks. *And no choice but to plunge through the door without knowing what is on the other side,* A'baht thought.

"Signal ferret reentry in ten," a tactical aide called out. "Nine. Eight—"

"Confirm alert level one," said Morano.

"Confirming," said the executive officer. "All defense systems ready to go active. Flash alert receivers are green. All weapons stations crewed. Flight Two and Flight Four are on the deck and hot, ready for immediate launch."

"Thank you, Lieutenant."

There was no outward sign that anything had happened when the count reached zero. Somewhere ahead of them, the tiny signal ferret and its complement of droids should have emerged into realspace and begun receiving and decoding any flash alerts and tactical updates from the Fleet Office. But they would not know if that had happened until *Intrepid* went through the door.

Another timer started counting down the short interval to the emergence of the pickets and scouts. The background murmur of activity on *Intrepid*'s bridge grew louder. Captain Morano turned away from the status displays on the viewscreen and crossed the bridge to his combat station, strapping himself into the flak couch. Shortly after, A'baht did the same.

"There go the pickets," Morano noted unnecessarily.

"How many combat jumps have you made, Captain?" A'baht asked quietly.

"Thirty-eight down in the roundhouse," Morano

said, referring to the combat operations center. "Nine on the bridge, all since the Empire fell."

"How many as captain?"

"Combat jumps? None."

"Then I suggest you begin telling yourself you've made a hundred."

"Why?"

"So that when your crew looks at you in the last seconds before we enter realspace, they will not see any reason to distract themselves with fear," said A'baht. "Whatever waits for us, whether princess or dragon, we are called to embrace it. I am mindful of a Dornean war prayer I heard my own mother offer—'I pray that my son does not die today. But if he should die, I pray that he dies well. But most of all, I pray that if he lives, it will not be dishonor which preserves him.' "

Captain Morano nodded. "Are you a betting man, General? Princess or dragon?"

The third and final timer was counting down toward zero. "Captain," said A'baht, "I am not certain I can always tell the difference."

All the major craft guilds had contributed to the processional car. The scale was grand, the lines flowing. The metalwork gleamed. The motor's hum was muted and musical. The mounting ladder was a wonder of design, its airily elegant treads and supports folding together and disappearing under the carriage the moment Nil Spaar's weight left it. The open cabin's cushions and wall panels were plush and finely embroidered with the shield of the Spaar clan, the symbols of the viceroy's house, the icons of auspicious blessing, and the glory-names of the Yevetha, all woven together in a design of spectacular beauty.

Even the car's driver and guards had been chosen to honor him. The driver was that rare genetic curiosity, a white-cast neuter—pale as the midday sky and neither male nor female. It sat tall and expressionless in the driver's crèche at the front of the car, a silent herald whose presence alone announced that a great man was coming. The guards were another curiosity: serial twins, grown from the same birth-cask and identical but for their ages. By tradition, serial twins were thought lucky, and able to pass that blessing at will by breath, touch, and blood.

"Proctor Raalk—" Nil Spaar said, looking down from the cabin at the small gathering in *Aramadia*'s ground-level loading bay.

The proctor of Giat Nor stepped forward. "Blessed."

"This pleases me greatly," Nil Spaar said. "See that the guildmasters know that their work was well received."

"Thank you, Blessed," said Ton Raalk, bowing his head gratefully.

Nil Spaar acknowledged the proctor's submission with a nod and a gesture. "I am ready. Driver, proceed."

The great curving doors ahead began to fan outward. As the gap widened, a sound filled the bay, a sound that grew moment to moment—the sound of voices suddenly raised in joy. Only part of the crowd could see the doors reopening, but the word spread quickly to those whose view was blocked.

As the car cleared *Aramadia*'s hull, Nil Spaar closed his eyes for a moment and drew a deep breath of the richly aromatic air. It seemed to him like the first breath in ages that was wholly free from the taint of the vermin. Even aboard ship, their impure stench seemed to cling to him, lingering in his nostrils like a reminder of their invasion of the All. It took the hot breezes of N'zoth to blow that contaminant away at last, just as it had taken the purifying fire of the fleet to rid the All of the vermin's poisonous presence.

Nil Spaar opened his eyes and stood, feeling renewed. There was a gripbar by his hand, but he had no

need of it. The processional car was accelerating so
gently and turning so smoothly as it glided across the
broad landing pad that he could hardly tell that it was in
motion.

The car circled *Aramadia* twice, affording the front
ranks of the crowd a glimpse of their hero and precipi-
tating two surges forward that the security forces met
with paralysis fields. Then the car headed down the wide
corridor leading to the city road. Nil Spaar sighed with
pleasure at the sight of Giat Nor ahead on the horizon.
The horror that was Imperial City faded from his memory. He was home.

As he passed down the corridor, the clamor from
the faithful beat at Nil Spaar from both sides. He looked
at their faces and saw rapture. He looked into their eyes
and saw soaring hope, profound gratitude, uncondi-
tional love.

"Stop," Nil Spaar suddenly called forward to the
driver. "Stop the car."

The vehicle eased to a stop as gently as a breeze dies.
The elder guard, in the forward crèche, was standing and
looking back at Nil Spaar with concern. "Is there a problem, Blessed?"

"No," said Nil Spaar. "There is something I wish to
do."

He opened the cabin's low door, and the mounting
ladder moved quickly into place to take his weight. At
the bottom, he walked toward the crowd on the right,
which fell eerily silent as he approached, struck mute by
the nearness of the Blessed. Signaling the car to follow,
Nil Spaar strode along the security line, appraising what
he saw beyond it.

Then he stopped and stepped closer to a young
nitakka, tall and strong, with a fine splay of crests and
ridges.

"You," Nil Spaar said, pointing. "Will you give
your blood to me?"

Surprise froze the *nitakka*'s expression, and then

wonder animated it. "Oh, yes, *darama*!" the young male cried, dropping to his knees without hesitation.

"Then come," Nil Spaar said, signaling the guards to pass him through the security line. When the *nitakka* was within reach, the viceroy lashed out and raked one cheek with his claw in a symbolic claiming, the bloody gash foreshadowing the sacrifice to come. The crowd chittered with a nervous excitement. The *nitakka* did not flinch.

"I accept your gift," Nil Spaar said. "Walk behind my car."

Then Nil Spaar turned away and crossed the pavement to the opposite side. The startled hush was dissolving quickly into noisy anticipation as the crowd began to guess his purpose. Ignoring the shouted pleas and offers, he walked parallel to the security line just as he had in selecting the *nitakka*. This time he looked only at the young females who still showed a mating ridge and the soft round bulge of a *mara-nas* carried high inside.

"You," he said at last, stopping and pointing at one. "Will you give your birth-cask to me?"

The *marasi* could not have heard his words over the screams of those around her, but she bowed her head and came to him all the same. With a claiming touch, Nil Spaar spun her around so that her back was to him and seized her head in the mating grip. She dropped to her knees without resistance, and he released her and stepped back, leaving her there.

"I accept your gift," he said. "Walk behind my car."

The processional car came forward and stopped for him, and Nil Spaar ascended once more to the open cabin. Once there, he spread his clenched fists wide, turned his face to the faithful, and roared the cry of the old imperatives, flesh and joy. They answered with the chant of grace to the All, as though approving his choices.

"Onward," Nil Spaar ordered the driver, then settled back into his seat. It was a profound power he had discovered, to know that his touch could change lives, his glance confer honor, his presence bring ecstasy, and his whim invite immediate gratification.

I shall have to be very careful not to let this distract me overly much, Nil Spaar thought as the car continued toward Giat Nor. *But it will be an agreeable enough distraction for the present.*

At a distance of half a light-year, Koornacht Cluster filled half the sky with a spectacular wash of stars and lit the hulls of the Fifth Fleet like a spotlight.

At the same time, local and hypercomm signals bombarded the vessels that had just emerged from hyperspace, lighting up stations all around *Intrepid*'s bridge.

"Captain, we have a priority one alert from the Fleet Office," the communications chief sang out. "Fleet Office has upgraded the conflict code to yellow-two. I have five, count five, attachments for General A'baht, security high."

Morano spun his chair toward the right. "Tactical—report!"

"All clear, Captain. Sensors report no targets. Pickets report no contacts. Prowlers report no contacts."

"Poll the task force."

"Polling them, sir." It was the first chance to discover whether any of the ships in the task force had been lost en route. "Picket *Wayfarer* and tender *Northstar* do not respond. All others reporting on station."

"Confirming that," called the task force coordinator. "Receiving notification that *Northstar* missed the jump due to navcomp failure, arrival now expected two-eight-forty. *Wayfarer* suffered hyperdrive failure at mission time oh-nine-sixteen and dropped out early. She's now under tow to Alland Yard for repairs."

"Scratch her from the list, Arky, and move *Vigilant* forward into that slot," A'baht said calmly.

"Aye, General."

"Tactical, update," Captain Morano called.

"Still clear, sir."

"Maintain active scanning." Morano turned to A'baht. "Nothing out there. Then why did they kick us up to yellow-two?"

"Let me have my attachments here, Comm," said A'baht, swinging a flat-panel display up and across in front of him.

The polarizers on the secure display guaranteed that Morano could not read it from where he sat, so he tried to read A'baht's face instead, with little more success.

"Interesting," A'baht said finally, returning the display to its recess. "The yellow-two is due to the fact that the Yevetha apparently knew we were coming."

"Then where are they?"

"Apparently they chose not to meet us," said A'baht. "Or to make any other aggressive moves, for that matter. All the inhabited worlds within ten light-years of here are reporting quiet skies."

"Well—that's good, eh? That's what we want, isn't it?"

"That's what the President wants," said A'baht. "I wish the Yevetha *were* here. I want a good look at their fleet. Chances are they're getting a good look at ours. Narth, what can we do to make it harder for them?"

The tactical aide rocked back in his chair. "Shuffle assets, rotate callsigns, hop and skip along the operational perimeter. I think we can keep them confused for a while, anyway. But it's hard to hide for long in the middle of nowhere."

"With all respect, General, the way I understood it, hiding was the last thing we were supposed to do out here," said Morano. "And that kind of maneuvering sends the chances of an operational accident way up. Remember the *Endor* and the *Shooting Star*?" The two Alliance frigates had collided after a mistimed jump, with the loss of all hands. "Let them get a good look at us, so they know what they're in for if they come out. If they have any sense at all, they'll see they don't want to tangle with us."

"It's much too early to know if the way they think qualifies for our definition of 'sensible,' Captain," said A'baht. "The viceroy of the Duskhan League had some very strong things to say while we were en route—some about us, some about Princess Leia, and all of it very public. You can hear for yourself—I passed that dispatch over to your queue."

A'baht looked out at the brilliant sprawl of stars. "They knew we were coming, and they don't want us here. Until we know just what they're capable of, I'm not going to be happy about sitting here. We're out in the open, and they're somewhere in the tall grass," he said. "You know how strategists are—no matter what their species."

Captain Morano sighed and glanced across at his own tactical team. "It's true—they're easily tempted. They can't resist trying to plan the knockout first strike," he said, and the tactical chief confirmed the truth of it with a guilty smile. "So how do we play this?"

With a practiced ease, A'baht unstrapped his restraints and stood. "We sit here and let 'em look, because that's what we've been asked to do. We move the prowlers as far forward as we dare and keep them moving along the perimeter. And we all work on being very, very watchful."

To himself A'baht added, *And then we hope the diplomats and politicians either work this out, or deal us a stronger hand—and soon.* "I'll be in my ready room, working up the entry report," he said. "Alert me the moment there's any change in the tactical situation."

In the privacy of his ready room, General Etahn A'baht learned that there were not five, but six attachments to the Fleet Office's flash update.

The sixth was an electronic hitchhiker. It had no identifying code and a length of zero. But when A'baht keyed in the code he had reluctantly and tediously memorized at Admiral Drayson's insistence, the attachment unfolded into a lengthy dispatch from Alpha Blue.

A'baht watched the images of the Yevethan colony ships landing on Doornik-319, of the Yevethan Star Destroyers over Polneye, of the burning fields at the Kutag factory farm, of the scorched valleys on New Brigia, and wondered why the Fleet Office had withheld them from him. All the important information had been in his update—that the Yevetha had Imperial-design Star Destroyers, that multiple colonies in the Cluster had been attacked by Yevethan forces, and so on—but it had been stripped of its reality, rendered as sterile, bloodless, and calculated as the raids themselves.

The Yevetha had swept across the bright stars of Koornacht with such black ferocity that the sterile battlefields could not properly bear witness to it. Their millions of victims now had only one face, that of the only known survivor—Plat Mallar, who had seen the fire come and barely escaped it on a foolish gamble. But the Fleet Office had kept Plat Mallar's face from A'baht as well. The reports called him simply "a Polneyan pilot," as if afraid to let him be seen as a brave young man who had lost everything, and whose words might prick a conscience or launch a cause.

"Recorder."

The little stenographic droid called SCM-22 trundled forward, twisting and turning within a circle twice its own diameter. "Optimizing," it said in a high, unmistakably artificial voice. "Ready."

"Record. Task force commander's entry report, append," said Etahn A'baht. "Personal to Admiral Ackbar: In my estimation, the present deployment of the Fifth Fleet is unlikely to be effective either as a deterrent to further aggression or in denying the Yevetha the benefits of their past aggression.

"Our presence at this position directly threatens no Yevetha assets and directly protects no friendly infrastructure. Nor can we effectively block a breakout with only a single Interdictor. The Yevethan fleet can go right over our head at any time, and we'd be left chasing them into the combat zone of their choosing."

He paused to collect his thoughts, idly tapping the bridge of his nose with the blunt tips of two fingers as he did. "It is my recommendation that vessels or detachments of vessels with combined combat ratings no less than strength three be sent to Galantos, Wehttam, and each of the other new protectorates," he continued. "This will make unmistakably clear what interests we're here to protect. It also may serve to remind the Yevetha that being able to reach these targets isn't the same thing as being able to have them.

"But we also need to try to make it harder for the Yevetha to reach them. The primary hyperspace nav routes out of the Cluster should all be under interdiction, and from as close a proximity to the Yevetha forward bases as possible.

"Astrographic analysis shows that there are no single-jump exit routes from N'zoth, Wakiza, and the other known interior worlds—the density of the Cluster makes things a little easier for us. But there are still too many ways out. We cannot blockade Koornacht from this position, with these assets. Do not allow anyone there to believe otherwise.

"With respect to the preceding recommendations, I formally request the following additional assets be attached to this command as soon as practicable: any and all available Interdictors. Any and all available prowlers. No fewer than four additional capital ships, frigate or above, for assignment to the protectorates—I don't want to pull anything back from here for that duty, lest we send the wrong message to the Yevetha.

"And, finally, we should be thinking about setting up a field supply and logistics center somewhere closer than Halpat. If our presence brings the Yevetha out, we're going to take losses, and I want something better than cold space for our casualties and cripples. A'baht, commanding, Fifth."

A'baht raised his eyes to the little droid. "That's it. Expand, end, and close."

"Done. Compressing—done. Encrypting—done. Ready for transmission."

"Send it," said A'baht, looking out his viewscreen at the curtain of stars and wondering if the predators concealed within were looking back out at him.

The north beach at Illafian Point, on the western shore of Rathalay's western sea, was wide, broad, and nearly deserted.

If it had been located on a recreation world like Amfar, or even anywhere in Coruscant's temperate zones, the chances were that the beach would have been bustling with activity and the dunes paved over with pleasure resorts. Humans were not the only species drawn almost worshipfully to the sun and the water.

But overlooked and underused had been exactly what Han had been looking for, and he was delighted by the long, empty expanses of gray basaltic sand. In more than two hours he had seen only two people, outside of the family. One was an older man prospecting along the water's edge for the tiny jewel-like shells of sea motes, who stopped to show the children the small handful of unbroken shells he had found. The other was a Thodian distance swimmer who had passed offshore, taking no notice of them at all.

Anakin, Jaina, and Jacen showed no sign yet that the novelty of playing in and along the sea was fading. None of them had ever seen a body of water so vast that it met the horizon, or one that was home to carnivores large enough to devour an adult in a few bites, and it made an impression on them. They allowed Han to tell them of the wreck of the starfreighter *Just Cause,* which lay nine hundred meters below the surface, its cargo of precious metals guarded by superstition and schools of razor-toothed narkaa. They even stood still for a visualization lesson from Leia, who asked them to imagine being creatures of the sea, looking on the land for the first time.

Then they were off to play, wading into the sea and leaving stories, lessons, and parents behind. Jacen was captivated by the idea of the narkaa and kept plunging below the surface in hopes of seeing one. Jaina loved the warm current flowing along the beach and said that floating in it and letting it carry her along made her feel as if she were flying. And even though the water was nearly as tranquil as Lake Victory, the little waves that broke at the shore and tumbled over themselves trying to climb up the beach proved a fascination to Anakin.

The only blemish in the picture was Leia. She was present in body but not in spirit. Her mind was on matters far removed from the beach—matters Han had brought her there to forget, at least for a time. Politics and diplomacy and statecraft and war were still taking her away from all of them. And Nil Spaar's reversal from potential ally to determined adversary was still an open wound.

"Dad?"

Han twisted his head toward Jaina, who had come up unnoticed to stand close enough to drip water on his leg. "I'm sorry, I can't rescue your brother from the narkaa," Han said, squinting. "I left my hero suit in the cabin."

Jaina just ignored his gibe, as she was wont to do when intent on her own business. "Jacen and I are going to go down the beach and look for sea motes. Okay?"

"Okay," he said. "But don't go out of sight. If you can't see me, I can't see you."

For a moment she gave him her impatient I-*know*-that-Dad look. But Jaina was learning not to throw away her victories, and said nothing more than a breezy "Thanks!" as she ran away to where Jacen waited.

Han's gaze flicked to Anakin, who sat at the edge of the water carving pools and rivers with his fingers for the waves to fill, then to Leia, who had gone twenty meters up the beach with her comlink. After a moment's hesitation, he bounced up from the sand cover and started toward her.

Leia's conversation ended before he was halfway to where she stood, so he heard none of it. He only saw her switch the comlink off and turn as if to come back to him. But when she saw him approaching, she waited for him there instead. "I'm sorry," she said, kissing him dutifully. "I didn't think that would take so long. Do you still want to go swimming?"

"You may as well tell me the news first."

"Admiral Ackbar says the Fifth has taken up station without incident. No sign of the Yevethan fleet."

"Good," said Han. "Maybe that business is over now."

"I don't think Nil Spaar makes empty threats. If anything, he understates them."

"Maybe he does, maybe he doesn't. I didn't kidnap you away from Imperial City so you could hold strategy sessions in a bathing suit."

"I know," she said, taking his hand as they started to walk. "Ackbar says that Senator Tuomi raised a challenge to my credentials this morning."

"Oh, here we go again—"

"Tuomi said the refugee population of Alderaan didn't constitute a state, and we're only entitled to non-voting membership and representation by a legate. And, of course, a legate can't be president of the Senate."

"Isn't that old news? Wasn't that issue settled when the Provisional Council was dissolved?"

"There are a lot of new members since then—Drannik is one of them. Members who weren't around when the Alderaan question was decided, who didn't have any part in the decision. I guess some of them want to have their say now."

"But can they actually *do* anything to you?"

"The Ministry Council could, in theory," she said. "But the chairman was a friend of my father's. I don't think he'll let this get very far."

Han shook his head. "I have to tell you, Leia—nothing makes my head hurt faster than trying to keep straight who's really in charge of what around here. It seems like every time I think I've got the gist of it, someone comes along to rename half the offices and rearrange the rest of them."

Leia laughed. "I guess it does seem that way sometimes. But you know that the first concern was to make sure there was never another Palpatine—to prevent any single person from acquiring too much power. Mon Mothma told me that the Senate worries more about success than failure. They'll tolerate ineffective leadership forever, but effective leadership frightens them."

"Which is nuts," said Han. "How is anyone supposed to get anything done in a system like that?"

"They're not. That's the whole point. No one's supposed to have the power that goes along with their responsibilities. I guess there are some in the Senate who think I've crossed that line," she said, clinging to his arm. "Ackbar said Behn-kihl-nahm would call me when all the shouting was over and tell me how many senators spoke in support of Tuomi's challenge."

Growling, Han snatched the comlink from Leia's other hand and broke away from her toward the water. After three long strides, he reached back and hurled the comlink out to sea with all the strength he could muster. It made a small white splash out beyond where the Thodian swimmer had been. A moment later, a sleek dark shape broke the surface near the splash, then slipped below again.

"Han!" Leia's tone carried both puzzlement and rebuke.

He turned back toward her. "I had to do it. It was trying to kill you."

"What?"

"Look at us. We're on vacation, for the first time in who can remember," Han said, slowly returning to her. "We're walking on a beautiful beach, hand in hand, with no kids climbing all over us—and we're talking about *politics*."

She sighed. "You're right. It's worse than I realized."

"Trust me. The New Republic won't fall if the President's out of touch for a day, or three. And they're not going to get that mess all cleaned up while we're gone— you'll get your share of mop and bucket time."

"Oh, *that's* comforting."

Han stopped and turned her toward him. "Leia, you've given them enough of you. Can't you give yourself—us—these few days? If this isn't where you want to be, or what you want to be doing with this time, tell me, and we'll do something about it. And if I have to take you farther from the castle to break the spell the Wizard of Duty laid on you—"

"Illafian Point is fine," she said. "It's beautiful here. And I doubt you could find a place that was any less like Imperial City."

"Then stop worrying already. Try to enjoy yourself. That's why you're here."

She started walking again and pulled him along with her. "I'll try. But you're going to have to be patient with me," she said. "I'm kind of new to this 'having fun' business."

"Oh?"

"Oh," she said. "Being a princess of the royal family of Alderaan was a pretty serious matter, all things considered. Bail Organa's idea of recreation was to take some subject you know nothing about and try to become an expert in it."

"You must have taken family vacations at drill school."

"Close. We'd go visit friends of my father, or have them as guests at the palace, and Bail would always be saying 'Leia, this is my old friend Farblemumble. There isn't anything he doesn't know about noodlefishing, and he's offered to teach you nineteen ways to make a trap net out of an old sweater—'"

Han was grinning broadly. "So that's why my clothes keep disappearing."

She poked him with a finger. "And then I skipped right over the part where I was supposed to be young and carefree—I was seventeen when I came here as a senator." She sighed weightily. "Oh, my stars—"

"What?"

"I just realized that I've been on Coruscant as long as I lived on Alderaan. A little longer, even." She shook her head. "Oh, I wish I hadn't realized that. I don't even *like* Coruscant that much, and now I've spent half my life there."

"Really—that much? Ever been to the Ice Crypts? Walked the mazes in the Trophill Garden in East Minor? Heard a performance in the Kallarak Amphitheater?"

"No," she said, and looked puzzled.

"I thought not. You don't know Coruscant, Leia. What you know is Imperial City. And mostly the inside of rooms, at that."

"You're right," she admitted. "I told you I wasn't strong on this 'fun' business. —Did I ever tell you my first impression of Imperial City?"

"I don't think so."

"I wrote my father that it looked like a colony of squibs had moved into the Queen's collection of braaken glass." Leia laughed quietly and slipped an arm around Han's waist. "Bail thought the braaken glass was hideous. He understood."

As they continued in an intimate silence, Leia cast

her gaze about her at the sea, the beach, and the sky. "This *is* nice, Han," she said, as Anakin looked up from his sand sculptures and came running toward them. "Thank you. I don't feel quite so much like one of the squibs out here."

Chapter 11

♦

"Admiral!" The nurse-medic saluted smartly. "Can I help you, sir?"

"I was informed that Plat Mallar has been removed from the bacta tank," said Admiral Ackbar, cocking his head slightly.

"Yes, sir—about two hours ago. He's doing well. Dr. Yintal was able to speak to him briefly."

"Where is Dr. Yintal now?"

"Emergency, sir. There was an accident out at Biggs Field, just a short time ago—"

"Yes," said Ackbar. "I know."

"Do you have any information about what happened, sir? All we've heard here are rumors—"

"A student in a TX-sixty-five missed his approach and crashed on a taxiway," Ackbar said. "Two other trainers and a command shuttle were hit by the debris. I have been told of three dead and sixteen injured."

"Thank you, sir. That gives us some idea what to get ready for up here."

"I will leave you to that in a moment," said Ackbar. "Did you say that Plat Mallar regained consciousness?"

"Just briefly, right after he came out of the tank. He

and Dr. Yintal exchanged a few words. But the prisoner's sleeping now."

"Mind your words—Plat Mallar is not a prisoner," Ackbar said sharply.

"I'm sorry, sir. I understood that he was an Imperial pilot, from an Imperial depot world—"

"You are mistaken," said Ackbar. "He is a brave young man who risked his life to try to help his people. And I have taken a special interest in his welfare. I expect him to receive the very best care this facility can offer—is that understood?"

"Yes, sir," the nurse-medic said contritely. "I understand, sir."

"I would like to see him now. Is he still in Unit Number Five?"

"Yes, sir. I'll take you there—"

"That is not necessary," Ackbar said. "See to your preparations."

The bacta tank in Intensive Care Unit #5 was vacant and drained. A young Grannan male lay in the IC bed nearby, monitor bands on his broad forehead, soft thorax, and left wrist.

Standing close by the bed, Ackbar leaned over the patient and studied him closely. Plat Mallar's fingers were drawn up short into his skin-cuff, and his eye crease was closed and sealed with a thin bead of a glistening secretion. A clear gas tube pumped methanogen into Plat Mallar's respiratory sacs; an opaque red tube carried his poisonous wastes away.

But his skin had regained the typical Grannan color and luster; despite the surroundings, he no longer appeared on the brink of death.

"Good," Ackbar said to himself. "Good."

Hoping that Plat Mallar's sleep was as restful as it appeared, Ackbar moved the self-adjusting chair over beside the bed, then settled his large body into it. Setting his comlink on the bed beside him where he could reach it quickly if called, Ackbar placed his hands on his knees in a familiar and comfortable posture.

"Sleep, little one," he said quietly. "Sleep and heal. When you are ready, I will be here."

Leaning forward across the control yoke, Han Solo peered sideways out the windshield at the steps leading to the main entrance to the General Ministry.

"Where are The Sniffer and The Shooter?" he asked Leia. "I don't see them. You didn't tell Nanaod you were coming back today, did you. Do you want me to come in with you?"

"No," she said, gathering up her robes so that she could climb out. "But I hope you'll be at home when I get there. I might need you then."

"We'll be there," Han said, nodding. "You sure you don't need me to come up, now?"

"I'm sure," she said. "I'm just going to go do what needs to be done, and we'll see what happens after that."

The entrance to the Grand Ministry had once been the reception entrance to the Imperial Palace. Forty polished stone steps led up to triple metal-mosaic doors sheltered under a great cantilevered stone awning edged with eight stars—symbols of the founding signatories of the Declaration of a New Republic.

The security monitors spotted Leia as soon as she stepped out of the speeder. A courtesy droid met her at the doors and opened one. Walking with long-strided purpose, she started down the main promenade, ignoring the expressions of surprise and whispers of curiosity she left in her wake.

By the time she was halfway down the main promenade, The Sniffer and The Shooter came running up from behind to join her. She did not break her stride, but continued into the General Ministry's central offices.

The office staff rose at once as she entered. An older

woman emerged from a back room and rushed forward to meet her.

"Madame President," said Poas Trell, the first administrator's executive aide. "We weren't told you were coming—the first administrator is over at the Senate this morning—"

"That's all right," said Leia. "No special preparations were called for. Where is the minister of state?"

"Minister Falanthas is meeting with the Vorkaan delegation. But I could have him paged—"

"No," said Leia. "That's not necessary either. Do you have the emergency petitions for membership?"

"The originals? Why, yes—they're in Minister Falanthas's secure file."

"I want them," said Leia. "And an endorsement tablet."

"Of course, Madame President. Won't you let me call the administrator and Minister Falanthas?"

"Completely unnecessary. They have their work to do, and I have mine," Leia said. "We'll use your staff conference room, if it's available. You can witness."

Plat Mallar stirred in the infirmary bed and made a noise that might have been a soft groan. Setting his datapad aside, Admiral Ackbar leaned forward and watched as the young Grannan's eye crease opened and his eyes sought to focus.

"Good morning," Ackbar said, patting Mallar's hand. "Don't be afraid. Do you know where you are?"

" 'ospital," Mallar said in a croak.

"Yes. You are in the New Republic Fleet Infirmary on Coruscant," said Ackbar. "And I am Ackbar."

Plat Mallar's eyes widened. "Cor'scant? How? I was—what about Polneye—what happened—"

"I will tell you everything, in time. Some of it is hard to hear," Ackbar said gravely. "But none of that matters today."

"Thought—I was dying," Mallar said. Each word was an effort.

"Today you start to live again. And, if you will allow me, I will be here to help you."

Mallar raised an unsteady hand a few centimeters and pointed. "Wha'r' you?"

"I am Mon Calamari," said Ackbar. "And you are Grannan. I have never met a Grannan before today. Have you ever met one of my people?"

Mallar shook his head slightly.

"Then perhaps we both can learn from each other."

"Uniform," Mallar said. "Wha'r' you? 'r'you my doctor?"

Ackbar glanced down at his battle dress. "I am just an old star pilot without enough sense to go home," he said, rising. "I'll bring your doctor now. He'll have more important things to talk about."

Poas Trell could not keep the frown off her face as she handed a seated Leia the stack of petitions. "Madame President, when you said that I could witness—"

"Do you have a problem with that?"

"Madame President, Minister Falanthas's aide alerted him to your arrival before I reached the office. He's on his way down now. Could I possibly impose on you to wait just a few minutes—"

"No," said Leia. "There's nothing to discuss. I have the authority to grant these requests, and I intend to do so. Where is the endorsement tablet?"

"My auxiliary is fetching one," said Trell. "It will be here shortly."

Leia raised a questioning eyebrow. "It looks like we've received some additional petitions."

"Yes, Madame President. There are twenty-three all told, eighteen from Farlax and five from elsewhere. The administrator and Minister Falanthas were discussing with Chairman Beruss a proposal that the four systems closest to the hostilities be placed in an accelerated approval process—"

"I can accelerate that process considerably if you'll just get that endorsement tablet in here."

Trell was openly squirming. "Princess, I'm very uncomfortable with this—"

"Are you questioning my authority to act on these petitions?"

"No, of course not, Princess Leia. I only thought you might see value to consulting with your senior ministers on your decision, and coordinate your timing with—"

"The endorsement tablet, please," Leia said firmly. "Or I take these with me to my own offices and deal with them there. And then I inform Nanaod that he will need to find a new executive aide, since the last one has been dismissed for insubordination."

Trell let her comlink slip down into her hand. Her fingers twisted the endpiece. "Faylee," she said evenly. "Have you located a tablet yet?"

A moment later the door to the staff conference room opened, and a clerk entered bearing an endorsement tablet. Trell nodded toward Leia, and the clerk placed the tablet on the table in front of her, then excused herself.

"Will you sit down?" Leia invited, indicating the chair opposite hers.

When Trell complied, Leia placed the first petition on the tablet and activated its recording system. The prism-shaped bulge at the top of the tablet contained three holo lenses—one to record the document itself, one to record the signer in the act of signing, and one to record the witness sitting opposite.

"President Leia Organa Solo, acting for the New Republic in the matter of the emergency petition of Galantos for membership," she said, taking up the endorsing stylus.

"Poas Trell, senior aide to First Administrator Engh, witnessing."

Leia signed the petition with a flourish. "Approved. President Leia Organa Solo, acting for the New Republic in the matter of the emergency petition of Wehttam for membership—"

When Leia reached the fifth document in the stack, Trell hesitated. "Do you mean to approve all the Farlax petitions?"

"I mean to approve all the petitions, period. Please continue."

Trell drew a long breath, thought something she decided not to say, and folded her hands on the table. "Poas Trell, senior aide to the first administrator—"

Minister Falanthas arrived just in time for Leia to hand him the stack of approved petitions as she left. "Good morning, Mokka," she said. "I'm sorry you were called away from your meeting for nothing. But since you're here, let me ask you to see that all the governments are notified as soon as possible. No, wait—do you happen to know if Councillor Jobath is still on Coruscant?"

"I believe he is at the diplomatic hostel."

"Then you can leave Galantos to me—I'd like to inform the councillor myself."

As she started to leave, Minister Falanthas looked down at the stack of documents in his hands, then up at Leia. "What should I tell Chairman Beruss?"

"Tell him that we've done the right thing," Leia called back to him. "Tell him we can move on to the hard decisions now."

"Dr. Yintal called you 'Admiral,' " said Plat Mallar as he and Ackbar walked slowly through the exercise garden in the courtyard of the Fleet infirmary. "He treated you like more than an old star pilot. He treated you like someone important."

"Dr. Yintal is unusually respectful for a doctor," Ackbar said. "How does it feel to be moving?"

"Better than it did to be in that bed," said Mallar. "Was I really in that tank for sixteen days?"

"I was there when you were brought in," said Ackbar. "You were terribly, terribly ill."

"Is a day here the same as a day on Polneye?"

"Just the same, I suspect—one sunset to the next," Ackbar said, and chuckled at his own joke. "Does Polneye still use Imperial System measures and the decimal clock?"

"Yes."

"A day here is fourteen hundred standard time parts long," Ackbar said. "You can adjust your expectations accordingly."

"That's shorter," said Mallar. "The Polneye day is eighteen hundred ST. Still, sixteen days—" His expression suddenly changed to one of worry. "How am I going to pay for all that?"

"You owe us nothing," said Ackbar. "Your care is a gift from the New Republic, one we are more than happy to give." He paused and gestured toward a nearby bench. "Would you like to stop for a while?"

"No," Mallar said, nodding. "It feels good to be walking."

"Then we will walk," said Ackbar, resuming his almost-shuffling pace.

"Dr. Yintal said he didn't know anything about what's been happening at Polneye," Mallar said after a time. "If you *are* an admiral, does that mean you might know more?"

"I'm afraid the last report we have from Polneye is yours," Ackbar said. "We have not been able to raise them, or to send a scout in."

"In sixteen days? Why not?"

"Plat Mallar, you must try to prepare yourself for the idea that you are the only survivor of that horrible attack," said Ackbar.

"But Ten South was still standing—and there was a transport on the ground—"

"We have analyzed the recordings from your interceptor," Ackbar said. "The transport was being loaded with droids and other equipment. I'm afraid there is little foundation for hope."

Mallar fell silent for more than half a lap around the courtyard. "Who did it?" he asked at last. "Can you at least tell me who killed my family?"

"The attack was carried out by the Yevetha," Ackbar said.

"The Yevetha?" Mallar asked, indignant. "Who are the Yevetha?"

"They are a species native to Koornacht Cluster. They were enslaved by the Empire but seem to have stolen the Empire's technologies, and perhaps a substantial battle fleet as well. Several other colonies were attacked at the same time. Our information is far from complete, but you are, in fact, the only known survivor."

"What are you doing about them?"

"We have taken steps to protect the other inhabited worlds near Koornacht," said Ackbar. "We are still looking at what we can do to respond to the Yevethan aggression."

"What I saw wasn't aggression," said Mallar. "It was murder. It was nothing but calculated butchery."

"Yes," Ackbar said, nodding. "It was."

"Then I don't understand. Is what I've heard about the New Republic wrong? You deposed the Emperor because of the injustices under his rule. You stood up against the whole Imperial Navy over principle. Is that true, or propaganda?"

"It is true."

"And you still have a great fleet of your own?"

"Yes."

Mallar stopped and turned to Ackbar. "Will you use it?"

"That decision is in the hands of the civil government," Ackbar said. "I do not know what they will decide."

"Why is this so difficult?"

"You may not understand this, Plat Mallar, but it is not easy to rouse a democracy to war," said Ackbar. "Not unless it has been attacked directly. Everything must be discussed. The provocation must be more compelling than the politics. And it always takes time." Ackbar shook his head. "Sixteen days is not enough time."

"What do you think will happen? Tell me what you honestly believe," said Mallar. "It's important."

Ackbar nodded. "I believe that, in the end, we will call the Yevetha to account. But there will be an ugly fight here first."

"Thank you," Mallar said. "Do you know when I can leave the hospital?"

"Whenever Dr. Yintal is satisfied with your recovery," said Ackbar. "I would think another day at least. Do you have plans already?"

"Yes," said Plat Mallar. "I'm going to volunteer to join your pilot corps. When you call the Yevetha to account, I want to be part of it. That's the only thing that matters to me now. That's all there is that's worth doing."

By the time Leia reached the executive suite on the fifteenth level of the Ministry Center, Alole and Tarrick were standing and talking just inside the suite's reception entrance, inconspicuously positioned to either greet or intercept her. Alole's face lit up as she turned toward Leia.

"Princess—we just heard that you were back."

"I'll bet you heard," said Leia with a wry smile. "How are you, Alole?"

"I'm fine, Princess."

"Tarrick?"

"Very well, Madame President."

"Then is there any reason we can't go inside and get to work?"

"None at all," Tarrick said, breaking into a smile.

Once in Leia's private office, both the formality and the familiarity quickly passed. "So—how does the damage look from your end of the lifeboat?"

"Better now that you're here again," Tarrick said.

"We've been having some trouble with the steerage," Alole said.

"Oh?"

"A lot of people trying to grab the wheel."

Leia nodded. "How long is my hot list?"

"Manageable," Alole said. "We've been handling everything we could on our own. But Nanny is pretty insistent on seeing you at the earliest opportunity."

"I'll keep that in mind," Leia said. "Alole, please call over to the Senate and see if Bennie has any time for me today."

"Right away," Alole said, fading back toward the door. "Your hot list is on your datapad."

"Thank you," Leia said, pulling the datapad toward her. "Tarrick, see if you can find Councillor Jobath and coax him in. Tell him I have news for him."

"He's been calling us every morning for a fortnight," the aide said with a lazy grin. "I think I can get him here."

Alole had paused at the door. "Princess—"

Leia looked up from the device. "Yes, Alole?"

"It's good to have you back."

"Run a tally sheet," Leia said. "I'm betting yours is the minority opinion."

Entering with a smile, Behn-kihl-nahm embraced Leia, then turned and closed the door to the President's reception lounge. "How are you, Princess?"

"Better," she said. "How am I, Bennie?"

Selecting the largest of the chairs, the chairman of the Defense Council made himself comfortable before answering. "You are safe for the moment. You still have the support of five of the seven Council chairs. There is no serious talk of convening the Ruling Council to consider a petition of no confidence."

"That sounds better than I had reason to hope. Who are the contraries? Borsk Fey'lya?" The opportunistic Bothan headed the Justice Council and had always been cool to Leia, not least because of her friendship with Ackbar.

"Of course," Behn-kihl-nahm said. "There's no possible advantage to him in supporting you—but if the tide turns, he has positioned himself as the leader of the opposition. Since Justice has no real responsibility for either war or diplomacy, Fey'lya is free to play both the inside game and the outside game."

"How so?"

"For now, the malcontents of the Senate will gather around him, simply because he stands taller than they do. He need not even promise them anything, though they may end up thinking he has. And when the grids come looking for what they call balance, he can be as provocative as he pleases."

"You're saying that I'll have to get accustomed to the sound of his voice."

"Whenever you are the subject of the grids' attention, there he will be. In a month, perhaps two, if it should happen that you *were* removed, he will have acquired enough power and status to have a chance at becoming acting President."

Leia nodded, frowning. "Surely you'd be in a stronger position than he would."

"In this scenario, I would be fatally damaged by having been your champion in a losing cause," said the chairman. "If you are recalled, whether by the Senate or the Ruling Council, they will not turn to me to replace you."

"And if I resigned now?"

Behn-kihl-nahm wriggled his shoulders, settling deeper into the chair. "There is no reason for you to do so—or even to contemplate it."

"You wouldn't be tainted," she pressed. "And he wouldn't have had a chance to enlarge his power bloc."

"We are already where we belong, you and I," said Behn-kihl-nahm. "There's no need to speak of change. It is an unnecessary distraction."

"I'll try to remember that when Borsk Fey'lya speaks of it from the Senate podium," Leia said. "Who's the other chairman to side with Fey'lya?"

"Chairman Rattagagech is the other, but I would not say he has sided with Chairman Fey'lya," Behn-kihl-nahm said.

On hearing the name, Leia immediately understood the reason for her mentor's distinction. The scholarly, thoughtful Elomin, who headed the Science and Technology Council, was in most respects the antithesis of the boisterous Bothan. "Do you know anything about his reasons?"

"As you would expect," Behn-kihl-nahm said. "The Elomin love order. After the events of the last few weeks, he views you as a font of social and political chaos rather than as a force for stability and order."

"I suppose I can hardly blame him for that," Leia said. "Is anyone teetering?"

"Chairman Praget has expressed some ambivalence to me," said Behn-kihl-nahm, naming the head of the Security and Intelligence body. "Of course, this is only the present. Much depends on what you do next. There is very little enthusiasm for war. Too aggressive a course could easily swing two, perhaps even three other members of the Council to support a petition of no confidence. And then there would be no protecting you from a vote by the Senate common."

"How much enthusiasm is there for justice?"

Behn-kihl-nahm shrugged. "Indifferent. The deaths

of strangers, conveniently out of sight in Koornacht Cluster, do not weigh heavily against the prospect of the deaths of patriotic Republic pilots and fighting on peaceful Republic worlds. There are some who find a cause in these events, but more, perhaps, who see only a political crisis."

"Which reminds me," Leia said. "What became of Senator Tuomi's challenge to my credentials?"

"Over. Forgotten. Chairman Beruss squashed it under a procedural mountain. And I was able to limit the parade to the podium to ten speakers."

"How many more would there have been if you hadn't shown up at the end of the line brandishing an ax?"

Behn-kihl-nahm waved away the question. "It's simply noise to be ignored. The more important question concerns the future. What do you plan to do about the Yevetha?"

"What are we strong enough to do?" Leia asked. "What options are there that don't lead to handing the presidency to Fey'lya or Praget or Cion Marook?"

"Perhaps you might consider the question of what *should* be done, and then we can work together on surviving it."

"What should be done—" Leia shook her head. "What we *should* do is drive the Yevetha back to N'zoth, then drop a planetary interdiction field over them, with the timer set for a thousand years. And that would probably be too light a sentence by half."

"You are kinder than I," said Behn-kihl-nahm. "The only justice I can imagine would be for them to suffer the sentence they imposed on *their* victims. Of course, that's impossible—for us to do such a thing would violate every principle in the Declaration." He plunked a bitter candy from the bowl on the side table. "But I could stand by and watch while someone else did it."

"You're stronger than I," Leia said. "I think I would have to look away."

Behn-kiln-nahm made the candy disappear with a snap of his jaws. "But while we are waiting for this avenger to appear—"

"Maybe I should meet with the Defense Council and get a sense of how far we're willing to go."

"I would rather see you come to the Council on a quest than with a question."

"If I come before them and insist that we have to use the Fifth Fleet to spank the Yevetha, every one of them will remember what Tig Peramis said about why we built that fleet, and what Nil Spaar said about my heritage. If we're going to do anything that risks the lives of those who wear New Republic uniforms, the initiative has to come from the Defense Council."

Behn-kihl-nahm shook his head. "There is no way it can come from anyone but you."

"Then it isn't going to happen," Leia said flatly. "Nil Spaar tied my hands. Senators Hodidiji and Peramis gave him the rope. And I stood still for it, because he was smiling while he did it."

"This decision does not have to be about Leia Organa Solo."

"How can it be about anything else?"

"It could be about Plat Mallar," said the chairman. "He could become the symbol of your cause."

Leia was shaking her head even before Behn-kihl-nahm finished speaking. "I will not use him," she said. "I won't exploit his tragedy. If the execution of a million or more sentient beings, the destruction of a dozen planetary communities, isn't enough—if the members of the Council need a living victim paraded in front of them to move them to act—then shame on them. And shame on us."

Making as to leave, Behn-kihl-nahm stood. "Shame is a scarce commodity in politics," he said, brushing down his clothes. "And there are more politicians than statesmen on Coruscant now."

"I don't want to believe that."

"Nevertheless, it is so. Think this through carefully, Princess. You will get only one chance to lead them," the chairman said. "If you forfeit it, you will have no choice but to follow where *they* lead. And I cannot promise you that they will choose an agreeable destination."

The hypercomm link showed nothing but static until General A'baht entered the decryption code Admiral Hiram Drayson had obliged him to memorize. Several seconds later—longer than the usual hypercomm transmission lag—the static resolved into the face of the Alpha Blue director.

"General A'baht," said Drayson with a nod. "Thank you for making yourself available—"

"Drayson," A'baht growled. "Perhaps *you* can explain what is going on back there."

"You may be hoping for too much," said Drayson. "This is Coruscant, after all. Which peculiarity in particular concerns you?"

"I requested additional support within the first hour of our arrival on station," A'baht said. "All I have heard in reply is silence. 'Under review by the Fleet Office Strategic Command,' I am told. But not one member of the command staff has contacted me."

"Strategic Command is waiting for guidance from higher levels," Drayson said. "Until those issues are resolved, I don't think you can expect any reinforcements—unless you should happen to come under direct attack."

"How long is it going to take to find some resolve?" A'baht said. "I've been forced to detach ships from the Fifth for Wehttam and Galantos. The other neighboring systems are still unprotected. And every day we sit out here patrolling empty space, the Yevetha dig in deeper on the worlds they took. We can't reward them for their aggression. We must do something to punish them."

"I am not the one who needs convincing."

"Then who is? Our presence is accomplishing nothing. By this time, the Yevetha must know that the Fleet is an empty threat."

"The Princess wants to do the right thing," said A'baht. "She will need our help to see that the right thing gets done."

"What kind of help?"

"You need to find more graphic evidence of the Yevethan atrocities," Drayson said. "Without it, Princess Leia will not be strong enough to overcome the resistance of the Senate."

A'baht drew his lips back in a silent snarl. "I don't know that we can do more than we have. I've put prowlers right up to the border, even a little beyond. Our sensing technology simply can't give us anything at that range. I'm having a difficult enough time getting good tactical information, much less documenting the massacres."

"I trust you're persisting, even though it's difficult."

"If you're asking whether the ferrets and prowlers are still out, the answer is yes," said A'baht. "But it's too late now for what you ask. From the looks of what you sent me, the Yevetha didn't leave much evidence behind. And why isn't what you have already enough for Leia?"

"It's not a matter of what Leia has or hasn't seen," said Drayson ambiguously. "It's a matter of what she's free to show the Senate. If she offers them independent intelligence, something that doesn't come from the NRI or the Fleet, the meaning of what she shows them will get lost in the questions about its origin."

"*I* have questions about its origin," A'baht said gruffly. "You have to have had assets inside Koornacht to get those holos—assets which were either in place undetected, or which could move fast enough to arrive before the fires were out. I would very much like to know what manner of ferret could accomplish that."

"And those are exactly the questions Leia cannot be asked," said Drayson. "She needs intelligence with a good, clear, and perfectly ordinary pedigree. General, I suggest you place a ferret in Zone Nineteen."

"Zone Nineteen?" A'baht consulted his tactical map. "That's a third of the way around the Cluster toward the Core—far outside the area we've been patrolling."

"Then I suggest you widen your patrol area."

"Why?"

"It so happens that Zone Nineteen sits on the line-of-sight vector connecting Wakiza and Doornik Three Nineteen, the Yevethan forward base. I think you may have an opportunity to acquire some signal intercepts with the hypercomm scanners."

"Yevethan signals?"

"Of course."

A'baht grunted expressionlessly. "And when might this opportunity arise?"

"Oh—I suspect there's a great deal of traffic between those sites," Drayson said lightly. "I wouldn't be surprised if you picked up something in the first few hours you were there."

"Which I'd be obliged to forward immediately to the Fleet Office."

"Of course."

"Will it get to Leia from there?"

"In fairly short order, I would think."

A'baht nodded. "It just might be that we've shown the Yevetha this patrol deployment long enough. If I extend the perimeter patrols by half, maybe it'll make 'em stop and wonder why."

"Thank you for considering my input, General," said Drayson, smiling genially. "Oh, and one other thing—"

"What is that?"

"Since there are probably still some days, even weeks, of work left to do at this end, perhaps you might consider whether you can spare a smaller vessel for each of the other inhabited systems."

"I'm convinced that nothing smaller than a frigate could withstand an initial Yevethan attack, and I have no more ships of that class to spare," said A'baht.

"You're right, of course," Drayson said. "A corvette or patrol escort probably wouldn't discourage the Yevetha, and certainly wouldn't be able to repel them. I only thought there might be some symbolic value in their presence—"

A'baht suddenly understood what Drayson was saying. —*Unless we should happen to come under direct attack, you say. And so you would like me to bait the Yevetha with an easy victory.*

"The only thing worse than leaving those populations unprotected is giving them an illusion of safety," A'baht said curtly. "And the only thing worse than asking men to risk their lives on your word is sending them into a fight you know they can't win. My pilots and crews are not symbols, Admiral Drayson. And I won't betray them by reducing them to that."

"I understand those feelings, General," Drayson said. "I share them. But I invite you to consider whether your status there is any different than that of an escort orbiting Dandalas or Kktkt. If the Yevetha attack your formation, many issues would be simplified."

"Are you saying that we were sent here to draw the Yevetha into a war?"

"I am saying that you may decide for yourself how much of your arm to place in the rancor's mouth," Drayson said. "Zone Nineteen, General. Whatever else you decide, please keep that rendezvous."

The on-site recruiting office at Fleet Headquarters was next to the main gate, a long walk from the infirmary. Mindful of the physical exam, Ackbar had been unable to persuade Plat Mallar to wait until morning. But the energy in Mallar's long strides on the way over had seemed to vindicate Dr. Yintal's judgment that the Polneye survivor could be released.

When they reached the small white dome with the Fleet insignia, Ackbar lost a second argument, this one over whether he would accompany Mallar inside.

"I have to go in there without anyone holding my hand," Mallar had said. "It's important to me. I don't want any pity, or any special favors from friends of old star pilots."

"As you wish," Ackbar had said, acceding to the stubborn will of the young Grannan. He settled in a waiting area ordinarily occupied only by civilians and let himself be amused by the surprised recruitment staffers falling over themselves to salute him.

Mallar was gone for the better part of an hour, but the process should have taken two. And when he returned, he looked worse than ill—his eyes were as empty as a discarded chrysalis, all the life having left them. Ackbar rose quickly and hurried to him.

"What's wrong?" he demanded. "Never mind— there's a speeder at the guard station. Come, I can have you back to the infirmary in a twinkling."

"I was turned down," Mallar said, his expression stunned and wondering.

"For pilot training?"

"For anything. For everything. He rejected me. They won't let me volunteer for *any* duty."

"That's absurd," Ackbar said. "Stay here."

Leaving a wake of unanswered salutes behind him, Ackbar stormed through the screening room and past the interview rooms to the office of the recruiting supervisor.

"Admiral Ackbar?" the supervisor said, rising from his chair in surprise as Ackbar entered unannounced. "Sir," he added, and saluted smartly.

"Major, one of your recruiters just processed an applicant named Plat Mallar," Ackbar snapped. "I want that person in this room now, to answer some questions."

"Right away, Admiral." The supervisor bent over his comlink and barked out an order. "I'm terribly sorry if there's been some mix-up, Admiral—"

The arrival of a tall human lieutenant interrupted the apology, as Ackbar turned away and ignored the major completely.

"What's your name?" Ackbar demanded, noting the Corellian insignia in the place above the right pocket reserved for an affiliation pin.

"Lieutenant Warris, sir."

"Would you care to explain to me your actions regarding Plat Mallar?" he asked.

The recruiter looked momentarily taken aback. "Sir, I don't understand. He was unqualified," Warris said.

"Unqualified?"

"Yes, sir," Warris said. "The guidelines clearly specify that an applicant's primary education must be through a certified school or program. Plat Mallar's program isn't even listed in the system."

"Of course it isn't, you dunderhead—did you happen to notice where he's *from*?"

"Yes, sir. But that's another problem, sir. He's ineligible to join the Fleet—he's not a citizen of the New Republic. In fact, it's worse than just not being a citizen—he's a citizen of Polneye, a planet that's still officially listed as aligned with the Empire. I couldn't possibly pass him through the interview, sir." The recruiter looked to the major for help. "Are there special circumstances I wasn't made aware of—"

"Admiral, Lieutenant Warris is quite right on the procedures," the major said. "If this applicant doesn't have a verifiable citizenship record with a member world, we can't even consider him."

"Bureaucratic nonsense," Ackbar raged, his voice

rising on a wave of righteous indignation. "Whatever happened to taking the measure of a man's courage, his honor—the fight in him, and the reasons in his heart? Do they all have to be as stamped-and-pressed alike as stormtroopers to get your approval?" He dismissed the recruiter with a wave. "Get out."

Grateful to be excused, Warris retreated as Ackbar focused his attention on the supervisor.

"Admiral, we could certainly reconsider the application if you could just give us the context for your concern—"

"The context," Ackbar repeated disbelievingly. "It's not enough that a man is willing to put on a uniform and fight alongside people he's never met, just because he shares an ideal with them—no, his offer must come from the right context, and his school papers must be in order, and his arms not too long, and his blood type stocked in the combat medivacs." Ackbar shook his head in disgust. "How things have changed. I can remember when we were glad for anyone willing to fight beside us."

"Admiral—there have to be standards—"

The major's tone was placating, and Ackbar did not wish to be placated. "Major, ask yourself how many of the everyday heroes of the Rebellion—not just the names everyone knows—would have qualified to fight for their freedom under your rules," Ackbar said, leaning in. "And then ask yourself if that answer doesn't make you look just a bit like a dewback's cloaca." Then Ackbar turned and stalked out of the office without waiting for a reply, much less a salute.

Halfway down the corridor, Ackbar's outburst was already making him feel a touch foolish. But what he found when he reached the waiting area left him feeling a deep sadness.

For Ackbar found that all the seats in the waiting area were empty. Seemingly crushed by the rejection, Plat Mallar had not waited for him. Without a word to clerk or guard, the young survivor had left the recruiting office, exited through the main gate, and faded away into the city.

Ackbar turned to the gate guard and pointed. "I'm going to need that speeder."

Chapter 12

◆

From experience on Coruscant and Mon Calamari both, Admiral Ackbar knew that the line that divided the inner circle from the outer circle in any government was access. If you were part of the inner circle, you could see the President simply by walking down a private corridor and through the back doorway into her office; when you called, the President spoke to you directly; when you transmitted a letter, you got a personal response.

Ackbar had enjoyed that status throughout Leia's tenure in the top office, first as chief of state under the Provisional government, then as President of the New Republic. Even under her comparatively open administration, that placed him in select company.

The private door was open to Han, of course. And Mon Mothma, who had chosen to distance herself from the Palace since her close call with an assassin led to her giving up the office. Nanaod Engh, who had not quite become a friend, but whose duties made him an everyday visitor. Behn-kihl-nahm, though he was too well-mannered not to observe the protocols of high office. Tarrick and Alole. And Ackbar.

Or so it had been before the Yevethan matter had

escalated to a crisis. But Ackbar had been jarred by the discovery that he was locked out of the President's residence, his key disabled, his status as a member of the family suddenly withdrawn. So he had chosen to approach the President's suite on level fifteen through the front door, and tried to prepare himself for another rebuff.

But the security guards outside the suite made no move to stop Ackbar, and though the staff inside showed some slight surprise at seeing him there, no one moved to bar him from the back rooms.

"Good morning, Admiral," Alole said, looking up from her greatdesk with a smile. "Go right on in—she's in her conference room, reviewing last week's Senate debate."

When he reached the doorway from the office to the conference room, Ackbar hesitated. Leia was standing at the end of the room with her back to him, hugging herself as she looked up at her holoviewer. The image on the screen was of Senator Tuomi. His tone was earnestly reasonable, his words subtly inflammatory.

"Is this door still open to me?" Ackbar's voice boomed in the confined space.

Leia turned away from Tuomi only long enough to steal a look back over her shoulder. "If you didn't have to shoot your way past Tarrick, then the door's still open."

"I shall try to remember to take a cue from the presence of weapons in the reception area."

Pausing the playback of the recording, Leia turned toward Ackbar. "Did you really think you might not be welcome here?"

"We have not had a chance to talk since you returned, and we only spoke once while you were away—a short and businesslike conversation, as I recall," Ackbar said. "Before that—well, I am not sure that I would have been included in the meeting the night of the pirate broadcast if it had been convenient to exclude me. I have been afraid to try my key again."

"Then you haven't seen Han, either? I told him to tell you it was fixed. And here I thought it was me you were avoiding," Leia said, coming to where he stood and hugging him. "I can't stay angry at you for long. And besides—you're one of the few people I've told myself I have to keep listening to, even when I am angry at you."

Patting Leia on the back with one large hand, Ackbar sighed. "That is good to know."

"I've missed you," she said, easing out of the embrace. "Anakin misses you. No one on the staff's caught sight of you for days. What have you been up to?"

"I have been preoccupied," Ackbar said, and gestured toward the viewer. "Why are you bothering with this? It can't be pleasant to hear yourself be talked about that way, and I cannot see the use of it."

Leia glanced back over her shoulder at Tuomi's face. "I suppose I have a morbid curiosity about whether anything is considered out of bounds."

" 'Greed has no limits, envy no boundaries, in the heart of a petty man.' A favorite quote from Toklar, a much-quoted Mon Calamari philosopher," Ackbar added.

"Was he also the one who said, 'Don't look back—something may be gaining on you'?" Leia asked lightly.

"I do not believe so," Ackbar said. "But Toklar did write, 'One sting is remembered longer than a thousand caresses.' For every voice that supported Tuomi's challenge, there were a hundred saying it was foolish, unjust, and cruel. Listen to them instead."

"I'm not offended for myself," Leia said, pointing her controller at the holoviewer and ending the projection. "But it's hurtful to those of us who are left to hear Alderaan spoken of that way. And it seems as though suddenly everyone's finding reasons to object to my being here."

"People find what they look for," said Ackbar. "Look to their motives, not their words."

"Tuomi says that his motive is justice," Leia said with a shrug. "Alderaan is a nation of refugees, sixty thousand people with no territory except for our embassies here and on Bonadan. Tuomi represents five inhabited planets and nearly a billion citizens. Why should Alderaan rule Bosch, he asks."

"But you do not lead us for Alderaan. You lead us for the New Republic."

"In which Alderaan is a member only due to misguided pity, according to Tuomi."

"Tuomi is an ignorant fingerling," Ackbar said with sharp contempt. "Alderaan's membership is neither a courtesy nor a violation of the Charter. The New Republic is an alliance of peoples, not planets."

Leia nodded an acknowledgment. "Something often forgotten, even here."

"Then I will presume to remind you that the structure of the New Republic was crafted to avoid dominance by the most populous worlds—to prevent what Kerrithrarr called a tyranny of fecundity," Ackbar said.

Leia laughed tersely, tossing her hair. "I remember that argument."

"Perhaps you remember another quote I am fond of," Ackbar said. " 'Today, we become a galactic family—a family of the great and the small, the young and the old, with honor to all and favor to none.' "

Leia recognized the words from her own Restoration Day address. "That's cheating."

"I trust you still believe what you said then."

"Of course I do."

"Then it does not matter if Alderaan now means sixty thousand, or six hundred, or six."

"No," agreed Leia. "The exact number matters only to the assessors and accountants. Our claim to membership is valid, and just, and moral—regardless."

"I am glad to hear you say that," Ackbar said, and

dug into a large flap pocket in his belt. "I have brought something here for your endorsement." He unfolded a single sheet of pale blue document vellum and handed it to her. "That is an emergency petition for membership for Polneye, offered by its representative on Coruscant."

Leia eyed Ackbar questioningly as she circled the table toward the window. "I think I've been manipulated."

"This claim, too, is valid, and just, and moral—regardless."

"Is there any reason at all to think that anyone else on Polneye survived the Yevethan assault?"

"There is no evidence either way," said Ackbar. "Why does it matter?"

"If Plat Mallar wants to sit in the Senate—"

"Plat Mallar wants to sit in the cockpit of a fighter. The Senate seat for Polneye will remain vacant, unless other survivors are found—as a reminder."

"I see your handprints all over this, Ackbar."

"I am trying to help the boy," Ackbar admitted. "But he has his own mind."

"Let me ask a different question," Leia said. "Have you made him aware of the offer from Jobath of Galantos, for sanctuary and membership in the Fia?"

"Plat has spoken with Jobath."

"And?"

"In the days after Alderaan was destroyed, how would you have looked on an invitation to become a citizen of Lafra or Ithor?"

Leia placed the vellum on the table and bowed her head, pressing her palms together and touching her fingertips to her mouth. "I'm being roundly criticized already for the applications I approved when I came back."

"If that's so, then one more can hardly make any difference," said Ackbar. "But it will make all the difference in the world to the Polneya. And I must add this—

for whatever it may be worth to you, I was proud of you for what you did."

Frowning, Leia leaned forward and rested her hands on either side of the document as she studied it intently. "You know," she said slowly, "I felt pretty good about it, too." She keyed her comlink with the remote. "Alole—bring me an endorsement tablet, please. Admiral Ackbar has called my attention to an application that was overlooked."

Belezaboth Ourn, extraordinary consul of the Paqwepori, paced restlessly in the sleeping chamber of his cottage in the diplomatic hostel.

For the tenth time, he checked to see that the tiny blind box the Yevethan viceroy had provided him was properly attached to the much larger hypercomm relay. That was the extent of Ourn's ability to determine whether there was some technical reason why, five hours after sending an urgent request to speak with Nil Spaar, he was still pacing and waiting.

And Belezaboth Ourn did not like being kept waiting.

His ship's engineer had examined the sealed box with all the means at his disposal, but after a discharge from the box had destroyed his test instruments, the engineer had returned it with a shrug. All Ourn really knew is that with the blind box attached, the hypercomm conversed with it, and the box conversed with a Yevethan hypercomm at an unknown location.

Muttering an imprecation against Nil Spaar's fertility, Ourn called for a toko bird and a slaughter knife to be brought to him. He had been stuck on Coruscant for weeks now, unable to leave, waiting on the viceroy to keep his promises. He was not about to let himself be stuck in his room, unable to eat, waiting on the viceroy to answer his calls.

Mother's Valkyrie was still sitting on the landing

pad where it had been battered by the departing Yevethan thrustship *Aramadia*. With the mission short of funds, Ourn had refused to authorize repairs, expecting to sell the cutter as scrap when the ship Nil Spaar had promised him was delivered. Then spaceport ground crews had covered *Valkyrie* with a bubble-like lien seal when the unpaid berth fees mounted.

It was embarrassing to have the Paqwepori consular ship sitting there under a debtor's lock for everyone to see. It would be humiliating to have to stand in line to leave Coruscant on a shuttle. And it was unthinkable for the delegation to return home penniless aboard one of the rattletrap commercial liners that came calling at Paqwepori.

There was only one acceptable resolution, and Ourn clung to it unwaveringly. Nil Spaar must keep his promise of a Yevethan thrustship in payment for the damage to the *Valkyrie* and other services Ourn had rendered to Nil Spaar. Then the delegation could leave Coruscant not only in grand style, but in such a way that everyone would know that the Paqwepori had powerful friends.

The only troubling matter was that Nil Spaar was so often unavailable when Belezaboth Ourn tried to reach him. The last two times he had called with information, Ourn had been relegated to speaking to underlings. And his three attempts since deciding to withhold what he knew and insist on speaking directly with Nil Spaar had gone completely unanswered.

For this, the fourth, Ourn had baited the hook, leaving a message that he had information about important developments near Koornacht. But, still, he had been waiting five hours.

The toko bird and a response from the Yevetha arrived at the same time, and Ourn rudely chased the former away so that he could receive the latter. To his delight, the face that appeared was Nil Spaar's.

"Belezaboth Ourn," Nil Spaar said. "What is that sound?"

The toko bird's squawking over being rejected was still audible from the outer room. "Viceroy! An honor and delight to have a chance to speak to you again. Disregard the noise—it is a wild animal outside, nothing more. What news do you have for me? Is there any further word on delivery of my ship?"

Ourn thought he saw regret in the Yevethan's expressive eyes. "Consul, this has become a matter of great awkwardness," Nil Spaar said. "My people and yours are nearly at war—"

"No, not our people!" Ourn said, dismayed. "Why, there is not a single Paqwepori citizen in the New Republic's armed forces—not one! The societor has forbidden it."

"And I hope that will be an example to other rulers," Nil Spaar said. "But there is a great fleet poised to invade our territory, and they do not seem to have been left wanting by your absence."

"Oh, that fleet is nothing but bluster," Ourn said dismissively. "The Princess hasn't the will to use it, or the support to do so."

"I find her a strong and canny dictator," Nil Spaar said. "I cannot believe that she would make empty threats."

"If you could hear the speakers denouncing her daily in the Senate, you would know how weak she is. There has been a challenge to her right to lead the New Republic. Why, there is even talk that she will be recalled."

"I am more concerned whether the fleet that threatens us will be recalled," said Nil Spaar. "You will understand that I can't look past that."

"But what about your promise? What about the favors I have done you?"

"We have a debt to the Paqwepori, it is true—but others in my government question whether we can trust an ally of Leia Organa Solo—"

"I would have denounced her myself, if the chairman would only have let me—"

"—and still others believe that we must keep *Queen of the Valkyries* for ourselves, to help us in our defense against the fleets and armies Leia is raising against us. Truly, I do not see how we can deliver the ship to you in such circumstances."

The consul's face had fallen farther with every word. "This is horrendous—unthinkable!" he sputtered. "Is there nothing you can do?"

Nil Spaar flicked his cheek in the Paqwepori gesture of resignation. "Perhaps it would be possible—but no. I am embarrassed to ask for more when a debt already exists."

"Ask! Please, ask! Is there some way I can help resolve this?"

"I thought only that if you could give me the means to persuade the others—if I could give them sufficient reason to trust you—to know that you are as honorable as I know you to be—"

"Yes, of course—but what will do that? Are you asking me to leave Coruscant? Are you asking us to leave the New Republic?"

"No, no—by no means. Just continue to be a friend to us there," Nil Spaar said. "Keep your eyes and ears open to the machinations of she who afflicts us. Provide us with an unbiased report of her actions. Give us the information we need to keep this confrontation from spinning out of control. That's the only way we can keep our promise to you. That will be all the proof they need of your loyalty."

"Of course," Ourn said. "Of course! I would have done so anyway. In fact, my first reason for contacting you was to tell you about Leia's newest abuse of her power. Even *her* friends are shocked by this—she came back from holiday and granted membership to more than twenty new systems, completely bypassing the established protocols—"

*   *   *

"No," Leia said emphatically, brushing past Nanaod Engh as though he were a street beggar. "I don't want to call a cabinet meeting. I have nothing to tell them yet. The Defense Council hasn't met yet. The viceroy hasn't shown his hand yet."

Engh appealed to Behn-kihl-nahm with his eyes. "Will you talk to her, Chairman?"

"Leia—you don't have to have answers for them yet," Behn-kihl-nahm said. "Just let them see you. Just let them see you taking command. A government is an organism—and this one has taken two shocks substantial enough to disrupt its systems."

"I'm sorry, but all that can't depend on me. There's a reason for having a cabinet, and the reason is so I don't have to concern myself with all those 'systems.' So let the ministers deal with their responsibilities, and I'll deal with the things that only the chief of state can."

"But you need to tell them that, and show them that you're present, aware, and active," said Behn-kihl-nahm. "You need to refocus their attention, or you'll have nine little kingdoms before you know it, all looking to their councils over in the Senate instead of to you. To a degree, that's already happened."

"There's a great deal of governing which has nothing to do with Koornacht, the Defense Council, black fleets, and matters of state," Engh said. "Perhaps the ministers and their staffs should not need reassuring, but they do."

"And I don't need to be hung by my heels and questioned for four hours."

"That won't happen," Engh said. "It will be your meeting, not theirs. Thank them for the work they've been doing. Call for their reports. Acknowledge the difficult times ahead. Ask them to remain diligent in discharging their responsibilities. Promise to tell them more when you can. Let them know that they are making it possible for you to do *your* job."

"They should know all that without being told," Leia protested. "Why does it require a pep talk from me? My stars, during the Rebellion, our pilots got in their fighters knowing they were outnumbered five to one and worse with less hand-holding than this."

"That was a different place and a different time," Behn-kihl-nahm said simply. "Leia—you have never served anywhere in government except at the top. Please trust those of us who are better acquainted with the view from the bottom to advise you in this."

Sighing, Leia looked to the first administrator. "When do you suggest we do this, then? This afternoon?"

"Oh, no—that would put the stamp of an emergency on it, which is the last thing you want. No, all you need do this afternoon is give the usual three-day notice. That will start sending the message you want heard. For the rest, three days from now is soon enough."

"All right. Three days, then," Leia said grudgingly. "Will one of you tell Alole on your way out?"

The first full cabinet meeting of the new era went surprisingly smoothly. Minister of State Mokka Falanthas showed signs—noticeable but not overt—of still being disgruntled over Leia's violation of his turf, but he kept those feelings out of his words when he reported on the work of the diplomatic corps. But the rest of them, Leia was forced to admit, did seem to relish the return to normalcy.

Even better, Leia was able to hold the meeting down to two hours, giving her a chance to get some real work done before meeting Han for lunch. But she didn't quite manage to escape cleanly—Nanaod Engh followed her out of the council hall and down the corridor toward the turbolifts.

"Do you have some time now, Princess?" Engh

asked. "There's something I'd like to bring up that wasn't appropriate for that venue."

"I was planning on taking a slow second look at some new material that came in from General A'baht overnight," Leia said. "I'm going before the Defense Council on the first, you know."

"Yes, I do."

"Well, you have from here to my office door to convince me that whatever this is is more important than that."

"I think perhaps this is *part* of that, Princess," said Engh. "Has Alole been showing you any of the traffic from the ministry channels?"

"I don't understand. She screens it all and shows me the dispatches and inquiries I need to handle. You know that."

"I'm sorry—I meant the public lines. The tallies from the message-handling droids that handle the unaddressed comments, the abstracts from the general call logs—that sort of thing? Or perhaps you've taken a peek in there yourself."

"No," Leia said, calling for the lift. "Why would I?"

"Well—to get an idea how this all is being taken on the outside, off Coruscant, away from the government. To see how people are reacting to the news."

"Go on," Leia said as the lift arrived.

"This matter of the new members, for example—perfectly within your powers under the Charter," Engh said, following her into the car. "Everyone here knows the new members had to agree to observe the Charter like any other member, and that what was done was done not only for a legitimate reason, but a noble one."

"I'd like to think that none of that needs explaining," said Leia as the doors knifed closed. "Except perhaps to Minister Falanthas."

"That's a matter of professional turf and personal style, which I'm sure you two will work out in time," Engh said. "But out in the capitals, there's a great deal of concern about recent events—talk of your having exceeded your authority, of special privileges being granted, and of your acting on a whim, even rashly."

"Are you talking about the home governments?"

"The home governments themselves in some cases, the technocrats in others. And not only the technocrats—this reaches nearly every quarter. Much of what's coming in from individual citizens on the public lines is critical—often crudely and ignorantly, but there it is."

"And you think I should be reading this?" Leia said wryly. "Look, Nanaod—I don't understand why you're calling my attention to this. *I'm* unhappy with the situation, so why would I be surprised if others are? What's there to do about it?"

"Well, we've been talking about this downstairs for several days now," Engh said. "The emerging consensus is that all of that mess is the result of our not having prepared the New Republic for what was coming, and not moving fast enough to educate them after the fact. I'd like to put a couple of staff members on the problem full-time, preferably in consultation with someone in your office—I was thinking that Tarrick would be the best suited."

The turbolift eased to a stop, and the doors flashed open on fifteen. "What do you propose to have them doing?"

"Why, to plan a program to buff up your public image a bit. I like to think that it's mostly a matter of getting the word out—informing rather than influencing. We might want to think about making you a bit more available to the grids, not only the big ones based here, but the regional and local nets—"

"Now you want me to give interviews? What next? Preside over spaceport openings? Endorse a line of little Leia dolls? Let myself be recorded dancing for Han in a Huttese slave-girl costume?"

"Now, Leia, no one is suggesting—"

"You'd get there, eventually. And that's not what

I'm here to do," Leia said firmly. "What's more, I'd be deeply discouraged to discover that you can take someone who's shown terrible judgment and get people to support her just because she has a nice smile. I earned whatever criticism's aimed at me right now, and I'm going to try to earn back the respect I've lost—not replace it with something false."

"That's not what we're talking about, Leia," Engh said. "We're talking about taking your case not just to the Senate, but to the people the senators represent. We're talking about combating misinformation and misimpressions before they take hold firmly enough to be mistaken for the truth. Leia, this can only strengthen your hand."

They were closing in on the presidential suite. "Am I supposed to do the right thing, Nanaod, or the popular thing? Where's the line between wanting to be understood and wanting to be liked?" She stopped and faced him, blocking him from coming further. "How does it help me provide the leadership everyone expects from me if there's a little man standing behind me whispering that the people aren't ready yet to go where I know we have to? Don't make it any harder than it is, Nanaod. Because I have to tell you, it's hard enough already."

"All I want is to give you all the tools you need to be successful," Engh said. "Your public image is one of them."

"Except it needs rehabilitation."

"In some circles—where you haven't been well served by gossip, rumor, and the news. This isn't about fogging the air with lies, Leia—it's about clearing away the fog that others create."

"Mon Mothma never had to resort to image strategists, and she led us through harder times than these," Leia said. "No. I'm not interested."

"Will you think about it? Perhaps if you sampled what's coming in, you'd understand why we're concerned—"

"I understand," Leia said. "I just don't want that kind of help. And I have work to do now."

Engh did not press the point further, but Leia had trouble leaving the conversation behind when she entered her office. Hours later, still burning over it, she repeated much of the exchange to Han when he joined her with the children for lunch at the indoor waterfall cascade.

She expected his sympathy, but Han's face acquired an uncomfortable expression as she talked.

"What? What is it?"

"Nothing. It's nothing—go on, I'm listening."

"No, I know that look," Leia insisted. "It's your 'I'm not going to say this because it'll just make things worse' trying-to-bite-your-tongue look. Except you always have to let me see how hard you're working to be nice. I don't know how you ever won a single hand of sabacc with that face."

"Just like I know that speech," Han said, his mouth twisting into a wry, crooked grin. "That's your 'I'm going to poke at him until he's just mad enough to blurt out what he's thinking' speech. And it doesn't work anymore."

"So why don't you just tell me, before we're both worn out from wrestling?"

"It really doesn't mean anything—"

"Why don't you skip the cushioning-the-blow part this time, too?"

"Women," Han sniffed in mock indignation. "They always want you to tell them what you're thinking, but whatever you say is wrong."

"As long as you understand the ground rules."

"Oh, yeah. What's scary is watching Jaina figure them out, too." Han sighed. "A couple of days ago I heard from an old smuggling buddy who's settled down to the straight life out on Fokask. Haven't had any contact with him in years."

"So why now?"

"He sent me a copy of a commentary and half a dozen letters from *The Fokask Banner,* which I guess is what passes for a newsgrid out there. The title on the commentary was something like 'Does Princess Crave Lost Crown?' "

"Mmm. What did it have to say?"

"Aw, I didn't read it that closely—why would I want to?" Her eyes prodded him gently. "Something about how they'd always thought of you as a steward of the best Old Republic values, but now you were starting to look like a fan of an even older idea, the divine right of monarchs—whatever that means. I probably got it at least partly wrong. You can read it yourself, if you really want."

"And what did your friend have to say?"

Han pursed his lips and avoided her eyes, clearly looking for a way to not answer.

"Just tell me."

"Well—he didn't have much to say, actually. After the last of the letters from the *Banner,* he just added a short note. 'Is there something in the water there on Coruscant? She seemed like such a nice girl.' " Han shrugged. "It doesn't mean anything, except that now I have to kill him."

"No, you don't."

He nodded, deadpan. "Do. Insulted my girl. Have to kill all of them."

"Stop that, before the children hear you," she said, punching his shoulder and then resting her head against it.

Han wrapped an arm around her. "I might let him off if he takes it back." After a long pause, he added, "But he has to mean it." There was another pause, during which his tone turned serious. "And, what you said—before the children hear him."

Leia said nothing then. But as she cuddled with Han and watched Jaina, Jacen, and Anakin playing by the waterfalls, four words burned in her ears: *before the chil-*

dren hear. When she returned to the fifteenth floor, she quietly asked Alole to find her a sample of the messages received in recent days on the ministry lines. Not long after Alole provided them, Leia called Nanaod Engh.

"I've thought some more about what you said," she said. "Please see what can be done."

"We'll get after it right away," Engh promised.

Young and old, fresh and seasoned, the Grannan and the Mon Calamari left their Fleet speeder and walked in unconscious lockstep across the parking apron toward the red-and-white snub fighter sitting high on its skids a dozen meters away.

"Here's what I wanted to show you," Admiral Ackbar said. "Have you ever seen one of these before?"

"Yes," Plat Mallar said, ducking under the locked foils and studying the wingtip spars. "In my grandfather's enemy vessel silhouette drill set. It's some variation on an Incom T-sixty-five X-wing, isn't it?"

"Correct. But notice the wider profile through the fuselage, and the side-by-side cockpit."

"Dummy laser cannon on the wingtips, too," Mallar said. "Trainer?"

Ackbar nodded. "This is a TX-sixty-five primary trainer. The X-wing may no longer be the Fleet's front-line fighter, but every pilot in the Fleet took his first hundred hours in one of these, and every new pilot probably will for some years to come."

Mallar crouched and peered under the fuselage. "A lot different from a TIE interceptor."

"Indeed. Including one difference you should be able to particularly appreciate—hyperdrive."

A wry smile creased the boy's face, then vanished. "One of these crashed the day I came out of the tank, didn't it? I heard the medics talking."

Ackbar turned and pointed across the field. "Right over there, on taxiway twenty-two. Not the first, or the last," he said with a little shake of the head. "Sometimes, despite everything we do, they come out of the simulators with the idea that if they make a mistake their mentor pilot will just reset the exercise." He shrugged. "And sometimes ships just break."

"My engineering instructor liked to say that stopping isn't hard, stopping gently is—and anytime you leave the ground, you'd better check twice to make sure all the nuts are tightened, because gravity flunks all the incompletes."

"It sounds like your instructor knew his business."

"Yes," Mallar said. "Bowman York did know his business. I miss him."

A fat-bodied military transport rose from the field beyond and roared overhead on its way to space. Wearing a wistful expression, Plat Mallar turned his head to watch it until it vanished from sight.

"So effortless—so much power, under such precise control." He looked back to Ackbar. "That's all I cared about before the Yevetha came, you know. Not the bombs and the laser cannon. Just flying. Just the ships, so graceful, dropping out of the clouds, disappearing into the sky. They came and went every day when I was very young. Mom said I'd sit at my window for hours and watch for them, and call out to the whole house when I saw one."

Ackbar inclined his head toward the trainer. "Would you like to go up?"

"I've been trying to convince myself that it would only make me feel worse, just in case you asked," Mallar said.

"How did you do?"

"Failed miserably. Yes, I'd really like to. Can we, sometime?"

As his answer, Ackbar climbed up the boarding ladder, reached inside the open cockpit, and tossed a flight helmet down to a surprised Plat Mallar.

"Now?"

"Why not?"

"Don't I need something more than this?"

"You need a mentor pilot," said Ackbar, reaching into the cockpit again and retrieving another flight helmet. "That's me."

"I meant—wait, we're just going for a ride, aren't we?"

Ackbar clambered down the ladder with his helmet under his arm. "You meant like a flight suit?"

"Well—yes."

"In the cargo area of the speeder," Ackbar said, nodding toward it. "Why don't you get them?"

Mallar hurried off to the speeder, returning quickly with an armful of folded brown fabric. "Which one's mine?"

"On top," Ackbar said. "The one with your name on it."

For a moment Mallar stared blankly, uncomprehending. Then Ackbar's bundled flight suit fell to the ground as Mallar shook his out and pawed over it with shaking hands, searching for the namestrip above the right pocket. When he found it, he looked up at Ackbar wonderingly.

"On your own merit," Ackbar said firmly. "On the merit you showed the day the Yevetha came to Polneye—the kind that counts more than any test score or transcript. And I mean to teach you the way I was taught, with an eye to what you already know, and a light hand on the stick. In the worst days of the Rebellion, we were putting pilots in combat on ten hours of simulator time, because we were at war. Well, Polneye is at war with N'zoth. And if it's still important to you, and there's any way it can be done, I will have you ready to go back to Koornacht before that war is over."

"Yes," Mallar said with a quiet fierceness. "Yes, I want it."

Ackbar nodded. "There is a corridor in pilot country—you will see it later—lined with small metal plaques, one for each pilot who's died flying out of this base. The walls and the ceiling of that corridor are nearly covered in metal. And if we were to hang a plaque for every pilot who came through here as a trainee and died somewhere out there, under enemy guns or in a ship that just broke, we'd have to cover the entire face of the tower."

"I understand," Mallar said.

"You only think you do—like everyone your age," Ackbar said, shaking his head. "Just listen to me for a moment. When old people start wars, young people die. And every hero every war has ever made went out that morning with comrades who were every bit as brave, but not quite as lucky. You've used up a lot of luck already getting here, Plat Mallar. And no one, no one anywhere, would ever say a word to you if you were to choose *not* to put on that flight suit, and chose instead to make a life here. You stole that life back from those marauders. You need not offer it up again."

"I know," said Plat Mallar, standing as tall as his frame would allow. "And I thank you for reminding me that there is a choice. But my choice is to wear this, and hope for a chance to do something that makes a difference—to me, if not to anyone else."

"Very well," Ackbar said. "Then let us begin. You have a great deal to learn."

Chapter 13

◆

As the last holoimage of the Yevethan attack on Morning Bell faded and the lights came back up in the Defense Council's hearing chamber, Leia studied the senators seated at the V-shaped table.

There was one new face among the eight, reflecting a small shift in the balance: the human Tig Peramis of Walalla was gone, and Nara Deega of Clak'dor VII, a Bith, had been seated in his place. After the confrontation at the activation briefing for the Fifth Fleet, it was a relief not to have to face the fiery Peramis, who had removed himself to a legal limbo by presenting articles of withdrawal for his homeworld.

But the intimidatingly intelligent Deega was, like the majority of his species, deeply committed to pacifism. A ruinous civil war had left Clak'dor VII an ecological nightmare, inhabitable only in domed cities. Because of those memories, Leia did not expect to find Deega any more tractable than Peramis had been.

Leia walked into the middle of the space defined by the V, and all eyes turned to her. On the recommendation of Engh's image specialists, she had forgone the flowing robes of Alderaan's royal house in favor of what Han had called street-fighting clothes—a simple garment suggestive of a flight jumpsuit. But she wore just one of the medals and honors she was entitled to: the small blue-fire crystal talisman of House Organa.

"The question I bring before you is a simple one," Leia said—the first words she had spoken in that room that day. "What shall we do about what you've just seen?

"These images document both the murderous brutality and the expansionist mentality of the current Yevethan government," she went on. "They've committed unspeakable acts of xenophobic genocide and been rewarded for it with new worlds to settle and new resources to exploit. Their success can only whet their appetite for more—but even if they are content now, they're profiting from crimes against peace and morality.

"Excluding the Koornacht Cluster, Farlax Sector contains more than two thousand inhabited systems, some three hundred of which are members of the New Republic. Not one of them is strong enough to resist the Yevetha on its own.

"We've already accepted our responsibility to protect the peaceable inhabitants of Farlax by sending the Fifth Fleet to stand between them and the Yevetha. But that's no more than a stopgap solution. We cannot undertake a permanent deployment at battle-group strength. Eventually we will face an unappealing choice between abandoning those systems, reinforcing them, and taking on the Yevetha for them.

"I think we must face that choice now, while the initiative remains with us—before the Yevetha find a way to force our hand. We must find some way to alter the Yevethan calculus, or what you saw just now will only be the beginning. We should try first to change their willingness to wage war, but we should be prepared to deny them the means to wage war.

"That's why I'm here today—to ask for your counsel in devising a plan to deal with the Yevetha, and your support in carrying it forward."

Leia's presentation was the only part of the meeting she could control, and it proved to be her best moment of the morning. As soon as she returned to her seat, Behn-kihl-nahm spoke briefly but supportively before laying out the ground rules for the discussion to follow. But as soon as that discussion began, the division in the Council became evident, and Leia's opponents began chipping away at the foundation she stood on.

"What is the source of these images you have presented to us?" asked Senator Deega.

Leia stood at her seat. "Senator, they were recorded by the Yevetha and intercepted by a ferret patrolling the perimeter of Koornacht Cluster."

"Then they are completely undocumented?"

"What do you mean, Senator? I can, if there's a legitimate reason to do so, bring someone in here who can testify to the time, manner, and location in which those images were recorded."

"You have misunderstood, President Solo," Senator Deega said patiently. "If you did not make the recordings, you do not know what was being recorded. You have said that these images document the eradication of certain settlements within Koornacht Cluster. But, objectively viewed, they document nothing. What planets were those? Who was aboard those ships? When did those events take place? Who assembled those images in that sequence?"

"If the Council feels it hasn't seen enough and chooses to commit the time, I can present the entire unedited intercept—all eleven hours of it."

"You still misunderstand, President Solo," said Deega. "For all you can prove, those images were recorded during the Rebellion, light-years away from Koornacht Cluster. If they were recorded at all—the quality of the images does not exceed the capabilities of the best image editors."

Chairman Behn-kihl-nahm intervened at that point. "Senator Deega, inasmuch as you're new to the Council,

I'm aware that you haven't had much experience evaluating military intelligence. Much as we would all like to have absolute certainty in these matters, technical espionage does not often allow us the luxury of the exacting standards a scientist has for evidence, or a mathematician for a proof. Sometimes we just have to trust our spies—or, if that asks too much, trust our eyes."

That brought chuckles from Senators Bogen and Yar, and effectively silenced Deega. But Senator Marook stepped up to fill the void.

"I have no doubt that terrible, shameful things have happened in Koornacht Cluster," said the Hrasskis, his air sacs pulsing slowly. "I do not question what Princess Leia has *shown* us."

Leia waited, knowing not to take his words as a vote of confidence.

"In truth, I found the presentation sufficiently real that I should not like to see any more, or see any more closely. It's enough to know that the dying are screaming—I don't find that listening to it adds anything to my understanding," said Marook. "What I question is the Princess's claim that this is a matter of great urgency. Perhaps she can help me understand."

"I'll do my best," Leia said, wary.

"These recordings—to the best of your knowledge, they were made days, even weeks ago, yes?"

"That's true."

"So what you've shown us is history. None of these tragedies can be prevented, or even tempered."

"No—"

"Then how is this any different from the unavenged atrocities of the Imperial era? Why are we not meeting to discuss how and when to invade the Core in search of the agents of Palpatine's rampages? Isn't the real urgency here the waning of your political power, and your desperate need for a dramatic victory to restore your prestige?"

That brought Tolik Yar roaring to his feet in Leia's

defense with accusations of his own. "Bold talk from a traitor who secretly visited *Aramadia* and plotted with Nil Spaar against his own. You have never explained what you were doing there—besides shaming your people and betraying your oath—"

Marook answered with a lunge and a clenched fist, which brought Senators Bogen and Frammel into it as peacemakers and sent Deega fleeing from the room. Meanwhile Senator Cundertol of Bakura and Senator Zilar of Praesitlyn sat back in their chairs, treating the contretemps as an object lesson and an entertainment, respectively.

"You see?" Cundertol said, leaning toward his companion. "These aliens are always fighting, on the least provocation. It's in their nature. You can't stop them—so why should we try? Why are we obliged to protect the weak against the strong? Why not let the weak fall, and then make our alliances with the strong?"

It took all Behn-kihl-nahm's persuasive skill to bring everyone back to the table and the session back to order. But by then, unanimity was hopelessly beyond reach.

The meeting dragged out for three more fractious hours. At the end of it, Leia was forced to settle for a compromise that pleased no one in the room, least of all herself and the chairman. The plan was too bold for Deega, too hasty for Marook, too interventionist for Cundertol, too far short of what Behn-kihl-nahm had thought possible, and too timid for Tolik Yar and the rest of the Council.

But all eight were willing to support it when they left the privacy of the hearing room, which made it the best Leia could hope for.

"Thank you, Chairman," Leia said after the consensus vote, pretending to a dignity far more elevated than the process deserved. "I'll give the Council advance notice of the announcement. I'll need to consult with Admiral Ackbar and notify General A'baht. But it should only be a matter of a few hours."

The preparation took longer than the execution.

"Here's a question for you, Princess," Han said, scratching his head as he peered at the holorecorder's reference screen. "How exactly will we know that Nil Spaar has gotten the message, since he's officially not talking to you?"

"We have three different holocomm codes from his visit here—two for *Aramadia* and one for the viceroy's staff," said Leia. "It'll go to all three."

"We'll be using Channel One to notify all the home governments," added Minister of State Mokka Falanthas. "Since the Yevetha used Channel One themselves for Nil Spaar's last address, we know they *can* monitor it—and if they can, it's likely that they do."

"We will also have prowlers broadcasting in high-band and laser directional from along the Koornacht perimeter," said General Rieekan. "Those signals will reach the Yevethan pickets in eight hours or less, and Doornik Three Nineteen thirty-four hours later."

"And if for some reason they willfully manage to ignore all that, they cannot fail to notice two days from now, when we repeat this message and allow the grids to carry it to the general citizenry, to prepare them for what may come," said Behn-kihl-nahm. "I have no doubt that the Yevetha still have spies on Coruscant. They will know what has transpired." He shrugged. "Indeed, they may already know."

Leia finished fussing with the drape of her robes and looked up. "Where is Ackbar? Has anyone seen him?"

"I did," Han said. "He was heading for his office with a big bundle under his arm, muttering something about too much ormachek. I think maybe he was having trouble with his dress uniform."

Leia's face relaxed into a smile for the first time in

hours. "If he went all the way back into his closet for the Mon Calamari battle tunic he wore at Endor, this may take a while."

Tugging uncomfortably at his own uniform, Han said wryly, "I could have used a tailor myself. I hope we don't look more silly than scary, standing behind you."

Behn-kihl-nahm patted Han on the shoulder. "Don't worry—the right message will come through. And your presence is as much for domestic eyes as for Yevethan ones."

At that point Ackbar arrived, resplendent in his white admiral's tunic.

"Is that everyone now?" called the young consultant from Nanaod Engh's staff. "Can I have everyone but the Princess here by the banner?"

The consultant quickly arranged the extras along the wall behind where Leia was to sit—Han, Ackbar, and Rieekan all in uniform to the left of the banner bearing the gold-trimmed New Republic insignia, Engh, Behn-kihl-nahm, and Falanthas all in diplomatic dress to the right. Then he brought Leia in and sat her down in the cupped-hand pedestal chair, which effectively vanished behind her robes. Backing up, he studied his handiwork, then peered at the tableau on the reference screen for a few seconds.

"That's all I can do," he announced. "Princess, you can go ahead whenever the technicians are ready."

The technicians were ready in short order. Then, at last, it was Leia's room, and Leia's moment.

"I am Princess Leia Organa Solo, President of the Senate, Chief of State of the New Republic, and Commander-in-Chief of the Defense Force. I address myself to Nil Spaar, Viceroy of the Duskhan League, to the governments of N'zoth, Wakiza, Zhina, and the other Yevethan worlds throughout Koornacht Cluster, and to the commanders of Yevethan armed forces everywhere.

"Whereas Viceroy Nil Spaar has freely and openly admitted to responsibility for grievous crimes against the inhabitants of Morning Bell, Polneye, New Brigia, Doornik Six Twenty-eight, and other legally constituted settlements in and near Koornacht Cluster—

"Whereas these crimes include the unprovoked wholesale slaughter of the inhabitants of these worlds, and the illegal and immoral seizure of their homes, goods, and territory—

"Whereas these acts grossly and wantonly violate the fundamental rights of sentient beings and peaceful worlds everywhere, as well as the fundamental principles of moral conduct—

"Whereas these are rights and principles to which the New Republic is wholly and unswervingly committed in both law and spirit—

"I do thereby instruct and advise Viceroy Nil Spaar and the ruling authorities of the Yevetha to immediately relinquish and withdraw from the systems you have seized, surrender any and all property confiscated, and release unharmed any and all prisoners now held. If you fail to do so in a timely and responsive manner, you will leave us no choice but to enforce this directive by every means available to us."

Her gaze burned into the lens of the holorecorder. "Do not misjudge this—our will and determination in this matter are unwavering. Withdraw from those worlds you illegally and immorally seized, or be removed from them. Those are the only choices. The New Republic will not allow you to profit from acts of such unbridled barbarism.

"Ordered and recorded this day and before these witnesses at Imperial City, Coruscant, by President Leia Organa Solo.

"End transmission."

When the technical staff signaled the recording was over, the gathering dispersed with surprising speed. Ackbar, Behn-kihl-nahm, and Han all came to her with words of support, but only Han lingered.

"Sounded great from where we were, Leia," he said,

catching her up in a quick hug. "If it was me you were talking to, I'd know you meant business. Now—how long do we wait?"

"I hope we don't have to wait very long," she said. "But there aren't any deadlines. We'll give them enough time to work through their decision. I'm sure we'll hear from someone at that end before long."

"What if we don't?"

"Then everything centers on Doornik Three Nineteen," she said. "It's the one site we can monitor closely enough to know whether the Yevetha are packing up or still moving in. That's where we'll be watching."

Waiting was hard.

An hour came and went, with the excitement of the moment making it seem like only a few minutes. The next hour lasted a day. The first day lasted forever. Anticipation became anxiety, and anxiety restlessness. Soon restlessness became impatience, and impatience a gnawing distraction.

The second day was even longer.

And nowhere was the waiting harder than along the Koornacht perimeter. All 106 principal vessels of the Fifth Battle Group were on round-the-clock combat-level alerts. Flights of fully armed fighters and interceptors came and went from the launch bays of the carriers as the defensive screens were brought up to full combat density.

At the end of the second day, the ultimatum was made public, along with selected still images from the Alpha Blue intelligence. The response was surprisingly muted and, overall, supportive.

"It is comforting, but illusory," Behn-kihl-nahm warned Leia. "The Senate is holding its criticism until there's some sign—in the form of news from Farlax—to tell them which side they want to end up on. In the meantime, they can nobly posture as loyal supporters of the President and defenders of the Charter. And the public response—I suspect you will find that most casual observers are applauding the principle without grasping the risk. They enjoy the show of strength, and it seems right and good to them for us to dictate to outsiders. They expect the Yevetha to meekly comply, and for this to be over in a few days. Most of all, they do not expect this to lead to war."

Two days became three, and three stretched to five. The ultimatum was retransmitted daily at 1700, but there was no response of any kind from inside Koornacht Cluster. It became increasingly clear that the Yevetha were ignoring the messages.

On the sixth day an Alpha Blue stationary probe came out of hyperspace near Doornik 319 and recorded the arrival of a small flotilla—three spherical thrustships and an Imperial-design Star Destroyer. The recording was relayed successfully to a repeater outside the Cluster, but the probe had been on station long beyond its endurance and disintegrated when it tried to disappear back into hyperspace.

As soon as they reached him, Drayson brought both the news and the dispatch to Leia at the residence.

"I'm afraid our probe will have left debris in real-space," he said apologetically. "That may complicate matters."

"All it tells them is that we're watching—and that they can't detect it when we are," Leia said. "Maybe that will help us a little."

"But the reality is that that was my last asset in that system," Drayson said. "And placing them is harder than hiding them once they're there. This is likely to be the last report from Doornik Three Nineteen for the foreseeable future. They're all going to be expiring."

"Let me get Han, and we'll take a look," she said. "And we should contact Behn-kihl-nahm and Ackbar."

"I took the liberty," Drayson said. "Bennie is on his

way over. But Admiral Ackbar is getting in some time in a TX-sixty-five and won't be here for at least an hour."

"All right. We'll wait for Bennie."

"He said not to."

"Well," said Leia. "Then I guess we won't."

Together Han, Leia, and Admiral Drayson watched the four minutes of data—twenty capture clips, each twenty seconds long, spanning a six-hour period. They documented the arrival of four ships and landings at widely separated sites by three of them. When the recording was finished, Leia looked up in surprise.

"That's not enough," she said. "We can't tell whether those ships went down empty or full. We can't see if they left or stayed."

"Wait," Drayson said. "The recording is ER—enhanced resolution. We can zoom on the last two clips, when the second thrustship was almost directly under the probe."

The enhanced images resolved the ambiguity. They revealed a glassy landing pad in the middle of an empty, undeveloped plain, and a train of cargo pallets, each nearly the size of a light freighter, being towed away from the thrustship.

"That's it," Leia said. "That's their answer."

Han shook his head and frowned. "I think the translation is 'Oh yeah? Make me.'" He drew a deep breath and released it noisily. "What now?"

"We wait for Bennie," Leia said. "In the meantime, I want to see it again."

Eventually the meeting at the residence grew to include Engh, Rieekan, Falanthas, Behn-kihl-nahm, and Ackbar. There were several showings of the recording, particularly the later clips. No one who saw it failed to be concerned.

"Bennie? What do we do?" Leia asked. "Send another ultimatum? Tell them we know what they're doing, insist that they stop? Maybe a firm deadline this time, and a clearly stated consequence for missing it."

Behn-kihl-nahm's jaws worked at her use of the nickname in that setting, but he said nothing of it. "It's difficult to see what magic words would make another warning any more credible than the ones we've already sent."

"We should give them more time," Minister Falanthas said. "There may be an internal struggle over this—a split between the military and the civilian government. What we see at Doornik Three Nineteen may not reflect the ultimate resolution. If we respond too forcefully, it could force them into an adversarial position."

"In the little we know, at least, there is no evidence the distinction is meaningful in the Duskhan League," Ackbar said. "Nil Spaar acts with the singular initiative and decisiveness of an autocrat—an absolute ruler."

"He's calling your bluff, Leia," Han said. "There's no other way to read this."

Rieekan nodded. "I agree."

"Yes," said Ackbar. "Those ships have hyperdrive. If they came from N'zoth, they left *after* we sent the first warning."

"I'll have to come back to the Defense Council, then," Leia said, looking at the chairman.

Behn-kihl-nahm inclined his head. "And if Senator Marook and Senator Deega prevail this time, now that the stakes are clearly higher? Do we call the Fifth Fleet home and walk away?"

Leia stood up and walked to the study's viewpane. From there she stared out into the quiet hedge garden, its sculpted shapes lit only by the nightglow of Imperial City. "We don't know what's happening on N'zoth," she said finally. "We only know what's happening on Doornik Three Nineteen, and that it's unacceptable." She turned to them, her arms crossed over her chest. "Will you support a blockade of Doornik Three Nineteen?"

One by one, they nodded or spoke their acquiescence. Drayson was the last to respond.

"I do not think the Yevetha will be easily persuaded of their vulnerability, or our resolve," he said slowly. "But it seems a reasonable next step, even if it should prove insufficient."

Leia nodded an acknowledgment, then moved away from the viewpane and rejoined them where they sat. "Admiral Ackbar, does General A'baht have what he needs to securely blockade that system?"

"We should consult with him on that," Ackbar said. "With at least one Yevethan Star Destroyer already there, the general will need to come in with overwhelming force or risk immediate hostilities."

"Let's pull up the rules of engagement for planetary blockade and review them with that in mind," Leia said.

Behn-kihl-nahm stood. "Madame President, if you will excuse me—the decisions that remain do not require my presence, and I would like to go home to be with my family. Minister Falanthas—will you walk with me? There is a small matter I need to discuss with you—"

With the seats on either side of him suddenly empty, Nanaod Engh found a reason to excuse himself as well. Leia looked questioningly at Ackbar when Engh was gone.

"These are hard enough decisions for soldiers," Drayson said. "You cannot blame them if they want to distance themselves enough so that they can sleep."

"Why should *they* be the lucky ones?" Han said grumpily, and sighed. "Oh, hell. Here we go again."

"No," said Leia firmly. "We're doing this to prevent a war, not to start one. But that means we have to teach Nil Spaar that he misread us. That's going to be General A'baht's real mission. Nothing more."

General A'baht turned away from the display with the blockade order. "Finally," he said. "Finally."

"What?" asked Captain Morano.

"We're going into the Cluster," A'baht said. "We're going to deny the Yevetha the use of Doornik Three Nineteen as a forward base." A'baht looked past Morano to the lieutenant at the comm station. "Call my tactical staff. Bring in the secondary screens. And alert all commands to prepare for redeployment."

Ultimately, thirty-one ships of the Fifth Battle Group of the New Republic Defense Force were chosen to make the entry into the six-planet blue-white star system cataloged as Doornik 319. Leading the deployment were the Fleet carrier *Intrepid*, the battle cruisers *Stalwart*, *Illustrious*, *Liberty*, and *Vigilant*, and the assault carriers *Repulse* and *Shield*. The blockade entry was prefaced three minutes in advance by a new hypercomm message from Princess Leia to the Yevetha.

"The Yevethan government's reckless decision to resupply the bases and settlements located on illegally seized territory is in clear defiance of our order to withdraw," Leia said. "I therefore declare an immediate blockade of such locations as we may choose.

"It is our declared purpose in this blockade to interdict any and all inbound traffic, and to peaceably oversee the withdrawal of Yevethan citizens and the removal of Yevethan facilities. But know this—in the event of any hostile acts directed at New Republic vessels taking part in the blockade, our commanders in the field are authorized to respond immediately with all necessary force.

"To avoid unnecessary bloodshed, I call on Viceroy Nil Spaar to promptly and clearly announce your intention to abide by the terms of the order of withdrawal, and to give unambiguous evidence by your actions of the sincerity of your words.

"Any other course you choose will lead to war."

Good words, General A'baht thought, with grudging respect. *Strong words. May the viceroy hear the steel in your voice, and spare the lives of our mothers' sons and daughters.*

*   *   *

"Signal ferret reentry *now*," sang out the jump manager.

"Confirm alert level zero," said Captain Morano.

"Confirming!" called the exec. "All defense systems active. Shields set to go automatic on reentry. Flash alert receivers in the green. All stations crewed. All weapons on standby. Interceptor Two, Five, Eight, Fighter Red, Gold, Black, are on the deck and hot."

"Picket line reentry *now*," sang out the jump manager.

Captain Morano nervously tightened the straps holding him in his flak couch. "So how many combat jumps have *you* made, General?" he said to A'baht.

"Too many, and not enough," said A'baht.

"I understand that," Morano said. "Say—what was that Dornean war prayer again?"

"I have already said it for us," A'baht said, nodding.

"Attention, all hands!" called the jump manager. "Realspace entry in five—four—three—two—"

"Remember, everyone, there's at least one big Star Destroyer out there—let's find it *fast*!" Morano called out.

"—one—"

The jump alarm sounded, and the bridge viewscreens blurred with streaks of white. When the streaks abruptly collapsed into a brilliant field of stars, a brown-and-white planet, two-thirds in night, filled a generous share of the forward view.

"Stang, look at them all," someone breathed, reacting to the spectacle of the Cluster viewed from within. "How are the gunners supposed to find their targets against *that* background?"

"Cut the chatter," A'baht snapped. "I want a head count."

"Polling the task force, sir."

"Tactical!" Morano called. "Where are you?"

"Sensors report no targets. Pickets report no contacts. Prowlers report no contacts."

"Where's that Star Destroyer?"

"I don't know, sir."

"Must be on the other side of the planet," Morano said to A'baht. "I don't know if that's lucky for them or for us."

Reports kept coming from stations all around the bridge of *Intrepid*.

"General, poll is complete—all ships reporting on station."

"Hangar boss reports all flights away, Captain. Fighter screen is moving to position."

"Let's push those lead pickets out and get a look at the other side," said A'baht. "Anything from the ground scans yet?"

"Located six—now seven—landing sites with adjacent structures," answered the sensor operator. "No grounded ships, any design."

Morano turned to look at A'baht. "Maybe they got smart and left before we got here?"

"Let's wait until we hear from the lead pickets," A'baht said, touching his combat comm. "This is task force leader, all units. Open the formation and take up assigned orbits configuration. Maintain your alerts."

Over the next half hour the furious, nearly frantic activity of the first few moments faded to a more manageable level. With an all-clear from the lead pickets, the ships dispersed into the blockade screen—the capital ships moving north and south in midlevel orbits, the secondaries east and west in high orbits, and the enclosing halo of pickets and prowlers expanding outward.

Through it all, the Yevethan Star Destroyer was nowhere to be found. Nor were any thrustships located, either on the ground or in orbit. Morano frowned into his hand as he studied the scan board. A'baht bounced a fist on the armrest of his flak couch, wondering if he believed their good fortune.

"No dragons today?" Morano asked finally. "The Princess will be pleased."

A'baht shook his head. "This doesn't feel right."

"Maybe at the end of the day, the Yevetha are the kind of bullies that back down when someone finally stands up to them."

"No," said A'baht. "No, that's not the right personality. They're tougher—and colder—than that. Operations! I want scouts sent immediately to the other planets in the system. I've got a feeling the Yevetha didn't go very far."

"Right away, sir."

But there was no chance for that order to be carried out. Contact alarms began to sound, and the tactical officer shouted over them, "Captain! I've got incoming hostiles, six, eight, ten, fifteen, all vectors, very high closing speeds—they must be microjumping in behind the pickets—"

Something detonated against *Intrepid*'s forward particle shields, bathing the bridge in blinding light until the dazzlers responded. The shield shock made the ship sway slightly underfoot.

"Where did that come from?"

"We're taking ground fire, General—ion cannon and high-velocity missiles. Three sites."

"Show me tactical."

The center viewscreen metamorphosed into a three-dimensional tactical display, which showed the task force's ships arrayed in three shells orbiting the planet. The attacking vessels were already inside the outer shell, diving in toward the larger ships from half the compass.

"This is task force leader," A'baht said grimly. "All ships, counterfire at will. Defend yourselves."

"All batteries, return fire, counterforce protocol," Morano ordered. "Tactical—report enemy strength."

"Count three, repeat, three *Imperial*-class Star Destroyers; six, repeat, six *Aramadia*-class thrustships; one additional capital ship, unknown configuration and design."

It all happened so quickly that surprise never faded from the bridge of *Intrepid*. The attacking Star Destroyers dove in at high speed, their forward batteries firing without cessation. A'baht watched the spherical thrustships with special interest. With their large silhouettes, the Yevethan-designed ships seemed as though they should be vulnerable, but they proved otherwise. Without ever seeming to drop shields, they launched volleys of torpedoes and released salvos of a type of side-steering gravity bomb not previously seen. All the time, heavy laser batteries fired from six concealed and widely spaced gun ports.

A cluster of four Yevethan gravity bombs targeted the light escort *Trenchant* in high orbit, overwhelming its particle shields with a coordinated detonation. Moments later a proton torpedo struck it forward of the bridge, and it disappeared inside a billowing fireball.

"All defense batteries, target those slow bombs," the ship's tactical officer ordered. "General, sir, *Liberty* is reporting six fighters down, lateral shields at one-quarter. *Repulse* is moving to screen her."

Morano pounded his fist on the armrest. "We've got numbers on them, but we're deployed all wrong for this kind of attack. We're sandwiched in between them and the planet with no room to maneuver."

"Patience, Captain," A'baht said. "We need a little more."

The tracking officer turned at his station. "General—the enemy vessels are not sustaining contact. They're making one pass only, then veering off to multiple headings. There may be more coming in behind them, sir."

"Hold your speculation unless asked for it," A'baht said. "Colonel Corgan, where do we stand?"

The tactical officer for A'baht's staff frowned over

his console. "Fifty seconds more, General. Then I'll be ready to transmit."

"Fifty seconds it is," A'baht said. "Task force leader—all secondaries prepare to break orbit to vector five-five-two. All primaries cover the withdrawal."

The comm chief signaled A'baht through his couch console. "Sir, the captains of *Illustrious* and *Liberty* are asking for permission to pursue."

"Denied," A'baht said. "Task force leader, all ships. Lock up on your debris and take it with you—I want bodies pulled before we jump out."

Now it was the ship tactical officer's turn. "Sir—we can take them. We just need to regroup and pursue—"

"At what losses, under these conditions? Lieutenant, we didn't come here to win at any cost, in a battle zone they chose and at a time that suited them," A'baht said. "We came here for the information we need to win the next time. And that next time is coming sooner than they think."

"Yes, sir."

"Transmitting," Colonel Corgan said. "Dispatch away."

A'baht nodded. "Task force leader—secondaries break orbit. We got what we came for—now the Yevetha will get what they deserve." He switched his hypercomm to the scrambled command channel and keyed the transmit code. "All groups, your authorization is kaph-samekh-nine-cipher-nine-go-daleth. Hit 'em hard."

The eighteen ships of Task Force Aster were waiting at their staging area two light-hours above the plane of the Doornik 319 system. The word was passed to them by the task force commander, Commodore Brand, aboard the star cruiser *Indomitable*.

"All ships, alert," he said. "The Yevetha have resisted the blockade. We're going in. You should be receiving updated target and jump vector data from Group

Tactical now. Countdown to the jump-in will begin on my call. All batteries, make sure you have positive target acquisition. It's going to be crowded down there."

Two light-hours below the planetary plane, similar directions were passed to the twenty ships of Task Force Blackvine by Commodore Tolsk. The word filtered quickly down through the ranks and out from the bridge, reaching even the crews waiting in the cockpits of their fighters and assault craft, which were arrayed for launch on the hangar decks.

"Are you keeping an eye on that number three engine?" Skids called forward to the pilot's cockpit of the K-wing. "It looks a little hot from back here."

"I'm on top of it," Esege Tuketu answered. "But everything in here is going to run a little hot till they throw the doors open and start pushing us out. She can take it."

"I just don't want to hear 'Oops' at the end of a power dive on one of those Star Destroyers," Skids said.

"I promise—you won't," Tuke said.

"Good."

"—I'll just think it to myself."

"Is it too late for me to find another pilot?"

Ahead of them, the great armored clamshell doors of Hangar Bay 5 began to open. "It's too late," said Tuke. "You just make sure all our eggs are safe. I don't want to crack one early."

"Point this thing straight and you won't have to worry about that."

Moving as one under the control of the floor chief, the assault bombers of the 24th Bombardment Squadron accelerated down the draglines—first Black Flight, its six K-wings in two rows, three abreast, then Green, then Red. The most dangerous part about cluster launches was executing the break on time—the spacing was so tight that impatience in the back rows could wipe out half the squadron.

"Red Leader clear," Tuke called back to *Indomita-*

ble's battle operations center as his tracking system lit. "Acquiring target."

"My, my, my—they sure turned all the lights on for us," Skids said on the local comm, craning his head to look in all directions. "I've never seen such a sky full of stars."

Red Flight broke down and away, toward the last of four Yevethan thrustships strung out in a line leading back to Doornik 319. In a few moments they picked up their cover fighters—the E-wings of the 16th Fighter Squadron's Blue Flight.

"That trailer's ours, Blue Leader," Tuke said. "Red Flight, arm your eggs and confirm acquisition by your targeting computers."

Each of the six bombers was carrying two fat T-33 plasma torpedoes, known among the crews as shield-busters or rotten eggs. Designed to detonate at the shield perimeter rather than to penetrate it, the plasma warheads of the T-33s created the most intense radiation burst of any New Republic weapon, several times the output of a capital ship's ion cannon batteries.

The focused cone of radiation was designed to overload ray-shielding generators, either burning them up with the feedback or pushing them overlimit with the bounceback. Once even one generator was down, the towers for the particle shields would be vulnerable to the turbolaser turrets on the gun frigates. If everything went according to plan, the carriers, already falling back behind the cruiser screen, would never come close to engaging the enemy directly.

Their system entry had placed them a startlingly close 16,000 klicks from their targets, and the thrustship grew quickly in the scopes and screens as the bombers accelerated to attack velocity. At a range of three thousand kilometers, Tuketu ordered Red Flight to move into the open hex formation, which would give them all room for evasive maneuvers on the way in and an unobstructed power pullup on the way out.

There was no sign of enemy snub fighters, but the flight began taking some fire from the thrustship at fifteen hundred kilometers. Hinking and jinking the K-wing violently, Tuketu alerted his weapons tech to the opportunity that created.

"They're firing through their shields, Skids—the beam scatter will give us the exact range to the boundary."

"Working on it now," Skids answered, his head down over his control displays.

"Hurry," Tuketu said. "Drop point coming up fast."

There was an induction crackle as an ion bolt passed within twenty meters of the bomber. "Red Leader, Red Five—are you hearing this stuff on the command comm?"

The moment the question was asked, Tuketu realized that there were other voices in the cockpit. "Cut the chatter, Red Flight," he said automatically. "C One has to stay open."

"Red Leader, that's not us—and it's all over the spectrum, C One, C Two, the task force frequency, the Fifth's hypercomm—are you listening to it, Red Leader? Do you hear what they're saying?"

The drop point was almost on them. Esege Tuketu forced himself to focus on the sounds he had been disregarding as extraneous.

"—I am the Kubaz called Totolaya. I reside in the colony Morning Bell. I am a hostage of the Yevetha. If you attack, I will be killed—"

On C2 the message was, "I am Brakka Barakas, an elder of New Brigia. I am a hostage of the Yevetha. If you attack us, I will be killed—"

"Red Leader, Red Four. Shall we break off?"

"Red Two here—Tuke, what do we do?"

The decision had to be made in an instant. "Stay on target. Make your drops," Tuke snapped.

Just then an ion bolt from one of the thrustship

batteries caught Red Four full on the port engine foil. The charge danced angrily over the surface of the bomber. Before it could reach the eggs, Red Four's weapons tech released them.

"Eggs away!" Skids cried.

"—I am Liekas Tendo, a Morath mining engineer. I'm in a security cell on some kind of starship. They say these creatures holding us are Yevetha. They say if you attack us, I'll be killed. Please don't attack us—"

Tuketu pulled the stick back sharply, kicking in the big slant-mounted third engine. The power of it quickly changed the bomber's attitude and trajectory, pushing it out and away from the ship, the shields, and the explosions to come. As always, the pullout took Tuketu right to the brink of unconsciousness.

"—I am Crandor Ijjix of the Norat Sovereignty. I have been taken hostage by invaders and held on their ship. To all vessels of the New Republic—do not attack, or we will be eradicated—"

Red Four never made its pullout move. Disabled by the ion bolt, the K-wing continued falling in toward the thrustship, trailing its own torpedoes by a fraction of a second. When the plasma eggs reached the shield perimeter, Red Four was enveloped by the double fireball. The fragments that were hurled out of the cloud were closer in size to dust than to a spaceship.

"Jojo—" Tuke closed his eyes for just a moment. "Skids, report results of bombing."

"Negative—negative, the shield's still up," Skids said disgustedly. "Red Two, Three, and Five did not drop their eggs, repeat, did not drop."

"Red Leader, this is Red Three weps. Tuke, I'm sorry—I just couldn't do it. Not with hostages begging me not to."

"Son of a—you're looking at a court-martial, Condor."

"I'll accept the consequences. But I wasn't going to help murder the people we came here to help."

"Blue Leader to Red Flight—you guys had better work it out back at the barn. Target is launching its own birds. Ten on the wing and more coming."

After one glance at the tracking display, Tuketu pushed the throttle forward and wheeled his bomber around so that the nose pointed back toward *Indomitable*. "Red Two, Red Three, Red Five, find a safe place to dump your bomb load. Everyone take it home, best possible speed. Red Leader to flight boss—five coming in, ETA four minutes."

It was four minutes of hell. The Yevethan fighters were fast and lethal, and the outnumbered E-wings couldn't hold them off. Red Three was picked off returning from its bomb dump. Red Five took a hit on the port wing and another just behind the cockpit, and exploded in flames just before it reached the cover umbrella of the cruiser *Gallant*. Blue Flight fared even worse—only one of the bombers made it back to the comparative safety of *Indomitable*'s hangar bays.

Helmet under his arm, his eyes hollow and his face drawn, Esege Tuketu stood near the flight boss as the casualties were posted on the status board. Jojo. Keek. Dopey and the Bear. Pacci. Nooch.

When Miranda's name went up, he no longer could stand the bloody litany and turned and slipped away.

With his skin cold and pale, General A'baht watched from the bridge of *Intrepid* as variations on the same theme played out all over the battle zone.

Every attack bomber, every cover fighter, every capital ship from both Task Force Aster and Task Force Blackvine received a continuous broadcast of hostage appeals on every comm channel used by the Fleet. Enough gunners hesitated and enough pilots turned away that not a single Yevethan capital ship was touched.

And in the retreat—both the confused one that

started spontaneously and the official one he ordered minutes later—nineteen of the Fleet's small warbirds were destroyed. A hangar fire on the carrier *Venture* consumed fourteen more and left all three portside bays unusable. The cruiser *Phalanx* took a bow shot while pulling a crippled E-wing inside its shields with a tractor beam, and the damage went all the way back to the number 14 bulkhead.

The cost in lives, counting the loss of *Trenchant,* ran to well over a thousand.

But the full cost of the defeat went far beyond that, A'baht knew. And the ultimate cost in blood was beyond measuring.

They are not afraid of us. They are not afraid of dying. There is nothing we can use to restrain their behavior but force—the war we didn't want to fight.

Intrepid lingered, hidden in the glare of Doornik 319's star, while the Fifth Fleet forces jumped out of the system in ones and twos. Only when the carrier was the last ship remaining did A'baht turn away from the viewscreens and descend to the main bridge on unsteady legs.

"Captain Morano," he said. "Take us out of here."

Behn-kihl-nahm walked the empty Memorial Corridor with long, impatient strides. Two maintenance engineers, neither accustomed to moving at that pace, struggled to keep up with him.

At the end of the corridor he turned right, stopping under the sign over the entrance to the Senate Hall. He glanced up at it only briefly, reading it with a sigh in his heart.

1000 DAYS WITHOUT
A SHOT FIRED IN ANGER
Remember,
Peace Is No Accident

Then the chairman turned and looked back, waiting for the maintenance men to join him. When they did, Behn-kihl-nahm pointed up at the sign.

"Turn it off," he said. "Take it down. Take it away."

One of the engineers squinted up at the sign. "Do you want it put in the Senate storeroom?"

Behn-kihl-nahm shook his head. "No. Just get it out of here, now. We won't have any more use for it."

Then he hurried away from the broken dream and toward the Defense Council hearing chamber. The emergency meeting on the situation in Koornacht Cluster was waiting on his arrival to begin.

Chapter 14

◆

The Senate messenger at the gate to the President's residence was as determined to be admitted as the security droid was determined to bar him from entering.

"I don't care what your protocols say—I am here on the authority of the acting chairman of the Ruling Council of the Senate, and my instructions are explicit," the messenger was saying as Leia approached the gate from the inner walk. "I *must* deliver this message, and I may *only* deliver it into the hands of the Princess herself."

"Very well. Here I am," Leia said.

"Princess," the messenger said, turning quickly and bowing his head slightly. "I apologize for the disruption—"

"It's not your fault," she said, reaching through the gate past S-EP1 for the stiff folder bearing the royal blue insignia. "Sleepy's programming didn't include the possibility of a summons. Someone will have to see to that, apparently."

The messenger bowed his head again. "My apologies again, Princess," he said, and backed away.

Leia did not open the folder before starting back toward the house. Of all the many bodies—councils, committees, commissions, and contractors—making up the complex organizational structure of the Senate of the New Republic, only one had the power to summon the President to appear before it.

That one was the Ruling Council.

Its name, which went back to the days of the Provisional government, was no longer descriptive of its role. Much of the power and responsibility of the transitional Ruling Council now rested elsewhere in the Senate, the General Ministry, or the Fleet Office. The New Republic had traded efficiency for democracy and oligarchy for bureaucracy—and had done so willingly and knowingly. A confederation of more than ten thousand systems could not be justly ruled by a self-elected few.

But the one element of its old power which the Ruling Council had retained involved a special responsibility regarding the President. The drafters of the Charter were wary about creating too strong an executive—one who, unchecked, might be able to accumulate more and more power over time and become a dictator in fact if not in name. The cold truth was that Palpatine's reign had begun not with a coup, but with his gaining power largely by legitimate means.

As a check against that history being repeated, the Charter preserved the Ruling Council in the form of a supercommittee made up of the chairmen of the Senate Councils. The founders gave it the power both to void the election of a President and to initiate the recall of a sitting one. Ackbar had dubbed the Ruling Council "the speed brake on the ship of state." But as often as it was spoken of, the Ruling Council met rarely, and had never been used for its intended purpose.

Until now.

The Council had already been seated, apparently arguing behind closed doors, for nearly an hour before Leia was brought in. Though a seat was provided for her, Leia chose to stand in the shallow well of the chambers. Even that only placed her at eye level with the seven senators seated around the arc of the panel. At the center was Doman Beruss, the crystal pyramid and striker resting near his hand. Behn-kihl-nahm was to his left, but would not look at her.

"Madame President—Princess Leia—in the normal rotation, it would be Senator Praget's turn to chair this session," Beruss said. "However, due to the present circumstances, the Council has decided to advance the rotation to the next designated chair, so as to avoid any procedural conflicts. Do you have any objection to my chairing this session?"

So that's what the delay was about, Leia thought. "I have no objection."

"Very well," said Beruss. "President Leia Organa Solo, you have been summoned before the Ruling Council for the discussion of a petition of recall against you.

"A duly constituted member of this body has presented articles calling for a vote of no confidence on the following grounds: One, exceeding your Charter authority. Two, recklessly endangering the peace and the lives of citizens of the Republic. Three, issuing illegal orders to initiate hostilities against a sovereign state. Four, incompetence to properly carry out the duties of office.

"Do you understand your rights and obligations in regard to a petition of recall? If so, please state them in your own words."

"I have the right to hear a specification of the cause of action. I have the right to present whatever witnesses and evidence I choose in defense of my actions and performance," Leia said. "I have the obligation to answer fully and truthfully all questions which may be put to me, as well as the obligation to appear before the Senate in assembly should you vote to sustain the petition."

"Very well," said Beruss. "Senator Praget has brought the petition, and will lay out the specific articles."

That took Leia by surprise—she had been expecting the complainant to be Borsk Fey'lya. "Senator," she said with a nod.

Krall Praget eyed her briefly before he began, his gaze measuring her, judging her, ultimately dismissing her. For the duration of his presentation, he looked down along the curving table from his seat at the right end, addressing himself to Beruss and the other Council members, virtually ignoring Leia.

Praget spoke for not quite an hour, then yielded back to Senator Beruss without asking Leia a single question. She could not tell whether he had decided he was unlikely to succeed in getting her to betray herself, or thought his case so strong that that was unnecessary.

In contrast, Senator Rattagagech had a long series of very specific questions, but they were far less accusatory in tone than Praget's exposition, or even his glances. The Elomin was trying to reconstruct the calculus of Leia's decisions in painstaking detail, and even Praget grew impatient with him.

"You either know what you stand for, or you don't," Praget said. "Relevance, Chairman, relevance—please instruct the Senator to be relevant or yield. The petition is offered on actions and results, not motives or intentions."

Rattagagech drew back in surprise. "Senator Praget, your fourth charge, of incompetence, demands a thorough assessment of the President's judgment—"

"Chairman, permission to amend the petition?"

Beruss nodded. "As you wish."

"I strike and withdraw the fourth article in its entirety," Praget said, then looked at Rattagagech. "Are you finished now?"

The Elomin showed a peevish expression. "In light of the amendment, Chairman, I have no further questions for Princess Leia."

"Very well," said Beruss. "Senator Fey'lya."

All along Leia had been expecting the gloves-off assault, the killing blow, to come from Borsk Fey'lya. Praget's obvious eagerness to give the Bothan the floor only confirmed that expectation. But Fey'lya changed direction abruptly, leaving their expectations falling to the floor as dust.

"President Organa Solo," Fey'lya said, smiling politely. "I'm sorry we've had to take up so much of your time at such a critical juncture. I have just one question for you this morning. If you could revisit any of these decisions of the last several days, with no more knowledge than was available to you the first time, would you change any of them?"

Leia blinked in surprise—Fey'lya might as well have laid his coat across a puddle for her. Praget gaped, then fell into a coughing fit.

"No, Senator," Leia said, unable to see a trap. "I believe we were right to demand that the Yevetha withdraw, and that I consulted properly with the Defense Council before doing so. I believe we were right to try to enforce the ultimatum with a blockade, and that I consulted properly with the Supreme Commander before doing so. I believe we were right to respond to the Yevethan ambush immediately with the forces available, and that General A'baht acted within his authority in doing so. The outcome wasn't what we wanted, but not for reasons we had any cause to anticipate."

Praget snorted derisively at the last, but Fey'lya accepted her answer with a nod. "Thank you, Princess. Chairman Beruss?"

The balance of the discussion was brief and inconsequential, and they voted with Leia still present. The vote was two to five against, with only Rattagagech joining Praget.

"The petition fails," said Beruss. "That being the only business before the Council, this session is adjourned."

Jaw set and an ugly look in his eyes, Praget headed directly for Fey'lya. Buoyed by relief, Leia headed for the corridor. Before she reached it, Behn-kihl-nahm joined her, and they walked away from the chambers together.

"I thought it would be Fey'lya," she said.

"It will be," Behn-kihl-nahm said. "Krall Praget got there first."

"Why?"

"Turf violation," Behn-kihl-nahm said. "You didn't consult with Praget before acting. And the intelligence you depended on didn't come through him."

"So why didn't Fey'lya support him? Did someone forget to bring the rope for the hanging?"

"Because the moment is premature. Because he knew that the petition would not carry, even with his vote," said Behn-kihl-nahm. "The outcome was foreordained, long before you were called in."

"How?"

"By the outcome of the vote on who would chair the meeting. When Fey'lya saw that Praget would not get to run the session, he knew that this was not the day."

"Would it violate the secrecy of the proceedings to tell me who raised that issue?"

A hint of a smile tugged tellingly at the corner of Behn-kihl-nahm's mouth. "I'm afraid I'm not at liberty."

Leia's answering smile was broad and affectionate. "Whoever it was, Bennie, please thank him for me."

"I'm sure he would not think that necessary. I'm certain he would say he was acting for the good of the Republic."

"Thank him anyway," Leia said. "So what happens now?"

"You have a little time. But not so much as you would like, or probably as much as is required," said the chairman. "When the air is saturated with fear, it needs only a seed around which it can begin to coalesce. The same is true of ambition. This is only the beginning of the challenges, Leia. And if nothing changes, the next time you may not survive."

*　　*　　*

Viceroy Nil Spaar's newly expanded breedery on the top level of the palace quarters now had sixteen alcoves. All but one of them contained a birth-cask, supple and fertile, or a maturing nesting, bulging and fecund.

The empty space had once been occupied by the *mara-nas* of Kei, who had been his first. Her birth-cask had brought forth two handsome *nitakka* and a strong *marasi* before succumbing to the gray death. He had left that alcove open to respect Kei's place as *darna* of his family, and to give her some comfort against her envy of his younger mates.

By design and custom, the breedery was a quiet, private place. But Nil Spaar had chosen to have his visitor brought to him there.

"So you are Tal Fraan," he said.

"Yes, *darama,*" the young proctor said, kneeling in submission.

"Rise," Nil Spaar said. "I am told you are the architect of the rout of the vermin at Preza."

"I am honored by the *darama*'s notice," Tal Fraan said, his glance jumping past the viceroy to the alcoves beyond. "But the opportunity for success was created by the *darama,* with the aid of our shipbuilders, who have given us such splendid weapons."

"Excessive modesty betrays calculation, and begs for excessive attention," said Nil Spaar. "Remember that and be guided by it, if you hope to continue your speedy advance."

"I wish only to serve the *darama* in reclaiming the All for the Pure—" Tal Fraan began.

Nil Spaar raised a warning finger. "You were not so eager to refuse credit when the primate of *Glory* advanced you to your new rank. Do you think that I surround myself with talentless flatterers? I have far more use for cleverness. You *are* clever, aren't you, Proctor Tal Fraan?"

"I try not to allow opportunities to escape me, Viceroy."

Showing an approving nod at being addressed directly, Nil Spaar turned and began to walk slowly along the line of alcoves. Both blood-scent and breeding-scent were bracingly strong in the air. "And how came you to the device which served so well against the vermin?"

"The directive sent by the vermin spoke of prisoners," said Tal Fraan, following a step or two behind. "That gave me cause to believe that their actions could be steered by seizing that concern."

"You risked much in surrendering the advantage over the blockade force in the hope of drawing out their reserves," Nil Spaar said, stopping and running his fingers lightly over the surface of a nesting that was nearly at term. "This device, this matter of regard for the fate of prisoners—it would not have stopped Yevetha. If it had failed, your entire force could have been lost."

"The vermin are not strong about death," Tal Fraan said. "I knew it would not fail."

"Ah! Then you feel you have pierced their habits so well that you would commit ten thousand lives to the proof?"

"The primate committed them, Viceroy."

"An incautious answer, Tal Fraan," said the viceroy, turning. "Would you commit *your* life on your confidence?"

The young proctor twitched, then shook his head to lift his crests. "Yes, Viceroy."

"Good," Nil Spaar said. "I can have no respect for one who will not gamble his own blood."

A breedery assistant had been discreetly keeping his distance throughout the meeting. Now Nil Spaar signaled to him, and he disappeared into the anteroom. He returned moments later, leading a *nitakka* prepared for the sacrifice.

"Wait," Nil Spaar said to Tal Fraan, and walked to where the *nitakka* stood on the grate above the drain pit.

The young male met Nil Spaar's eyes without fear.

"I ask for your blood for my children," the viceroy said softly.

"The *darama* honors me," said the *nitakka*, dropping to his knees. "I offer my blood as a gift."

"I accept your gift," said Nil Spaar. His killing claws appeared and slashed air and flesh with silent precision. As the sacrifice collapsed to the grating, the viceroy turned away to rejoin his now pale visitor.

"I have pierced your habits, Tal Fraan," he said. "They are familiar to me. You look at what I have, and you see yourself. No, I have warned you already—do not deny it. I respect cleverness, and courage, and most of all success. I will keep you here, close by, to serve me. If you understand the opportunity, you can expect to profit from it." Nil Spaar smiled. "And if you err, you can expect to serve my new children instead."

"Yes," Lieutenant Davith Sconn said, and blew a puff of smoke from his hoat-stick. The brisk breeze blowing across the north yard of the Jagg Island Detention Center carried the acrid scent away. "I've been to N'zoth."

"I've read the deposition you gave to the Intelligence examiner a few months ago," Leia said. "His evaluation says that in his judgment, you were just trying to earn favors by making something up—that you knew we didn't have any way to confirm or refute what you said."

"Then there's obviously a shortage of intelligence at Intelligence," Sconn said, turning toward where she sat. His gaze flicked past her to The Sniffer and The Shooter. "You must be someone pretty important. I've never seen them let a weapon in here before. What if one of us dangerous war criminals got that firestick away from him and took you hostage?"

Leia smiled sweetly. "I do think they'd enjoy it if someone tried. It's been more than a year since the last time a fool gave my bodyguards a chance to use deadly force."

"There ain't no justice in this galaxy," Sconn said, and came to sit opposite her. "They get paid for the same thing I'm getting punished for. So who are you? You look a little like Princess Leia, only older."

She ignored his gibe. "Lieutenant Sconn—"

"Davith," he corrected. "I was forcibly retired from the Imperial Navy, you know."

"I've also reviewed your trial record, *Davith* Sconn," Leia said evenly. "You were the executive officer of the Star Destroyer *Forger* when it suppressed a rebellion on Gra Ploven by creating steam clouds which boiled alive two hundred thousand Ploven in three coastal cities."

"On the orders of Grand Moff Dureya," Sconn said. "For some reason, people are always leaving that part out. Don't you Rebels believe in discipline? I still can't figure out how you managed to defeat us."

Despite herself, she let him goad her into a reply. "Perhaps it has something to do with having the freedom to refuse immoral orders."

"Immoral? The little finbacks had refused to pay their defense assessments, making the Grand Moff rather cranky." Sconn drew hard on his hoat-stick and held the smoke for long seconds. "But, then, that was late in the day for the Empire, and Grand Moff Dureya was cranky rather a lot of the time."

"Was it with *Forger* that you visited N'zoth?"

"Oh, no. I was on *Moff Weblin*—second watch bridge commander of a Fleet tender," he said, hooking one leg over the other. "Why should I talk to you about N'zoth?"

"Why did you talk to the NRI?"

"Because it didn't matter," Sconn said, shrugging. "Because it was a novelty. Because Agent Ralls was such a clueless young tad that I thought I might have fun shocking him with tales of my travels with Papa Vader."

He leaned forward in his chair. "You're different. You matter. For some reason, you really care about what I know. And you're not going to be any fun at all to shock. So I'm afraid you'll have to show me a little more consideration than Ralls was able to."

"But you forget, Sconn—I already have the deposition," Leia said. "You don't have much left to sell."

"Oh, but you don't know what I left out—"

"Sconn, I ought to warn you that I'm already way over my quota of self-serving lies for the year," Leia said, her gaze intent. "If you want consideration, you give me something first. I have some questions about N'zoth—about what you told Agent Ralls. Answer my questions honestly, to the best of your ability, without games, and then I'll tell you how much what you've said is worth to me."

Sconn sat back in his chair. "I have no reason to trust you," he said. "Or, when it comes to that, to help you."

It took all the self-control Leia had not to reach across the space separating them with her thoughts and slide in behind his smugness with the full power of the Force, looking for some fragile place to grab and twist until something snapped. Instead, she gathered the folds of her robe in her hands and stood.

"Even in prison, Sconn, you always have choices," she said. "If that's yours, so be it."

She turned and started to go, fully expecting that he would let her.

"Wait," Sconn said quickly. "Look, can you find us someplace more private to talk? Somewhere away from here. We're in the middle of the yard, for gaol's sake. I can't be seen cooperating with the keepers. Especially not with you."

"The war is over, you know."

"Not in here," he said. "Never in here. Have them send me to isolation, as though I'm being punished for giving you a hard time. They can take me out from there without anyone knowing."

"You want us to take you off Jagg Island?" Leia asked, her eyebrow cocked skeptically. "Tell me, do I look particularly gullible today?"

"That's all I really want. That's all I was going to ask for, anyway. Just a few hours out."

"So you can try that escape plan you've been working on, no doubt."

"Much as I hate to say it, your blue-hats don't seem prone to losing track of us," Sconn said. "Stang, they can take me out in a stun-box, if you want. It doesn't matter."

"Any particular place you had in mind to go?"

"Since you're asking—" Sconn's head twitched skyward. "How about three hundred klicks straight up, with a view that goes the rest of the way?"

"Stop—please."

His wrists cross-bound against his chest, Davith Sconn stared out the cutter's viewport at the sunrise racing toward them.

"In twenty-four years in the navy, the longest I was ever dirtside was forty days' forced leave on Trif one year," he said, blinking away tears that came freely but silently. "I never found a good enough reason not to go right back out. Now I've been tied down on that rock for twelve years, and I've gotten a lot closer to crazy than I ever wanted to on account of it. You wouldn't think you could, but I was starting to forget. I'd forgotten almost everything but the feeling—this feeling."

Sconn turned back to Leia. "Sit me where I can look out," he said. "I'll answer whatever questions I can."

With a broad sweep of her hand, Leia guided Admiral Ackbar to a chair in the President's briefing room.

"This is the part I thought you should see," she said, and started the holoprojector.

"Black Fifteen was used mostly for new construction and finish work, not as a repair depot. But it had a reputation for the tightest work in the whole sector. Any captain who had a choice put in there. We took *Moff Weblin* in there for a rebuild on a blown number four power cell.

"That's not an overnight in any yard, so the captain told me to look into shore leave. The station morale officer laid out the rules: enlisted restricted to the yard and the station, officers permitted but discouraged from going down to the planet.

"I asked him what was up, since Black Fifteen had been there for three years at that point, and it didn't usually take the troopers that long to bring the locals in line. He told me that one out of two Imperial personnel on the planet was a stormtrooper.

" 'There's been very little trouble for a few months now, but I don't trust them,' he said. 'They're crazy,' he told me. 'More blood than rain fell in the streets before we got here, and it will again when we leave.' "

Leia heard her own voice asking, "What did he mean by that?"

"That's what I asked him. But it turned out he wasn't trying to show off his metaphors. He meant it just like he said it. More blood than rain."

"There's that much fighting among the Yevetha?"

"No, they hardly fight at all with each other—not what we'd call fighting, anyway. I got in with a security captain who fancied himself a xenobiologist, a fellow who'd been down on the surface a lot. He told me about dominance killing, blood sacrifice, and some weird ideas he had about blood and Yevethan reproduction."

"Dominance killing?"

"The way he told it, the only killing the Yevetha consider murder is when a lower-status male kills a higher-status male. The other way around, it's expected.

You offer your neck every time you approach someone higher up the ladder than you, and you'd better really mean it; they have every right to take what you're offering and rip you open with those claws of theirs. And there's something about doing it well that adds to your status."

"Claws?" Leia winced as she heard the surprise in her voice. "What are you talking about? Nil Spaar didn't have any claws—"

Sconn rubbed his wrists together. "Right here. One big curved claw above each hand, on the inside. This I saw with my own eyes—all the males have them. They retract down to a bump, come out backward—it looked backward to me, anyway—for slashing and grabbing on. That's why none of the males wear long sleeves, I guess. It would just get in the way."

"Nil Spaar wore a long-sleeved tunic to our sessions," Leia remembered. "And gloves."

"There you go," said Sconn. "After I heard all this, I had to go down to the surface myself and see. There were Yevetha all over the yard, and no sign of any of this. The yard boss told the captain they were hard workers—especially since they'd figured out we weren't leaving soon."

"So did you spend some time on N'zoth, then?"

"About five days, all together, in three trips." Sconn dropped his eyes and drew a deep breath. "I saw one male put his hands on another's shoulders, drive those claws through, and lift that screaming devil right off the ground. I saw what they call the proctor—means kind of like mayor, I guess—of Giat Nor nearly take off the head of a *nitakka* who was a little slow to take the knee. There must have been fifty Yevetha who witnessed that one. Not one of them said a word, or even showed any surprise."

Sconn shook his head. "When the yard started losing Yevethan workers to this stuff, having to retrain new ones all the time, I guess the Imperial governor told the troopers to try to put a stop to it. But they never really managed to, unless it happened after *Moff Weblin* left. And I ended up the only one of my crew to go down. After he heard my report, the captain restricted the officers to the base."

"Make sure you don't miss this part," Leia said to Ackbar.

"Is there anything else you can think of that might be useful?" she asked Sconn.

"Just the other thing that the morale officer warned me about my first day in," Sconn said. " 'They're crazy, but smart. Don't show them anything you don't want them to start building for themselves.'

"You see, the quality ratings for Black Fifteen had nothing to do with the engineering staff or the foremen and everything to do with the Yevethan guildsmen. They've got the gift of understanding how a thing is put together practically on a first glance. Then they draw it from memory the next day, and by the third they've figured out everything that's wrong about it and started making you a better one."

Oh, my stars, Leia thought, hearing it for the second time. *The droids at the Imperial factory farm—*

"Did you see that for yourself, too?"

Sconn nodded. "That number four power cell we were in for? It was replaced by one the Yevetha had rebuilt—and the replacement ran twenty percent over rated capacity at a hundred degrees below the redline, with absolutely no start-up surge. The chief engineer used to say that he expected it'd still be running when the rest of the ship was rust dust."

"Did the Yevethan conscripts work on every part of the ships in the yard?"

"No, of course not," Sconn said. "The Empire was very fond of secrets. Stang, there were systems on board the *Moff Weblin* that *I* wasn't cleared to know the details of. Conscript workers were never let near anything on the secure list—that was true anywhere. And the yard boss at Black Fifteen was especially careful about not letting the Yevetha near the sensitive stuff—hyperdrives, turbolasers, shield generators, reactors."

Then Sconn smiled with wry amusement. "At least, you'd better hope he was. If you end up having to fight the Yevetha, and what they have looks anything like what we had—well, all I can say is I wish I was going to be there to see it. Nothing personal, mind you," he added. "Just an old rooting interest I haven't quite managed to shed."

"General A'baht."

The Dornean's gaze was level. "Madame President."

"General, before you start, I have some information to pass along to you. Within the hour, the *Gol Storn* and the *Thackery* will be en route to Galantos. *Jantol* and *Farlight* will be detached from the Third Fleet no later than twenty-two hundred for duty at Wehttam. And the Fourth Fleet will be sending two cruisers to Nanta-Ri by the end of the day."

"All welcome news, Madame President. So far, I have no reports of any Yevethan incursions in those systems. I hope we will be able to keep it that way."

"Yes," Leia said. "General, what do you need from us?"

"That depends entirely on what you want me to accomplish. But before we can even contemplate a course of action, I *must* have better information about the enemy. Can I assume that Admiral Drayson is not in a position to expand his assistance?"

"I'm afraid that's correct. Drayson tells me that his assets inside Koornacht Cluster have been 'extinguished,' " Leia said.

"Then I need authorization to send in my own," A'baht said.

"Tell me what you propose."

"There are eleven members of the Duskhan League. We know of thirteen habitable worlds which the Yevetha may have attacked. I want to put a ship within a thousand kilometers of every one of them, on a flash pass."

"Do you have enough drones?" The pilotless ferrets were the first choice for forays into hostile territory.

"No," A'baht said. "I have to commit all my prowlers as well—and put X-wing recon fighters out on patrol to replace them. Or I can send the recon fighters themselves into the Cluster. I would prefer to do the latter."

"Why is that?"

"A recon-X is somewhat faster than a prowler, which I hope will increase their chance of survival. And a recon-X has a smaller crew than a prowler, minimizing any losses."

"Well—you've obviously had your tactical staff working on this already," Leia said. "Do you have any projections?"

"The only reasonable way to go is to synchronize all the contacts. Stagger departures so everyone jumps in-system at the same time—five minutes later, everyone jumps out—"

"Five minutes! That's a long exposure for a flash pass."

"It's necessary to get maximum coverage of the primaries," A'baht said. "We have to be able to see what's in orbit on the back side."

"What does the estimate look like, then?"

"Seventy-five percent getting at least a one-minute partial report out. Forty percent overall mission survival."

"My word—"

"That's under the least-risk mission profile, without direct return. Most of the scouts would continue more or less straight through to the other side of the Cluster and return the long way around. That's another reason to use a recon-X instead of a prowler—fewer hours without that detection capacity on *our* perimeter."

"You're planning to send out twenty-four scouts, and you expect to lose fourteen or fifteen of them."

"Based on what we encountered at Doornik Three Nineteen—yes. The losses will probably be heavier among the recon-X's than the drones, on account of speed and size," A'baht said. "Do I have your authorization, Madame President?"

"Have you considered putting this off until we can get some additional drones out to you?"

"We did consider it. I would be uncomfortable with waiting, Madame President. We need information now. We're vulnerable without it."

Thinking about the pilots of those recon-X fighters, Leia drew a deep breath and let it out slowly. "Very well. You may proceed, General," she said. "What else do you need from us?"

"Replacement fighters," he said without hesitation. "What's the status of the first ferry flight?"

"Assembling now at Zone Ninety East," Leia said, glancing at the report Ackbar had supplied to her. "Twenty-four E-wings, X-wings, and B-wings to cover the losses at Doornik Three Nineteen."

"Don't hold them up on this account—I wish we had them here already," General A'baht said. "But you can get ready to send us some more."

"How long?"

"I took the liberty of prepositioning several of the drones," A'baht said. "We'll be launching the first scout into Koornacht in ninety minutes."

The delta-winged Yevethan fighter banked more sharply than Plat Mallar expected and bore in toward his X-wing's port side. That quickly, he was trapped. No maneuver he knew—no twisting roll, no amount of climbing or diving—could carry him clear of the Yevetha's fire zone.

In desperation, he turned away from the enemy

fighter and tried to run from it. Twenty seconds later a pinpoint laser bolt blasted through the armor on the tailplate. The aft end of the fuselage exploded, sending all four stabilizers spinning wildly away. Moments later Mallar's displays went black.

Mallar tore off his helmet and mopped the perspiration off his face as the scoring came up.

> SIMULATOR MODULE 82Y—SINGLE COMBAT
> T-65 VS. YEVETHAN D-TYPE
> PILOT: MALLAR, PLAT 9938
> DURATION 02:07
> LASER CANNON SHOTS FIRED: 0   HITS: 0
> PROTON TORPEDOES FIRED: 0   HITS: 0
> OPPONENT SHOTS FIRED: 6   HITS: 3
> COMBAT RESULT: YEVETHAN VICTORY

As he climbed disgustedly out of the simulator, Mallar found Admiral Ackbar waiting for him at the bottom of the ladder.

"I see you were trying the new simulation."

An embarrassed look crossed Mallar's face. "Did you watch?"

Ackbar nodded. "Your last three runs. You're not alone. Several of our pilots made similar miscalculations at Doornik Three Nineteen," he said. "It appears the Yevetha have a greater tolerance for g-forces than the pilots for whom New Republic fighters were designed."

"Than *human* pilots, you mean," Mallar said.

Ackbar's mouth worked. "Yes. It is occasionally frustrating to be held back by their limitations." He nodded toward the simulator. "Are you going back in?"

"No," Mallar said, and started down the ladder.

"I see—"

"There's just no way, with an X-wing." His tone was both annoyed and discouraged. "It's not quick enough against a D-type. And the operator won't let me start training on an E-wing yet."

Ackbar snorted. "He must belong to that stodgy old order of instructors that believes in mastering one skill before taking on another." Reaching up toward Mallar, Ackbar held out a data card. "I was in the Mission Planning Office and saw this come up for you," he said. "I was coming this way, so I signed for you. I think you should look at it now."

"What is it?"

"Your orders," Ackbar said. "You've been placed on alert."

"Me? Why?" He fumbled with the data card reader. "Ferry pilot?"

"Do you have a problem with that?"

"Problem—no! It's terrific. I just didn't expect—"

"Most of the available pilots went with the ferry flight that just left. Why do you think it's so quiet here? But another flight will go out in the next fifty hours. You'll be the last called—but you may be called on all the same, to take a recon-X out to the Fifth Fleet."

"Gladly. It's something," Mallar said. "It counts for something. Thank you, sir."

Ackbar frowned crossly. "Airman Mallar, if you *are* called, it'll be because someone with considerably more experience did no better out there against the real thing than you did in here against the simulator. Does that make your orders any more clear?"

Mallar paled. "Yes, sir." Slipping the data card and reader back into his pocket, he grabbed the handrail and hastened back up the ladder to the simulator.

"Eighty-two-Y, please," he called to the operator as he opened the cockpit hatch. "And put me in a recon-X this time."

Chapter 15

◆

Strapped securely in the cockpit of his recon-X fighter, Lieutenant Rone Taggar went through his prepass checklist with unusually exacting care.

His target was N'zoth, the capital of the Duskhan League—the most important objective of the 21st Recon Group's targets, and quite probably the best defended. But it was not the danger ahead, on the other side of the hyperspace wall, that concerned him. What mattered was gathering the information he had been sent to collect and kicking it back out unjammed to the hypercomm receivers and data recorders waiting in the Fleet.

The beveled nose of the recon-X concealed six separate flat-scan imaging systems, each with its own independent pan and zoom. The scanning radar, infrared imager, and stereoscopic imagers were programmed to keep the planet centered in the data frame, filling it edge to edge. The other two systems were under the control of the R2-R recon droid, which would evaluate the images in real time and select both particular targets and the best scanning wavelength.

All six systems were linked to the hyperdrive controls and would begin operating the moment *Jennie Lee* entered realspace. The hypercomm data relay was automatic as well, even to the selection of alternate channels if jamming signals were detected. The pass trajectory was programmed into the autopilot, which would take over the controls if there was a deviation of more than one percent without pilot inputs.

It was said, jokingly, that all a recon-X pilot was really needed for was to keep the R2 unit company, and that a pilot could have a heart attack in hyperspace and still fly a perfect mission. The unit's second-in-command, Sleepy Nagelson—who was flying the Wakiza intercept—had gotten his nickname when cockpit monitors recorded him sleeping through a recon run, back during the Thrawn affair.

But Taggar shrugged all that off. In heart and mind both, he believed what he had told his pilots before they set off on the mission: that the irreplaceable quality the pilot brought to the cockpit was caring about the outcome. A pilot would keep trying when a machine would quit, because he understood the concept of failure, and the consequences mattered to him.

"There are no great stories told about drones that fought their way home with vital information, or rose above themselves to complete a perilous mission," he had told them. "You're there because you can make a difference. That's what I'm asking of you—make a difference, and make sure the job gets done. That's why there is a Twenty-first Recon Wing. Pilots—to your ships! I'll see you all on the other side."

The mission synchronization clock was counting down toward zero. For a moment Taggar paused to picture the other pilots, in other claustrophobic cockpits, nearing other targets scattered halfway across the Cluster. Even though 21st Recon had been newly formed to serve the Fifth Fleet, he had flown with several of them before in other units, other wars. He could picture all their faces, guess at all their moods.

00:15

Good recon, he thought, sending the wish at them. *And good luck.*

Taggar's nose had begun to itch, and he wrinkled it up in an unsuccessful attempt to salve it. He licked lips that had gone dry, flexed hands that had begun to stiffen from being held too tensely, checked systems that he had already checked three times.

00:05

Taggar's mother, a Y-wing pilot, had died attacking a Star Destroyer in the frightful clash at Endor. His own good-luck ritual, performed before the start of every mission, was to rub his thumb left to right across his mother's wings, which were taped above the navicom.

Mother, I hope I make you proud today.

00:00

The universe suddenly expanded around Taggar's recon fighter. Ahead lay a gray-green marble frosted with swirls of pale yellow clouds. The mission timer started to count upward as the imaging systems stirred in their mountings. Taggar flew a steady line as he read the reports from R2-R on his cockpit display.

IDENTIFIED: *ARAMADIA*-CLASS THRUSTSHIP
IDENTIFIED: *ARAMADIA*-CLASS THRUSTSHIP
IDENTIFIED: *VICTORY*-CLASS STAR DESTROYER
IDENTIFIED: *ARAMADIA*-CLASS THRUSTSHIP
IDENTIFIED: *IMPERIAL*-CLASS STAR DESTROYER
IDENTIFIED: *EXECUTOR*-CLASS STAR DESTROYER

The list grew longer as N'zoth grew larger ahead. Rone Taggar wanted to be afraid, but he did not have that luxury. He told himself he could be brave for five more minutes. In five minutes—perhaps less—it would be over.

Taggar tried to whistle past the graveyard, but his mouth was suddenly too dry.

*　　*　　*

There had been a tug-of-war between Leia and Ackbar over who would be invited to be in the War Hall at Fleet Headquarters when the data from the Koornacht recon incursion came in.

"This is not the time to repay favors or curry favor," Ackbar had said, holding out for keeping the list as short as possible. "You cannot control information that's already been freely distributed. We will need time to evaluate the data and place it in context."

"Everyone on that list has a legitimate right to know what's going on in Farlax," she had argued. "They're all going to have to be part of the decisions to come—Defense Council, Security Council, the rest of the Ruling Council, Rieekan from NRI. It's not as though I'm trying to bring in outsiders."

"No," Ackbar said. "You are only bringing in a senator who just tried to have you removed from office, and another who is likely to try in the near future. They are part of the same government as you, Leia, but they are not your allies."

Behn-kihl-nahm's opinion had settled the question in favor of Leia's side. As the intercepts neared, the room was full of extra bodies, and there was more than enough to occupy them.

The full-wall display in the War Hall had been divided into twenty-four identical rectangles. Each contained an intercept chart, with a blank circle representing the target planet and a red line marking the expected path of the scout. As the contacts proceeded, the charts would change to show the position of the ships and the progress of the scans.

Beside each chart was space for a flat-screen feed from the scout's imagers. At the moment the name of the target world and the type of scout assigned to it were displayed in that space.

Ackbar, Leia, and Han stood together at the back of the room, leaning on the railing at the edge of the raised observer's platform and watching twenty-four timers counting down in synchrony.

"It kind of reminds me of a tout board I saw at a million-credit betting parlor on Bragkis," Han said, "and everyone standing around waiting for the race to begin. 'Who's got a favorite?' 'What odds will you give me on Wakiza?' "

Leia usually found Han's irreverence refreshing. But she had no patience for it just then and walked away after shooting him a hot sidewise glare. Han's first instinct was to follow, but Ackbar stayed him with a touch.

"Let her be," he said. "This is a hard time. She does not have much water under her."

The room quieted dramatically in the last seconds, as everyone working attended to the console before them, and everyone watching turned away from their conversations and looked up toward the display. As zero turned to plus-1, the entire wall came alive with moving images as the charts began to change and the first images arrived.

It almost seemed to Han as though the wall were a squirming mass of tiny creatures made of light. Unless he focused his attention on just one area, the effect made his stomach turn and his nerves jangle.

Ackbar raised a hand and pointed to the lower right corner of the wall. "One casualty already," he said. Number 23, a pilotless ferret, had missed its rendezvous at Doornik 207, which at last report had been host to a nest of Corasgh. But all the other charts were beginning to fill in—the flight tracks changing from red to green, the faces of the planets beginning to be shaded in.

The early images from N'zoth caused a buzz in the room. They showed the unmistakable shapes of Star Destroyers, singled out by the R2-controlled imaging systems on Rone Taggar's *Jennie Lee*. After leaving Han, Leia had gone to stand by Ayddar Nylykerka, who was busily capturing individual frames from the data into a collage of ship portraits. She listened in while the intense little analyst from the Asset Tracking Office talked aloud to himself.

"That could be the *Redoubtable*," he muttered, consulting his lists. "It's definitely early *Imperial*-class, despite the modifications to the forward superstructure—"

The buzz turned into a dark murmur a few seconds later, when the view from Number 1 changed and another, sleeker dagger shape snapped into focus. There was hardly a person in the room who could not identify that profile, and the exceptions quickly learned the significance in a hasty whisper from a companion: there was a Super Star Destroyer in orbit around N'zoth.

From the beginning, the New Republic had opted to build a larger number of smaller vessels—Fleet carriers, *Republic*-class Star Destroyers, battle cruisers—rather than adopt the Imperial design philosophy. Mon Mothma had given orders to scrap rather than repair or make a museum piece of the sole SSD captured from the Empire. Consequently, the eight-kilometer-long behemoth circling N'zoth had anything in the New Republic Fleet badly outgunned.

"Now, that, that can only be *Intimidator*," Nylykerka pronounced. "All of the late-production Super-class had that additional shield tower located on the centerline—"

Shocking as that discovery was, the attention of the audience in the War Hall was quickly drawn elsewhere. As the counters approached the two-minute mark and the scouts raced toward the midpoint and closest approach of their passes, the display wall was filling with images of warships, until it resembled a larger version of the collage at Nylykerka's station.

There were Star Destroyers at Wakiza, at Zhina, at New Brigia and Doornik 881, where the Imperial factory farm had been. The Yevethan fleet at Morning Bell now numbered at least sixteen vessels, including four Star

Destroyers, six *Aramadia*-class thrustships, and a queer-looking Dreadnaught-scale ship, which Nylykerka excitedly identified as a long-missing Imperial testbed, the *EX-F.* Other thrustships seemed to be everywhere—orbiting all the other Duskhan League worlds, at Polneye and the former Morath mining operation on Kojash.

Conspicuously missing from the entry scans were the three Imperial shipyards named in Lieutenant Sconn's deposition: Black Fifteen, which had been located in orbit at N'zoth; Black Eleven, which had been at Zhina; and Black Eight, at Wakiza. Ackbar noted their absence to Han and added, "I do not think we will find them—I do not put it past the Yevetha to have moved the shipyards to concealed locations. I suspect that that is what *Astrolabe* stumbled on at Doornik Eleven Forty-two."

At 02:05, the signal from Number 16 at Polneye abruptly terminated, the tracking chart freezing with only forty-two percent of the planet scanned. Moments later Number 19, at Morning Bell, and Number 5, at the Duskhan world Tizon, also went dead.

The losses did not stop there. All over the wall, the individual displays were going blank almost as quickly as they had come to life. Only half the scouts reached the midpoint of their runs. Three more winked out almost as one as Leia drifted away from Nylykerka and toward the middle of the War Hall.

"What's going on out there?" she breathed to no one in particular as she stared up at the displays.

The signals from Z'fell, Wakiza, Faz, N'zoth—all assigned to the 21st Recon Group's X-wings—were among the last to vanish, but vanish they did. No scout managed to scan more than three-fourths of a Duskhan League target before being destroyed.

There was not a sound in the War Hall other than a muffled cough or a furniture creak as the five-minute timer expired. Only four scouts survived to jump out of their target systems—all drones. None had found anything during their passes, save for newly dead worlds. Eyes began to turn from the frozen images on the wall to the woman standing alone in the center of the room.

"Now we know," Leia said simply. "Controller, put the pilots' visual IDs up while you queue the data from Number One for replay. I'd like us to remember who we owe for this."

The blast that disabled Rone Taggar's recon-X came from behind and below, without warning. Even before the cockpit went dark, he could tell from the blue lightning dancing over the cockpit that it was a powerful ion cannon bolt that had overwhelmed the fighter's shields. Twisting in his harness, he tried to look back and find his attacker. There'd been no fire from the ground during the close approach, and he was now out of range for any ordinary ground-based antiship battery.

"Come on, where are you?" he muttered. "Where'd you come from?"

There were dozens of stars bright enough that Taggar could not look directly at them without squinting—more than enough dazzle to hide an interceptor or a defense buoy from his eyes. But he didn't understand why his targeting system had missed it. The recon-X had the smallest blind spot to the rear of any Republic fighter, and on a normal threat acquisition—at fifty thousand meters or more—he would have bet a month's pay that he could have held off any equal opponent long enough to finish the run.

Taggar silently counted off the restart interval, fully expecting the killing shot to come before he reached 100. The absorbers worked passively, soaking up the excess surface charge and using it to feed the restart cell. Its momentum unchanged by the blast, his fighter was still speeding away from N'zoth. With a successful restart, he could grab the last thirty seconds of data on the unscanned far side and jump away to safety.

The count had reached eighty-seven when he felt the lurch of the tractor beam grabbing hold of his ship. With the spoiler shaking and the fuselage chattering around him, Taggar fished in his chest pocket for the purge stick. Another ship, corvette-size, was visible ahead of him as he rammed the stick home into the socket on the control panel.

The purge charge that jumped from the stick raced through the computer memories of the fighter, erasing every coherent bit. Its final stop was the R2 interface, where it passed to a shape charge under the droid's sensor dome. The small explosion that followed was surprisingly loud and briefly lit the inside of the cockpit. Glancing back, Taggar confirmed that the charge had completely and thoroughly decapitated the droid.

That left only one duty—the suicide needle now available at the other end of the purge stick, and the dead-man grip of the ship's self-destruct trigger. Taggar looked out at the Yevethan warship, measuring the closing distance. He knew that he was taking a chance by waiting, especially after they'd seen R2-R blow its top. But he also knew that the corvette would have to lower its shields to bring him alongside.

When the ship had drawn close enough to loom over the fighter, Taggar closed his left hand around the trigger and let his head roll to one side as though he were unconscious. Watching through slit eyes, he saw light spilling from the underside of the corvette, between the opening doors of the docking berth. There was no pinnace inside—the berth was meant for his fighter.

Gambling, he waited longer still, until the coupling lines grabbed the spoilers and drew the recon-X upward, until the doors began to close under him. Then he lifted his head, rubbed his thumb across the pilot's wings taped to the console, and jammed the palm of his right hand against the end of the purge stick.

A few moments later his head lolled forward against his chest and the hand closed tightly around the trigger began to relax, his tired fingers yielding against the pressure of the springplate. Taggar was peacefully elsewhere when the destruct charge ripped the belly of the corvette open along the centerline, spilling a churning cloud of debris from both ships into space.

As bright fire enveloped *Beauty of Yevetha,* Nil Spaar averted his eyes from the sight, then turned and searched the chamber for the proctor of defense for the spawnworld.

"Kol Attan!" he bellowed.

His fighting crests shrunken almost to invisibility, Kol Attan shuffled forward. "Viceroy, I—"

Nil Spaar silenced him with a glare and pointed at the floor. Trembling, the proctor lowered himself to one knee, closed his eyes, and bared his neck. The viceroy circled him slowly, flexing his right hand in a motion that brought the dewclaw curling out to its full length.

"You are a coward as well as incompetent," Nil Spaar whispered at last. "Your blood is not worth spilling. It would be beneath me to touch you. I declare you *to-mara,* a shamed one. Go home and beg your *darna* for death."

When the proctor did not move, Nil Spaar drew a deep breath that brought a flush to his crests, then sent Kol Attan sprawling with a vicious kick. "You will not provoke me into giving you an honorable exit," he said through clenched teeth. "Go!"

As the proctor scrambled away on all fours, Nil Spaar turned his back to him. "Tal Fraan," he said.

The *nitakka* came forward with strength in his strides and pride in his carriage. "Sir."

"You anticipated that the vermin would violate the All in an attempt to know us. How is it you come to your prescience?"

"I have spent time with them, in the camps on Pa'aal, and aboard *Devotion of Yevetha,* where they

serve us," said Tal Fraan. "I have seen how they hunger
to debase even the smallest mysteries, instead of embrac-
ing the mysteries as they present themselves. The pale
ones, especially, seem to me driven this way."

Nil Spaar nodded slowly. "You failed to anticipate
that the vermin who came would choose death over cap-
tivity. That failure has cost my fleet a useful vessel, and
wasted Yevetha blood."

Drawing a hard breath, Tal Fraan dropped immediately to one knee. "Yes, *darama*. I know my error."

"Rise," Nil Spaar said, and the younger Yevetha
complied. "I shall not hold you to account for the failure
of Kol Attan to seize the hostage you brought to him.
Nor for the offense of the vermin in killing above their
station."

"You are gracious, Viceroy."

"There are many kinds of vermin," Nil Spaar said
offhandedly. "Perhaps those that were sent here are
more like Commander Paret, who at least had the courage to defy me when I took this ship from him, than they
are like those we hold in service. Otherwise, I would
have judged them as you do."

"I do not deserve your mercy, *darama*."

"No," Nil Spaar said. "But you will help me think
on how to answer the vermin for their boldness, and to
strike at this one called Leia, for commissioning such
sacrilege. And perhaps I will forget the other after a
while, on such pleasures of revenge as you devise."

Ackbar stood before the briefing room viewscreen
holding one hand behind his back and pointing with the
other.

"This seems workable to me," he said. "If we tap
Task Forces Apex and Summer from the Fourth Fleet,
Task Forces Bellbright and Token from the Second Fleet,
and Task Force Gemstone from the Third, we should be
able to maintain our current patrols through the rest of

the New Republic while building the force in Farlax to the strength of two battle groups."

"Meanwhile, the Home Fleet will be left at full strength to defend Coruscant," Leia said. "Which may not sit well with the border sectors, but seems only prudent."

"Well—General A'baht will be happy," Han said, leaning back in his chair. "This is what he's been saying he needed ever since he got there."

Turning half away from the viewscreen, Ackbar exchanged glances with Leia. "General A'baht will not be in command of the combined force," Ackbar said, and turned back.

"No? Well—he might not mind too much," Han said, folding his hands on his lap. "A combined command like that is kind of like being put in charge of a zoo. Who are you going to pull off the line? Admiral Nantz is senior flag officer now, right?"

Ackbar turned back toward the viewscreen, both hands tucked behind him. "No," he said. "Not Nantz."

A crooked smile creased Han's face. "You'll do fine, Admiral," he said. "It's like riding a—it's something you don't forget how to do."

"Han, Admiral Ackbar will be staying here with me," Leia said quietly. "I'm putting you in charge of the forces in Farlax."

The smile faded quickly. "Didn't we take this class already?" he asked, sitting forward and dropping his forearms on the table. "I'm not the grand admiral kind. And this'll just make it look like you can't make up your mind—Etahn, me, Etahn, me—"

"Han, she had no choice," Ackbar said without turning. "The Defense Council, led by Senator Fey'lya, insisted on approving the commander. He's lost confidence in General A'baht."

"So why me?"

"Because you've already spent some time with the Fifth. Because you're already familiar with the geography and logistics out there. But mostly because you're not tainted," Leia said. "Fey'lya wanted Admiral Jid'yda—"

"A Bothan—of course."

"—and Bennie offered you as a compromise. As he explained it, the pro-Leia senators see you as supportive of me, and the anti-Leia senators think you're independent enough to deal with me."

Han shook his head. "I can tell that *that* must have been an elevated debate."

"You can't begin to know how absurd it was at times," Ackbar said, turning away from the viewscreen and approaching the table. "Senator Cundertol actually supported you on the grounds of—and I quote the great man verbatim—'He's not doing anything else, is he?'"

"A heartwarming recommendation," Han said. "Remind me to thank His Denseness." He pulled Ackbar's datapad toward him and studied the list of force assignments. "I suppose it's a little late at this point to consider negotiating a truce."

"I can't believe that the Yevetha will ever consider us their equals at the table," Leia said.

"I suppose not," Han said, and pushed the datapad away. "For a while there, Leia dear, I actually let myself think that we'd have a chance for that normal life you told Luke you wanted. I let myself believe that we were through with this sort of thing. And I have to tell you— leaving the uniform in the closet really agreed with me."

Leia and Han exchanged rueful smiles at that. "Well—seems like going all the way back to Yavin," he added, "I've made you coax, wheedle, guilt, and shame me into volunteering for dirty jobs. I won't make you do it this time. Fact is, the Yevetha disgust me—and they scare the stang out of me, too. If we don't control them now, the future could get very messy. So I'll take this job, because it needs to be done."

"The hard jobs are usually necessary ones," Ackbar mused.

"This isn't hard," Han said. "Those pilots who flew into the Cluster, knowing the odds on coming back— that's hard. All *I* have to do is give men like that a reason. What's the timetable, Admiral?"

"There is a ferry flight of recon-X's leaving for the Fifth Fleet in fifteen hours. They will fly escort for your shuttle," Ackbar said. "You should arrive not long after the task groups from the Fourth Fleet reach Farlax. Oh, and you will take the temporary rank of commodore for the duration of this assignment."

"Commodore, eh?" He tried a cheerful smile on Leia, but she was no more persuaded by it than he was. "Does that come with a hat?"

Even though he was caught in legal limbo—not quite a full member of the Senate, nor quite a former one—Tig Peramis of Walalla retained some of the usual courtesies of office. Behn-kihl-nahm would not allow him to speak or vote in the Assembly and had removed him entirely from the Defense Council. But Peramis's access keys still allowed him entrance to all but the Council chambers and restricted records. And that meant access to the other senators, whose gossip he thought worth nearly as much as a senatorial record search.

Months ago he had denounced the Fifth Fleet as a weapon of conquest and tyranny and warned the Defense Council about the ambitions of Vader's daughter. He had been reprimanded by Behn-kihl-nahm and ridiculed by Tolik Yar, but events had proved him prophetic, confirming his worst fears. And the lightning annexation—on the flimsiest of pretexts—of eighteen formerly independent worlds in Farlax seemed to Peramis to foreordain a dramatic escalation.

The middle-of-the-night gatherings in the Defense chambers, Leia's secret meeting with the Ruling Council, the "bungled" blockade attempt, the nakedly emotional appeals on behalf of tiny alien populations, and the open and deliberate provocation of the Yevetha at every turn all appeared to Peramis as pieces of an elaborate plan to justify annexation of Koornacht itself. Even the periodic outbreaks of criticism in the Senate seemed calculated, the critics themselves buffoons doing more discredit to their cause than damage to the Princess.

But something a drunken Senator Cundertol carelessly said to him alarmed Peramis to the point that he could no longer be satisfied with rumor and gossip.

"A Corellian pirate with two battle groups to command," Cundertol had giggled. "He'll show you goon-faces something about fighting. Old Eating-a-Boat didn't want to kill other goon-faces, so he's goon-goon-gone—"

Peramis fed him more doan wine in the hopes of coaxing Cundertol to tell him more, but the Bakuran only grew more childishly self-amused at being in the superior position.

"Should have been a good boy," Cundertol said, swaying on his feet as he shook a finger. "You can't come to the party."

Half an hour later Cundertol was glassy-eyed with doan shock, and Peramis was entering the Senate office complex with both his and Cundertol's voting keys in his hand.

Cundertol's key alone would not be enough to give Peramis access to the Defense Council records, but Peramis knew from experience that security on senators' personal logs was much more lax. Convenience demanded it. A personal log kept behind too many barriers would never be used. Of course, nothing classified Secure was supposed to be kept in something as unsecured as a personal log. But Peramis thought Cundertol someone who was likely to place more value on convenience than confidentiality.

The Bakuran's voting key opened every necessary door and every damning file. It was all there, in a xenophobic rant that demonstrated the surprising fact that the senator actually *did* temper his words in public.

A battle group–strength force was headed to Farlax to reinforce the Fifth—but piecemeal, a clever stratagem that would help conceal what was happening by allowing all the other battle groups to remain visible on their patrol stations. And the Corellian who was to take charge of the war fleet was, as Peramis had suspected, Princess Leia's husband, Han Solo.

Peramis stayed in Cundertol's office only long enough to watch the log once and copy it to a data card. Then he returned to the private dining room where he had left Cundertol, replaced the voting key in the senator's valise, and left him to ride out his pleasure trance alone.

In the privacy of his own quarters in the Walallan mission, he retrieved the small black box Nil Spaar had given him from its hiding place in a chest of his eldest son's toys. There was no one to see him—he had sent his family home months ago, and the modest staff that served him knew better than to intrude in the middle of the night.

Seated at a table in his office, Peramis connected both the black box and his datapad to the hypercomm. At that point he paused. The furtiveness, the physical act of readying the devices, made him uncomfortable. He had not used the black box before. He had told himself that he never would. Peramis did not think of himself as a spy, much less a traitor.

But he had kept the box nonetheless.

He told himself he was an honorable man, with an honorable cause—to contain the militarism that threatened all that had been won in the Rebellion. After a successful adventure in Farlax, Leia would be untouchable. The Yevetha had to be warned.

And it appealed to Peramis's vision of cosmic irony that Senator Cundertol would be the one to warn them, in his own words.

But when Peramis activated the hypercomm, he left his office so that he would not have to hear those words again.

Three hours short of reaching *Intrepid,* the commodore's Fleet shuttle *Tampion* and its ferry flight escort abruptly dropped out of hyperspace. They found half a dozen Yevethan ships waiting for them—the Interdictor Dreadnaught that had yanked them down, two thrust-ships, and three smaller vessels.

The ambush had been perfectly planned. Before the dozing recon-X pilots and startled shuttle passengers even understood what was happening, their ships were bracketed in a furious ion-cannon crossfire. The fighters were disabled almost at once, then left drifting, ignored. The unarmed but better-shielded shuttle took more subduing but was soon dead in space, unable to maneuver or escape.

Shortly after, *Tampion* was moving away from its escorts on a new course, under tow alongside one of the spherical thrustships. Raging over his impotence, unable even to signal the other pilots, Plat Mallar watched the pair jump out toward Koornacht. The Cluster filled the entire sky on the starboard side of his ship, like a painting of a swarm of night sparks.

Mallar was never so sure of death as he was when the shuttle vanished. Helpless as the fighters were, any one of the five remaining ships could have dispatched them at leisure.

Instead, the five ships gracefully arrayed themselves in a V, with the Interdictor in the lead position. Moments later they jumped away from the ambush point, their mission seemingly complete.

Why did they leave us alive? Mallar wondered.

An answer came to him almost at once, and it made him feel sick inside. *So we could tell the Fleet, tell Corus-*

cant, what happened to the commodore. So we would know that they have him.

Han was brought before Nil Spaar not as a trophy, but as an object of curiosity.

The encounter was in private, with no one else present except for Han's guards—two immensely strong male Yevetha who carried no weapons and seemed unlikely to need any, given how Han was bound. And the setting for the encounter was puzzling—not a throne room or arena of humiliation for the conquered, but a tile-wrapped chamber with floor gutters and valve jets mounted high on the walls. It made Han think of a shower stall, or an abattoir—and he wished he hadn't thought of the second possibility.

As the Yevethan viceroy slowly circled his prisoner, he took particular interest in the bruises and burns Han had acquired by resisting when the soldiers boarded *Tampion*. Nil Spaar leaned in close to study the marks but was careful not to touch Han, even with gloved hands.

"You are the mate of Leia."

"I guess that secret's out," said Han, deciding to try to take his captor's measure. "And you're Nil Spaar. I've heard a lot about you, all of it bad. You've moved right to the top of my least favorite people list. I had to drop Jabba the Hutt off to make room for you. It's only fair to tell you that my number one goal in life is to outlive everyone on the list. I was halfway there before you replaced Jabba."

The Yevethan ruler did not seem to take any notice of Han's goading. "What sort of vermin are you?"

"I think the word you're looking for is 'scoundrel,' as in 'Corellian scoundrel,' " Han said. "I've also answered to 'rascal,' 'pirate,' 'smuggler,' 'wretched scum,' 'toad-licker,' and a few others. Not all of those are considered polite where I come from, though—so I don't always answer politely. Just so you'll know, 'vermin' probably counts as impolite."

"You are stronger than she," Nil Spaar said, cocking his head. "Why do you follow her? Why do you not lead?"

Han answered with a contemptuous gaze and a shake of his head. "I was gonna tell you that grabbing me was the biggest mistake you ever made," he said. "Now I see it's the second biggest. You've misjudged Leia from the beginning. Day in and day out, she might just be the strongest person I know. And you're gonna find that out the hard way now."

Saying nothing, Nil Spaar retreated to the far end of the chamber, as if to leave. Then he gestured to the guards and spoke a few words in an unfamiliar language. One guard stepped away from Han to stand against the wall. The other, the crests at his temples swelling, stepped in front of Han and swung on him with such speed that Han could not duck away.

The blow fell on his right arm, right above the blaster burn from Captain Sreas's panicky, mistimed shot. The force of the blow drove the ball into his shoulder joint, leaving the arm suddenly numb. The next was aimed at his face, and Han was able to soften the impact by turning with it. But it still scalded him with pain.

The beating seemed unpracticed, experimental. Nil Spaar stood calmly watching, as though waiting for something—an almost clinical curiosity, with no sign of gloating. Han wondered if the guard had ever seen a human before and tried to make note of how and where he was struck, thinking it might offer clues to Yevethan vulnerabilities.

It lasted only until a head shot left Han crumpled on his side on the floor with blood running from his mouth and nose. Then Nil Spaar spoke sharply to the guard, who immediately backed away. The viceroy approached Han and crouched down beside him, peering curiously at the injuries. He reached out with one gloved hand and dabbed the fingertips in the small pool of blood collecting by Han's head. Bringing the glove up to his face, he passed the bloody fingertips through the air over the ridges of his face, as though sniffing them.

"Your blood is weak—as weak as any vermin's," Nil Spaar said. "It does not cause the heart to rise. It does not feed the *mara-nas*. It does not ripen the birthcask. I do not see why she has given herself to you. I do not see why you did not die unmated."

Then he stood, stripped off his gloves, and dropped them on the tile. *"Tar makara,"* he said to the guards. *"Talbran."*

Both knelt and offered their necks to the viceroy. *"Ko, darama,"* they murmured.

When Nil Spaar was gone, the guards scrubbed Han and the chamber down with equal diligence and vigor, then took him away, back to the cell where Lieutenant Barth and the body of Captain Sreas were waiting.

Admiral Ackbar returned to the family room wearing a longer face than he had when he left a few moments before. He looked at Leia, who was sitting in the middle of the floor, her arms wrapped around Jaina, whispering words of hope and comfort to her, and knew that those words could not possibly reach the anguish in Leia's own heart.

"Leia." Ackbar cleared his throat. "Will you come with me, please? There is something you must do, and I'm afraid it cannot wait."

She looked at him with a plaintive look that said, *Please. No more.* But she let Winter take Jaina and followed Ackbar out of the room and into the yard.

"Have you heard something more about Han? Something from the Yevetha?"

Ackbar shook his head and gestured down the walk toward the gate, where a messenger stood waiting outside.

Throwing Ackbar a disbelieving look, Leia moved down the path to where S-EP1 was vigilantly guarding the entry.

"Princess Leia, I have been sent by the acting chairman of the Ruling Council of the Senate to deliver this summons into your hands."

She reached out and took it from him. As she did, she saw Behn-kihl-nahm standing a few steps behind the messenger, hovering at the edge of the shadows.

"I'm sorry," he said, moving forward. "There was nothing I could do."

"Let Bennie in, Sleepy," Leia said, stepping back to make room on the path. "Who? Who would do this to me now?"

Behn-kihl-nahm's face wrinkled, as though he was reluctant to answer. "The summons is at the initiative of Chairman Beruss."

Bail Organa's old friend, and second only to Bennie as her ally. The name hit her like a roundhouse punch. "Why?" she asked plaintively.

"Doman feels that someone less personally involved must make the decisions now," Behn-kihl-nahm said gently. "He hopes you will understand this and step down on your own. He fears that you may act—precipitously."

"Precipitously!" Her laugh had a bitter edge. "Oh, he knows me—I'd like nothing more than to send the Fifth in to burn the Yevetha off the face of N'zoth. But how can I? How can I do *anything*, Bennie?" she asked, her voice pleading for an answer. "The Yevetha have my husband. My children's father is in the hands of Nil Spaar."

About the Author

Michael P. Kube-McDowell* is the pen name of Philadelphia-born novelist Michael Paul McDowell. His highly praised prior works include the star-spanning 1985 Philip K. Dick Award finalist *Emprise* and the evocative 1991 Hugo Award nominee *The Quiet Pools*.

In addition to his eight previous novels, Michael has contributed more than two dozen short stories to leading magazines and anthologies, including *Analog, The Magazine of Fantasy & Science Fiction, After the Flames,* and *Alternate Warriors.* Three of his stories have been adapted as episodes of the horror-fantasy television series *Tales from the Darkside.* Outside of science fiction, he is the author of more than five hundred nonfiction articles on subjects ranging from "scientific creationism" to the U.S. space program.

A popular guest at SF conventions, Michael is also a member of the cheerfully amateur folk-rock group The Black Book Band, in which he plays guitar, keyboards, and viola. A live album, *First Contact,* was released in 1995 by Dodeka Records.

Michael resides in central Michigan with artist and

* "Kube" is pronounced "CUE-bee."

modelmaker Gwen Zak, children Matt and Amanda,
cats Doc and Captain, and "entirely too many books."
At various times he has called Fairview Village (Camden), New Jersey; East Lansing, Sturgis, and Lansing,
Michigan; and Goshen, Indiana, home.

The World of
STAR WARS Novels

In May 1991, *Star Wars* caused a sensation in the publishing industry
with the Bantam Spectra release of Timothy Zahn's novel *Heir to the
Empire*. For the first time, Lucasfilm Ltd. had authorized new novels
that *continued* the famous story told in George Lucas's three block-
buster motion pictures: *Star Wars*, *The Empire Strikes Back*, and *Return of the Jedi*. Reader reaction was immediate and tumultuous: *Heir*
reached #1 on the *New York Times* bestseller list and demonstrated that
Star Wars lovers were eager for exciting new stories set in this universe, written by leading science fiction authors who shared their passion. Since then, each Bantam *Star Wars* novel has been an instant
national bestseller.

Lucasfilm and Bantam decided that future novels in the series would
be interconnected: that is, events in one novel would have consequences in the others. You might say that each Bantam *Star Wars*
novel, enjoyable on its own, is also part of a much larger tale.

Here is a special look at Bantam's *Star Wars* books, along with
excerpts from the more recent novels. Each one is available now wherever Bantam Books are sold.

SHADOWS OF THE EMPIRE
by Steve Perry
Setting: Between *The Empire Strikes Back*
and *Return of the Jedi*

*Here is a very special STAR WARS story dealing with Black Sun, a
galaxy-spanning criminal organization that is masterminded by one of
the most interesting villains in the STAR WARS universe: Xizor, dark
prince of the Falleen. Xizor's chief rival for the favor of Emperor
Palpatine is none other than Darth Vader himself—alive and well, and
a major character in this story, since it is set during the events of the
STAR WARS film trilogy.*

In the opening prologue, we revisit a familiar scene from The Empire Strikes Back, *and are introduced to our marvelous new bad guy:*

He looks like a walking corpse, Xizor thought. *Like a mummified
body dead a thousand years. Amazing he is still alive, much less the*

Xizor stood four meters away from the Emperor, watching as the man who had long ago been Senator Palpatine moved to stand in the holocam field. He imagined he could smell the decay in the Emperor's worn body. Likely that was just some trick of the recycled air, run through dozens of filters to ensure that there was no chance of any poison gas being introduced into it. Filtered the life out of it, perhaps, giving it that dead smell.

The viewer on the other end of the holo-link would see a close-up of the Emperor's head and shoulders, of an age-ravaged face shrouded in the cowl of his dark zeyd-cloth robe. The man on the other end of the transmission, light-years away, would not see Xizor, though Xizor would be able to see him. It was a measure of the Emperor's trust that Xizor was allowed to be here while the conversation took place.

The man on the other end of the transmission—if he could still be called that—

The air swirled inside the Imperial chamber in front of the Emperor, coalesced, and blossomed into the image of a figure down on one knee. A caped humanoid biped dressed in jet black, face hidden under a full helmet and breathing mask:

Darth Vader.

Vader spoke: "What is thy bidding, my master?"

If Xizor could have hurled a power bolt through time and space to strike Vader dead, he would have done it without blinking. Wishful thinking: Vader was too powerful to attack directly.

"There is a great disturbance in the Force," the Emperor said.

"I have felt it," Vader said.

"We have a new enemy. Luke Skywalker."

Skywalker? That had been Vader's name, a long time ago. Who was this person with the same name, someone so powerful as to be worth a conversation between the Emperor and his most loathsome creation? More importantly, why had Xizor's agents not uncovered this before now? Xizor's ire was instant—but cold. No sign of his surprise or anger would show on his imperturbable features. The Falleen did not allow their emotions to burst forth as did many of the inferior species; no, the Falleen ancestry was not fur but scales, not mammalian but reptilian. Not wild but coolly calculating. Such was much better. Much safer.

"Yes, my master," Vader continued.

"He could destroy us," the Emperor said.

Xizor's attention was riveted upon the Emperor and the holographic image of Vader kneeling on the deck of a ship far away. Here was interesting news indeed. Something the Emperor perceived as a danger to himself? Something the Emperor feared?

"He's just a boy," Vader said. "Obi-Wan can no longer help him."

Obi-Wan. That name Xizor knew. He was among the last of the Jedi Knights, a general. But he'd been dead for decades, hadn't he?

Apparently Xizor's information was wrong if Obi-Wan had been helping someone who was still a boy. His agents were going to be sorry.

Even as Xizor took in the distant image of Vader and the nearness of the Emperor, even as he was aware of the luxury of the Emperor's private and protected chamber at the core of the giant pyramidal palace, he was also able to make a mental note to himself: Somebody's head would roll for the failure to make him aware of all this. Knowledge was power; lack of knowledge was weakness. This was something he could not permit.

The Emperor continued. "The Force is strong with him. The son of Skywalker must not become a Jedi."

Son of Skywalker?

Vader's son! Amazing!

"If he could be turned he would become a powerful ally," Vader said.

There was something in Vader's voice when he said this, something Xizor could not quite put his finger on. Longing? Worry?

Hope?

"Yes . . . yes. He would be a great asset," the Emperor said. "Can it be done?"

There was the briefest of pauses. "He will join us or die, master."

Xizor felt the smile, though he did not allow it to show any more than he had allowed his anger play. Ah. Vader wanted Skywalker alive, *that* was what had been in his tone. Yes, he had said that the boy would join them or die, but this latter part was obviously meant only to placate the Emperor. Vader had no intention of killing Skywalker, his own son; that was obvious to one as skilled in reading voices as was Xizor. He had not gotten to be the Dark Prince, Underlord of Black Sun, the largest criminal organization in the galaxy, merely on his formidable good looks. Xizor didn't truly understand the Force that sustained the Emperor and made him and Vader so powerful, save to know that it certainly worked somehow. But he did know that it was something the extinct Jedi had supposedly mastered. And now, apparently, this new player had tapped into it. Vader wanted Skywalker alive, had practically promised the Emperor that he would deliver him alive—and converted.

This was most interesting.

Most interesting indeed.

The Emperor finished his communication and turned back to face him. "Now, where were we, Prince Xizor?"

The Dark Prince smiled. He would attend to the business at hand, but he would not forget the name of Luke Skywalker.

THE TRUCE AT BAKURA by Kathy Tyers
Setting: Immediately after *Return of the Jedi*

The day after his climactic battle with Emperor Palpatine and the sacrifice of his father, Darth Vader, who died saving his life, Luke Skywalker helps recover an Imperial drone ship bearing a startling message intended for the Emperor. It is a distress signal from the far-off Imperial outpost of Bakura, which is under attack by an alien invasion force, the Ssi-ruuk. Leia sees a rescue mission as an opportunity to achieve a diplomatic victory for the Rebel Alliance, even if it means fighting alongside former Imperials. But Luke receives a vision from Obi-Wan Kenobi revealing that the stakes are even higher: the invasion at Bakura threatens everything the Rebels have won at such great cost.

STAR WARS: X-WING
by Michael A. Stackpole
ROGUE SQUADRON
WEDGE'S GAMBLE
Setting: Two and a half years after *Return of the Jedi*

Inspired by X-wing, *the bestselling computer game from LucasArts Entertainment Co., this exciting series chronicles the further adventures of the most feared and fearless fighting force in the galaxy. A new generation of X-wing pilots, led by Commander Wedge Antilles, is combating the remnants of the Empire still left after the events of the STAR WARS movies. Here are novels full of explosive space action, nonstop adventure, and the special brand of wonder known as STAR WARS.*

In this very early scene, young Corellian pilot Corran Horn faces a tough challenge fast enough to get his heart pounding—and this is only a simulation! [P.S.: "Whistler" is Corran's R2 astromech droid]:

The Corellian brought his proton torpedo targeting program up and locked on to the TIE. It tried to break the lock, but turbolaser fire from the *Korolev* boxed it in. Corran's heads-up display went red and he triggered the torpedo. "Scratch one eyeball."

The missile shot straight in at the fighter, but the pilot broke hard to port and away, causing the missile to overshoot the target. *Nice flying!* Corran brought his X-wing over and started down to loop in behind the TIE, but as he did so, the TIE vanished from his forward screen and reappeared in his aft arc. Yanking the stick hard to the right and pulling it back, Corran wrestled the X-wing up and to starboard, then inverted and rolled out to the left.

A laser shot jolted a tremor through the simulator's couch. *Lucky thing I had all shields aft!* Corran reinforced them with energy from his lasers, then evened them out fore and aft. Jinking the fighter right and left, he avoided laser shots coming in from behind, but they all came in far closer than he liked.

He knew Jace had been in the bomber, and Jace was the only pilot in the unit who could have stayed with him. *Except for our leader.* Corran smiled broadly. *Coming to see how good I really am, Commander Antilles? Let me give you a clinic.* "Make sure you're in there solid, Whistler, because we're going for a little ride."

Corran refused to let the R2's moan slow him down. A snap-roll brought the X-wing up on its port wing. Pulling back on the stick yanked the fighter's nose up away from the original line of flight. The TIE stayed with him, then tightened up on the arc to close distance. Corran then rolled another ninety degrees and continued the turn into a dive. Throttling back, Corran hung in the dive for three seconds, then hauled back hard on the stick and cruised up into the TIE fighter's aft.

The X-wing's laser fire missed wide to the right as the TIE cut to the left. Corran kicked his speed up to full and broke with the TIE. He let the X-wing rise above the plane of the break, then put the fighter through a twisting roll that ate up enough time to bring him again into the TIE's rear. The TIE snapped to the right and Corran looped out left.

He watched the tracking display as the distance between them grew to be a kilometer and a half, then slowed. *Fine, you want to go nose to nose? I've got shields and you don't.* If Commander Antilles wanted to commit virtual suicide, Corran was happy to oblige him. He tugged the stick back to his sternum and rolled out in an inversion loop. *Coming at you!*

The two starfighters closed swiftly. Corran centered his foe in the crosshairs and waited for a dead shot. Without shields the TIE fighter would die with one burst, and Corran wanted the kill to be clean. His

HUD flicked green as the TIE juked in and out of the center, then locked green as they closed.

The TIE started firing at maximum range and scored hits. At that distance the lasers did no real damage against the shields, prompting Corran to wonder why Wedge was wasting the energy. Then, as the HUD's green color started to flicker, realization dawned. *The bright bursts on the shields are a distraction to my targeting! I better kill him now!*

Corran tightened down on the trigger button, sending red laser needles stabbing out at the closing TIE fighter. He couldn't tell if he had hit anything. Lights flashed in the cockpit and Whistler started screeching furiously. Corran's main monitor went black, his shields were down, and his weapons controls were dead.

The pilot looked left and right. "Where is he, Whistler?"

The monitor in front of him flickered to life and a diagnostic report began to scroll by. Bloodred bordered the damage reports. "Scanners, out; lasers, out; shields, out; engine, out! I'm a wallowing Hutt just hanging here in space."

THE COURTSHIP OF PRINCESS LEIA
by Dave Wolverton
Setting: Four years after *Return of the Jedi*

One of the most interesting developments in Bantam's Star Wars *novels is that in their storyline, Han Solo and Princess Leia start a family. This tale reveals how the couple originally got together. Wishing to strengthen the fledgling New Republic by bringing in powerful allies, Leia opens talks with the Hapes consortium of more than sixty worlds. But the consortium is ruled by the Queen Mother, who, to Han's dismay, wants Leia to marry her son, Prince Isolder. Before this action-packed story is over, Luke will join forces with Isolder against a group of Force-trained "witches" and face a deadly foe.*

Luke stood in a mountain fortress of stone, looking over a plain with a sea of dark forested hills beyond, and a storm rose—a magnificent wind that brought with it towering walls of black clouds and dust, trees hurtling toward him and twisting through the sky. The clouds thundered overhead, filled with purple flames, obliterating all sunlight, and Luke could feel a malevolence hidden in those clouds and knew that they had been raised through the power of the dark side of the Force.

Dust and stones whistled through the air like autumn leaves. Luke tried to hold on to the stone parapet overlooking the plain to keep from being swept from the fortress walls. Winds pounded in his ears like the roar of an ocean, howling.

It was as if a storm of pure dark Force raged over the countryside, and suddenly, amid the towering clouds of darkness that thundered toward him, Luke could hear laughing, the sweet sound of women laughing. He looked above into the dark clouds, and saw the women borne through the air along with the rocks and debris, like motes of dust, laughing. A voice seemed to whisper, "the witches of Dathomir."

HEIR TO THE EMPIRE
DARK FORCE RISING
THE LAST COMMAND
by Timothy Zahn
Setting: Five years after *Return of the Jedi*

This #1 bestselling trilogy introduces two legendary forces of evil into the Star Wars *literary pantheon. Grand Admiral Thrawn has taken control of the Imperial fleet in the years since the destruction of the Death Star, and the mysterious Joruus C'baoth is a fearsome Jedi Master who has been seduced by the dark side. Han and Leia have now been married for about a year, and as the story begins, she is pregnant with twins. Thrawn's plan is to crush the Rebellion and resurrect the Empire's New Order with C'baoth's help—and in return, the Dark Master will get Han and Leia's Jedi children to mold as he wishes. For as readers of this magnificent trilogy will see, Luke Skywalker is not the last of the old Jedi. He is the first of the new.*

The Jedi Academy Trilogy:
JEDI SEARCH
DARK APPRENTICE
CHAMPIONS OF THE FORCE
by Kevin J. Anderson
Setting: Seven years after *Return of the Jedi*

In order to assure the continuation of the Jedi Knights, Luke Skywalker has decided to start a training facility: a Jedi Academy. He will gather Force-sensitive students who show potential as prospective Jedi and serve as their mentor, as Jedi Masters Obi-Wan Kenobi and Yoda did for him. Han and Leia's twins are now toddlers, and there is a third

Jedi child: the infant Anakin, named after Luke and Leia's father. In this trilogy, we ~~discover the existence of a~~ powerful Imperial dooms-day weapon, the horrifying Sun Crusher—which will soon become the centerpiece of a titanic struggle between Luke Skywalker and his most brilliant Jedi Academy student, who is delving dangerously into the dark side.

In this scene from the first novel, Jedi Search, *Luke vocalizes his concept of a new Jedi order to a distinguished assembly of New Republic leaders:*

As he descended the long ramp, Luke felt all eyes turn toward him. A hush fell over the assembly. Luke Skywalker, the lone remaining Jedi Master, almost never took part in governmental proceedings.

"I have an important matter to address," he said.

Mon Mothma gave him a soft, mysterious smile and gestured for him to take a central position. "The words of a Jedi Knight are always welcome to the New Republic," she said.

Luke tried not to look pleased. She had provided the perfect opening for him. "In the Old Republic," he said, "Jedi Knights were the protectors and guardians of all. For a thousand generations the Jedi used the powers of the Force to guide, defend, and provide support for the rightful government of worlds—before the dark days of the Empire came, and the Jedi Knights were killed."

He let his words hang, then took another breath. "Now we have a New Republic. The Empire appears to be defeated. We have founded a new government based upon the old, but let us hope we learn from our mistakes. Before, an entire order of Jedi watched over the Republic, offering strength. Now I am the only Jedi Master who remains.

"Without that order of protectors to provide a backbone of strength for the New Republic, can we survive? Will we be able to weather the storms and the difficulties of forging a new union? Until now we have suffered severe struggles—but in the future they will be seen as nothing more than birth pangs."

Before the other senators could disagree with that, Luke continued. "Our people had a common foe in the Empire, and we must not let our defenses lapse just because we have internal problems. More to the point, what will happen when we begin squabbling among ourselves over petty matters? The old Jedi helped to mediate many types of disputes. What if there are no Jedi Knights to protect us in the difficult times ahead?

"My sister is undergoing Jedi training. She has a great deal of skill in the Force. Her three children are also likely candidates to be trained as young Jedi. In recent years I have come to know a woman named

Mara Jade, who is now unifying the smugglers—the former smugglers," he amended, "into an organization that can support the needs of the New Republic. She also has a talent for the Force. I have encountered others in my travels."

Another pause. The audience was listening so far. "But are these the only ones? We already know that the ability to use the Force is passed from generation to generation. Most of the Jedi were killed in the Emperor's purge—but could he possibly have eradicated all of the descendants of those Knights? I myself was unaware of the potential power within me until Obi-Wan Kenobi taught me how to use it. My sister Leia was similarly unaware.

"How many people are abroad in this galaxy who have a comparable strength in the Force, who are potential members of a new order of Jedi Knights, but are unaware of who they are?"

Luke looked at them again. "In my brief search I have already discovered that there are indeed some descendants of former Jedi. I have come here to ask"—he turned to gesture toward Mon Mothma, swept his hands across the people gathered there in the chamber—"for two things.

"First, that the New Republic officially sanction my search for those with a hidden talent for the Force, to seek them out and try to bring them to our service. For this I will need some help."

"And what will you yourself be doing?" Mon Mothma asked, shifting in her robes.

CHILDREN OF THE JEDI
by Barbara Hambly
Setting: Eight years after *Return of the Jedi*

The Star Wars *characters face a menace from the glory days of the Empire when a thirty-year-old automated Imperial Dreadnaught comes to life and begins its grim mission: to gather forces and annihilate a long-forgotten stronghold of Jedi children. When Luke is whisked onboard, he begins to communicate with the brave Jedi Knight who paralyzed the ship decades ago, and gave her life in the process. Now she is part of the vessel, existing in its artificial intelligence core, and guiding Luke through one of the most unusual adventures he has ever had.*

In this scene, Luke discovers that an evil presence is gathering, one that will force him to join the battle:

Like See-Threepio, Nichos Marr sat in the outer room of the suite to which Cray had been assigned, in the power-down mode that was the droid equivalent of rest. Like Threepio, at the sound of Luke's almost noiseless tread he turned his head, aware of his presence.

"Luke?" Cray had equipped him with the most sensitive vocal modulators, and the word was calibrated to a whisper no louder than the rustle of the blueleaves massed outside the windows. He rose, and crossed to where Luke stood, the dull silver of his arms and shoulders a phantom gleam in the stray flickers of light. "What is it?"

"I don't know." They retreated to the small dining area where Luke had earlier probed his mind, and Luke stretched up to pin back a corner of the lamp-sheath, letting a slim triangle of butter-colored light fall on the purple of the vulwood tabletop. "A dream. A premonition, maybe." It was on his lips to ask, *Do you dream?* but he remembered the ghastly, imageless darkness in Nichos's mind, and didn't. He wasn't sure if his pupil was aware of the difference from his human perception and knowledge, aware of just exactly what he'd lost when his consciousness, his self, had been transferred.

In the morning Luke excused himself from the expedition Tomla El had organized with Nichos and Cray to the Falls of Dessiar, one of the places on Ithor most renowned for its beauty and peace. When they left he sought out Umwaw Moolis, and the tall herd leader listened gravely to his less than logical request and promised to put matters in train to fulfill it. Then Luke descended to the House of the Healers, where Drub McKumb lay, sedated far beyond pain but with all the perceptions of agony and nightmare still howling in his mind.

"Kill you!" He heaved himself at the restraints, blue eyes glaring furiously as he groped and scrabbled at Luke with his clawed hands. "It's all poison! I see you! I see the dark light all around you! You're him! You're him!" His back bent like a bow; the sound of his shrieking was like something being ground out of him by an infernal mangle.

Luke had been through the darkest places of the universe and of his own mind, had done and experienced greater evil than perhaps any man had known on the road the Force had dragged him . . . Still, it was hard not to turn away.

"We even tried yarrock on him last night," explained the Healer in charge, a slightly built Ithorian beautifully tabby-striped green and yellow under her simple tabard of purple linen. "But apparently the earlier doses that brought him enough lucidity to reach here from his point of origin oversensitized his system. We'll try again in four or five days."

Luke gazed down into the contorted, grimacing face.

"As you can see," the Healer said, "the internal perception of pain and fear is slowly lessening. It's down to ninety-three percent of what it was when he was first brought in. Not much, I know, but something."

"Him! *Him! HIM!*" Foam spattered the old man's stained gray beard.

Who?

"I wouldn't advise attempting any kind of mindlink until it's at least down to fifty percent, Master Skywalker."

"No," said Luke softly.

Kill you all. And, *They are gathering* . . .

"Do you have recordings of everything he's said?"

"Oh, yes." The big coppery eyes blinked assent. "The transcript is available through the monitor cubicle down the hall. We could make nothing of them. Perhaps they will mean something to you."

They didn't. Luke listened to them all, the incoherent groans and screams, the chewed fragments of words that could be only guessed at, and now and again the clear disjointed cries: "Solo! Solo! Can you hear me? Children . . . Evil . . . Gathering here . . . Kill you all!"

DARKSABER by Kevin J. Anderson
Setting: Immediately thereafter

Not long after Children of the Jedi, *Luke and Han learn that evil Hutts are building a reconstruction of the original Death Star—and that the Empire is still alive, in the form of Daala, who has joined forces with Pellaeon, former second in command to the feared Grand Admiral Thrawn. In this early scene, Luke has returned to the home of Obi-Wan Kenobi on Tatooine to try and consult a long-gone mentor:*

He stood anxious and alone, feeling like a prodigal son outside the ramshackle, collapsed hut that had once been the home of Obi-Wan Kenobi.

Luke swallowed and stepped forward, his footsteps crunching in the silence. He had not been here in many years. The door had fallen off its hinges; part of the clay front wall had fallen in. Boulders and crumbled adobe jammed the entrance. A pair of small, screeching desert rodents snapped at him and fled for cover; Luke ignored them.

Gingerly, he ducked low and stepped into the home of his first mentor.

Luke stood in the middle of the room breathing deeply, turning around, trying to sense the presence he desperately needed to see. This was the place where Obi-Wan Kenobi had told Luke of the Force. Here, the old man had first given Luke his lightsaber and hinted at the truth about his father, "from a certain point of view," dispelling the diversionary story that Uncle Owen had told, at the same time planting seeds of his own deceptions.

"Ben," he said and closed his eyes, calling out with his mind as well as his voice. He tried to penetrate the invisible walls of the Force and reach to the luminous being of Obi-Wan Kenobi who had visited him numerous times, before saying he could never speak with Luke again.

"Ben, I need you," Luke said. Circumstances had changed. He could think of no other way past the obstacles he faced. Obi-Wan had to answer. It wouldn't take long, but it could give him the key he needed with all his heart.

Luke paused and listened and sensed—

But felt nothing. If he could not summon Obi-Wan's spirit here in the empty dwelling where the old man had lived in exile for so many years, Luke didn't believe he could find his former teacher ever again.

He echoed the words Leia had used more than a decade earlier, beseeching him, "Help me, Obi-Wan Kenobi," Luke whispered, "you're my only hope."

THE CRYSTAL STAR
by Vonda N. McIntyre
Setting: Ten years after *Return of the Jedi*

Leia's three children have been kidnapped. That horrible fact is made worse by Leia's realization that she can no longer sense her children through the Force! While she, Artoo-Detoo, and Chewbacca trail the kidnappers, Luke and Han discover a planet that is suffering strange quantum effects from a nearby star. Slowly freezing into a perfect crystal and disrupting the Force, the star is blunting Luke's power and crippling the Millennium Falcon. These strands converge in an apocalyptic threat not only to the fate of the New Republic, but to the universe itself.

The Black Fleet Crisis
BEFORE THE STORM
SHIELD OF LIES
by Michael P. Kube-McDowell
Setting: Twelve years after *Return of the Jedi*

*Long after setting up the hard-won New Republic, yesterday's Rebels
have become today's administrators and diplomats. But the peace is
not to last for long. A restless Luke must journey to his mother's
homeworld in a desperate quest to find her people; Lando seizes a
mysterious spacecraft with unimaginable weapons of destruction; and
waiting in the wings is an horrific battle fleet under the control of a
ruthless leader bent on a genocidal war.*

Here is an opening scene from Before the Storm:

In the pristine silence of space, the Fifth Battle Group of the New
Republic Defense Fleet blossomed over the planet Bessimir like a
beautiful, deadly flower.

The formation of capital ships sprang into view with startling sud-
denness, trailing fire-white wakes of twisted space and bristling with
weapons. Angular Star Destroyers guarded fat-hulled fleet carriers,
while the assault cruisers, their mirror finishes gleaming, took the
point.

A halo of smaller ships appeared at the same time. The fighters
among them quickly deployed in a spherical defensive screen. As the
Star Destroyers firmed up their formation, their flight decks quickly
spawned scores of additional fighters.

At the same time, the carriers and cruisers began to disgorge the
bombers, transports, and gunboats they had ferried to the battle. There
was no reason to risk the loss of one fully loaded—a lesson the Republic had learned in pain. At Orinda, the commander of the fleet carrier
Endurance had kept his pilots waiting in the launch bays, to protect the
smaller craft from Imperial fire as long as possible. They were still
there when *Endurance* took the brunt of a Super Star Destroyer attack
and vanished in a ball of metal fire.

Before long more than two hundred warships, large and small, were
bearing down on Bessimir and its twin moons. But the terrible, restless
power of the armada could be heard and felt only by the ships' crews.
The silence of the approach was broken only on the fleet comm channels, which had crackled to life in the first moments with encoded
bursts of noise and cryptic ship-to-ship chatter.

At the center of the formation of great vessels was the flagship of the Fifth Battle Group, the fleet carrier *Intrepid*. She was so new from the yards at Hakassi that her corridors still reeked of sealing compound and cleaning solvent. Her huge realspace thruster engines still sang with the high-pitched squeal that the engine crews called "the baby's cry."

It would take more than a year for the mingled scents of the crew to displace the chemical smells from the first impressions of visitors. But after a hundred more hours under way, her engines' vibrations would drop two octaves, to the reassuring thrum of a seasoned thruster bank.

On *Intrepid*'s bridge, a tall Dornean in general's uniform paced along an arc of command stations equipped with large monitors. His eye-folds were swollen and fanned by an unconscious Dornean defensive reflex, and his leathery face was flushed purple by concern. Before the deployment was even a minute old, Etahn A'baht's first command had been bloodied.

The fleet tender *Ahazi* had overshot its jump, coming out of hyperspace too close to Bessimir and too late for its crew to recover from the error. Etahn A'baht watched the bright flare of light in the upper atmosphere from *Intrepid*'s forward viewstation, knowing that it meant six young men were dead.

The Corellian Trilogy:
AMBUSH AT CORELLIA
ASSAULT AT SELONIA
SHOWDOWN AT CENTERPOINT
by Roger MacBride Allen
Setting: Fourteen years after *Return of the Jedi*

This trilogy takes us to Corellia, Han Solo's homeworld, which Han has not visited in quite some time. A trade summit brings Han, Leia, and the children—now developing their own clear personalities and instinctively learning more about their innate skills in the Force—into the middle of a situation that most closely resembles a burning fuse. The Corellian system is on the brink of civil war, there are New Republic intelligence agents on a mysterious mission which even Han does not understand, and worst of all, a fanatical rebel leader has his hands on a superweapon of unimaginable power—and just wait until you find out who that leader is!

Here is an early scene from Ambush *that gives you a wonderful look at the growing Solo children (the twins are Jacen and Jaina, and their little brother is Anakin):*

Anakin plugged the board into the innards of the droid and pressed a button. The droid's black, boxy body shuddered awake, it drew in its wheels to stand up a bit taller, its status lights lit, and it made a sort of triple beep. "That's good," he said, and pushed the button again. The droid's status lights went out, and its body slumped down again. Anakin picked up the next piece, a motivation actuator. He frowned at it as he turned it over in his hands. He shook his head. "That's *not* good," he announced.

"What's not good?" Jaina asked.

"This thing," Anakin said, handing her the actuator. "Can't you *tell*? The insides part is all melty."

Jaina and Jacen exchanged a look. "The outside looks okay," Jaina said, giving the part to her brother. "How can he tell what the *inside* of it looks like? It's sealed shut when they make it."

Anakin, still sitting on the floor, took the device from his brother and frowned at it again. He turned it over and over in his hands, and then held it over his head and looked at it as if he were holding it up to the light. "There," he said, pointing a chubby finger at one point on the unmarked surface. "In there is the bad part." He rearranged himself to sit cross-legged, put the actuator in his lap, and put his right index finger over the "bad" part. "Fix," he said. "Fix." The dark brown outer case of the actuator seemed to glow for a second with an odd blue-red light, but then the glow sputtered out and Anakin pulled his finger away quickly and stuck it in his mouth, as if he had burned it on something.

"Better now?" Jaina asked.

"*Some* better," Anakin said, pulling his finger out of his mouth. "Not *all* better." He took the actuator in his hand and stood up. He opened the access panel on the broken droid and plugged in the actuator. He closed the door and looked expectantly at his older brother and sister.

"Done?" Jaina asked.

"Done," Anakin agreed. "But *I'm* not going to push the button." He backed well away from the droid, sat down on the floor, and folded his arms.

Jacen looked at his sister.

"Not me," she said. "This was your idea."

Jacen stepped forward to the droid, reached out to push the power button from as far away as he could, and then stepped hurriedly back.

Once again, the droid shuddered awake, rattling a bit this time as it did so. It pulled its wheels in, lit its panel lights, and made the same triple beep. But then its holocam eye viewlens wobbled back and forth, and its panel lights dimmed and flared. It rolled backward just a bit, and then recovered itself.

"Good morning, young mistress and masters," it said. "How may I surge you?"

Well, one word wrong, but so what? Jacen grinned and clapped his hands and rubbed them together eagerly. "Good day, droid," he said. They had done it! But what to ask for first? "First tidy up this room," he said. A simple task, and one that ought to serve as a good test of what this droid could do.

Suddenly the droid's overhead access door blew off and there was a flash of light from its interior. A thin plume of smoke drifted out of the droid. Its panel lights flared again, and then the work arm sagged downward. The droid's body, softened by heat, sagged in on itself and drooped to the floor. The floor and walls and ceilings of the playroom were supposed to be fireproof, but nonetheless the floor under the droid darkened a bit, and the ceiling turned black. The ventilators kicked on high automatically, and drew the smoke out of the room. After a moment they shut themselves off, and the room was silent.

The three children stood, every bit as frozen to the spot as the droid was, absolutely stunned. It was Anakin who recovered first. He walked cautiously toward the droid and looked at it carefully, being sure not to get too close or touch it. "*Really* melty now," he announced, and then wandered off to the other side of the room to play with his blocks.

The twins looked at the droid, and then at each other.

"We're dead," Jacen announced, surveying the wreckage.

STAR WARS®

A LITERARY TIME LINE OF BESTSELLING NOVELS AVAILABLE FROM BANTAM BOOKS

SF 3 7/96

JOIN

STAR WARS®

on the INTERNET

Bantam Spectra invites you to visit the Official STAR WARS® Web Site.

You'll find:

< Sneak previews of upcoming STAR WARS® novels.

< Samples from audio editions of the novels.

< Bulletin boards that put you in touch with other fans, with the authors, and with the Spectra editors who bring them to you.

< The latest word from behind the scenes of the STAR WARS® universe.

< Quizzes, games, and contests available only on-line.

< Links to other STAR WARS® licensees' sites on the Internet.

< Look for STAR WARS® on the World Wide Web at:

http://www.bdd.com

SF 28 6/96